A BEAUTY AT THE HIGHLAND COURT

THE HIGHLAND LADIES BOOK 7

CELESTE BARCLAY

SUBSCRIBE TO CELESTE'S NEWSLETTER

Subscribe to Celeste's bimonthly newsletter to receive exclusive insider perks.

Have you read *Their Highland Beginning, The Clan Sinclair Prequel?* Learn how the saga begins! This FREE novella is available to all new subscribers to Celeste's monthly newsletter. Subscribe on her website.

Subscribe Now

THE HIGHLAND LADIES

A Spinster at the Highland Court

A Spy at the Highland Court

A Wallflower at the Highland Court

A Rogue at the Highland Court

A Rake at the Highland Court

An Enemy at the Highland Court

A Saint at the Highland Court

A Beauty at the Highland Court

A Sinner at the Highland Court

A Hellion at the Highland Court

An Angel at the Highland Court

A Harlot at the Highland Court

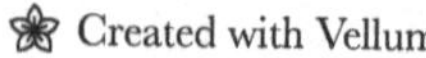 Created with Vellum

When you hit the bottom, you can only go up from there.

Happy reading, y'all,
Celeste

PREFACE

The Highland Ladies series is a spin-off to my first series, *The Clan Sinclair,* and follows the lives of ladies-in-waiting at King Robert the Bruce's court. If you are a fan of Highlander romances, then you have surely encountered the time period that spans the Wars of Scottish Independence, along with the rise and reign of Robert the Bruce.

While I was intentionally vague about the time period and royal couple in *The Clan Sinclair,* there is little way to avoid the history of Robert the Bruce when this series takes place predominantly at Stirling Castle after he was crowned king. I have taken creative license in a number of areas, especially the creation of characters, but the events and clan dynamics are true to history.

A Beauty at the Highland Court tackles more than one social issue. Never one to shy away from a challenge, I've jumped in with both feet to create a story that depicts social pressures and expectations based upon beauty, anxiety, and alcoholism. Arabella Johnstone is once again a product of my imagination, but she mirrors the struggle many women face when reality can never live up to expectation.

All locations in this story are real, just as in all my

other books. The exception are the taverns mentioned. Those are also a product of my imagination. I've had readers ask how I estimate the time it takes for characters to travel from place to place. I work on the premise that a horse can travel on average 20 miles per day given the terrain our medieval characters would have faced.

Inchcailleoch Priory is a setting mentioned in more than one book in *The Highland Ladies* series. It was supposedly referred to as the "island of old women," but there is no historical record to specify what monastic order of nuns may have resided there. The name is what leads historians to speculate there was a monastic house on the island of Inchailleoch, located in Loch Lomand.

It often seems like clan rivalries and alliances changed with the wind. Given Scotland's notorious weather, this meant often. Depending upon the political climate and relationships with other clans, friends became enemies just like enemies became friends. The enemy of my enemy is my friend. Clan Gunn is featured prominently in this book, and their discord with Clan Keith and Clan Mackay was true to fact, but it happened in the 15th century rather than the 14th. Their adversarial relationship with the Mackays, who were rivals with the Sinclairs, begins in *The Clan Sinclair* series. I "solved" the real animosity between the Mackays and Sinclairs with Mairghread and Tristan's story in *His Highland Lass*, making the Mackays and Sinclairs allies. Fictitious members of Clan Gunn become enemies to the Sinclairs in *His Bonnie Highland Temptation* and *His Highland Prize*.

Clan Gunn and Clan Sutherland allied during the 16th century, but there is not significant record of their relationship during the 14th century, so for the purposes of my storytelling, they did not get along.

Clan Sinclair and Clan Sutherland had a shifting relationship depending upon the century. To weave my stories, I chose to focus on the time when there was no feuding. The marriage between Kyla Sutherland and Liam Sinclair in *Their Highland Beginning* lays the foundation for their alliance, which meant Clan Gunn became the Sutherlands' enemy too. Complicated? Just a little, but alliances and feuds were a way of life for the rugged Highlanders who fought for their land and their clan's survival.

Clan Johnstone was a border clan and were well known reivers. They battled the English, often crossing the border to steal or reclaim (depending upon whose side you take) livestock. For more than six centuries, they held considerable power and influence in the West Marches, protecting the land from the English. This is briefly mentioned in this story as well as the clan's one-time allegiance to King Edward I in the late 1200s. A member of their clan was appointed Warden of the Western March nearly one hundred years later in the late 1300s, which is well past the setting for this series, but this is another instance where I took creative license on dates.

I hope you enjoy this tale that's been foreshadowed since *A Wallflower at the Highland Court*. Please consider leaving a review to share with other readers to let them know enjoyed this installment in *The Highland Ladies*.

Happy reading,
Celeste

ONE

Arabella Johnstone gripped the back of the chair and tried not to groan as her maid cinched her kirtle tighter. She'd already suffered through more than an hour of Eliza curling and pinning her hair. While her maid created some of the most exquisite coiffures Arabella had ever worn—in fact, ever seen—she didn't have a gentle touch. More than once Arabella was grateful that her hair was auburn, because surely her scalp bled from being a pincushion. Arabella took one more shallow breath as she felt her maid tie the ends of her gown's laces.

"There you go, my lady. You're a right bobby-dazzler, if I may say so," Eliza beamed.

"Thank you, Eliza." Arabella smiled. She looked across her chamber as Blair Sutherland's maid brushed out her mistress's velvet kirtle for the last time. Arabella breathed a wistful sigh. She and Blair had grown closer since Blair's older sister Maude married and moved to the Isle of Lewis. Arabella had befriended the reserved Maude when the sisters arrived at court. Taunted mercilessly for being unfashionably curvaceous, Maude became the victim of her future sister-by-marriage's venom. With Kieran

"

MacLeod's support, Maude emerged from her wall-flower ways and found a love match.

"I just need a few moments more," Blair looked over her shoulder at Arabella.

"You needn't rush. We still have time," Arabella reassured as she dabbed rose water behind her ears and into her cleavage. She knew the Great Hall would be sweltering, and the fresh scent was as much for her as it was for anyone else. It would offer her a reprieve from the stench of too many unwashed and overheated bodies.

As Arabella watched Blair, she wondered when her friend would find her match. She suspected that it would happen soon, since Blair and Hardwin Cameron were inseparable. It wouldn't surprise Arabella if Blair and Hardi (as she called him) hand-fasted before a priest could read the banns. Thoughts of Maude and Blair inevitably turned her mind toward their older brother, Lachlan. Arabella stifled her sigh as she thought about the handsome, dark-haired man who appeared at court every few months. She didn't envy him his lengthy rides south from Dunrobin. The keep was along the north-eastern coast of Scotland, almost as far north as that of the Sinclairs, and marriage linked the two clans. Arabella had long admired Lachlan's easygoing nature and protectiveness of his sisters. The three siblings were extremely close, and both Maude and Blair had looked forward to his visits. Arabella knew Lachlan looked for excuses to see them. She couldn't help the sadness she felt when she realized Lachlan would rarely make the long trip to court once Blair left.

"I'm almost done," Blair said as she bent to pull up her stockings and slip on her shoes. She disliked wearing stockings, so she put them on last.

Arabella thought about her other friends who

had left over the past three years. Nearly all her original friends were gone, one after another marrying and leaving court. First to go had been Elizabeth Fraser, a woman everyone assumed would remain a spinster. Despite her beauty, her father made and broke four betrothals, all for the sake of politics. But when Robert the Bruce's adopted brother Edward came to court, she snared his attention. Edward's single-minded focus on wooing her eventually won Elizabeth over.

Isabella Dunbar stunned many people when she married the dashing English knight sent to spy on King Robert. Her husband was half Scottish; after his English father married a MacLellan, his father switched his allegiance to Scotland. But both of his parents died while the knight was still a child, and English soldiers captured him in the name of King Edward "Longshanks." Raised in England, he longed for his Scottish home and found it when he married Isabella.

Maude had been the next to marry, and Arabella rejoiced as she thought about her former roommate and close companion. Then she tried not to grin when she recalled how Allyson Elliot bolted from court when she learned she was to marry the roguish Ewan Gordon. What a merry chase she had led him on! But Arabella sobered when she recalled how Allyson was kidnapped and nearly tortured and what Arabella later learned of Allyson's family secrets.

Cairstine Grant convinced Ewan's rakish twin Eoin to pretend to be her betrothed so her younger sister could marry, only for them to marry in truth. Arabella regretted the unkind thoughts she'd had about Cairstine once she discovered Cairstine's painful past, which explained why she'd kept everyone at arms' length. Cairstine and Eoin were as much a love match as Allyson and Ewan turned out to be. Arabella wished she could say the same for the start of her friend Cairren Kennedy's marriage.

Cairren was soft-spoken and kind, but she'd always stuck out at court. Her Arab heritage was apparent in her olive skin, a stark contrast to the creamy Scottish complexions that the other ladies-in-waiting shared. Her appearance had immediately put her at odds with her new clan, the Munros, when King Robert and her father agreed on her marriage to Padraig Munro. Fortunately, he realized what a gem he'd been given and fell in love with his wife. Arabella was glad to know they were no longer enemies, but deeply in love.

Arabella's thought's returned to Lachlan. He had returned to Stirling when he accompanied Cairren and Padraig, who needed an audience with the king. Taxes had brought him back most recently. Arabella hadn't seen him in more than a moon, and she tried to distract herself with the various events at court and the budding romance between Blair and Hardi. While she danced with one suitor after another, she resigned herself to the knowledge that her father was arranging her marriage to a stranger. She didn't know who her father had in mind, but she was certain it was a Lowland laird who would make a powerful ally to her clan. While life at court wasn't what Arabella wanted for her future, she didn't look forward to moving home to the dangerous border territory. The supposed truce between the Scottish and English kings was yet to be seen. The English continued to cross the border and harass the Scots, then cried foul when the Scots retaliated.

"Are you ready?" Blair interrupted Arabella's thoughts. "We shouldn't keep the others waiting. Laurel will wonder where we are." Blair grinned, knowing she was the one who delayed them.

Laurel Ross was the only other lady-in-waiting

who had been at court as long as Arabella. She'd once been friends with Madeline MacLeod, Maude's former nemesis and now sister-by-marriage. She had a razor-sharp tongue, but nowadays she used it to be a fiercely protective friend. Arabella hadn't pried into why Laurel became friends with Madeline, but she suspected the latter held some influence over Laurel, and she had either bribed or threatened Laurel into following Madeline's lead. Now that Madeline had been away from court for years, Laurel was much easier to get along with.

"I'm ready. Are we to meet her at her chamber or in the Great Hall?" Arabella asked.

"The Great Hall. She shall save us seats at our usual table. After my run-in with Henry and Daniel MacMillan, Laurel wants to be certain we sit closer to the king and queen," Blair explained. It was a little-known secret that Blair, Maude, and Lachlan, along with their Sinclair cousins, were the godchildren of King Robert and Queen Elizabeth de Burgh. The royal couple never played favorites, and the Sutherland and Sinclair siblings never asked for favors. Laurel's suggestion had been coincidental, but Arabella was privy to the secret and agreed with the wisdom of proximity.

The women thanked their maids and left their chamber, winding through the passageways until they entered the Great Hall. Arabella watched as Hardi and Blair exchanged private smiles, and Arabella was certain it was only a matter of a brief time before the couple saw what everyone else did: they were already in love. They took their seats beside Laurel just as the meal began.

"You're fortunate that Laird Cameron arrived just as your brother left," Laurel mused halfway through the meal. "You aren't as glum as usual when your brother departs. I'm glad for you."

Arabella caught Blair's darting glance, and she knew her friend was aware that something existed between her and Lachlan, but it was nothing that either would ever act upon. It was by silent agreement that neither dared to make their relationship more than friendship. Arabella didn't want to jeopardize her friendships with Blair and Maude, and she intuited Lachlan felt the same. It made it painful to watch him leave Stirling without acknowledging their connection, but Arabella resigned herself to it.

"Aye. It has been wonderful to have Laird Cameron here," Blair agreed. "It was a surprise how easily we picked up our childhood friendship. It pains me to see his grief over losing so much of his family and having to assume the lairdship, but I believe he has the fortitude and courage to be a powerful leader."

"And he's not hard on the eyes either," Arabella teased, happy to move the conversation away from Lachlan.

"No, he isn't," Blair responded noncommittally. She studiously kept her eyes on her trencher, though Arabella watched her fight the urge to turn and look in Hardi's direction.

"He must plan to leave soon," Laurel pressed. Arabella shot her a warning glare, but Laurel's eyes sparkled with mischief.

"He will have to. He has duties to return to, and he's settled his taxes," Blair nodded. Blair's bowed head told her friends she was through discussing her relationship with the handsome, broad-shouldered laird, but Arabella knew their relationship was far from over.

The conversation turned to more mundane topics such as fashion, gossip, and the queen's plans for a picnic the following week. Arabella watched as people moved about the Great Hall as the music began. She partnered with one man after another; some were courtiers she'd known throughout her time at court, while others were visitors. She danced with Hardi once, happily fulfilling her promise to Lachlan that his friend would have more partners than just Blair. She forced her mind away from Lachlan and focused on learning more about Hardi, realizing once more why he and Blair were so well suited. It was a long evening, and Arabella welcomed the silence and dark of her chamber once she fell into bed.

TWO

Only two months after leaving Stirling Castle, Lachlan Sutherland rode through the gates of Stirling Castle, conflicted between his dread of being at court but excited to see the woman he'd often dreamed about while in Sutherland. It had relieved him to see both Blair and Maude earlier that month. He'd met Maude's newborn daughter, and it reassured him and his family that Blair was safe after she disappeared for nearly a moon. She'd left court to aid Hardi as he learned to read and write while taking on his lairdship.

No one in the Sutherland family was surprised to learn Blair and Hardi were in love. They'd been inseparable as children when Hardi and his older brother fostered with the Sutherlands. Lachlan shook his head as he considered the conspiracy against Hardi that had nearly gotten his childhood friend and his sister killed. It had been a tumultuous month when no missives came from Blair. He and his family were exhausted but ecstatic to find Blair well and handfasted to Hardi.

Now he was returning to court alongside Blair and Hardi as they paid the last of their taxes, and to report to the king what happened once they arrived at Tor Castle. Lachlan represented his father, Laird Hamish Sutherland, and would explain his clan's role in the truce settled between the Mackintoshes and Camerons. The Sutherlands were only witnesses, but he understood that his clan's overwhelming presence after the Mackintoshes' planned attack had spurred Laird Mackintosh to accept Hardi's terms.

He glanced at Blair and Hardi, and he smirked as he watched tiny Blair whisper advice to her mountainous husband. His youngest sister had always tended toward being bossy, but it made Lachlan smile to see her protectiveness over her husband. Still new to being a laird and never trained for the position, Lachlan's worries were soothed knowing that his sister offered sage advice to their lifelong friend. Other than his parents, he'd never seen a more balanced and equal partnership. He saw many of his mother's qualities in both his sisters, and he prayed he held many of the qualities he admired in his father.

"Bella!" Blair called out as they entered the bailey and watched the queen and her ladies-in-waiting enter the royal gardens. Lachlan's heart flipped as he caught sight of the red-haired beauty. He couldn't deny that she was the most stunningly attractive lady-in-waiting. Many argued she was the most beautiful woman at court, and Lachlan was apt to agree. He schooled his expression as he dismounted, and Arabella rushed to greet Blair. The women embraced and chattered until Arabella's gaze shifted to Lachlan. He watched her swallow as she turned her eyes back to Blair. The hair on Lachlan's arms stood up as he felt the connection between them, a connection he felt every time they saw one another. And just like every other time, they would both pretend as though it didn't exist.

When it was Lachlan's turn to greet Arabella, her

hand hovered over his as he bent to proffer a kiss just above the back of her hand. He longed to clasp her fine-boned fingers and bring them to his lips, but he obeyed the rules of decorum. Lachlan and Arabella exchanged the amiable smiles of longtime friends, ignoring the undercurrent that passed between them. Lachlan caught Blair's sly glance and worried what his sister was about to say. He knew he wouldn't like it, and the words that flowed forth were a wrenching blow to his gut.

"Has your father made any advances in that betrothal you suspect?" Blair asked innocently. She offered a serene smile as Arabella and Lachlan scowled before catching themselves. Not usually given to violence, Arabella wanted to smack the smug smile from Blair's face. She was aware her friend noticed what passed between her and Lachlan, but she hadn't played matchmaker. Though Arabella didn't doubt that Blair was tempted, she suspected the comment was meant to nudge Lachlan into action. Arabella wondered if that was as close to getting Blair's blessing as they would come.

The women separated from the men and followed Queen Elizabeth into the gardens while Lachlan and Hardi went to secure chambers. Arabella was relieved to see Blair after hearing about the treacherous plot that some of Hardi's family members concocted to oust him.

"Have you settled into life at Tor?" Arabella asked Blair as they walked with their arms linked and heads close together.

"I have. Now that the tumultuousness is over and the new clan council has accepted me as a regular member, it is much easier. The Camerons have welcomed me with warmth and kindness," Blair explained. It was too warm for an arisaid, but Blair wore a sash of Cameron plaid over her shoulder with a twinkling ruby brooch that signified her role as Lady Cameron. "How have things been at court with just Laurel as a confidante?"

"I don't know that I would call her a confidante as yet, but I appreciate her company in a way that I never did before. The newer ladies are the upstarts they were a moon ago, and now that there are so few of us experienced ladies, they believe they shall have the run of the place. Laurel and I are content to remain out of their way."

"How does the queen receive these new attendants?" Blair asked.

"The same as she always does. She appreciates being surrounded by young and attractive women who entertain her and do her bidding. She is just as any queen is, I suppose. With the bairn on the way, she is even more fervent in her prayer, but fortunately for all of our knees, she spends much of that time alone."

"How do you fill that time?" Blair wondered.

"The same way we always do." Arabella looked away as she considered how she'd spent much of her time as of late. It was something she would never admit, not even to Blair. "Sewing, reading, archery, riding. The endless cycle of being pretty and smiling."

"I must admit I don't miss that. I didn't realize how much my cheeks ached each day from plastering a smile on my face until I no longer had to do it." Blair grinned. "Now when I smile, it's because I mean it."

"That must be nice!" Arabella chuckled but lowered her voice when several heads turned back to watch the two friends. "How long will you be here?"

"Not long at all. Less than a sennight. It's a sennight each way, and Hardi doesn't want to be away that long. Things are better, but the strife with the Macphersons hasn't been resolved, and neither

Hardi nor I are convinced the Mackintoshes won't get up to naughty tricks again. I swear, Laird Mackintosh was like a petulant child when Laird Shaw insisted they sign the truce. I'm positive I saw him pout," Blair giggled. "I suggested to Maude that a nap alongside her weans might make him more agreeable."

"I hope no one overheard you," Arabella pretended concern.

"Only Lachlan. And he laughed before shaking his finger at me. He was standing beside me, and I snapped my teeth at him; nearly took off the tip of his wagging finger." This time Blair laughed and didn't bother trying to sound ladylike. Arabella's stomach clenched at the mention of Lachlan's name. She could picture the sisters with their brother. Their closeness was so unlike Arabella's relationship with her siblings. She and her brothers had little to do with one another, and she was younger than her sisters by nearly a decade. None of them had batted an eye when she left for her position at court.

"How is your family?" Arabella hedged.

"Maude and Kieran are blissfully happy. Kieran's sister Abigail just entered a handfast with Laird Lathan Chisholm, so she is no longer at Stornoway. She'd come around quite a lot from when Maude first met her, and I suspect my sister misses her. Madeline, as I'm sure you know, is still at Inchcailleoch Priory. I don't know that she will ever see the light of day," Blair explained.

"And at Dunrobin?" Arabella pressed. Both women knew what Arabella hinted at.

"Much the same as usual from what I understand. Lachlan, Mama, and Da went home after visiting Tor. I'm so happy that they and Maude, Kieran, and their weans could come. I know it was because they were frightened not knowing what might have happened to me, but they were there to see Hardi and me marry in the kirk. Lachlan came back to Tor just before we were set to leave and said Da wanted him to accompany us. He is to stand witness to what happened with the Mackintoshes, Shaws, and MacThomases." Blair turned to look at her friend and met Arabella's gaze. "Hardi and I shall be here for nearly a sennight to settle the last of the taxes. But I don't know that Lachlan plans to leave with us. I don't know his intentions."

The pointed comment made Arabella want to squirm, but she nodded once and smiled before turning her gaze back to the path before them. Her stomach churned as she prayed Lachlan would remain longer, but she knew she was a glutton for punishment if he did. It would only make saying goodbye that much harder. With her father's plans in the works, it might be the last time they ever said goodbye.

THREE

"I canna believe the Master of the Bedchamber thought to separate a mon from his wife. A newlywed mon from his bride!" Hardi fumed. With little time spent at court and Blair's tutoring as his only formal education, the Highland laird never attempted to hide his brogue as others did when they visited Stirling. He'd teased Blair that she would sound like a "bluidy Lowlander" once they rode through Stirling's gates. He warned her not to lose her plaid, lest she forget she was really a Highlander. Lachlan roared with laughter at his sister's scathing set down that she made sure only her brother and husband could hear.

"At least he offered to let us share," Lachlan reasoned. "If worst came to worst, I could have found somewhere else to sleep, and Blair could have come to you."

"And where would that have been?" Hardi waggled his eyebrows. Lachlan shot him a warning glare as he looked around him to ensure no one could hear. They were moving through a busier part of the keep as they went in search of Blair. Lachlan didn't want gossip flying around the castle that he was looking for a bedmate. He wasn't entirely celibate at home, but he always was at court.

"In the barracks or next to my horse," Lachlan grumbled.

"Worried she'd hear of it?" Hardi pressed.

Lachlan cast another mutinous stare in Hardi's direction. Arabella was exactly the reason he never sought female companionship while at court. He was uninterested in anyone at Stirling Castle or the surrounding town, and he wouldn't slight her by choosing someone else in her presence. Neither spoke of their feelings, and neither ever would. But they were there, and they both knew it. He found diversion from time to time at Dunrobin, but he was far from being the rogue people assumed he was because of his looks and charm.

"Ye can cast that brooding sulk somewhere else," Hardi grinned.

"Leave be, or I shall tell my sister that you were the one who filched her bannocks this morning," Lachlan threatened.

"She already kens, and I've promised to make it up to her." Hardi waggled his brows again.

"Disgusting. It's bad enough I ken the two of ye are just like Maude and Kieran. I dinna need reminding," Lachlan's burr slipped into his voice as he turned his nose up. "That's ma wee baby sister."

"The only bairn is the one Blair is carrying," Hardi guffawed.

The men shaded their eyes as they walked into the brilliant late morning sunlight. Hardi elbowed Lachlan and pointed toward a group of women emerging from the gardens. The men caught sight of Blair and Arabella and joined them at the end of the path.

"Ye look weary, *mo ghaol*," Hardi murmured as he tipped Blair's face up. His thumb brushed the dark shadows under Blair's eyes. Arabella tried not to stare; she lowered her eyes and twisted away, embarrassed by her longing for such tenderness from a man. One particular man, who happened to be standing on the other side of the couple. "Do ye wish to retire?"

Blair nodded, and Arabella regretted dragging her pregnant friend on such a lengthy walk after a week on horseback. It was still early in Blair's pregnancy, and she'd shared with Arabella that she found herself exhausted for no reason other than rising from bed. Hardi wrapped his arm around Blair's waist, but she hung back to look at Arabella.

"Will you sit with us at the evening meal? I've missed you," Blair pleaded.

"Of course," Arabella nodded. She watched the couple walk away before turning toward Lachlan. His expression was speculative, almost as though he were assessing her. She opened her mouth, but he spoke first.

"Must you join the queen?" Lachlan kept his voice low.

Arabella shook her head as she observed Queen Elizabeth and her ladies enter the keep. She looked back at Lachlan. "No. My absence won't be noticed since the queen knows Blair is here. She will assume I'm with her."

"I ken you've just been for a walk, but would you humor me and accompany me on another? I've been on horseback for nearly a fortnight straight. I arrived at Tor in the evening, and we departed the next morning. I would like to stretch my legs."

Arabella forced herself not to look at the bare knees and calves that showed below Lachlan's plaid. The muscular limbs covered in black hair seemed indecently masculine compared to the leggings that courtiers wore. While the leggings left nothing to the imagination, the sight of his bare skin felt like an illicit treat to the Lowland lady-in-waiting. She nodded, then gulped as Lachlan wrapped her arm through his.

They moved toward the garden path in silence. While Arabella sensed Lachlan wanted to speak, neither broke the companionable silence. They strolled together until they reached the center of the gardens and stood beside an enormous bed of hydrangeas. The bright blues and purples were in full bloom, and bees quietly buzzed from one bud to another, industriously working while ignoring all else around them.

"You look well, Bella," Lachlan commented softly.

"Thank you." Arabella smiled but couldn't hold his gaze. "You don't look like you've been on horseback for a fortnight." Arabella's eyes widened as she snapped her mouth shut. She realized she'd made more than one faux pas with that comment. She shouldn't have commented on a man's appearance, and she shouldn't have offered such a backhanded compliment. Lachlan's deep chuckle eased her misgivings, and she returned his smile.

"What is the news of court since last I was here?" Lachlan released her arm and turned to look at the flowers. Arabella wanted to sigh, but she understood he did it more for her reputation than because it was something he wanted. Anyone walking by would surely comment if they saw the couple standing arm-in-arm while engaging in a private conversation.

"There's not much to report. People are still buzzing aboot Blair and Hardi, but mostly it's those who supposedly predicted their marriage who have plenty to say. The initial surprise has worn off, and with the royal couple acknowledging their marriage, there's no scandal. They are back to being boring," Arabella grinned.

"Blair is hardly ever boring, but I'm certain she'll be glad there isn't too much gossip. I was worried," Lachlan confessed.

"I'm sure that you were, but Blair proved quite clearly that she has a sharper mind and a sharper tongue than most. I think there are few who will challenge her, be it out loud or behind her back. And God's mercy on them if they make Laird Cameron their target. We'll need a priest to give last rites."

"My sister is a little protective of her husband." Lachlan glanced over his shoulder as if to see whether Blair might spy them. He lowered his head to whisper to Arabella. "Repeat a word of this, and I will deny it. But I have seen nothing more endearing than the way my sister defends Hardi. And he isn't insulted or embarrassed. He's proud to have the little termagant stand up for him."

"So she's really as happy as she seems?" Arabella wondered.

"More so. Besides my parents, I don't think there has ever been a better matched couple," Lachlan nodded.

"Even more than Maude and Kieran?" Arabella challenged with a smile.

"Aye. Maude and Kieran trust one another implicitly and understand one another as only soulmates can. But Kieran still fears for Maude and is overprotective. Between what she endured at court, the cold welcome at Stornoway, and the wildcat attack, he barely wants her out of his sight. I don't blame him, but I know Maude feels suffocated at times. She doesn't say aught because she knows he's doing the best he can to show his love the only way he knows how. She doesn't want to hurt him."

Lachlan shook his head but smiled softly as his thoughts moved to his youngest sister. He was overjoyed to know both of his sisters had found partners who loved them unconditionally.

"Blair and Hardi are just different. I can't explain other than they're two sides of the same coin. It's not just that they understand one another and accept each other for it. It's as though they share the same thoughts and way of thinking on everything." Lachlan shrugged and raised his hands. "I don't really know how to explain it."

"I understand what you mean. I saw it when they were here," Arabella agreed. "Maybe it's because they grew up together. Their way of thinking is so similar because they were with each other so much. From what Blair says, it was always you and your cousin Michael while Laird Cameron had his older brother Dougal. But whenever there was trouble with the other boys, Dougal and Laird Cameron made themselves scarce so they wouldn't anger your father. It meant Laird Cameron spent a lot of time with Blair."

"It did. And they had a great deal in common even then. They both loved archery, climbing trees, throwing knives, and being a pain in my arse," Lachlan chortled. "Bella, I'm certain you can call him Hardwin, if not Hardi. You're like a second sister to Blair."

A second sister. All the more reason naught can happen between us. If Blair thinks of me as her sister, it would horrify her if Lachlan were to pursue me. And does that mean he thinks of me like a sister? Have I completely misread everything?

"Bella?" Lachlan nudged her. Arabella turned a blank stare toward Lachlan before she realized he'd continued talking. She hadn't a clue what he'd just said. From his grin, she understood he knew that. "Where did you go just now?"

"Nowhere that interesting," Arabella grinned.

When she didn't say more, Lachlan shrugged and returned to looking at the flower bed. It was Arabella's turn to find something to say, having pushed Lachlan into silence when he assumed she was no longer paying attention. She struggled to find something to say. "How are Laird and Lady Sutherland?"

"Mama and Da are well, but it hasn't been easy for them now that Maude and Blair are married. My sisters seem to cause more trouble as married women than they ever did as lasses. I don't think my parents worried as much about sending them here as they do now that they belong to new clans."

"I can understand that. Your father is no longer responsible for them. He has to trust his sons-by-marriage to protect his lasses. Laird MacLeod and Laird Cameron are up to the task, but it must be hard to ken that neither of them will return to Dunrobin and call it home."

"It is. The keep is empty without them. For two such small women, they filled the keep, and their absence is keenly felt by everyone."

Arabella glanced up at Lachlan, her brow furrowed as she considered what he didn't say. On a hushed voice, she asked, "Are you lonely?"

Lachlan started, then nodded as he looked down at Arabella. "Aye. At times. First Hardi and Dougal left when they finished fostering. Then a couple of years later, my cousin Michael left to join the priesthood. Then Maude and Blair came here. But their position as ladies-in-waiting was always meant to be temporary. They still felt part of our clan, even if they were away. Now they belong elsewhere." Lachlan shrugged. "I never thought I would feel left behind when I ken I'm to one day become Laird Sutherland, but Dunrobin seems empty now."

"No keep is ever empty," Arabella teased.

"The family quarters then," Lachlan conceded.

"It does sound ridiculous since Dunrobin is rather large, and there are servants buzzing aboot everywhere."

"Rather large?" Arabella giggled. Dunrobin was one of the largest keeps in Scotland, and easily the largest in the northern Highlands.

"It just isn't the same," Lachlan grumbled in mock consternation. Their eyes locked, and their smiles slipped. The charged energy between them was palpable. Lachlan dredged his mind for something to say, but when the words came out, he realized he'd erred. "How is your family?"

Arabella stiffened. "All is well. Thank you for asking."

"Bella?" Lachlan was unaccustomed to such a perfunctory response from Arabella. He knew he'd misstepped, but he thought he would have gotten more than such a curt answer. When she turned a studiously innocent expression on him, he didn't press the matter.

"I am glad for the extra time outdoors, but the nooning approaches. The queen will notice if I'm late for that." Arabella dipped her head and offered a fleeting smile before sweeping from the garden. Lachlan was left staring and wondering how their conversation went adrift so quickly.

Because ye mentioned her family. She never likes talking aboot them. And bluidy hell, her father may be arranging a betrothal. Christ on the cross, I dinna want to ken if that's the case.

Lachlan rubbed his fist over his heart, but it did nothing to ease the ache. When Arabella was no longer in sight, Lachlan wandered through the gardens. He needed to clear his head and stretch his legs. He was stiff after so much time on horseback, but his mind felt addled as he kept returning to the notion that Arabella might soon be another man's bride.

Can I live with that? Do I have a choice? Aye. There's always a choice, but what if Bella isnae the right one and it ruins her friendship with Blair and Maude? What if I ruin things with them? Why canna I get the bollocks to make a move? I can slay an enemy, but I canna let a wisp of a lass ken that I love her.

Lachlan wound his way through the gardens until the noon meal bells pealed, and his stomach rumbled in response. He entered the Great Hall and searched for Hardi and Blair, but they were nowhere to be seen. He noticed Arabella immediately. She sat with Laurel Ross and a handful of ladies Lachlan recognized but didn't know. He sighed and made his way to where the Sutherland and Cameron guardsmen sat together.

FOUR

Arabella slipped into her chamber and pressed the door closed without a click. She rushed across the room and kneeled beside the head of her bed. Arabella leaned below the mattress and stretched to pry away two loose stones from the wall. She sighed as she pulled the jug of whisky from its hiding place. Pulling the stopper loose, Arabella inhaled the deep aroma of the distilled liquor. She didn't care for the taste of whisky, or even the scent, but she knew she was only minutes away from the soothing relief it offered. The first taste bit into her tongue and burned her throat, and soon everything was numb: her taste buds, her throat, and her mind. She shifted until she sat with her back resting against the bed, her legs out before her.

I look like a bluidy drunkard left to rot beside a dock. But a true drunkard is none the wiser to what's happening around him. Sotted and forgetful. Lucky bastard. I need just a wee more liquid courage before I face the evening. I'm both eager and dreading dancing with Lachlan. I want to be in his arms, and dancing is my only choice. It keeps me away from all the others. But it's so bluidy hard to let go. And if one more person calls me Bonnie Bella, I shall scream. I don't give a damn how I look. Why does everyone else? What has being beautiful done for me but send me away from my clan to serve as a trinket for the queen? I can't do aught or say aught without people chiming in or straining to hear. What would they do if I came out of this chamber less than perfectly presentable? Would time stop if I wasn't perfect? If only I could make that happen.

Arabella took another long drag from the jug as the afternoon's conversation in the queen's solar replayed in her mind.

"Aren't you excited that your father is finally arranging a betrothal?" Laurel asked.

"I can't say that I am," Arabella murmured.

"I do hope it's to a man as handsome as you are beautiful. Just imagine what a perfect couple you would make, and the perfectly cherubic bairns you'll have," Laurel gushed but then turned wistful. "To be as bonnie as you, Bella. We should all be so fortunate. God made his masterpiece with you."

"I hardly think God was paying attention to my looks when I was in my mother's womb," Arabella scoffed.

"But he must have," Caitlyn Kennedy chimed in. A fellow Lowlander, Caitlyn arrived the previous year to replace her sister Cairren, who left court to marry. "How else could you always be so flawless?"

"I have plenty of flaws," Arabella chuckled, but she felt no mirth. She wished they could all see her flaws, then they might leave her alone.

"Nay. Not a one," Caitlyn answered with such surety and sincerity that Arabella felt a twinge of guilt for not graciously accepting the compliment. But as Caitlyn continued, Arabella felt the guilt evaporate as the weight of more expectations piled upon her. "You make the rest of us look like poor country cousins. Everyone says you're the most beautiful woman at court. We're lucky you're so kind and selfless, but then again, that just proves you are above reproach. We'd all do well to be more like you."

As Arabella took another long swig, tears pricked the back of her eyes. She wanted to lean her head back, but she didn't dare disturb her hairdo. She swallowed her tears along with the whisky. People expected her to be enchanting and outgoing even though she would have rather hidden with her sewing than venture into the Great Hall. And she loathed sewing.

Get yourself together, Belle. You do the same song and dance every night. This is no different. You've been doing it for more years than you have fingers on one hand. Don't be maudlin, and don't cry. Puffy eyes and a red nose will draw more attention. The last thing you need is gossip. Gossip that somehow always reaches Mother and Father. I swear they know more aboot what happens at court than I do.

Arabella pushed the stopper back into the jug and ducked beneath the bed to return it to its hidey hole. She stood and shook out her skirts before breaking off several mint leaves that she chewed. Between the mint and the wine served with the evening meal, she'd successfully hidden her penchant for liquor for months. As she spat out the leaves, she looked once more at the bed.

Mayhap one more sip? I feel calmer and a little more at ease, but I'd hardly say relaxed. Do I dare? Do I have time? Sod it. I have time if I make time. I need a little more.

Arabella crawled back onto her hands and knees before retrieving the jug. She shook it, disappointed to realize it was nearly empty. The flasks weren't lasting nearly as long as they used to. Arabella recognized that was because she drank more often and needed to drink more of the liquid fire to get the numbing escape she longed for. When she was certain she'd drained the last drop, she hid the empty container and grabbed a handful of mint leaves. She would have to chew them on her way to the Great Hall and find somewhere along the way to dispose of them. She would most certainly be late. But it would be worth it, Arabella decided as the warmth spread throughout her body.

That's all I needed. I just needed to move around a tad and get the whisky in my blood. I shall feel much better now.

Arabella grinned to herself as her cheeks took on the telltale tingle before they grew numb. She knew the effects of imbibing were imminent, and she was confident she could muster her way through the meal and the dancing to come.

Lachlan's heart raced as he watched Arabella glide toward the table where he sat with his sister and brother-by-marriage. He watched her greet those who called out to her, always gracious. As she approached, Lachlan watched her blink several times as though she needed to clear her vision. Blair and Hardi sat with their backs to her, but Lachlan noticed that her cheeks seemed flushed, and even the tip of her nose was a touch red. He worried that she was ill when she cast her bleary gaze at him, but her warm smile set him at ease.

"Forgive me for being tardy," Arabella murmured as she took a seat beside Blair, putting her across from Lachlan.

"I was wondering where you were," Blair responded before taking a bite of bread.

"I had a couple of loose curls to fix," Arabella fibbed.

"You haven't a hair out of place," Blair grinned as she swept her eyes over Arabella. "Picture perfect as always."

I ruddy well hate that word. Perfect. No one would be calling me perfect if they saw me guzzle down a pint of whisky not ten minutes ago. Arabella laughed to herself. *I wish they would. Perhaps I should bring some down tomorrow and see what everyone has to say when Bonnie Bella drinks most of the men in here under the table. Why is Lachlan staring at me? He's usually discreet. Can he tell? Does he ken I've been drinking? Nay. He can't. Calm down, Belle. You'll give yourself away.*

"Thank you," Arabella stated as a servant placed a trencher before her. She focused on her food, but she was careful not to eat too much or anything too heavy. It would dull the effects of the whisky sooner, and she wasn't interested in sobriety if she still had hours ahead of her. She reached for her chalice at the same time that Lachlan reached for his and the backs of their fingers grazed one another. She felt singed, and her eyes flew to his face. Their gazes locked, and Arabella read the concern in his.

Mayhap I did have a wee too much. Mayhap I shouldn't have gone back for the second round. Lachlan is too perceptive by half. I may not be able to dance with him tonight lest he discovers what I've been aboot. I can't afford him giving me away. And I don't want to answer his questions. And I don't want to lie to him either. The best thing is to avoid him. But I don't want to. Wheest, you sound like a spoiled wean. You can't have everything. Everyone else might think you do, but you know you don't.

Arabella felt a headache developing by the middle of the meal as her mind wouldn't cease its constant internal monologue. She was sick of the sound of her own voice, even if it was only in her head. As the servants cleared away the last of the meal, Lachlan drew Arabella's attention when he asked her to dance. She nodded as she rose from the bench. She recognized the concern in his eyes and knew questions were inevitable. She still wasn't prepared.

"Are you unwell, Bella?" Lachlan whispered as they grasped hands for the first dance.

"I'm hale," Arabella assured as she turned away, then returned to face Lachlan and dipped into a curtsy, matching the other women in her row as the reel began. It was an energetic dance, and it required they change partners, so while she was spared Lachlan's questions, she wasn't spared attention from other men. She was relieved when the dance steps brought her even with Lachlan, even if she wished to avoid his questions.

"Bella, you're very flushed," Lachlan worried. "And your eyes are glassy again."

"Too much wine, I'm sure." Arabella tried to explain away her appearance with a half-truth, but Lachlan shook his head.

"You didn't have more than you usually do. I'm concerned."

"I'm not your concern," Arabella snapped. Her eyes widened at her curt reply. She felt her temper bubbling not far beneath the surface. Generally, alcohol soothed her, but every once in a while, the anger and resentment seemed to be forced higher, making room for the whisky in her belly. "I apologize."

Lachlan nodded, a stony expression on his face. As the music shifted, Lachlan twirled Arabella to the large doors that led to a terrace. He grasped her hands and pulled her into the shadows.

"You're drunk," Lachlan stated. It wasn't an accusation. It didn't even sound like an observation. His tone was flat, stating a fact.

"I am not." Arabella jerked free and shook her head. She was feeling more defiant that she ever had, and she knew she was risking her friendship with Lachlan, but he felt like a safe outlet for her repressed anger and anxiety. "I was, but now I'm not. Killjoy." She hissed the last word. She didn't fail to see the shock and hurt that flashed in Lachlan's eyes before he raised his chin.

"Why? Were you meeting someone? Did he give you too much to drink?"

"What?" Arabella gawped at him. "You think I slipped off with a mon and let him get me soused. Am I too perfect to do something so imperfect on my own? Or am I not smart enough to come up with such an idea on my own?"

"Bella, you're not making sense," Lachlan tried to cup her elbow, but she shied away.

"Of course, I'm not. I'm drunk. Remember?"

"Bella." The exasperation was obvious in Lachlan's voice.

"Lach," Arabella mocked. She witnessed heat flair in his eyes before he tamped it down and narrowed them. "You've accused me of being drunk and of meeting a mon alone. You don't have the right to be indignant in this conversation."

"Mayhap I'm only half right, but it doesn't change that you've been drinking."

"So you say. I had wine at the meal and didn't eat very much. It's gone to my head."

"Why weren't you eating?" Lachlan pressed, but he knew every word he spoke pushed Arabella further from him.

"I'm not a wean, Lachlan. I don't have to explain myself to you. I didn't care for the food, and I didn't feel like eating. I rarely eat much at the evening meal. You know that. You've commented on it before."

Lachlan's chin jerked back in surprise. "I have?"

"Aye. You've made me sound finicky and wasteful. You've drawn attention to how much I eat before, and I didn't appreciate it then. I don't appreciate it now," Arabella blurted.

"That was never my intention." Lachlan was aghast. He had no idea he'd offended Arabella so deeply, and from the sound of it, on more than one occasion. "I offer my most humble apologies, Lady Arabella, for slighting you."

Arabella heard the sincerity, and this time she couldn't ignore the pain in Lachlan's gaze. She'd cut him deeper than he had her. She glanced toward the doors, ensuring no one was watching them before she took Lachlan's hand in hers and squeezed.

"I know you didn't. I just don't like having attention drawn to what I eat. People expect me to eat like a sparrow and comment if I eat what most other women would. When you comment aboot how little I eat, I feel trapped."

"Why is how much you eat anyone's business, including mine?" Lachlan demanded. "Aren't you starving then most nights?"

"People like to have something to talk aboot," Arabella said dismissively. "And my maid usually has a heel of bread and a chunk of cheese for me when I return to my chamber."

"That's it?"

"I haven't wasted away yet, Lach," Arabella chuckled.

"But you are thinner," Lachlan blurted before snapping his mouth shut. Even in the dark, Arabella could tell he was blushing.

"Most would say that's a good thing," Arabella whispered. She was unprepared for Lachlan to step closer. If it had been any other man, she would have felt crowded. But it was Lachlan, and she yearned for him to pull her into his embrace. He never had, and he never would. Dancing was the closest they ever came to Arabella being in his arms. She swallowed the lump in her throat, resigning herself to not receiving the consolation she realized she needed.

"Bella, you haven't an ounce to spare. I noticed earlier that you look like you're withering away, but I didn't dare say aught. But you worried me when you arrived with rosy cheeks, a red nose, and glassy eyes. I thought you might be suffering from the ague."

Arabella's fingers flew to her nose. She hadn't thought that her nose would be evidence of her imbibing. She wondered if that happened every time she drank and if others noticed. She assured herself that it mustn't or someone else would have pointed it out.

"Bella," Lachlan squeezed her hand before bringing it to his lips. He pressed a kiss to the satiny skin, and it was the first time his mouth made contact with any part of her. "I wish you trusted me enough to tell me what's wrong. Will you at least speak with Blair? Something isn't right."

Arabella nodded, ensnared by the intensity of Lachlan's gaze. The inky summer night with only torchlight for illumination made it difficult to see his whisky-hued irises, but Arabella knew that staring into Lachlan's eyes was like looking into a barrel of aging liquor. In the daylight, it suffused the same warmth into her as the drink. But in the dark, it sent a shiver along her spine, their potency as strong as the drink.

"There wasn't much time to talk today, but I am looking forward to seeing Blair this sennight. I've missed her and Maude dreadfully." As though her words were a bucket of icy water, Lachlan stepped back and released Arabella's hands. The reminder that the woman he desired above all others was a dear friend to his sisters brought reality crashing back down. Lachlan nodded as he cast a glance over his shoulder.

"We should return before too many people notice we've both disappeared," Lachlan suggested.

"Aye." Arabella agreed, but she couldn't make her feet move. She bit her bottom lip as she worried that she'd driven a wedge between them. If he was to be here such a brief time, she didn't want to squander it with ill temper. "Lach, I'm sorry for being so rude. I ken you're speaking to me as a friend and with good intentions. I'm testy of late, and you stepped in front of my target, I guess."

Lachlan paused and waited to see if Arabella would offer more. She sighed and relented. She could at least tell him part of what caused her such upset. She wouldn't confess to her secret habit because she still didn't think it was any of his business, but she could tell him part of what drove her to drink.

"My father has made it clear that it's time I marry. I never opposed him, but he acts as though I've failed him and my clan. I've been here almost the longest now, and I have drawn no proposals he's been willing to accept. He says I haven't been trying hard enough. 'God didn't give you a bonnie face just for it to be useless'."

Arabella shuddered as she recalled her father's last visit to court nearly a year ago. She knew there had been many offers for her hand over the years, but none were acceptable to her father's matchmaking and political intentions. He blamed her for not charming men she never knew came to court, and he'd hinted more than once that she should have used her attractiveness to trap a man alone, forcing him to marry her.

"Bella—"

"Belle," Arabella whispered.

"What?" Lachlan squinted as though seeing her more clearly would make the single word make more sense.

"I don't like the name Bella. I never have," Arabella offered as though it explained everything.

"I don't understand," Lachlan admitted. "It's part of your name. Do you not care for your name?"

"Not particularly. 'Yielding to prayer.' I don't mind its meaning, and the Lord honestly kens I have yielded hours of my life to prayer, since the queen is so devout. But I just have never liked Bella. I ken it's Latin, but I don't speak Italian or Spanish and neither does anyone I ken. We speak French and Scots. You and your family and Laird Cameron all speak Gaelic. I don't see why it and Isabella are so popular. Since I speak French and so does my family, Belle makes more sense. And there have been entirely too many Arabellas and Isabellas all nicknamed Bella since I've arrived here. I detest being called Bonnie Bella. I'd like to give the next person who calls me that a bonnie black eye."

Lachlan's deep chuckle rumbled in the quiet night air. Its pitch was like thunder, but rather than ominous, it was contagious. Arabella giggled before catching herself.

"I don't think you'd care for the Gaelic version of 'yielding to prayer.' It's *toradh gu ùrnaigh*."

"I agree. I don't care for that," Arabella giggled again.

"I think you prefer Belle because you're a wee rebellious. You don't want to be what everyone expects." Lachlan cast a shrewd look over the silhouette of Arabella's visage. "You are more than what people expect."

Arabella gasped. No one had ever seemed to expect her to be more than pretty. That expectation often felt suffocating, but she wanted people to know her for more than her appearance. It felt as though nothing else about her meant much to most. She knew her friends like Blair and Maude saw more to her than her auburn hair and green eyes, but she was certain it took a while for at least Maude to move past Arabella's appearance. She'd seen the insecurity in Maude's eyes countless times, and other people pointing out the differences in their looks only made both women feel worse. Maude felt inadequate, and Arabella felt guilty and resentful. Maude had become a respected healer at court, and her value was seen more for her knowledge than the superficial. Arabella wished the same were true for her.

"I take it I might be a little right," Lachlan broke into her thoughts once more.

"How did you become so insightful?" Arabella whispered.

"How many years have I known you? You have been by my sisters' side each time I visit. I think we've spent enough time together to say we're well acquainted, Belle."

Arabella felt the heat rise from her belly into her chest as her preferred nickname rolled off Lachlan's tongue with a pronounced burr. He slipped his hand to her waist but did nothing more. When she didn't pull away, his fingers flexed, encouraging her to step closer. It was the slightest nudge, but all she needed. She stepped into his embrace as his hands came around her waist. With nowhere to put her hands but at his waist, she noticed she clung to his leine. She could feel the heat building between them. She always tended toward being too warm, and it felt like an inferno broiling her. She tilted her head back and caught Lachlan observing her. She didn't understand his expression, but she understood what she wanted.

"I don't think you're so tipsy anymore," Lachlan murmured. "Will you remember this in the morning?" Without waiting for her response, he brushed his lips against hers. Arabella swayed against Lachlan's much larger frame, finally where she'd longed to be since she first met him. There was open passion here rather than the desire they ignored when they danced. She opened her mouth to his pressing tongue and moaned when she felt it pass her teeth before swiping along hers. She felt intoxicated all over again, and she preferred this to whisky. She prayed she wouldn't wake up with the same regret and headache that she did when she drank.

Lachlan was certain his knees shook. He feared Arabella would hear them knock together and discover how nervous he was. He wasn't without experience, but he'd longed to kiss Arabella for more than five years, and his head felt as though it floated above his shoulders as fantasy became reality. He struggled not to press for more, knowing that Arabella wasn't familiar with such intimacy. As her tongue flicked out to meet his, the threads of his control frayed further. The feel of Arabella pressing her breasts against his chest as her mouth opened wider hinted at her curiosity. Lachlan tightened his hold around her waist, and Arabella sighed at they stood with their torsos fused together, only their clothing keeping them apart.

A musical crescendo broke the spell they found themselves under, and both heads turned toward the open doors. For the first time, they both seemed to realize the precariousness of their position. Anyone could spot them, and there would be little choice but for them to marry. Both secretly thought that wouldn't be such a horrendous outcome, but the scandal would mar both of their families' names. Lachlan eased his hold and took a step back. Arabella nodded as she sucked air into her dry lungs. Without a word, no acknowledgement of what they'd just shared, they returned to the Great Hall.

FIVE

Lachlan stood to Blair's left while Hardi stood as her champion to her right. They were in the king's private solar, and Lachlan appreciated that Robert the Bruce, godfather to Blair and her siblings, opted for a private audience. As Lachlan listened to Blair and Hardi regale the king with details of the plot to not only usurp the lairdship from Hardi, but for enemy clans to invade through a secret tunnel, Lachlan's mind wandered back to the previous night. He could still feel Arabella's lips against his, like a phantom pain, except the sensation was one of pleasure. Despite breaking his fast, he could still taste her mouth, and his tongue ached to explore every inch of her.

He'd said a hasty goodnight to his family and Arabella before hurrying back to his chamber, where he'd stripped bare and taken himself in hand twice before he felt soothed enough to sleep. It was the same predicament he always found himself in when he was near Arabella, but the sampling only made the agony of not having her worse. It was the epitome of bittersweet.

Now standing before the king, he appreciated the yards of wool and heavy leather sporran that hid his arousal from everyone's eyes. He was torn between wanting to endure more torture by finding Arabella or racing back to his chamber to ease his need with his hand and memories of the night before.

"Lachlan, what say you?" King Robert asked. Fortunately, he'd been paying just enough attention to keep track of the conversation and had an answer prepared. From the speculative look on the king's face, he was aware the discussion didn't hold Lachlan's full attention.

"We were fortunate to arrive when we did, Your Majesty. Blair and Hardwin devised a brilliant strategy to outwit and foil their attackers. The battle was avoided, but the MacLeods and Sutherlands were only too happy to stand witness to the truce the Camerons signed with the Mackintoshes, Shaws, and MacThomases. It is unfortunate that those clans lost any mon, but such was their choice when they plotted against my sister and brother-by-marriage. Perhaps the Clan Chattan Confederation will think twice before setting their sights on the Camerons."

"And do you think the peace will hold between the Camerons and their enemies?" King Robert pressed.

"Aye. The fear and awe on their faces was genuine when they emerged from the tunnel to discover the Sutherlands and MacLeods camped within spitting distance. There can be no doubt which clans stand beside the Camerons. Perhaps they didn't understand what it meant to plot against the clan that now includes a Sutherland, but they do now."

"So the Sutherlands are prepared to march into battle to protect the Camerons," King Robert mused.

"I will protect my sister and her future bairns, but the Camerons don't need our protection. They have our support," Lachlan clarified as his eyebrow arched and his chin came up.

"Don't be testy," King Robert warned with a grin. The monarch cast his amused expression at Blair. "I expected Lady Cameron to have something to say aboot who protects the Cameron."

Blair's cheeks sucked in as though she'd bitten into a lemon, but she remained silent as she glared at her godfather. The nuance of his phrasing didn't escape her, and she knew he was taunting her about Hardi and not their clan. This only made King Robert laugh harder. Blair did little to hide her protectiveness of her husband, and Hardi basked in his wife's attention. While such comments were an annoyance, neither Blair nor Hardi intended to change the dynamic of their relationship. Hardi admired his wife's sharp mind and gumption as much as he appreciated her loyalty and kindness when she taught him to read and write. Blair never doubted Hardi's ability to defend himself by word or deed, but she tolerated no belittling or besmirching of her husband's name because he didn't come to his position with the training most lairds received.

"Your Majesty, the MacLeods of Lewis are of a like mind. They stand beside the Camerons," Lachlan drew them back to discussing the truce. "While they are a greater distance from Tor Castle than we are, they are also prepared to bring warriors to fight alongside the Camerons should there ever be a need."

King Robert steepled his fingers as he considered the three young people before him. He'd known Lachlan and Blair since their births, and he'd met Hardi when the young laird arrived at Dunrobin to foster as a ten-year-old boy. Between the Sinclairs and the Sutherlands, a web of alliances had formed in the Highlands that could have threatened a lesser king. But the Sinclairs and Sutherlands were as loyal as any clan could be, and the Bruce was grateful for his ties to them. There had been less strife in the northern Highlands since the Sutherland and Sinclair siblings married. After years of living in mud and grime as he clawed his way onto his throne and defended his country from the English, Robert the Bruce was ready for peace and tranquility among the more contentious Highlanders. He needed a unified country if he hoped to preserve Scotland's independence. His mind wandered to an unresolved matter, and he seized the opportunity to ask for trusted opinions.

"How do things stand with the Gunns?" King Robert's abrupt change of topic made the others jump.

"As they always do. We get along well enough, but we like them aboot as much as they like us," Lachlan explained.

"Which is not at all," Blair muttered.

"It's been years since Siùsan's ordeal," King Robert pointed out, referring to the kidnapping and abuse Callum Sinclair's wife suffered at the hands of her stepmother's family. Siùsan Mackenzie was the neglected oldest child of Laird Mackenzie, and the man never noticed how his second wife's brother coveted Siùsan. When she and Callum travelled to visit her mother's clan, the MacLeods of Assynt, Siùsan was kidnapped by James Gunn, the younger brother of the then-Laird Gunn. He died for his choices, and it wasn't long after that Laird Tomas Gunn died for taking the wrong side against the Sinclairs.

Tomas Gunn allied himself with a border laird and a man with loyalties to England who conspired to kill Brighde Kerr, Alexander Sinclair's wife. Brighde's father and her suitor concocted a plan to split riches that would only become theirs if Brighde died. Tomas Gunn died on the battlefield at Tristan Mackay's hand. Thus, the Gunns were as problematic for the Mackays as they had been for the Sinclairs.

"It wasn't just Siùsan," Blair reminded. "They tried to kill Brighde, and then they tried to take her from Alex. And we all heard aboot what happened with Cairstine."

Blair shuddered as she thought about the former lady-in-waiting. She'd been part of the group of women who plagued Maude, but they discovered that Cairstine's attitude was a facade to push away potential suitors. Arlan Gunn had attacked her years earlier, and because of his assault she believed she was unsuitable to become any man's wife. It was with support from Eoin Gordon, who pretended to be her betrothed, that Cairstine Grant discovered that Arlan's attack didn't define who she was. She and Eoin were happily married, and the couple was deeply in love. But Arlan and his father, Laird Farlane Gunn— Laird Tomas's younger brother—died for their roles in Cairstine's abuse.

In a handful of years, James, Tomas, Farlane, and Arlan died because of their nefarious connections and the sides they chose. Clan Gunn had been in turmoil for more than a year as they attempted to rebuild from their losses in battle and the decimation of the lairds' family. Beathan Gunn was Arlan's younger brother, but he held little in common with the former heir. As the new laird, Beathan was making strides in redeeming his clan to their neighbors. He'd brokered peace with Clan Keith, and he'd gone out of his way to build accord, rather than just tolerance, between his clan and the Sinclairs and Sutherlands. He wasn't yet on steady footing with the Grants or Gordons, but those two clans lived a fair distance from the Gunns, whose territory was in the far northern reaches of Scotland.

"Young Beathan is proving to be a promising

leader, and his clan has prospered over the year that he's been in charge. He couldn't be more different from his brother, father, and uncles. He's not hot-headed or impulsive. He doesn't feast off of rancor and acrimony. He's done much to foster good relations with your Uncle Liam, and both Callum and Alex see the potential for even an alliance in the future. I don't think their father is quite so convinced."

Lachlan, Blair, and Hardi said nothing. The brother and sister didn't trust their neighbors after the trouble the Gunns caused their cousins, and Hardi wasn't familiar enough with any of the players to hold an opinion. The king looked at Blair before continuing.

"Do you think Lady Arabella can withstand the weather in Caithness?" King Robert asked.

"Lady Arabella?" Blair furrowed her brow, uncertain why the topic changed until she realized the subtly of the question. "Are you marrying her to Beathan Gunn?"

"No!" Lachlan blurted. All eyes swung toward him as he racked his mind for something to say. "Lady Arabella is from the border. She lived through constant skirmishes and attacks. The Gunns aren't much better. Beathan may be trying, but his clan still believes in raiding the Sinclairs. He hasn't curtailed their thievery nearly enough, and there have been clashes along their border with the Sinclairs and the one they share with the Mackays. Da and Uncle Liam have discussed this on more than one occasion. It's why Uncle Liam doesn't completely trust him. For a clan boxed in by two of the most powerful clans in the Highlands, they haven't the sense God gave a gnat to know they shouldn't keep antagonizing all of us. They may be proud of their Viking heritage and claim their name means 'war,' but they're far too fond of conflict to ever have stability."

"Besides," Blair cut in. "Why would a border laird need an alliance with a clan at the very opposite end of the country? The Johnstones are one of the most powerful border reiver clans and hold much of the West Marches. Why wouldn't he find a husband for Lady Arabella from one of the Lowland clans?"

"Because the clan has spent far too much time siding with that bluidy bastard. Laird Johnstone swore his fealty to Longshanks, and he has much to make up for," King Robert snarled. Like many border lairds, Arabella's father switched alliances as he sought to protect his clan from the ongoing turmoil between King Robert the Bruce and King Edward of England.

"Isn't Lady Arabella's tenure here part of their reparations for—" Blair trailed off. She didn't want to say treason, but disloyalty seemed too benign. Laird Johnstone was a powerful man who intended to exert his influence in Scotland and England. From pieces of information she gathered from Arabella, Blair knew the king didn't completely trust her father. Laird Johnstone's ambition kept him from accepting any proposals for Arabella's hand. It surprised Blair that Beathan Gunn was aware of Arabella and held any interest in her. She couldn't see how the alliance would benefit either clan.

"Johnstone is eager to prove that he has mended his way and is now my humble servant. He thinks marrying Lady Arabella to a Highland laird will prove how Scottish he is."

"We're not Scots," three voices grumbled under their breaths. King Robert's uproarious laughter only made the three faces scowl more. While the Bruces were a Lowland clan, King Robert had relied heavily on Highland forces to win the war against the English. He saw himself as more of a Highlander now, but it was small comments such as this that proved he wasn't, truly, one of them.

"Either way," King Robert waved a dismissive hand. "He is looking for a husband for Lady Arabella, and Laird Gunn is looking for a wife."

Blair stepped forward and lowered her voice, even though there was no one in the chamber besides her brother and husband. "Uncle Robert, I understand you consider the political ramifications for each of these noble marriages, but Arabella is my friend. She's a wonderful woman who deserves a mon who kens her and appreciates her for more than her appearance. She will be naught but a trophy to Beathan Gunn. He'll use her beauty and put her on display to prove his position among the other Highland lairds. He will preen and claim that you must favor him above others to have arranged such a marriage."

Blair clasped her hands before her and leaned forward. Her eyes were as beseeching as her tone. She feared for more than her friend's happiness. She feared for Arabella's life.

"Please, Uncle Robert. Don't do that to Arabella. She'll be miserable. The clan will reject her because she's naught like them. Highlanders aren't keen on outsiders, and she'll stand out because of her beauty and her Lowland customs. Beathan may be a good laird, but we've known him since we were weans. He won't make a good husband."

"Who would you suggest instead?" King Robert cast a calculating glance at Lachlan before returning his eyes to Blair. She wanted to squirm and look back at Lachlan, but she didn't dare. When her brother didn't speak up to nominate himself, Blair lifted her chin.

"A mon who already kens she's more than just a pretty face. A mon who will make her welcome among her new people, and a mon from a clan who won't cast judgement without giving her a chance. A mon with a family who will make Arabella belong in a way her own never has." Blair's nostrils flared as she dared the king to disagree with her.

"I shall take that into consideration, Blair," King Robert nodded before offering her a kind smile. He shot a pointed look at Lachlan, who had stood in rigid silence as the king and his sister discussed the woman he wanted for his own. With their business concluded, King Robert leaned back in his chair, giving a clear sign that the trio was dismissed. Blair curtseyed while Lachlan and Hardi bowed. They left the private solar in silence, Lachlan and Blair deep in their own thoughts and Hardi unsure of what to say.

SIX

"You're going to spring such news on me and then in the next breath tell me you're leaving?" Arabella demanded as she tried to calm her anxiety. She and Blair stood outside the Great Hall as people filed in for the evening meal. In low tones, Blair recounted her audience with King Robert and what she learned about Arabella's future. Then she informed Arabella that she and Hardi would depart the following morning.

"I'm sorry, Bella. We can't linger," Blair sighed.

"But it hasn't even been a sennight. I thought you were staying a few more days," Arabella insisted.

"We only planned to stay that long assuming we wouldn't meet with the king so soon," Blair explained. "There is still much to do at home to ensure a unified new clan council that's prepared to defend the clan. Hardi heard a few men talking in the lists this morning, and there are rumblings that the Mac-Phersons have plans for another raid. We have to get home."

"But…" Arabella swallowed the bile forcing its way up her throat. Her eyes darted around the crowd, fearful that people could hear their conversation. She noticed those who were watching her, but it was the same attention she drew every evening. She struggled to convince herself that she shouldn't panic, but she had an overwhelming need to escape. She wanted to return to her chamber and seek solace as she had the night before. With only a tippling left in her other hidden flask, Arabella had her customary dram of fortification before arriving at the Great Hall, but now she wished she could return to her chamber and console herself with the warmth and comfort only whisky offered her. She wanted nothing more than to drink until her lids grew too heavy to stay open and then slip into the abyss of sleep.

"Blair, Lady Arabella." Lachlan's voice made Arabella jump. She hadn't heard Lachlan and Hardi approach, and she was unprepared for his proximity. Only moments ago, the few sips of liquor she'd had felt like not nearly enough to survive the news of a potential marriage to Laird Beathan Gunn. But now the alcohol, mixed with the fresh pine scent of Lachlan's freshly washed hair, made her head swim. She felt unsteady on her feet as she turned to face the men as they joined her and Blair. When she wobbled, Lachlan's hand shot out to steady her by gripping her elbow. She hurried to explain away her lack of balance.

"Blair just told me what the king said. I wasn't prepared for the news. And now she's leaving." Arabella enunciated each word, fearful of slurring her words. She glanced at Blair before shaking her head. The walls were closing in, and she knew there was no way she could remain in the Great Hall and maintain her mask of serenity and grace. "Excuse me."

Arabella made to step around Lachlan, but his hand on her elbow kept her in place. She glanced down at it, and Lachlan must have realized he still held her, because his hand fell away with haste. She drew her gaze up to his, their contrasting emerald and amber eyes meeting. She sucked in a breath through her teeth, feeling too exposed to Lachlan's perceptive and inquisitive stare.

"Are you not well?" Lachlan whispered. Arabella shook her head, her eyes darting to Blair. She didn't want to miss her last evening with her friend, but she felt her heart racing. Her hands were growing clammy, and her lungs ached. She swept her eyes over the growing crowd settling at the tables. The meal would begin soon, and she would lose her opportunity to flee if she didn't leave immediately.

"I'll go back to your chamber with you," Blair offered.

"You need to eat," Arabella countered.

"We can request a tray," Blair argued.

"I—" Arabella could only shake her head. She watched as Blair sent a look at Lachlan before nodding.

"I'll escort you to your door, Belle," Lachlan whispered. Arabella knew decorum called for her to decline. It was inevitable people would notice her leaving with Lachlan, but she felt her unease strangling the breath from her. Casting one more look around the Great Hall, she ignored the judgmental gazes as people watched her speaking to her friends. She felt the eyes assessing her coiffure, her kirtle, the jewelry she wore, looking for any flaw that would be the seed to a new rumor. Arabella nodded, and Lachlan turned to walk to the doors with her. They entered the passageway in silence, both out of discretion and discomfort. They hadn't seen one another all day, and neither was certain whether they should mention the kiss from the previous night. The quiet drew out between them until they reached the passageway that contained the ladies'-in-waiting chambers. Torches in sconces illuminated their path, and when they stopped at Arabella's door, it made it easy for Lachlan to notice the telltale signs he was certain he'd seen the night before.

"Thank you," Arabella murmured. With none of the other scents from the masses of people in the Great Hall, Lachlan was certain he caught a whiff of whisky on Arabella's breath. He blurted his suspicion before he thought better of it.

"Where did you get whisky, Belle?" Lachlan demanded.

Arabella made to take a step back, but Lachlan's arms shot out and pulled her against his chest. His mouth descended and pressed against hers. His tongue swiped the seam of her lips, and despite her better judgement and wariness, she opened to him. Their moans and sighs blended into a melody of passion. Arabella slid her hands over his chest until she could wrap her arms around Lachlan's neck, but she had to stand on her toes to reach. Lachlan's arms encased her in a solid shield where she felt protected from the world. His tongue caressed the insides of her cheeks as it swept over her tongue. Arabella was certain her legs would give out if Lachlan weren't supporting her. An ache took up residence in her low belly as her core tingled with a need to press her hips against Lachlan. His sporran kept her from finding what her body searched for. But it felt like a bucket of ice was dumped over her when they broke apart, and the accusation slipped into Lachlan's eyes.

"I can taste it," Lachlan whispered.

"Is that why you did it? Is that why you kissed me last night too?" Arabella hissed.

"I kissed you then and now because I've wanted to kiss you since the first time I met you. Five years I've waited, Belle. I couldn't last any longer. That's why. But it doesn't change that I know you drink."

"So what if I do? It's not your concern. Mayhap

you should have had the bollocks to kiss me sooner.
Before I'm practically betrothed to someone else. I'm
not your problem, Lachlan."

"I never thought you were a problem. But you
are my friend. You're my sisters' friend too. You
know that's why we've—I've—" Lachlan trailed off.

Arabella inhaled deeply as she pulled her lips into
a flat line. She nodded. The truth was finally spoken
aloud. "I know," she whispered.

"Why?" Lachlan pressed.

"I don't drink much. Just enough to sooth my
nerves before the evening meal. It makes it easier to
ignore people watching me and to endure the endless
attempts at seduction when I'm dancing. It makes it
easier to forget everyone's expectation that I'm perfect." Arabella shook her head. "Clearly, I'm not."

"Belle, is it that bad? I never knew until last night
that they call you Bonnie Bella."

"Aye. I don't ken who started it, but it stuck.
Women comment on my gowns and my hairstyles.
Men go on and on about my hair and eyes. It's all
they can say to me. It's all they see. Women ask what
soap I use and what oils I rub into my skin. I do
naught but stay clean. I would happily be plain if it
would let me lower my guard."

"Plain like they thought Maude was?" Lachlan's
voice held an edge.

"Your sister isn't plain," Arabella snapped.

"But others thought she was. You know how she
fared. You'd prefer the relentless jabs and insults?"
Lachlan reminded her.

"What Madeline and the others said was cruel,
but the attention she received wasn't that different
from what I get. Everyone has something to say. No
one sees me as more than my appearance. My family
expects me to catch a wealthy and titled husband,
and my parents have even alluded to me seducing a

mon if I have to. They don't believe I can find a mon who might be interested in me for who I am. I doubt they've even considered it."

"And so you drink?" Lachlan heard the skepticism in his voice, and he knew Arabella did when she pulled loose.

"I don't drink because I pity myself," her clipped tone putting more space between them. "It makes me less anxious when I have to be among the crowd of people. It makes it easier to bear all the stares, all the comments. They don't bother me as much because I'm mercifully numb."

"Where do you get it from?" Lachlan asked for the second time.

"I have a guard who fetches it for me," Arabella confessed. "Lachlan, I don't want to talk aboot this. I told you, I'm not your problem."

"And I told you, you aren't anyone's problem. But that doesn't mean that I don't think this is problematic."

Arabella felt her defensiveness building, and she felt backed into a corner. What did Lachlan know? He wasn't the one who felt himself being ground down by the weight of expectation for something as trivial as his good looks. Her anger increased with every word he spoke, so she lashed out.

"I'll be another mon's bride soon enough. I doubt I'll be wanting whisky when I'm with him." Lachlan didn't miss the innuendo as he glared at her.

"You'll crave it even more after the first time you go to Beathan Gunn's bed. Too bad your guard won't be there to feed your habit."

"You don't ken what you're talking aboot," Arabella sniffed.

"Don't I? Have you met him? I've known him since I was a wean. He may be a good laird, but he's not a good mon."

"Bah," Arabella waved a hand. "How can he be a good laird if he isn't a good mon? That makes no sense."

"His brother Arlan wasn't the only one with a reputation for forcing women."

Arabella gaped at Lachlan. Nothing he said eased her fear of marrying the stranger. His words added to her anxiety and only made her want to escape into her jug of whisky. She narrowed her eyes at him.

"Why would you tell me that? You're jealous, that's why. I have no choice but to marry him if that's what my father decides. You want to scare me to punish me."

"This is to punish you," Lachlan growled as he pulled Arabella back against him and spun her, so her back was against the wall. His mouth crashed down to hers with no mercy. She opened to him without hesitation. Their anger fueled their passion as Arabella flicked her tongue into Lachlan's mouth, taking control of the kiss before he could. His chest pinned her against the wall as his hand grazed along her ribs until he cupped her breast. He kneaded the firm mound as his hips pressed forward. He ripped his mouth away long enough to growl, "This is to remind you of who wants you. Who's always wanted you. I don't give a bluidy damn aboot your looks. But it'll be me you think of when he's rutting on you."

"Then you should have done this sooner because it doesn't matter. You're right. I'll be in his bed soon enough," Arabella panted before their mouths fused together again. Lachlan felt Arabella's nipple pebble beneath his palm. He pinched it until she moaned with need.

"You wouldn't have let me," Lachlan countered. "Not until now you know you can't have me. But it will be me you wish was buried inside you. Can you see me when you close your eyes? It'll be my face you're looking at."

"Am I who you see as you tup other women?"

"Yes." Lachlan snapped. He could be as spiteful and proved it with his next words. "They're so well pleasured they don't care when it's your name I call out with my release."

Arabella pushed against Lachlan's chest, but he didn't budge. "I despise you. I'm not humping anyone, but you seem to be more than happy to toss any skirt that will rise for you."

"You'll be humping someone else for the rest of your life sooner than I will."

Arabella grunted as she tunneled her fingers into Lachlan's hair and tugged hard. Her other hand fisted his leine as she pulled him back to him. "Then give me something to remember, Lach."

Lachlan gazed down at her and regretted what he said. He knew his words would last longer in her memory than the feel of his kisses. "I was being cruel. Arabella, I'm no monk, but there is rarely anyone else. But I didn't lie when I said it's you I call out to."

"You can tell I've kissed before. Never like this. But it's you I've thought of." Their kiss was gentler, more like the previous night. Their anger fizzled as regret took its place. Regret for wasted time and wasted opportunity. Regret for a future that would keep them apart. Lachlan's touch as he ran his hand over her back was soothing rather than needy. As Arabella ran her fingers through his hair, her touch was so tender that Lachlan's heart ached. Laughter from nearby forced them to separate. Arabella slid along the wall until her door was at her back. She reached behind her for the door handle, but she couldn't bring herself to open it. She was certain her heart was breaking as she looked at Lachlan. When the voices drew too close to ignore, Lachlan shook his head.

"It'll always be you," he whispered before he spun on his heel and disappeared into the shadows where Arabella knew he would hide until the passageway was empty.

She entered her chamber and closed the door without a click. Her new roommate Rebekah would return some time later that night, but for now Arabella knew the meal was still going on. She didn't know which ladies were in the passageway, and she didn't care. She scrambled to reach under her bed. As she pried the stones loose, she held her breath, eager for just one sip. But she knew she wanted far more than one. She wanted to drink until she no longer felt anything, until she passed out on her bed and wouldn't dream of Lachlan.

She pulled out the jug she'd drained before going to the Great Hall and set it on the floor before moving aside the one that she'd finished the night before. She had one more hidden in the hole she'd discovered several months ago. She sighed as her fingers wrapped around it, but it was a whimper that she made next when she shook it and no liquid swished inside. She sat down heavily as she banged her head back against her bed thrice.

Sard! Now what? I can't ask Edwin to fetch more yet. It's too soon. But what am I going to do? I need more. Need more? Have I turned into a bluidy drunkard? Nay. I just like a little tipple here and there.

Arabella felt her heart speed up as her agitation grew with each thought. She wasn't sure she'd be able to sleep if she continued to get more worked up. Her eyes prickled with frustrated tears. On trembling legs, she rose and stripped off her gown before releasing her hair from the combs which kept it swept up. She crawled into bed and pulled the covers practically over her head as the tears fell. She cried from loathing the person she was becoming, the angry words she'd spewed at Lachlan, the hurtful things he'd said, and her frustration that she held from not being able to slip into an oblivion where no dreams of a dark-haired Highlander could plague her.

SEVEN

Arabella awoke with an aching head and a heavy heart. She slipped from her bed and tiptoed across the chamber, glancing at Rebekah to ensure her roommate was still asleep. She was grateful to Eliza, her ever-efficient maid, for the ewer of fresh water that sat on the table beside her combs and ribbons. She dipped a linen square into the icy water and folded it before slipping back into bed. She cringed when the bed creaked under her weight, but her roommate's light snores didn't pause. She placed the cool compress over her eyes as she tried not to think about the previous night. But try as she might, her mind insisted upon reliving every moment of the tense conversation with Lachlan.

She'd never imagined that a kiss, let alone all the ones they shared, could be so passionate. They'd both been angry and hurt, but neither shied away for once. She felt a certain freedom in finally showing Lachlan that she wanted him, and she reveled in knowing he felt the same. But it was agony to know that she couldn't have a future with him. She feared that his emotions were rooted more in lust than love, even if he'd told her he didn't care about her appearance. She wanted to believe that he felt as deeply for her as she did for him, but she knew it would pain her even more if he did. She dreaded a future with a man other than Lachlan, and his comment about Beathan terrified her. She would go to her husband's bed willingly, whoever he might be, because it was her duty. But she didn't want to be forced. She didn't want to be abused. She pushed her mind away from Beathan and the possible betrothal. It hadn't happened yet, and she wouldn't buy trouble where there was none.

But her mind jumped to Lachlan's musings about being with other women. It stung to think he wasn't chaste like she was. But how could she expect him to be? It hadn't been love at first sight, even if there had been an attraction from the start. It had taken time for her feelings to develop into the strong ones she possessed now, and she suspected it had been the same for Lachlan. They had no commitment between them, and until two nights ago, neither intended to act upon their emotions. She couldn't begrudge him for living his life. But she envied him the touch, the release, the distraction. He was a man, and no one would question him arriving at his wedding without his virginity. Arabella had no such freedom. But she wouldn't deny the pleasure she derived from knowing that while his body was with another woman, his mind and maybe his heart were with her.

As the pain behind her eyes eased, she lifted the cool compress from her face. She once again crept to the ewer and poured more water into the basin. She splashed the chilly water on her face and rubbed the sleep from her eyes. She soaked the cloth once more before climbing back into bed. She knew it was still early, but she no longer felt sleepy. She hadn't woken so early since before she'd discovered the soporific effects of alcohol. Once more her mind replayed the events from the night before. She could feel Lachlan's body against hers and taste his tongue in her mouth. Her body grew warm as the ache returned to between her legs. She understood what her body wanted. So many years at court had given her an education on how men and women enjoyed one another's bodies. She might still be a maiden, but she'd heard and seen enough to know her body was keenly aware of Lachlan's masculinity.

Rather than torture herself, she opted to dress and slip from her chamber. She would find her guards before they went to the lists and ask them to accompany her on a ride. Fresh air and the wind through her hair would wipe her mind clear of her troubles. As she approached the barracks, an all-too-familiar form walked out of the door. Lachlan, accompanied by his four guards, turned toward the lists. She knew the moment he spotted her. His back went rigid, and his head snapped up. He offered her a curt nod, but did nothing to change his course. Arabella could do nothing more than return the brief acknowledgement before continuing toward the barracks. She knocked on the door and stepped back. She recognized the swath of Kerr plaid slung over the man's shoulder who answered.

"Aye?" The man greeted her. She knew when he recognized her because his eyes widened. "I beg your pardon, Lady Arabella. If you're in search of your men, they've already gone to the lists."

"Thank you." Arabella turned in the direction that Lachlan had travelled and found him watching her. If she wanted to go for a ride, she had no choice but to search for her guards at the lists. She clamped her jaw shut as she prepared herself for the inevitable confrontation. When she was within speaking distance, Lachlan turned away and walked through the entrance to the lists. Arabella's stomach clenched with a sharp pain that nearly made her double over. The air she inhaled burned her nose and throat and seemed to get lost before it found her lungs. Lachlan had snubbed her in the most obvious way.

"Lady Arabella?" A voice called to her. She shifted her gaze from Lachlan's back to the men approaching. It relieved her to see her guards moving toward her. When they left the lists and stood before her, she doubted whether she wanted to go for the ride after all. The desire to flee back to her chamber and hide there until the day she drew her last breath consumed her; from the pain in her chest, she suspected it would be that very morning. Guilt tugged at her for drawing her men from their training, but she would appear a fool now that they waited for her to speak.

"When you finish training, I would like to go for a ride, please." The men before her might have served her, but they were still clan members, and she was always mindful of treating them with respect.

"Would you rather go now, my lady?" her guard, Duncan, asked.

Arabella bit her bottom lip as she peered past the men to the lists. "I don't want to take you from your training. I can wait."

"It's nay trouble, my lady," Duncan assured.

"Very well. If you don't mind." She smiled, but then wanted to grimace when she saw the men's inevitable reaction. She was their laird's daughter, but none were much older than her, and she recognized their appreciative expressions. They didn't offend her, but she was tired of having to always be mindful that she never gave the wrong impression to any man. She turned toward the stables, not waiting to see if the men followed.

Arabella asked a groom to saddle their horses as they milled about in the bailey. She darted a glance toward the lists, and it surprised her to find Lachlan watching her. She was too far to read his expression, but she would recognize him anywhere, even if the Sutherland plaid didn't give him away. She grew warm, and her skin prickled. She knew he could see her no more clearly than she could him, but the scrutiny set her on edge. She willed the grooms to hurry and barely waited for her men to mount once she was in the saddle. She charged through the gates, forcing herself not to look in Lachlan's direction one last time.

Lachlan watched Arabella surrounded by her men; for the first time, he had a consuming wave of jealousy wash over him. He knew they were her kinsmen and her guards, but knowing she would spend time with other men away from the castle made him want to roar with envy. He wanted to be the one taking her for a ride. Of more than one sort. His cock throbbed with frustration as he recalled the night before for the umpteenth time that morning. He'd barely slept, restless even after bringing himself to release each time his rod swelled. He was grateful that he didn't have a roommate, or he wouldn't have been able to ease his discomfort. He wondered if Arabella had suffered even a smidge of what he had. He wondered if she knew how to touch herself to bring about a climax. If she didn't, he found he wanted to be the one to teach her how. He already knew the ways he wanted to do it for her. He'd fantasized about it countless times.

Lachlan forced himself to focus upon the man who now stood before him, ready to cleave him in half if he remained distracted. Even with a blunted sword, it would be painful if his opponent got the better of him. As he swung his sword and blocked his partner's thrusts, he found his mind easing and his body loosening. He centered himself, and by the time practice was over he felt more relaxed. He even realized he'd gone hours without thinking about Arabella or what had passed between them. But the moment he stepped out of the lists, his mind returned to her. He wondered if she'd returned from her ride yet. He was torn between wanting to rush to her side to ask where she'd gone and what she'd done, and wanting to hide from her to avoid the discomfort of seeing her and not having her. He wanted to avoid an uncomfortable conversation, even if they ignored the encounter in the passageway.

It was nearly time for the noon meal, and Lachlan stepped into the barracks to complete his rushed ablutions rather than winding through the castle to his chamber. He heard three Lowland voices as he stood beside his guards at the bucket of water and passed the bar of soap. He knew immediately they were Arabella's guards.

"She never rides recklessly, but you would think the Devil bit her arse," one man said.

Lachlan wasn't happy to hear what she'd been doing, or that her guards discussed her where anyone could overhear.

"Aye. She's lucky she didn't break her bleeding neck or cripple her horse. I don't know what's gotten into her lately, but I want no part of this. She asks too much these days. Her father will murder me if he ever finds out that I get her—" the second man trailed off when Lachlan stood with his arms crossed and eyes narrowed.

"Perhaps you could find somewhere else to gossip like fishwives. Somewhere that all and sundry don't get to listen," Lachlan growled. The men's heads whipped around until all three faced him. Their embarrassment was obvious, and Lachlan drew it out by not budging. He stood with his arms crossed and the most menacing gaze he could muster. "If you don't want the lass's father to ken, I would keep your gob shut."

"Aye, Sutherland. As you say." The third man cleared his throat, and the three Johnstone warriors hurried to finish dressing before trying to squeeze past Lachlan, but he filled the doorway to the room the men were in. He caught the eye of the man who nearly admitted he supplied Arabella with alcohol. He tilted his head from one side to another, knowing that it would crack in both directions.

"I know what you're doing." Lachlan said no more. The warning was implicit in his tone, even though he said nothing else. He turned and walked away. His anger percolating just beneath the surface as he made his way to the Great Hall. His eyes swung toward the feminine chatter to his left, and he recognized the ladies-in-waiting. He noticed Arabella standing with Laurel Ross and Caitlyn Kennedy. She had her back to him, but almost as though she sensed him entering the gathering hall, she shifted so she could look back.

It was Arabella's turn to give him the cut, as she spared him not even a nod before returning her attention to the other women. Lachlan knew he deserved it, but he'd been in a hurry to avoid her that morning lest he make a fool of himself by falling to his knees and begging for her attention. He made his way to the table where his men already sat before enduring what felt like the longest midday meal of his life.

With no reason to linger at court other than his wish to spend time with Arabella, he had nothing to fill his afternoons. He opted to go for a ride much like Arabella had, and he found himself riding like a daredevil, much like her guards had described her. But his time away from the castle ate away the hours until the evening meal forced him to return to the Great Hall. While he never looked directly at Arabella, he was aware of her presence the entire night. She never turned to him or acknowledged him. It stung, but he knew he was acting no better. They studiously avoided each other, and he never approached her for a dance. Lachlan abandoned the gathering early. His moroseness must have shown since each of his dance partners scurried away as soon as their set ended. He noticed that Arabella avoided dancing as often as she could, finding ways to entrench herself in conversations with the other ladies.

So began their game of pretending to be strangers to one another. They avoided one another for the next three days, ensuring they never ran into each other in the Great Hall or partnered for any of the dances. Lachlan entered the lists as one of the first men to arrive, certain he could make his way there before Arabella began her day. She took seats at the dining tables that placed her with her back to Lachlan.

By the third evening, Lachlan was miserable, and he could tell Arabella grew more tense with each day. He couldn't tell if she'd continued drinking, but her drawn face and pinched expression made him think she wasn't. Not if she claimed the whisky settled her and made her relax. He wondered if he'd been the reason she ceased or if she'd no longer been able to procure her secret vice. He felt driven to drink, and he needed to escape the castle. His frustration tempted him to find solace in a woman's arms at one of Stirling's taverns, but he abandoned the idea as soon as it came to him. He didn't want another woman, even if he was able to pretend she was Arabella. He intended to take a page from her book and drown his sorrows in a barrel of whisky.

When his men finished eating, he surprised them by offering to treat them to several drams at one of the taverns in town. The men's enthusiasm cheered him as they made their way out of the keep and walked into the surrounding town. The thought of finding a woman once more floated through his head, and he decided to go where the night took him. They entered the Merry Widow, the unofficial name for a tavern renowned for being the location of illicit liaisons among the experienced women at court. Perhaps he would find his own merry widow for the night.

EIGHT

Arabella pulled her cloak closer around her neck as she adjusted her hood with the other hand. She kept her head down to ensure the light breeze didn't blow back the cowl that would reveal her auburn tresses. She didn't intend for anyone to discover her as she secretly ventured into Stirling. She'd slipped into her plainest gown, one she used for traveling, and removed all of her jewelry. She attempted to look as little like a lady from the royal court as she could. She wound her way through the streets to the tavern where she knew her guard could buy her flasks of whisky.

When she arrived at the Picked Over Plum, nicknamed such for the aged whores who worked there, she made her way around to the back of the building. She would never be brazen enough to enter through the main door and wander up to the counter to make her request. She took a deep breath before raising her fist to knock on the door. It swung open to a grizzly man who grunted at her.

"What have we here? You're a ripe one, I'd say," the man sneered as he reached out to push back Arabella's hood. She jerked away, but the man followed her outside as she tried to retreat. "Changed your mind aboot whoring, have you? I don't think so, lass. You're too fine to let go."

Arabella feared she'd wet herself, she was so terrified. She never imagined this would be the response she would receive. She'd sorely underestimated what went on at the tavern if her mere presence as a woman meant the man assumed she was a whore.

"I'm only here to buy whisky for my mistress," Arabella clarified.

"Then she should come in and make herself comfortable. Perhaps she'd find more than just the whisky to her liking," the man cackled. Arabella understood he referred to the whores, and it wasn't the first time she'd heard of women fornicating together. She was only interested in the whisky.

"She sent me to buy whisky," Arabella insisted. She drew a sharp blade from within the folds of her cloak. She and the man knew he could disarm her, but the blade was long and sharp. She would do some damage before he took it from her.

"Bah. I don't need a virgin here. And I don't sell whisky for the taking. Go back to your mistress before a mon takes what you aren't offering." With a lip curled in disgust, the man turned back to the door, leaving Arabella alone in the dark.

Now what? Where else do I try? The Wolf and Sheep or the Merry Widow? If you had any sense, you'd return to the castle and never take another sip of whisky again. But I can't do that. I need more.

Need more? Listen to me. I am a drunkard. But I don't bluidy well care. I already knew that anyway. They don't call it uisge beatha *for no reason. It is the water of life, or at least mine. I must get more. I can't face seeing Lachlan for another day or the questions that are pressing me to explain why I'm acting different if I don't get something to calm my nerves. What do I care if he's disappointed in me? He's not my husband and never will be. Like I told him,*

I'm not his problem. Then why am I so anxious each time I see him?

Arabella's mind swirled with doubt as she rationalized her choices to herself. She made her way to the Merry Widow and went around back, just as she had at the last tavern. A woman opened the door this time and invited her in. She slipped into the kitchens and inched closer to the door that allowed her to peek into the main room. Men in varying states of inebriation filled the tavern. She glanced around the room, but her eyes fixed on the dark-haired warrior who grinned as a serving wench leaned over as she placed a drink before him. Arabella watched Lachlan grin as the women's breasts nearly tumbled out of her blouse. She dropped the coins he handed her down the front of her top and offered him a salacious smile. Lachlan chuckled and waggled his eyebrows. The woman took his reaction as an invitation and dropped into his lap, pressing his face into her cleavage. Lachlan pulled away immediately but laughed again.

Arabella thought she would be ill when she saw him tweak her nipple. It was over in a matter of a blink, unlike how he'd played with her breast the night before. He pushed the woman off his lap, and it was that moment that he looked in Arabella's direction. He was out of his seat in a flash, and Arabella let go of the door. She fled through the kitchen and ran back into the pitch-black night. She glanced around, looking for somewhere to hide. If Lachlan followed her, there was no way she could outrun him. Arabella made for the shadows between two buildings, but she clawed at the man who captured her arm.

"Cease, Belle. It's me," came the angry growl. "Cease or I shall spank your perfect little derriere."

Arabella froze. "You wouldn't dare."

"Wouldn't I? You're not the only one who likes a little whisky at night."

"I noticed. Go back to her. Go back to your whore and see if she likes the name Arabella."

"Why do that when the woman I want is standing right in front of me?" Lachlan grinned, and the light from the moon allowed her to see what would have been a jovial expression in other circumstances.

"I don't want you," Arabella spat. The words hung in the air. It was a lie, and they both knew it. "You're the one who's drunk."

"Don't like it?" Lachlan taunted. "Perhaps you'd like to know what it tastes like to kiss someone with whisky on their breath. Or do you taste of it too?"

"I'm sure you'd like to ken, but you won't."

"Won't I, Belle? Have the past three days been even a bit of torture to you? They've been pure agony to me." Lachlan eased his hand to her waist, then onto her back before sliding to her backside. "I'd only spank you if you wanted me to."

"Why would I want that?" At the confusion and disgust in her voice, Lachlan leaned next to her ear.

"Because you want my hands on you as much as I want to put them there. Because you're risking your pretty little neck, and I'm livid. Because you haven't screamed or tried to run away," Lachlan whispered against her cheek, the smell of whisky wafting to her nose. The scent was welcome and familiar, and she wanted to taste it as much as she wanted to taste Lachlan. As though he sensed her temptation, he squeezed her backside. "You want a taste. You can't have the whisky without the mon."

"I want both," Arabella breathed.

Their bodies collided as Lachlan pulled her toward him. Arabella's hands flew up to brace herself, but as soon as they felt the scorching heat through his leine, she fisted the material. She tugged until Lachlan bent low enough for her to find his mouth. The kiss was savage as they both tried to master the other. Inspiration struck Arabella as Lachlan pushed his sporran out of the way and ground his length against her mons. She thought of something Blair told her that a woman could do with her mouth to please a man. She'd heard of it before, but Blair had convinced her it was enjoyable for both partners. While Arabella wouldn't drop to her knees like a doxy, she sucked Lachlan's tongue into her mouth. His response was immediate. He lifted her off her feet and moved them further into the dark before pressing her against a wall.

"If you weren't a maiden, I would be inside you," Lachlan ground out as his hips rocked against Arabella's mound. "It's your kisses that make me drunk."

"If I'm no longer a maiden, I can't marry him. I won't stop you." But Arabella's words stopped Lachlan. He released her and yanked her arms from around his neck.

"You want me to fuck you because you don't want to marry Beathan. You'd make me your whore for the night to escape him. Use your whisky to escape your life, not me." Lachlan gripped Arabella's arm and dragged her from between the buildings. He knew his guards would be waiting for him. He swung Arabella around until she stood before him. He dropped his voice until only she could hear. "They will take you back to the keep. I have unfinished business to conduct. At least the whore inside doesn't want me for aught more than my coin."

Arabella's hand flew toward his face, but he caught her finely boned wrist. "Go fuck her, but she will never be me. And Beathan will never be you. You deserve the same misery I do."

Lachlan heard the pain he felt in Arabella's voice.

He had no intention of following through with his threat of bedding the woman inside the tavern, and he couldn't go through with letting Arabella think he would. He glanced at his guards before guiding Arabella back into the shadows.

"I can't let you leave thinking I'm going in there. I'm not. I don't want her, or anyone else," Lachlan admitted.

"Why are we trying to hurt each other? We've never argued, and now we're spewing horrid, venomous things at one another," Arabella's voice trembled.

"Because we're frustrated over a situation we created."

"I didn't want to upset your sisters. I was scared it would ruin our friendships if things didn't work out with you," Arabella confessed.

"I feared the same. I didn't want to cause a rift between you and my sisters, and I didn't want to disappoint them if you turned me away."

"I wouldn't have turned you away," Arabella whispered.

"I know that now," Lachlan replied.

"Now what?"

"I don't know." Lachlan shook his head. "King Robert said your father is working on that betrothal. We can't keep doing this if you're to be promised to another mon."

"I don't want him," Arabella's voice croaked.

"I know. Belle, will you let me speak to King Robert? May I ask him to intervene?"

"To what end?" Arabella asked cautiously.

"So I may make an offer for your hand. I think it's what we both want," Lachlan said slowly.

"It's what I want," Arabella nodded.

"I will try to gain an audience with him tomorrow, but I can't guarantee he'll see me that soon."

The pair looked at one another, the moonlight offering enough illumination to see each other's face. Lachlan tucked hair behind Arabella's ear, then cupped her cheek. "You are so precious to me, Belle. I don't want to keep hurting you. I never imagined I could say the things I've said this sennight."

"I'm sorry," they said in unison. They smiled, and Lachlan wrapped his arms around Arabella. She encircled his waist with her own arms and laid her head against his chest. The embrace was meant to offer comfort, and both reveled in the feel of holding one another. Lachlan rested his cheek on the crown of her head, and Arabella sighed, content for the first time since Lachlan and his family arrived in Stirling.

"I don't want to move," Lachlan murmured.

"Me neither," Arabella mumbled against his chest.

"But I need to get you back to the castle. It's not safe out here for you."

Arabella's stomach clenched. She knew Lachlan was right. The situation at the Picked Over Plum already taught her that, but she hadn't gotten what she set out for. They might have resolved things between them, but she was still in need of more whisky. As Lachlan drew away, she sighed. She would have to ask her guard Edwin in the morning to fetch more. There was nothing she could do that night, and she didn't want Lachlan to know why she'd left the castle.

"Belle, why were you out here tonight? Why were you in a tavern kitchen?" Lachlan asked as he slipped his hand around Arabella's while they walked back toward the guards. The Sutherland men averted their eyes and pretended as though they hadn't seen the couple emerge from the shadows twice, nor that they found Arabella outside a tavern. She dreaded answering the question, and she suspected Lachlan already knew. But he wanted her to confess. She felt her defenses rise again, and it made her wish all the more for the calming escape whisky brought. She would be better able to answer the question if she didn't already feel so testy.

"Lach, you know why," Arabella muttered.

"You're that desperate?" Lachlan demanded.

"Don't use that tone with me. I don't need your condescension," Arabella spat.

"But you need my common sense. Someone could have attacked you. For what? A little libation? It's not worth your life."

Arabella clenched her jaw to keep from answering. She had nothing nice to say, and she didn't want their argument to flare again. She nodded, but her jaw hurt from how her teeth ground together. She forced herself to keep her thoughts to herself as they moved through the night.

NINE

A rabella and Lachlan walked in silence through the town until they entered the keep's bailey. Lachlan bid his warriors goodnight and escorted Arabella back into the castle through the silent kitchens. Before they reached the passageway that held her chamber, Lachlan guided her into an alcove with a tapestry hung at the entrance.

"Belle, you frighten me with your recklessness. I don't want to know if you've slipped out before. Finding you in that tavern was the worst thing I've ever experienced. All I could think aboot was getting to you before someone else found you. Those men in there wouldn't have thought twice aboot molesting you, and you're neither large enough nor trained to fight them off. I'm calm enough now to realize my anger came from fear. I—I care for you."

Lachlan knew those weren't the words he wanted to say, and they sounded lame to his ears. But he wasn't certain yet that Arabella's feelings matched his. She'd spoken in anger too, but he knew it didn't come from fear. He worried she didn't love him as he did her.

"Lach, I care for you too. Very much. I was humiliated and scared that you found me. I didn't know what you would do. As much as I didn't want to be found, I feared you would leave me. You threatened to do just that."

"I'll never leave you, Belle. Never," Lachlan swore.

"You will when you have to leave for home," Arabella croaked as the lump rose in her throat.

"Belle, I'm not leaving Stirling until you're my betrothed. If you'll have me, I will marry you, Belle. You won't be any mon's wife but mine."

"You mean that?"

"With every ounce of honor I possess in my Highlander soul. I've waited five years to tell you that. I should have been braver and spoken to you and my sisters. I should have confessed my wish to marry you sooner. We could already be wed."

"I don't know that I would have let you. Not while either Maude or Blair were here. Their friendship kept me afloat, and I was too frightened to lose that."

"I think Blair knows how we feel. It wouldn't surprise me if Maude figured it out, too. Now that I'm not keeping my feelings a secret, I can acknowledge what Blair hinted at more than once. I think my sisters would have encouraged us, had we let them."

"Mayhap you're right. Good Lord, our denial was for no reason. So much time wasted, Lach," Arabella said as tears streamed down her cheeks.

Lachlan kissed them away, tasting the salt on his tongue, before trailing kisses to her jaw then her neck. He peppered her skin with scorching but light kisses until Arabella moaned. She tilted her head back as her fingers wove through his hair. When she couldn't resist the need to return his kisses, she tugged on his hair, pulling his mouth from the sensitive flesh where her neck met her shoulder. Their mouths sought one another, and Lachlan sighed as his tongue dipped into her mouth.

Lachlan's hands squeezed her soft backside, and he groaned to feel the flesh fill his palms. Arabella mimicked his action, and her hands cupped his taut buttocks. It was as hard as the stone walls Lachlan had pressed her against more than once. Her hands slid over the rounded surface until she discovered grooves at his hips.

"They were made for your hands, Belle. Made to hold me as I bury myself in you and pleasure you," Lachlan whispered. His mouth was running away from him once more as he remembered this woman he held was a virgin, not one of the wenches or widows he'd bedded in the past. "I shouldn't say such things. I'm sorry."

"Don't you dare apologize. I've been curious for so long to discover what your body would feel like against mine, and my body aches for you to do just what you said. I don't ken why, but I need to hear you desire me as much as I desire you. I need to know I'm not the only one who feels this way," Arabella confessed. "I've wondered and doubted for so long."

"Belle, you must know that I want you more than any woman. You're all I think aboot, all I want."

"I ken, but it still feels good to hear it," Arabella mumbled as Lachlan launched another assault on her neck. One of her hands strayed from his backside as it roamed over his back and then around to his chest. His broad shoulders meant that there were hard planes to run her hand over even as he was pressed against her. Her cool fingers found the blazing skin where the ties to his leine were loose.

"The feel of your skin on mine is nearly too much, Belle. Will you let me touch you? I can intro-

duce you to pleasure, but I won't take your innocence," Lachlan asked.

"I hope by the time we leave here, I'm not as innocent as I was when we came in," Arabella grinned.

"I can assure you of that, but I will leave you a
maiden still. We can't be sure of what will come,"
Lachlan admitted.

"I'll be like Allyson Elliot and run away if my father tries to force me."

"I'll be like poor Ewan Gordon and chase after
you," Lachlan chuckled as he gathered the material
of her skirts.

"Poor Ewan naught. She was running from him.
I'd bring you along with me," Arabella grinned until
she felt Lachlan's fingertips graze the back of her
thighs and his hand cup her bare bottom. The time
for jesting ended when Arabella moaned and dug her
fingers into Lachlan's back. Spurred on by her excitement, Lachlan kneaded the globes as he dipped his
fingers between her legs. His fingers slid across her
damp seam, and he returned her moan with his own
groan. His fingers pressed further into her entrance
as his other hand retreated and moved to pluck loose
the ribbons of her kirtle.

When there was enough give for one sleeve to slip
down her shoulder, he bared her breast. Her rasp-
berry nipple puckered in the chill air and from his
attention. He ran his thumb over it until it was a taut
bud. He cupped her breast much like he had her
backside, her nipple fitting between his fingers. With
each squeeze, his fingers pinched her nipple until it
elongated, and he lowered his head to suckle. Arabella gasped as his tongue rasped over the sensitive
tip. She was certain he was trying to swallow her
alive as most of her small, pert breast fit into his
mouth. The moment he began to suckle, her knees
went limp.

Lachlan's other arm, wrapped around her with his fingers still working her sheath, braced her. Paying rapt attention to her breast, Lachlan's now-free hand gathered the fabric of her gown in the front. When he could reach, his hand caressed her bottom, then her hip, until his fingers brushed the curls at the juncture of her thighs. Arabella fumbled to flip her skirts over her still-covered shoulder. Lachlan slid his thigh between hers and lifted her leg to hook over his hip. With his fingers and his solid tree-trunk thigh, he aroused Arabella to a state where she was certain she would soon be delirious. She grasped the hem of his plaid and pulled up, but Lachlan's hand snagged one of her wrists.

"Do that, and my cock will find your cunny," Lachlan warned. "I won't ruin you, Belle. I will make you my wife, and I will fight tooth and nail to do it. But you can't risk me failing."

Arabella leaned her forehead against Lachlan's shoulder and nodded. She knew he was right, but her body demanded attention in a way her mind couldn't overrule. Lachlan's hand pressed her against his thigh in a rocking motion until she realized the arousing effect it had on her. He returned his mouth to her breast as Arabella moaned. She'd never felt anything like what Lachlan was doing to her body. It felt like it was alive and humming with a need, for what she didn't know. She knew it was a climax since she'd heard women speak of it, but she couldn't imagine how it would feel.

Arabella tugged at the back of Lachlan's leine, sliding her hands beneath the linen until her nails could glide along his back. With each darting sensation to and from her pleasure bud, Arabella's fingers pressed harder as though she might push Lachlan's body to consume her, making them one.

"The feel of your fingers, your nails on me. Mark

me as yours," Lachlan panted, and Arabella realized that his need was as strong as hers. She ran the nails of her left hand up his thigh as she rocked against it. When they reached his plaid, she flattened her hand and slid it beneath the wool. The back of her hand brushed Lachlan's rod, and he sucked in a whistling breath. Taking it as a sign that he enjoyed her touch, she ran her knuckles along the smooth skin, barely touching him. When he groaned, she pushed back his plaid, exposing his length. But the dim light only allowed Arabella to see a shadow.

"Belle, that isn't wise. I want you too much. You're too much temptation. At least one of us should be covered, or we will end up joining," Lachlan warned.

"And you know this for sure?" Arabella questioned.

"Aye." Lachlan felt her tense, and he knew she assumed he meant from his previous experiences. While that was true, it wasn't what he was thinking. "Because my body is in control, Belle. I'm struggling. I want you so much I'd throw caution to the wind to have you. There is only a wee bit of sense trying to make me do the honorable thing. And I'm ready to tell it to shut its gob."

Lachlan resumed his assault on her senses, and Arabella clung to him. But as a tightening began in her core, she refused to ignore Lachlan and focused on what he admitted he needed. Her hand wrapped around his now-covered length, her thumb rubbing along the ridge on the underside.

"Tell me what to do, Lach. Let me."

Lachlan groaned as he continued to suckle her. He encouraged her to increase her pace as he pressed her more firmly against his leg. His other hand wrapped around hers as he showed her how to stroke him. Their mouths connected as Lachlan thrust his tongue into her mouth as though he were starved and looking for succor. Arabella's core spasmed as the bundle of sensitive nerves under Lachlan's thumb seemed to explode. Her hips moved of their own volition, jerking and twitching as she craved something to fill the hollowness in her sheath. As she stroked Lachlan, she understood what she needed.

"Tighter. Faster," Lachlan croaked, and Arabella gladly obliged. Lachlan buried his face in Arabella's shoulder and hair as he grunted once. His teeth bit into where her shoulder met her neck, and her core released another tidal wave of pleasure. Arabella felt Lachlan's cock throb in her hand. Then something wet and cool coated it. Lachlan hurried to use his plaid to wipe her hand clean, but Arabella didn't let go. She continued to stroke him until she was certain she'd milked him dry.

"Belle," Lachlan breathed before pressing the most tender kiss Arabella ever imagined. It was the opposite of the kisses from just moments earlier, but just as exquisite. His arms wrapped around her waist and drew her higher on his thigh. They clung to one another as their breathing slowed, and the pounding of their hearts eased. Arabella rested her head against Lachlan's shoulder.

"What I wouldn't give to be in a bed right now," Arabella whispered and yawned. "I have never felt so comfortable or ready to fall asleep as I do now."

"One day soon I will make that wish come true. Then I will make sure you fall asleep every night just like that," Lachlan promised. He felt Arabella still, so he rubbed his hand over her back. Her fingers pressed against his jaw, turning his head so she could kiss him.

"Do you really believe that's true?"

"I told you, Arabella, I will fight tooth and nail to

make you my wife. I will run away with you if I must. I've cared aboot you for too long to just walk away."

"Run to where? Dunrobin? You're the Earl of Sutherland's heir. You can't go anywhere but home."

Lachlan eased Arabella back and shifted so the shaft of light that peeked past of the edge of the tapestry made it possible for them to see one another's faces. It surprised Arabella to see how stern and earnest Lachlan's expression was.

"Do not doubt I will give up everything for you, Belle. I've imagined it so many times. But it was doubt and loyalty to my sisters that kept me from acting upon it. But given the choice, now that I ken you return my feelings, I would pick you over all else. Without hesitation. I never thought I would have the chance, but now that I do, I won't give up."

"Lach, I wasn't jesting when I said I would run if my father or the king try to force me to marry Beathan, or anyone else for that matter. I've been—I've cared aboot you since we met. I won't accept anyone else now that I ken you want the same thing I do."

"We will solve this together. But promise me, Belle. You won't do aught impetuous or reckless out of fear or frustration. Let me be at your side, so we face this together. Allyson may have run to avoid Ewan, but she nearly died for it. I don't want that for you." Lachlan brushed his lips against hers in a brief kiss before he pulled away. "If your roommate awakes, she will wonder where you've gone. You don't need her to be suspicious or a gossip."

"True. But I was still incredibly comfortable a moment ago. I'd rather go back to that. Or better yet, what we were doing right before that, what left me feeling boneless." Arabella laughed, and Lachlan pinched her backside.

"Cheeky," he growled.

"Only for you." Arabella stood on her toes and

pressed a kiss to Lachlan's jaw. He tilted his head so she could kiss his cheek. Lachlan checked the passageway and waited to spy any movement. When he was certain the corridor was empty, he stuck his hand out behind him. Arabella didn't hesitate to place her hand in his, and he drew her out of the alcove. Still holding her hand, they slinked along the wall until they reached Arabella's door. Lachlan cupped her face in both hands and pressed a butterfly-soft kiss to her puckered lips.

"You are so precious to me, Belle," Lachlan whispered. For a moment Arabella thought he might confess his feelings, but with another quick kiss, Lachlan released her and stepped back. "I will try for that audience with King Robert tomorrow."

Lachlan kissed her forehead, and Arabella knew he was lingering. But eventually, Lachlan stepped into the center of the passageway, where Arabella was unable to reach him. He waited until she opened her chamber door, and she looked back over her shoulder. He slipped into the darkness as Arabella closed the door behind her.

TEN

Lachlan struggled not to tap his toes in irritation and impatience. He'd arrived early to the king's Privy Council chamber and was waiting outside. He'd succeeded in being among the first to gather, but the chancellor still hadn't granted entrance. He was loath to use his personal relationship with the Bruce, but as his frustration grew, so did the temptation. He clenched his fists behind his back and remained in place, stoic rather than pacing. The hours ticked by until the bells rang for the evening meal. Lachlan felt tempted to punch the chancellor when he announced that the king would receive no one else for the rest of the day. The pugnacious man looked directly at Lachlan as he made the announcement, and Lachlan would have been happy to knock the smug expression from the short man's face.

Lachlan weaved his way through the crowd, in a lather from nervousness, disappointment, and annoyance. As he entered the Great Hall, he scanned the gathering people, but didn't see the usual group of young ladies, nor was the queen at her seat. With no one to notice, he gave into the impulse and tapped his foot. He heard the gaggle of women before he saw them as he turned to look at the doorway. He spotted Arabella immediately, her movement a give-away. Her auburn hair rarely caught his attention; he'd long since overlooked her unique features and saw the woman he'd admired from a distance. As he waited for her to approach, he thought about what attracted him to her like a loadstone. She had a cutting and dry sense of humor, but she was never malicious or cruel with her jests. She was astute and possessed wisdom beyond her years. He was also taken by her kind heart and open-mindedness when she befriended Maude, and he'd seen her with Cairren Kennedy, who the other women alienated because of her olive complexion and Arab heritage. She'd not batted an eyelash at either woman and became friends with them soon after they arrived.

"Lach?" Arabella's fingertips tapped his elbow. He glanced down to find Arabella's brow wrinkled. "Looking for someone?"

"You, but I got lost in thought thinking aboot you," he grinned. But his smile faltered as he steeled himself for the disappointment Arabella would inevitably feel when he shared his news. "I wasn't able to gain an audience with King Robert."

Lachlan watched as Arabella's face fell. Tears filled her eyes as she looked at her feet. Her hand crumpled something within it that looked like parchment.

"Belle? I'll try again tomorrow, and if I can't be seen, then I'll use my relationship with my godparents to get me in."

"It'll be too late," Belle choked. She handed Lachlan the wadded piece of vellum. "Beathan and my father will be here in a day to sign the betrothal contracts. I'm to leave with Beathan within a sennight."

Lachlan felt like he'd been felled by a poleax. Try as he might, his lungs didn't seem to fill with air as panic replaced his irritation. He drew Arabella out of the Great Hall as they navigated their way back to the antechamber the king and queen often used for private meetings. He would either find his godfather there and address the matter, or they would have privacy. When no guards stood in his way, he assumed the chamber was empty. He yanked open the door and guided Arabella in. They both came to an abrupt halt as they found the king and queen locked in an embrace. Lachlan and Arabella spun on their heels, but King Robert's voice filled the otherwise silent room.

"What's the point in leaving now?" King Robert snapped.

"Robert," Queen Elizabeth hissed. She cocked an eyebrow and tilted her head toward the couple's hands. Neither realized that King Robert's booming demand had made them entwine their fingers.

"He's too late. He shouldn't have kept leaving his bollocks at Dunrobin," King Robert huffed.

"And I think our godson loves his sisters more than almost anyone," Queen Elizabeth observed.

"What do Maude and Blair have to do with it?"

"My dear, Maude, Blair, and Lady Arabella were —are—very close. Lachlan wouldn't have wanted to ruin the few friendships Maude had. Blair relied on Lady Arabella once her sister was gone," the perceptive queen explained, and the king grunted.

"Lachlan, you're still too late," King Robert cast a gimlet eye at the younger man.

"Is Lady Arabella already wed?" Lachlan waited until the king replied no. "Are the betrothal contracts signed?" The king answered no once more. "Then I am not too late."

"Laird Johnstone and Laird Gunn have already come to an agreement. The signatures are a mere formality. The betrothal is set," King Robert argued.

"If Laird Johnstone is marrying Lady Arabella off to a Highlander to prove his loyalty, he can't do much better than the future Earl of Sutherland," Lachlan countered as he narrowed his eyes at the king.

"On that point I would agree. But the future Earl of Sutherland dragged his feet. Now your mithering won't do you any good. Upset or not, Lady Arabella is set to marry Laird Gunn." Robert the Bruce grinned once more, knowing that his next comment would bother Lachlan the most. "And don't be mardy."

Lachlan's cheeks sucked in as he fought not to respond to the king's taunt. He'd detested the word "mardy" since he was a child. He didn't appreciate being called petulant and awkward. He had a genuine reason for requesting the king's intervention. He loved Arabella. He wasn't a dog in a manger.

"Your Majesty, the Queen is correct. I didn't move forward on my interest in Lady Arabella because I feared to do aught that would upset my sisters' relationship with her. I wasn't here every day. I couldn't protect Maude. How could I jeopardize the one friendship she had? There's naught I won't do for my sisters, and that includes sacrificing my happiness for them. But both of my sisters are wed now, and I believe they want Lady Arabella and me to be together."

Lachlan and Arabella watched the royal couple grimace. They knew the king and queen regretted not intervening on their goddaughter's behalf when a group of ladies-in-waiting ostracized her. Lachlan felt bad for the remorse that entered Queen Elizabeth's eyes, but he took guilty pleasure in seeing King Robert grow uncomfortable.

"Lachlan, it's not that simple, and you know that. Laird Johnstone and Laird Gunn have struck an agreement. You and Lady Arabella don't have a say in it," King Robert reminded.

"But you do," Lachlan asserted.

"I do, but I won't," King Robert replied. Lachlan narrowed his eyes before looking at Queen Elizabeth. He sent the queen a silent plea to intervene on their behalf, but she gave a slight shake of her head. Lachlan nodded once and turned away from the royals, taking Arabella's hand in his. She looked back over her shoulder, aghast that Lachlan would leave without being dismissed.

"Lach," she hissed, but he ignored her. It wasn't until they reached the door that the king spoke again.

"Do something foolish, and it won't just be you who's punished, Lachlan," King Robert called. Lachlan slowly turned around, his disgust evident as he looked at the man who was present on the day he was born. He'd known King Robert his entire life, but the man had just threatened Arabella and his family. He wouldn't easily forgive or forget that.

ELEVEN

Arabella was certain she would be ill. She trembled once she and Lachlan left the royal antechamber. Lachlan's disregard for etiquette and protocol scared her, and her stomach was in knots from learning that the Bruce wouldn't support her relationship with Lachlan. She wanted nothing more than to slip into her chamber and have a tipple of whisky. But she had none left. Frustration at both the king's decision and her lack of alçohol made her temper flare. She bit her tongue to keep from turning it on Lachlan.

"I will speak to your father as soon as he arrives. I will reason with him and remind him that the Sutherlands have far more to offer in an alliance than the Gunns," Lachlan assured her, but Arabella shook her head.

"You don't know my father. If he's made up his mind, then it may as well be written in blood and stone. He won't reconsider," Arabella explained.

"Even if he learns what type of mon Beathan is?"

"Don't you think he kens? He will have learned everything he can aboot Beathan to ensure he could outmaneuver the mon when they negotiated. He doesn't care. He wants to secure our clan lands in the West Marches, and he wants King Robert to absolve him of his past alliance with Longshanks. He doesn't worry aboot being in the king's favor. He wants the king to forget aboot him, so he can do as he wants."

"But does he ken that I want you? That I've always wanted you to be my wife?" Lachlan demanded.

"Then you—we—should have spoken up sooner." Tears filled Arabella's eyes, but she refused to cry. She wouldn't turn into a watering pot in front of Lachlan. If she did marry him, one day she would be the Countess of Sutherland. She would show Lachlan that she could face adversity with calm. But her mind roiled with the need to find whisky or even wine and ale. She smiled wanly at Lachlan. "This may be our last evening together."

"I refuse to accept that," Lachlan countered.

"I don't want to waste it, Lach." They looked in the Great Hall's direction, and they sighed, which brought a smile to both of their faces. They knew they couldn't sit together for the meal, but they could find one another once the music began.

"I would dance every set with you, Belle." Wistfulness filled Lachlan's voice.

"That would cause quite the stir," Arabella pointed out.

"Aye. I would make it clear that we are a couple."

"A couple of fools. It would only cause a scandal that would greet my father and Beathan at the gates," Arabella countered.

"I wouldn't want a scandal to tarnish your name, Belle. You're good and pure. But it might be what makes Beathan turn back to the hills and ride away."

"But my father would remain. I could never face him again. A scandal would force him to acknowledge I'm not perfect. To him, I have to be perfect.

He'd never forgive me if I'm not. What value would I be to him or my clan if I'm not?"

"Och, Belle." Lachlan didn't know what else to say as he wrapped his arms around her. When she didn't pull away, Lachlan knew she needed him more than she cared if anyone saw them. Their mere standing together alone would ignite a scandal, so being found in one another's arms would ruin Arabella. He would come out unscathed, and he knew how unfair that was. He kissed her forehead before leaning back. He took her chin in his fingers, glancing around him before bringing their mouths together. It was a light and brief kiss, but there was affection and tenderness in it. "Let us dine. Then we will dance. We will figure this out. I promise, Belle."

Arabella nodded, trying to appear as though she was confident in what Lachlan pledged, but she wasn't. Lachlan was underestimating her father's tenacity. They went their separate ways once they entered. Arabella joined the ladies-in-waiting, and Lachlan made for the table where his guards sat. Both were reserved during the meal, but they had eyes for no one else, and they found one another once the music began. Their movements were flawless after years of dancing together. Their bodies glided together with ease, much as they had the day before in the alcove. Lachlan held Arabella as close as he dared and was loath to let her go at the end of the set. They partnered with others, but they came back together every third set. They were aware that people watched them and whispered. While they weren't scandalous by dancing so often, they toed a fine and dangerous line.

By the end of the evening, Arabella had nearly forgotten about her father and future betrothed. A night of dancing mostly in Lachlan's arms had eased the tension between her shoulders and between her brows. But when it was time to retire, she was forced to leave Lachlan's arms. She looked over her shoulder as Rebekah tugged her toward the doors. Laurel and Caitlyn were soon by her sides, and the crowd swallowed her. She suspected Lachlan could still see her from his superior height, but her heart sank when she could see him no longer.

Eliza awaited her when she returned to her chamber, helping her take down her hair before easing the gown down her arms. She scrubbed her face and crawled into bed. It wasn't long before Rebekah's rhythmic breathing signaled that she'd fallen asleep, but Arabella laid in her bed. She was fully awake, and her eyes didn't want to remain closed. She thought about their impromptu audience with both the king and the queen. She considered how she would feel when she saw her father after nearly a year. She worried about what it would be like to meet Beathan Gunn, knowing he believed they would marry. She feared how Lachlan would react when her father refused to consider his troth.

The more she thought about the next day, the more her chest tightened. Sweat broke out along her brow. She felt like she couldn't breathe, even when she sat up in the dark. Impending panic only made her feel worse.

I need a drink. I can't do this without something to ease my fear. It would put me to sleep and a dram in the morning would make it easier to face Father. Damn it. What I wouldn't give for a jug right now.

Arabella glanced at the shadowy form of the woman across the chamber from her. Once she was certain Rebekah was fast asleep, Arabella slipped from her bed. She crept to the pegs on the wall and lifted off two gowns. One was her plain kirtle, and the other was a day dress she hung over the plain gown to hide it. It laced on the sides, so she slipped into it without needing her maid. She picked up the riding boots that sat at the end of her bed and lifted her cloak from where it lay across her chest. She eased her way out of the chamber on bare feet. When she made it into the shadows of the passageway, she hurried to put her shoes on and close the cape around her. Even inside, she drew the hood up. She couldn't risk a glimmer of light catching her reddish-brown tresses. She was the only woman at court with that shade of hair, and it would give her away.

Arabella slipped through the passageways, trying not to jump when she heard noises from behind closed doors or wooden floorboards creaked beneath her feet. She left the keep through the kitchens and hurried to the postern gate. She kept her head down as she slipped a small pouch of coins into the guard's hand. He opened it without hesitation, and she found herself able to breathe freely. She picked her way through the streets, staying where light from the buildings illuminated her path. She walked past the Picked Over Plum, not sparing it a glance. She'd had success being admitted into the Merry Widow's kitchen. She knocked and prayed she would be received as cordially as the night before.

"Then now, lass. You're back," said the woman who greeted Arabella the night before. "You were gone in less than two shakes of a lamb's tail. I didn't even have a chance to ask my husband if he would sell you the whisky."

"I ken, and I'm sorry for inconveniencing you last eve. I saw someone I recognized, and my lady wouldn't want it known that she seeks whisky."

"Dinna fash. I figured as much. And it was nay inconvenience. Wait here a stitch, love, and I will find my husband."

"Thank you." Arabella kept her cloak tightly wrapped around her, even though the temperature was sweltering in the kitchens. As the minutes ticked away, Arabella wondered how busy the tavern must be if it took the woman so long to return. Angry voices outside made her turn back toward the door she'd used to enter. The wood suddenly splintered as the door swung open. Burly men burst through the doorway, some with clubs. The kitchen wenches shrieked, and Arabella looked on, stunned into motionlessness. The tavern keeper's wife pushed open the door to the kitchens, but pivoted the moment she laid eyes on the men.

"Raid!" The older woman bellowed. "Raid!"

"A raid?" Arabella asked anyone who might answer.

"Aye," one man grunted. "Your employer doesn't pay his taxes, so we are here to collect. One way or another. You look like you're worth a pretty penny."

"That she does," said another man whose front teeth were missing. "She might be the amount Timothy owes the crown. Find the sod."

While the two men spoke to Arabella, she could hear the furor happening in the main dining room. Furniture crashed; other women's shrieks reached a crescendo over deep, angry, male voices. The number of men swarming the kitchen seemed to continue to swell. The first man who spoke to her seized her arm in a vicelike grip. He swung her around, yanking her arms behind her back. Arabella felt something cold and ungiving encase first one wrist, then the other. She strained to see the manacles the man placed on her. She looked around and witnessed men doing the same to the other women.

The door from the dining room swung open. The woman who let her in and a man Arabella presumed was her husband were shoved through. They wore manacles too, but someone had cuffed their hands in front of them.

Bluidy hell. What have I gotten myself into? Where will they take me? I have to get out of this. I have to be let go before anyone discovers I'm here. But I have to tell someone who I am.

Arabella peered back at the man whose hand was once more wrapped around her upper arm. She kept her voice low as she pleaded her case. "I'm Lady Arabella Johnstone. I'm a lady-in-waiting to the queen. I was merely here on an errand. I can't be taken to the gaol."

"And I'm the bleeding queen of England," the odoriferous man laughed in her face. "Ah reckon nowt ter that."

Arabella hadn't heard a commoner speak during most of her time at court. Even her maid's speech was refined, but she understood the man said he didn't believe her. She wanted to stomp her foot, but acting like a spoiled child would only draw more attention to her. She tried to pull away from him, throwing her body weight in the other direction. She landed against the chest of the man who was clearly the sheriff. He was a stocky man who carried a club, with a pouch swinging from his waist. Arabella knew the sheriff's job was to collect rent and fines, and it was clear he was there for the latter. She wondered briefly how much of the coin in his pouch was for revenue and how much was from bribery.

She darted her gaze at the tavern owner and took in his worn linen shirt and scruffy breeks. She took a closer look at his wife and noticed the frayed hems and cuffs of her gown. Her eyes swung around the kitchen, noting the poor condition of the wenches' clothes, and the old, chipped crockery. The Merry Widow may have been popular, but it wasn't profitable. The man had no money to bribe the sheriff.

Arabella considered the money hidden beneath her cloak and wondered if she could bribe her way to freedom. She needed to speak to the sheriff without everyone taking an interest. She also needed to be set free before they reached the castle. Otherwise someone would recognize her, or she'd be thrown into gaol with no way to get help.

Why didn't I listen to Lachlan?

"Ahm happy as pig in mud," the sheriff grinned as he pulled Arabella against him. He ground his pelvis against her. Arabella's skirts kept her from being able to kick the man's shins. "She's a right bonnie tart."

"Claims she's a lady-in-waiting, she does," the one who manacled her chortled.

"Mayhap she is, or mayhap she's some rich mon's leman. Her clothes are fine, and she's clean. A good rut with a clean whore is worth being slow to return to the castle."

Arabella fought to break free, her feet kicking out as she hoped to make contact despite her skirts. The man wasn't as tall as Lachlan, so she threw her head forward. Her forehead made contact with his nose, and she heard a loud crunch before blood splattered on her forehead.

"You bluidy bitch. You will pay for that. I shall take you extra rough now. Then I'll pass you along."

"And my father and betrothed will murder you in your sleep. They're both lairds. One's a Highlander," Arabella threatened. She felt the moment the man hesitated. She suspected it was hearing that a Highlander might come to avenge her that gave him pause.

"I don't have time for this," the sheriff said as he pulled a dirt-smeared linen from his sleeve and pinched his nose with it. The sheriff slapped Arabella, making her eyes sting and her cheek hurt from where she bit it. Arabella saw him raise his fist even though her eyes watered. "Tha'll get a clip rahnd yer heid if tha carries on like this."

Arabella understood the colloquialism, and didn't doubt the man would drive his fist into her head if she fought him again. She swallowed the blood she could taste and nodded her head. The sheriff dragged her through the door into the main dining room. Arabella kept her head down, thankful for small mercies—her cowl and hood were still in place despite the manhandling. She surreptitiously glanced around to see if she recognized anyone. She prayed Lachlan might have returned, but she knew he wouldn't. He'd come to the tavern the night before because of their argument. She looked to see if any of the women the tavern was nicknamed for were present. If she could find another lady from court, she would sort out her reputation later. An acquaintance could become an ally. But much to her dismay, the only women were the whores and serving wenches.

The sheriff dragged her across the room. She noticed none of the men called one another by name, and Arabella wondered if that was on purpose. If so, she wondered why. It was clear which man was in charge. There would be no anonymity for his enforcers. The sheriff flung her through the front door, and for a moment she considered breaking into a run. She'd been fleet-footed as a girl, but with her hands cuffed behind her back, she had no way to lift her skirts out of the way. The sheriff laughed as though he knew what she contemplated. He used his club to nudge her into walking. He kept a step behind, and Arabella knew he did it so he could swing his club at her. Once bitten, twice shy. He wouldn't let Arabella get the better of him again.

"Sheriff, I can pay my bail and resolve this before

we enter the castle's bailey," Arabella spoke barely above a whisper.

"And how would a woman such as you have the amount I would ask? I haven't paid you yet for a tumble." The man roared with laughter.

"As I told the other man. I'm Lady Arabella Johnstone. My father is Laird Johnstone, and my betrothed is a laird." Admitting twice that Beathan might be her betrothed left a sour taste in her mouth, but she hoped she could use it for leverage. After she spoke, she realized she would have been wiser to say her betrothed was the son of an earl. But she so rarely thought about Lachlan's position that she'd not remembered it before she spoke.

"Is that so? Then all the more fun I'll have exploring you as I look for your coin," the sheriff taunted. Arabella opted for silence. She would do what she could to ensure he didn't lay a hand on her, and she would save her coin to either bribe the guards at the gate or to bribe the guards at the dungeon.

TWELVE

Arabella knew the guard at the castle's gate recognized her because his eyes widened in recognition, but he said nothing. Arabella glared at him as the repugnant sheriff pushed her into the bailey. The uneven dirt and stones made her stumble, and her hood shifted. It tempted her to shake her head and free it of the cover. She wasn't certain if her hair would help or hurt her; either way, people would recognize it. But she waited too long to decide. The sheriff steered the group toward a doorway she knew led to the dungeons. She couldn't even enter the castle and hope to spot someone familiar. The steps were slick, and had the sheriff not gripped her arm, she would have tumbled head over heel. The creak of the dungeon door opening was the most ominous sound she'd ever heard.

Arabella gasped at the stench in the fettered air. She'd never imagined anything could smell so foul. As her eyes adjusted to the dim light, she looked around. She noticed cells lined the walkway ahead of her. With the sound of so many people entering, the prisoners came to their doors and pounded on them. Some of the doors had rectangles cut out to serve as windows the imprisoned men peered through, shouting jeers and profanity as Arabella and the others walked past. She searched for a prison guard, but none appeared. She knew the men who'd led the raid weren't guards because they didn't wear the king's livery or crest.

Arabella spotted the large ring of keys hanging from a peg in a wall above an empty chair. She strained to look into the shadows to discover whether a guard was nearby. Heavy booted footsteps approached from Arabella's left, but she could see little in the dark. She jumped when a hulking figure suddenly emerged, much closer than she expected.

The guard looked as unfriendly as anyone might imagine a man who oversaw the incarceration of criminals. Except Arabella wasn't a criminal. She admitted to herself that she was foolish, but she hadn't committed a crime. She realized that she should point that out.

"What crime have I committed?" Arabella asked. She attempted to keep her tone pleasant. "I was at a tavern behind on its rents, but I'm not related to the owner, and he is not my employer."

"Shut up, bitch," the dungeon guard snarled. Arabella jerked back, unprepared for his aggressive response. She raised her chin, straightened her spine, set her shoulders back, and cast the most imperious glare she could muster while her heart pounded and her bladder threatened to fail.

"You will refer to me by my title, Lady Arabella Johnstone. I am a lady-in-waiting to Queen Elizabeth. I am the daughter of Laird Mitcholm Johnstone and betrothed to the Earl of Sutherland's son."

"And I'm King Robert's long-lost son," the guard sneered.

"Perhaps you should make yourself known to him as I have made myself known to you," Arabella snapped.

The sheriff shook her arm and spat beside her. "I thought your betrothed was a laird. Now he's the son of an earl. I don't believe either. You upstart wench. You've learned to sound like your lady, but if you were one yourself, you wouldn't have set foot in a tavern's kitchen. And you wouldn't have been there alone. Where is your mon? If you have one."

Arabella twisted to look back at the sheriff. She took her time looking up from his feet to his face. She didn't have to feign her disgust. "Wake Lachlan Sutherland and discover who I am. Do it now because if he finds out you've kept me down here, you're forfeiting your life."

Those within earshot hooted with laughter, the sound mocking Arabella. She knew no one believed her. She would have to hope that they would present her to the king for her crimes and that he would exonerate her. But she knew she could rot in the dungeon for years before that ever happened. For all she knew, King Robert had already passed judgment on the tavern owner, and this was his sentence.

No more was said before the dungeon guard led the way down the corridor. He unlocked several doors, before unlocking her manacles and tossing Arabella into a cell. She reeled back from the stench from an unemptied chamber pot, rotting hay, and unwashed bodies she knew were there but she couldn't see. She stepped further into the cell as people entered behind her. She moved to the side wall and inched along it until her foot nudged something. A hand wrapped around her ankle. She didn't scream. Instead, she drew back her other foot and drove her boot into whoever grasped her.

"Touch me again, and I'll kill you," Arabella hissed. She wasn't convinced it was an empty threat now that her hands were free. She realized in that moment there was little she wouldn't do to stay alive, to see Lachlan again. In the dark, she fumbled to withdraw the blade she carried on her any time she left the castle grounds. She carried a smaller dirk while she remained in the keep. While she rarely walked through Stirling Castle alone, it was inevitable at times. She was prepared to defend herself.

It was Lachlan who insisted that she carry a dirk and taught her how to use it. They'd known each other a month, and she'd listened to Lachlan speaking to his sisters about their knife skills. He'd worried for his sisters, but he was speechless when he learned she neither carried one nor knew how to use one. He'd mumbled things under his breath about her father and brothers, but she hadn't caught all of it. She suspected it was nothing polite.

The hand released her ankle, and Arabella inched away. Several tavern patrons were imprisoned with her, and there was little space to be had. She listened to the voices and noted that she didn't hear any other women's tones.

Sard! They tossed me in here with all men. They expect me to be raped. They're punishing me. I should have kept my mouth shut. Arabella tipped her head back and closed her eyes. *If you panic, you'll draw attention to yourself. Remain still and think through this.*

There was a small window near the ceiling, far too high for anyone to reach. In the morning, the light would illuminate the cell enough for the men to see her. She needed to get free before then. She wouldn't be able to hide once the others could see. With the odor of human waste hanging in the air, she knew she couldn't use the need for relief as an excuse. Her stomach churned, and she felt her gorge rising. She wondered if casting up her accounts would be enough to get her away from all these men. It would either get her moved, or it would get her killed. She couldn't be certain which would happen first.

Arabella coughed a few times, making sure she gagged with each one. She eased her way to the door, ensuring the guard could hear her. In between, she made herself sound as though she were choking. She ignored the warnings, then the threats to be quiet. As the earliest rays of light shone through the window, she scratched. She scratched her arms, her legs, pretended to struggle to reach her back, and her belly. She writhed as she did it. She was careful to keep her face and any hair from showing in the light. But as soon as she coughed and scratched at the same time, the other prisoners in the cell complained that she brought sickness with her. The racket from their voices, stomping feet, and those next to her thumping the door finally forced the guard to investigate.

"She's pox ridden," a man proclaimed when the guard stood at the door.

"She'll be giving it to us if she stays," another complained.

"Get her out," one of the few women in the cell demanded.

"The bitch isn't going anywhere," the guard said lazily.

Arabella had scratched the back of her hands and her wrists enough to leave red marks. She pushed her sleeve back enough to bare her wrists as she reached out for the opening in the door. She made her voice croak and rasp as she spoke. "There's naught wrong with me."

But it was only a moment before the people standing close enough noticed the scratches. She gagged a couple more times until she could throw up what was left of her evening meal.

"Get her out," the others in the cell demanded. Their cries grew louder until people in the adjoining cells joined in. The guard unlocked the door and grabbed Arabella by the hood of her cloak and hair. He pulled her from the cell, then shoved her toward the darkest part of the dungeon. She could see the end of the corridor of cells, but the man continued to march her toward it. When they reached the stone wall, he reached past her shoulder and pushed a stone. A door opened that led them into a pitch-black space. The guard lifted a torch from a sconce before grunting at Arabella. She took that as a signal to keep walking. At the end of this hidden corridor, they reached a door the man unlocked.

Before Arabella could say anything, the man pushed her hard enough that she lost her footing. She landed hard on her hands and knees as the door slammed shut and the lock turned. When she looked up, she realized her nose nearly touched the far wall. She eased herself onto her feet and looked around. There was no window in the wall and no light coming in from the door. There was no opening to the outside world. Arabella realized the vindictive guard had thrown her into the oubliette. Her head dropped as the sobs began. She knew no one could hear her. Even if Lachlan came, he wouldn't be able to hear her scream. She wouldn't hear anyone enter the dungeon, so she wouldn't know when to even try.

The name's fitting. Oubliette. I will be forgotten. Lachlan won't know where I've gone. No one believes me. They'll leave me down here until I die of starvation, thirst, or succumb to illness. There is little likelihood aught else will happen now. They will conveniently keep me in here, even when they take the others before the king. You eejit, Belle. You haven't the sense of a coo. At least a coo has a bell around its neck, so it can be found. This is exactly what you deserve for your vices and stub-bornness. God will have me pay my penance here. Bonnie Bella locked away. Hardly so perfect now.

Arabella sobbed until her throat was raw, and her eyes burned. The single benefit of the oubliette was that it didn't stink. At least not yet.

It will once I've been down here a day. It'll be even worse than the first cell since it's so small.

Arabella stuck her foot out and swept it across the floor, touching each wall. There was no chamber pot. Her tears began again as she considered the life she'd given up for a jug of whisky, a jug she never even got. She wanted more than anything to see Lachlan, but she would marry Beathan Gunn without dissent if it meant she was free and safe. Grateful she still had her cloak, she slid down the wall until she sat on her haunches, propped up by the stones behind her. She closed her eyes, at least grateful she was not at risk of being attacked by a cellmate.

Her exhaustion hit her with the force of a tidal wave, carrying her away to an ocean of nightmares. She slept off and on; each time she dozed, it was fit-ful. But her body was too weary to fight the need for sleep. A banging on her cell door woke her fully. She caught the stale heel of bread thrown at her, re-joicing that at least they fed her. She could survive for quite a while on bread alone. She just prayed that the bread would come at least once a day. Forgotten in her hellhole, she didn't know if she'd be fed again.

THIRTEEN

Lachlan glanced sideways at the king as they rode over hill and dale accompanied by an entourage of guards and courtiers. King Robert invited Lachlan on the royal hunt that morning, and Lachlan wasn't sure if it was meant to be conciliatory or a distraction. Either way, it kept him from Arabella, and it made him feel testy. After leaving Arabella at her door, Lachlan had felt unsettled as he returned to his chamber. There was so much still left unsaid between the two of them, and he had no way of knowing whether he would have a chance to say any of it before Arabella's father and Beathan arrived that day.

As the hours ticked by and they still had found little more than grouse and rabbits, Lachlan was frustrated and irritable. He wanted to return to the castle since the hunting seemed to be a wasted effort. He sensed King Robert felt much the same way in spite of all his boasting how he would bring down the largest stag of the day. Lachlan breathed a sigh of relief when the king relented and ordered their party back to Stirling. As his luck would have it, just as they turned south to ride back to the castle, a herd of deer sprang from the trees into the meadow that stretched before them.

Lachlan drew an arrow from his quiver and knocked it. It flew straight and steady, piercing the side of a large doe. His sharp sight and quick thinking allowed him to choose between two female deer, one clearly pregnant and the other simply large. A man a few horses down from him was not as conscientious and felled the pregnant animal. King Robert's oaths were so loud that Lachlan expected them to scare away the other animals, but arrows zipped through the air, striking a stag and several other does.

"*Sard*!" King Robert bellowed as he spurred his horse around to trot in front of the offending hunter. "Can you not tell the difference between a doe that's with fawn and one that's fat?"

"I beg your pardon, Your Majesty. It wasn't until after I let go of the arrow that I realized my error," the courtier confessed.

"Not only is that cruel, but you've wasted an animal that could have grown and fed the keep in a year or so. You are no longer welcome on hunts. Return to the keep before I stick an arrow through you," King Robert ordered.

Lachlan was only partially paying attention. His eyes tracked a stag with a ten-point rack of antlers as it remained in the tree line away from its fallen and skittish comrades. When it moved within Lachlan's shooting range, he released his arrow. He heard the snickers and chides that he shot at nothing. The voices went silent at the thud and snap of twigs the animal's body made. Lachlan nudged his horse forward as he hooked his bow back onto his saddle. He wasn't interested in listening to the king's foul temper since it was only making his own mood worse. His four guards followed him as he went to retrieve both the stag and the doe he'd shot.

Sensing his mood, he and the Sutherlands worked in silence as they strung up the animals by their hooves, pushing a branch between the front and back feet that they used to carry the animals back to the castle. Lachlan felt much of his tension relax from between his shoulders. He looked forward to telling Arabella about his success and hoped that she would be impressed. He'd never felt compelled to impress her before, but he felt an overwhelming desire to know she was proud of him.

"Well done, Lach," King Robert beamed as he maneuvered his horse alongside Lachlan's. "Certainly better than Baird. Eejit that he is. I never should have welcomed him to court after drawing and quartering his cousin for treason. The family isn't right in the head."

"Thank you, Your Majesty," Lachlan responded, ignoring the commentary. He knew the king didn't expect him to acknowledge the derisive assessment, only listen to the lament.

"What say you the kitchens prepare your catches for the evening meal tomorrow? There shall be a celebratory feast," King Robert offered. Lachlan turned an angry glare at the king. He understood King Robert alluded to Belle's betrothal announcement. He didn't appreciate the thinly veiled reminder.

"As you wish, Your Majesty," Lachlan nodded.

"I wish there was more I could do, Lach," King Robert lowered his voice to barely more than a whisper. "Your family is dear to me, but you keep putting me in tenuous positions when it comes to your marriage prospects. I did what I could as both King Robert and Uncle Robert for Maude and Blair, but Lady Arabella and Laird Gunn's betrothal is too close to being settled. It's too late."

Lachlan kept his eyes forward and counted to ten before he answered, but he still snapped, "It's never too late when you're king."

"You may think that, but I prefer not to abuse my power. I like to keep my subjects loyal," King Robert retorted. Lachlan didn't answer. Antagonizing the king would get him nowhere. "Besides, Beathan will get a few bairns on her, then entertain himself elsewhere."

Lachlan's head whipped around, his loathing so clear that King Robert jerked away. "Raping her isn't the same as getting a few bairns on her. Even if she goes willingly to his bed, he will mistreat her simply because he enjoys abusing women. He's had no power until recently, and he used his strength and size over women to compensate. Now he does it to impress his men, claiming no woman turns him away. Uncle Robert, King Robert, it matters not to me. I can't forgive you for this. Even if I didn't care about her, I would say no woman deserves that."

"It's not rape when they're married. You ken that," King Robert condescended.

"Ask Isabella MacDuff if she thinks the same." Lachlan spurred his horse on, leaving the king and his entourage behind without a proper dismissal. Isabella MacDuff had crowned King Robert at Scone Abbey, fulfilling her clan's legacy. But the presumed mistress of the king had done it at the expense of forsaking her child and the safety the Buchans could have offered, even if only temporarily. King Edward of England captured her alongside the king's sisters, daughter, and Queen Elizabeth, then ordered she'd be hung in a cage outside Berwick Castle for four years. She'd escaped an abusive husband and fulfilled her duty, but at a cost greater than anyone expected.

Lachlan drummed his fingers on the table as he ignored the noon meal before him. The other ladies-in-waiting were seated, but Arabella was nowhere in sight. He hadn't seen her all morning because he'd been on the hunt. He'd hoped to catch her in the Great Hall and pull her aside to at least say hello. He wondered where she was since Queen Elizabeth sat on the dais, and he could see her friends. Laurel Ross and Caitlyn Kennedy sat chatting together, and the woman he recognized as her roommate was engaged in a lively conversation with some other younger members of the queen's attendants.

The meal progressed, but Arabella never appeared. The queen rose, and the ladies followed before Lachlan could slip over to ask Laurel and Caitlyn about Arabella. He worried that she was unwell when he spied her guards seated at a table nearby. She hadn't gone for a walk or a ride alone. Despite her ill-advised adventure to the Merry Widow, he trusted she wouldn't leave the castle again unaccompanied.

He forced himself to be patient and returned to his chamber, where he read a recently arrived missive from his father asking how the meeting went between King Robert and Blair, Hardi, and him. He drafted his response, which didn't take long. He sealed the vellum and found a page to dispatch the correspondence. IIe laid down on his bed, wondering how he might while away the afternoon. He soon drifted off to sleep. He never napped, but exhaustion from spending two weeks traveling on horseback plus worry over his relationship with Arabella along with concern for her wellbeing, caught up to him. He was soon in a deep sleep.

FOURTEEN

L achlan woke with a start from a deep sleep and immediately reached for the sword beside his bed. He blinked several times before he realized someone was pounding on his door. He glanced at the window embrasure and saw that early morning light was already streaming in. It was nearly time for him to rise, anyway. He wrapped his plaid around his waist and carried his sword with him. Generally, attackers wouldn't knock, but he reasoned it would be best to be prepared for anything. He pulled the door open and found a young lady staring up at him. He recognized her as Arabella's roommate. His heart raced.

"What happened?" Lachlan demanded.

"I don't ken, but she wasn't there when I woke in the middle of the night the night before last. I heard her slip out, but I assumed she was—ah—here," the woman blushed. "When I woke yesterday morn, she was still gone. I assumed she slipped back into our chamber later and slept, but I didn't see her all day. It's nearly morning, and she still hasn't returned. I'm scared."

"You did right to come to me, Lady—" Lachlan couldn't remember the woman's name for the life of him, and as he struggled to remember, he doubted they'd ever been introduced. She was fairly new.

"Lady Rebekah," she supplied.

"Thank you. Please, don't mention this to anyone. If someone asks, say Lady Arabella isn't well."

"I will," Rebekah agreed, nodding her head. But Lachlan felt uneasy about trusting her, and she must have been able to tell. "I won't betray her. I'm a poor liar, but I will try. I haven't been here long, and I've only been her roommate since your sister—err, Lady Blair—I mean, Lady Cameron, left. Arabella has been so generous and friendly since I arrived. Everything terrified me at first, and she's helped me to fit in. I would never do aught to harm her."

"Good," Lachlan answered, his deep voice filled with authority. Rebekah bobbed a curtsy before running back up the passageway and out of the bachelor quarters. Lachlan understood she risked a great deal coming to his door, so the lady-in-waiting must have been genuinely fearful for Arabella.

What have you done, Belle? Where are you?

Lachlan hurried to dress before rushing to the barracks. He shook his guards awake. One glance at his face and each man scrambled off his cot and pleated his plaid in record time. They left the barracks in less than five minutes, Lachlan not saying a word until he was certain they were alone.

"Lady Arabella is missing. She left her chamber the night before last and hasn't returned," Lachlan whispered. He'd had a chance to think, and he suspected he knew where to look first. "We start at the Merry Widow."

The gates to the castle weren't yet open, so it took Lachlan some negotiating and a few coins to grease the wheels that lifted the portcullis. He and his men set off on foot. Lachlan had them fan out since there was more than one route to the tavern, especially if

Arabella had passed through the postern gate. He met his men at the front door of the tavern, but each one shook his head. The acid in his stomach felt as though it would eat a hole through his insides. His trepidation mounted with each moment she was missing.

Lachlan reached out to open the tavern door but found it locked. He glanced at his men, and they appeared as puzzled as he did. Lachlan pounded on the door and waited. When there was no sound, let alone anyone opening the door, he pointed for one of his men to look through the window.

"It's empty, Lachlan. Nay one sleeping or aught. It looks like there was an almighty brouhaha. Tables turned over and chairs look smashed," the Sutherland warrior noted. Lachlan stepped to the window. With no glass, it was easy to see in, and the panic that he'd been suppressing took hold. He returned to the door and banged with both fists. When there was still no answer, not even a sign of life, he stepped back, prepared to break the door down with his foot or his shoulder. He'd use both if he had to.

"Lad," a weak old man's voice called out. Lachlan turned to find a shopkeeper standing in his doorway, a cane in his right hand. "You won't be finding anyone there. Them been raided two nights past. MacStevens hasn't paid his rents and fines, and the piper has come for him."

"There was a fight?" Lachlan asked.

"Nay exactly. The sheriff and his men roughed up the men and women, but he only dragged the owner, his wife, the kitchen and serving wenches, and the tavern watchmen to the gaol. Been closed ever since."

Lachlan was prepared to breathe a sigh of relief, thinking Arabella must have gone elsewhere, but the old man raised his hand.

"There was some talk of a lass claiming to be a lady. But thems figured she would say aught to be free. Others said she was a lady's maid sent to buy whisky for her mistress. I don't ken which it is, but they took her with the others."

"Where?" Lachlan demanded.

"The castle's gaol," the man answered. Lachlan looked in the castle's direction. While there was little to find reassuring about the news, at least Arabella was at the castle, in not in the town's gaol.

"How long ago did you say?"

"Och, middle of the night two nights ago, it was. I'd say a wee after midnight. The kerfuffle woke the entire street, it did."

Lachlan crossed over and reached out to hand the man a coin, but the shopkeeper shook his head. "I'd venture you're looking for the lady. If she was part of that, you'll need every coin you have to get her out of the prison."

Lachlan nodded and mumbled a "thank you." He was speechless. He was angrier than he'd ever been in his life. He was angry at Arabella for her foolish choices, for no longer being able to trust her, and for endangering her life. And he was petrified that she'd be dead by now. At the least, he expected her to have been assaulted at least once.

Lachlan's men wisely remained silent as they wound their way through the town and toward the castle. Lachlan's mind reeled with how he would get Arabella released and what he would do to keep from throttling her. He was absorbed in his thoughts, so he didn't notice the guard who tried to signal him.

"Sutherland! Sutherland!"

Lachlan looked up to find a royal guard running along the battlements. The man disappeared as he took the steps down to the bailey. The guard was out of breath when he came to a stop before Lachlan.

He panted for a moment and swallowed as he caught his breath enough to speak.

"Sutherland, I saw Lady Arabella the other night," the guard whispered. "Sheriff Angus Stirling —he's cousin to Lord John de Strivelyn, you ken— had her manacled and was dragging her by the arm. She was with the tavern owner from the MacStevens Inn and his lot. The Merry Widow," the guard clarified when he saw Lachlan's look of confusion.

"And you didn't think to come tell me a wee sooner?" Lachlan demanded.

The guard raised his chin toward the battlements, then swung around to cast a glance at the gate. "I couldn't very well abandon my post. Not for a lady who found herself in trouble for leaving the safety of the castle. Alone."

"Did you see her leave?" Lachlan snapped.

"Well, no, but—"

"Then how do you ken she was alone when she left?"

"Sutherland, Harris—" the guard pointed to a man watching them from the wall walk. "He was posted at the postern gate when she left. He told me she was alone."

Lachlan gestured for the man to join them. It was clear it wasn't a request. "Do you make a habit of letting ladies out of the castle with no protection?"

"It's not for me to say no," came the curt reply.

"It is when she isn't greasing your palm, but you conveniently forget your duty when you get paid," Lachlan snapped. He muttered under his breath, "Bluidy Lowlanders. No honor."

He looked at both men, trying to keep his loathing and frustration under control. He couldn't blame the men for Arabella's decisions. And he understood why neither left his post to inform Lachlan. Though, had he been in their place, he would have.

He wouldn't let any lady leave the castle at night un-escorted.

"You didn't seek me out yesterday." Lachlan growled.

"We figured she'd be released sharpish. It was seeing you pass through the gate this morning and watching you go toward the taverns that made me realize you must be looking for the lady," replied the guard who'd been at the front gate.

"Do you ken the men who guard the gaol?"

"Aye," the guard from the postern gate hedged.

"What?" Lachlan had just steadied his breathing, but his heart raced again.

"There's only one. He's not known to treat women well."

Lachlan lunged at the guardsman and grasped his collar. He lifted the man onto his toes and shook him. "Bluidy bleeding hell. You're to protect those within the castle as much from what happens in the walls as you are to protect them from what's outside the walls. You should have fetched me or sent someone else to. I swear to you both, if anyone harmed her during that time, I will rain down holy hellfire on you and anyone within reach."

Lachlan pushed the man away and spun on his heel so abruptly that his plaid swished around the back of his thighs. He knew where the dungeon was, and he knew what he would find down there. As he approached the door at the bottom of the steps, he steeled himself for the state in which he would find Arabella. She'd been down there for two nights and a day. He expected the worst, if she was even still alive.

FIFTEEN

"You will let me in, or I will sever your head from your shoulders," Lachlan threatened as he tried to gain entry to the dungeon. The guard met him at the door and refused to budge. They were matched in size, their glares menacing, their posture prepared for attack.

"If you aren't the king, then you don't give me orders."

"I am Lachlan Sutherland, the heir and son of Laird Hamish Sutherland, the Earl of Sutherland," Lachlan growled.

"So?" the guard sneered.

"I doubt my godfather will be pleased when I interrupt him in the Privy Council chamber. Imagine his displeasure to learn you've locked away one of his wife's favorite ladies-in-waiting," Lachlan kept his voice low, and it lent a gravelly pitch to it. He saw the moment the guard wavered, but the man didn't relent.

"Nah, yous nobles allus mitherin' aboot sommat," the guard grumbled. "There's nay lady in yon cells. And you aren't anyone's godson, you heathenous Highlander." The guard tried to slam the door shut, but Lachlan and his four guards barreled past him, pushing the man to the ground. Lachlan's foot landed against the guard's ribs, making him wheeze.

"What do they call ye, ye bag of shite? Give me yer real name, and I willna kill ye. Play me for a fool, and I will come back, tie a rope around yer cods, and hang ye from them like a slaughtered lamb." Lachlan was so furious that he didn't notice his brogue replaced his courtly accent. He kicked the man once more for good measure.

"Donnach," the guard spat.

"Vera well, Donnach. Mayhap ye will live to see tomorrow morn. Take me to her."

"The bitch you want isn't here. We don't hold feasts for lairds and ladies."

Lachlan pulled the man back onto his feet before driving his fist into his belly. "Yer lies stink as much as yer breath, ye foul swine. Tell me where she is."

"Not in any of these cells, she's not," Donnach taunted.

"Then which cell is she in?" Lachlan insisted.

"There's no lady, real or pretend, in any of these cells. See for yourself, my lord," Donnach sneered.

Lachlan dropped Donnach and spoke over his shoulder as he walked away. "Stay with him. Gut him if he says a word that isnae to tell ye where Lady Arabella is."

"Arabella!" Lachlan called out. The inmates howled and ranted, but he couldn't hear Arabella's voice. He yelled louder, "Belle!"

Lachlan walked to each cell door with a window and peered inside. The conditions were worse than deplorable. His fear for Arabella's safety pulsed through him as he caught sight of a man thrusting into a whore he recognized from the Merry Widow. He couldn't imagine how anyone would want to couple in such a place. He walked past one cell where there was enough light to see a man lying in a puddle of blood. The other men in the cell acted as if there wasn't a corpse among them. Not one flinched or looked guilty. Lachlan knew then that the guards didn't check prisoners for weapons. They were just as content to let them murder one another as they were to torture the inmates. Lachlan was certain Arabella carried her dirk, but he was also certain most of the people in the dungeon carried one too, and they would be far more experienced using one.

Lachlan continued to call out to Arabella, but the women's voices who reached him were not the refined tones of a lady. He came to the end of the cells and hadn't found Arabella. He turned around, unsure of how he didn't find her, unless the guard was telling the truth. He didn't believe that for a moment. She had to be somewhere in the dungeon. As he made his way back toward his guards and the door to the outside, a woman's hand stuck through an opening in a cell door.

"Laird," the woman called to him. "They done carted her off yesterday morn. I don't ken where to, but she was here. She was at my tavern—" a muffled voice behind her interrupted. "Hush, mon. Your tavern, my tavern. It doesn't bluidy matter. Anyway, laird. His nibs took her somewhere, but she was here. She came to our tavern looking for whisky. Said she was getting it for her mistress. I kenned she wasn't a maid. I kenned she was a lady." The woman's voice grew smug, proud of herself for realizing what no one else had.

"Thank you," Lachlan nodded before running back to his waiting men. He drew his sword and pointed it at Donnach. "Where's the oubliette?"

"We don't have one," Donnach grinned as he lied. Lachlan sliced the man's arm, and Donnach howled.

"Wrong answer. Where's the oubliette?" Lachlan repeated.

"We don't have one," Donnach mocked.

"My blade will last longer than your life," Lachlan warned before he slashed Donnach's thigh. "Where is she?"

"Why should I tell you?"

"Because you'll live." Lachlan fished into his sporran and pulled out a small pouch that he shook. Coins clinked together. Lachlan waived it before Donnach's face but yanked it out of his reach as soon as Lachlan saw his interest. "You could live and have some extra coin."

"Bah. You'll kill me anyway," Donnach growled. Lachlan knew he would get nowhere with the man. He could take the time to torture the man, but that was time better spent seeking King Robert's help.

"I won't, but they will." Lachlan snatched the key ring and nodded for his men to follow him. Two of them escorted Donnach down the corridor behind Lachlan. He stopped at the cell that held the most hardened of the men he'd seen locked away. He unlocked the door, and the Sutherland men tossed Donnach in. It was like watching a rabid pack of animals as they attacked Donnach. Lachlan felt no remorse for sentencing the man to death. He'd done the same to Arabella by not telling Lachlan where to find her. He spun on his heels, his men once again following. He would have an audience with the king in the Privy Council chamber, and God protect the chancellor if he thought to turn Lachlan away.

SIXTEEN

King Robert glanced toward the door at the sound of a scuffle. Laird Johnstone and Laird Gunn followed his gaze as the door flew open and slammed against the door. The three men watched as five men in Sutherland plaids forced their way past the guards. Lachlan had the chancellor by the front of his doublet as he dragged the man into the Privy Council chamber, then tossed him aside.

"They've taken her," Lachlan declared. He lifted the sheath that held his sword from his back and dropped it and several dirks on the ground beside it before storming toward King Robert. He wouldn't let the king's personal guard run him through for arriving well armed without being announced. He recognized Beathan Gunn and a man he assumed was Mitcholm Johnstone from his plaid sash and brooch. He would deal with the fallout of the two men listening once he was certain Arabella was safe.

"Where? Who?" King Robert snapped. "You were not summoned, Lachlan. This isn't the time--"

"To your gaol. She's been down there since the night before last," Lachlan insisted. He noted the confusion on Beathan and Mitcholm's faces. He would keep from saying Arabella's name if he could.

Understanding registered on the king's face as his eyes shifted between the two lairds who stood before him. The men had just been about to sign the betrothal contracts when Lachlan burst in. King Robert narrowed his eyes at Lachlan before lifting a quill and handing it to Mitcholm. Lachlan strode across the chamber and ripped the quill from Mitcholm's hand. He glanced at the parchment on the table but knew what it was without looking. Lachlan reached for the inkpot and poured the black liquid across the vellum, ruining it.

"Lachlan." The king's voice warned Lachlan that he treaded dangerous water. "How?"

"She was in the wrong place at the wrong time. If you'd listened to me, this wouldn't be happening," Lachlan snarled.

"Sutherland," Beathan interjected. "This is a meeting between two lairds and the king. You don't belong. Leave before I'm insulted."

For a long moment Lachlan stared at Beathan. Then he laughed. There was no merriment in the sound, but his laughter filled the chamber. Lachlan sneered at his neighbor. "Go home, Beathan. Hasn't my family beaten you often enough?"

Beathan turned more fully toward Lachlan, taking measure of the man he rarely saw off the battlefield. His eyes narrowed to slits before he sniffed and turned his back on Lachlan. It was meant to insult Lachlan, but he was glad that he could return his attention to King Robert.

"She was taken down to the cells, but your guard has her locked in an oubliette. She wasn't in any of the cells I saw. How do I get to her?" Lachlan demanded.

"Who are you talking aboot?" Mitcholm demanded. "Your Majesty, what is the meaning of this? Can this not wait until later?"

Lachlan shot King Robert a warning glare. For a moment, Lachlan feared King Robert would reveal to Arabella's father where she was. "It's a pressing matter," was all the king answered.

Lachlan pulled the pouch of coins from his sporran and dropped it on the table. The three men stared at him. "Her bail. Now have her released."

"You still haven't told me why she's there," King Robert countered.

"I told you, she was in the wrong place at the wrong time."

"Did she not tell them who she is?" King Robert asked.

"I'm sure she tried. But if you were the sheriff, would you believe a woman claiming to be a lady-in-waiting?"

"Sheriff?" King Robert's russet brows lifted. Lachlan watched him draw in a breath before nodding. King Robert waved one of his guards over and whispered in the man's ear. Lachlan watched the guard draw away, confusion on his face but nodding. "What was she doing there? Did you take her?"

"Of course not," Lachlan answered defiantly. "If the lass would listen to me, she would be safely tucked away in her chamber."

"Perhaps you aren't the right mon for her then if you can't keep her in hand," King Robert suggested.

"She's not a dog or a horse," Lachlan snapped. "I don't command her."

"Whoever this woman is," Mitcholm snickered. "That's your first mistake."

Lachlan fisted his hands at his side as he fought to control his temper. He feared he would say something he couldn't take back, or something that would give away Arabella's plight. He would keep her drinking a secret and spare her the shame of her father and Beathan learning where she was.

"Your Majesty, please order her release. I will see to her," Lachlan begged. He would get down on his knees if he had to. He'd send his men for the coin in his chamber if it would buy her way out. He would pledge his service directly to the king in trade for her freedom. The king shook his head and turned his attention back to the two lairds standing before him.

"My scribe will draft new contracts, they will include the newly negotiated terms," King Robert addressed Mitcholm and Beathan.

"No," Lachlan growled.

"Lachlan," King Robert warned once again.

"No. This wouldn't have happened—" Lachlan snapped his mouth shut when he realized he'd just revealed Arabella was the woman on whose behalf he was pleading.

"What has my daughter done?" Mitcholm demanded as he turned a murderous glare on Lachlan.

"Naught. She was mistaken for someone else."

"Who?" Beathan interrupted. "I demand to know what my betrothed has done."

"She isn't your betrothed," Lachlan growled. "The contracts aren't signed."

Beathan opened his mouth, but before he could say anything, a side door to the chamber opened. Arabella passed through it, and the rest of the world fell away for Lachlan. He rounded the table, sprinting toward her.

"Belle."

"Arabella?" Mitcholm demanded as Lachlan reached her.

Lachlan pulled her into his arms and held her, never so relieved to see anyone in his life. He thought learning of Maude's injuries from a wildcat attack had been the most fearful he'd ever been. Then Blair had disappeared for nearly a month, and he was certain nothing worse could befall him. But fearing for Arabella's life showed him how deeply he could love someone. He kissed the crown of her head as she clung to him, her petite frame trembling against him. His anger melted away as he rejoiced in having Arabella safely encircled in his arms.

"I'm so, so sorry," Arabella whispered. Lachlan leaned back and cupped her face in his hands.

"I love you, Belle. I always have," Lachlan professed.

"I love you too," Arabella admitted. She glanced around Lachlan's shoulder and recognized her father and a man she assumed was her soon-to-be betrothed.

"Shh," Lachlan comforted her as her body shook with fear. "We'll sort it out. I'm not leaving your side. They haven't signed the contracts yet."

Movement drew their attention away from one another. Mitcholm tried to pull Arabella from Lachlan's arms, but Lachlan's snarl made the older man lower his hand. But it didn't deter the laird from having his say.

"What is the meaning of this? You are disgusting and stink like a gutter rat. You were to be properly attired and groomed to meet Laird Gunn. Instead, you show up like a beggar, and we ken they locked you away. You're a disgrace, Arabella."

"Speak to her like that again, and I will cut out your tongue," Lachlan threatened. "This isn't the place for your admonishment. Don't you think you should ask if she's well?"

"Obviously she is if she can fawn over you. Arabella, release him. You are another mon's bride. You are humiliating us. Such a disappointment," Mitcholm sighed as though he expected nothing better from Arabella.

Arabella released Lachlan and tried to pull away, but he didn't loosen his embrace. She glanced up at him before looking at her father. "Yes, Father. Lach, let me go."

She could tell Lachlan was hesitant to release her, but he respected her request and dropped his arms. She inhaled deeply as she faced her father. She kept her attention on him, not daring to look in Beathan's direction. She could only imagine what he must have been thinking.

"What did you do?" Mitcholm demanded.

"I told you, she—" Lachlan slid his hand into Arabella's and gave it a squeeze as Mitcholm interrupted.

"I didn't ask you, Sutherland. My daughter will answer for her crimes."

Arabella looked up at Lachlan, remorse filling her eyes. Then she looked at Beathan, and fear replaced her guilt. His furious expression made her wonder what he would do to her once they wed and she was his chattel. Her eyes darted to King Robert and took in his impassive expression. She would admit what she'd done and shoulder the consequences.

"I was arrested during a raid on a tavern."

"What the devil were you doing there?" Mitcholm demanded.

Beathan shifted and stalked toward them. "Whoring. What else does a woman do in a tavern?"

"Gunn," King Robert's censorious tone made them all pause.

"I'm not a whore," Arabella defended herself. "Have a midwife check me. I was there to buy whisky." Arabella felt as though someone lifted the weight of the world from her shoulders even as her stomach continued to churn. She never imagined she would admit to her vice, but the confession relieved the burden of her secret.

"Whisky? Why?" Mitcholm asked in a whisper. Arabella could tell her father was genuinely perplexed.

"To drink, Father."

"You tried to marry me to a drunkard." Beathan growled. "Absolutely not."

"Ladies don't drink," Mitcholm stated. "You don't drink. You could never do something so improper."

"Why? Because I'm supposed to be above reproach at all times? Because it's not possible that I'm aught but perfect?"

"Aye," Mitcholm snapped. "You do not drink. You were not at a tavern."

"You can deny it to yourself all you want, Father. But I was at the Merry Widow, and I do drink. It calms my nerves."

"Calms your nerves?" Mitcholm mocked. "You spend your day swanning around the royal court, feasting and dancing every night. It's not as though you have a single care or responsibility. You're weak and a failure."

"You really have no idea what life is like here, do you?" Lachlan asked. "You sent your youngest child into the lion's den without knowing what she faced. The only failure here is you. You failed to care for her and protect her, as is your duty both as her father and as her laird."

"Shut your gob. No one asked you. You don't belong here. Who are you to tell me what my daughter's life is like? You don't even know her."

Arabella squeezed Lachlan's hand, silently begging him not to argue with Mitcholm. He glanced down at her and shook his head. Someone had to advocate on her behalf because Lachlan knew she feared her father too much to say any more.

"I had two sisters who served the queen. During their time here, no more than three months went by without either my father or me coming to see my sisters. We didn't abandon them for a year at a time," Lachlan's pointed comment registered with Mitcholm as the older man grimaced. "I have spent more time with Belle than you have in the past five years. I understand her more than you ever have."

"Understand? Bah. I understand my daughter has let her clan down, let me down. I sent her here to represent Clan Johnstone. All she had to do was be pretty and laugh at men's jests. She was to spend her days sewing and her nights dancing. She was to find a husband willing to pay her bride price and form an alliance for our clan. She is useless to us now. There will be an almighty scandal."

"I'll not have her. Midwife or not," Beathan interjected. "She's a drunkard and loose. Look at how she carries on with Sutherland. She's disobedient at best and feral at worst. She won't shame me among my people. The betrothal is off, Johnstone." Beathan curled his lip in disgust as he looked at Arabella. "But I'll take her as my leman if you want to be done with her."

"No," Arabella whimpered. Everything had spiraled out of control. Her father was furious with her, Beathan was disgusted with her, and worst of all, Lachlan was disappointed in her. She feared he stood by her only for appearance's sake and would turn away from her once they left the Privy Council chamber. Then what would she do? She'd never wanted a drink as badly as she did now. She wanted to lock herself away and drink until she drowned herself in whisky.

"She won't be any mon's leman, since she will be

my wife," Lachlan enunciated each word. Arabella snapped her head up in surprise. She hadn't expected Lachlan to still wish to marry her, and she hadn't anticipated him announcing it. "I will pay whatever bride price you demand, and a priest will read the banns this Sunday."

"Nay." Mitcholm shook his head before turning to Beathan. "Let the midwife examine her. When she's proven to be a maiden, we'll finalize our agreement. We both stand to profit from this union. Don't throw that away, mon. My daughter may be a foolish chit, but you are the mon to take her in hand. You heard Sutherland. He won't do it."

"The bride price is half," Beathan countered.

"Fine," Mitcholm nodded.

"You Majesty," Lachlan looked at his godfather, catching the monarch's stunned silence. "Lady Arabella isn't a broodmare to be haggled over. I ken you're aware of the Gunn's reputation with women. Is the queen?"

"Are you threatening me, Lachlan?" King Robert crossed his arms.

"I would never dare to do such a thing. I just wondered if my godmother was aware of what awaits one of her favorite ladies. I wouldn't want to be the cause of upset to Her Grace while she's in such a fragile condition. Being so close to her confinement." Lachlan cocked an eyebrow, and he was certain King Robert understood he sought retribution for the king's threat against Arabella and Lachlan's family the evening they found the royal couple in the antechamber. "I believe my godmother would be most disturbed to learn of Beathan's reputation."

"My reputation?" Beathan hissed.

"Aye. The one for beating your leman. The one for strangling a whore while you rutted. The one for liking girls young enough to be your daughter. That one."

"Sutherland!" Beathan bellowed as he pulled a hidden dirk from his belt. In the same moment, Lachlan drew his own knife from his belt. He may have left most of his weapons on the floor, but he was never completely unarmed.

"Lach," Arabella whispered. She looked at the four angry men, focusing on Lachlan and Beathan. They looked ready to murder one another, and Arabella realized this went deeper than just her possible marriage. Her betrothal was the scab that had been scratched off an old wound. Neither man continued to pretend that acrimony didn't exist between the Sutherlands and Gunns. Exhaustion, fear, and withdrawal made Arabella's mind grow cloudy. Black spots danced at the corners of her eyes, and the ground seemed to shift under her feet. She grabbed Lachlan's arm, and managed to say his name again. "Lach."

Lachlan heard the desperation in Arabella's voice and turned to her in time to see her eyes shut as she crumpled. He dropped his knife and caught her. He swept her into his arms, and without sparing a glance at anyone, he marched out of the Privy chamber. He heard the others calling his name, but he was unwavering in his course. He carried Arabella to his chamber, finding a page and summoning the healer along the way.

Sitting on the end of the bed with Arabella in his lap, Lachlan unfastened the clasp of Arabella's cape and loosened the ties at the sides of her kirtle. He wouldn't go so far as to undress her, but he hoped the loosened gown would make it easier for her to breathe. He noticed scratches on the back of her hands for the first time. When he pushed her sleeves back, he discovered more on her wrists and arms.

There were red marks on her neck, and he pushed her sleeves down her shoulders to examine them. He could see more marks, but none had broken the skin like on her hands and wrists.

"Belle, what did they do to you?" Lachlan moaned. He reached down and pulled off her boots, surprised to find her bare feet. He recalled that she must have dressed in the dark and not bothered with stockings. "*Mo chridhe*, you're safe now. Safe from it all."

SEVENTEEN

Lachlan stood and carried Arabella to the side of the bed and laid her down before moving to the pitcher and ewer that held fresh water. He soaked a cloth in the cool water, then lathered soap onto it. He returned to Arabella's side and with a gentleness he didn't know he possessed, he washed her face, neck, and hands. When he was satisfied that at least the dungeon grime was removed, if not the stench, he carried a chair to her bedside. He sat and held her hand until someone knocked at his door. He recalled how his morning began with Rebekah pounding on his door. This was softer and less demanding. He sighed, knowing it wasn't Mitcholm, Beathan, or a royal guard come to drag them apart. He eased the door open and found a withered monk standing before him. He recognized the man as the castle's healer. Maude was well versed in medicinals, so she had worked with the man often. She'd spoken of the priest often and introduced Lachlan to him on more than one occasion. While a little doddering with age, he still had a fine memory as a physician.

"Father Gormal, thank you for coming," Lachlan nodded as he let the monk into the chamber.

"The lad made it sound like it was life or death.

Something aboot an angel dying." Father Gormal stopped short when he noticed Arabella on Lachlan's bed. He cast a suspicious glance at Lachlan before limping to Arabella's side. "She does look like an angel. But a fallen one."

"Nay, Father. She is still pure, and she is an angel. But she's unwell. She hasn't been eating much lately, and she spent two nights in the dungeon."

"The dungeon?" Father Gormal held up a hand and shook his head. "I don't want to ken. But I will pray for her soul all the same. Why is she here instead of her own chamber?"

"I don't trust her father to ensure she receives proper care." Lachlan didn't add that he didn't trust Beathan not to take advantage of Arabella.

"She needs her maid to undress her, and you must leave," the old priest insisted.

"I will send for her maid, but I'm going nowhere. I will turn my back or stand behind the screen, but I'm not leaving as long as Lady Arabella is unwell. She is under my protection."

"Your protection, lad? And who does she need protecting from in this chamber? I'm an old mon, but you're a healthy young stripling. I think she's safer with me," Father Gormal grinned.

"Be that as it may, I'm not leaving," Lachlan insisted.

"Very well. Send for the maid."

Lachlan followed the priest's instructions and stuck his head out of the door. He caught sight of another page and summoned him. The messenger boys weren't usually so easy to find, but Lachlan thanked God for His intervention. With his request on the way, Lachlan turned back to the priest who was running his withered fingers over Arabella's throat and neck.

"How long has she been asleep?" Father Gormal inquired.

"She collapsed aboot a half an hour ago. She's unconscious, not asleep, Father."

"She might have been when she keeled over, but she's sleeping now. I tried to wake her while you were at the door, but she batted my hands and attempted to roll away." Lachlan walked back to the bed, and Father Gormal stepped aside as Lachlan took Arabella's hand. He leaned over and pressed a kiss to her forehead. Her contented sigh encouraged him. He brushed his lips against hers, ignoring the priest's throat clearing. Arabella's eyes fluttered open until their mouths joined. She returned Lachlan's kiss and even lifted her hand to his shoulder.

"I love you, Belle," Lachlan whispered.

"Still?" Arabella questioned.

"Always. I'm not well pleased with you at the moment, but I will always love you," Lachlan promised.

Arabella smiled wanly before looking around. Her brow furrowed in confusion. "Where am I?" She tried to lift her head but winced. "And I love you, too."

"You're in my chamber. I feared your father would go to your chamber and what would happen if he did. Your maid is on her way to help you undress. I will send for a bath, and Father Gormal will examine you."

Arabella shook her head and tried to sit up. As soon as she put weight on her arms, they buckled. She fell back against the pillow and groaned. "A bath and something to eat will set me to rights. I need not be examined."

"But your hands and wrists. I saw the scratches. Who did that? Or rather, what did that? Rats?"

"Nay." Arabella had the audacity to grin, and she

thought Lachlan's teeth would chip away as he ground them. "I did them to myself. I pretended to be ill to get out of the cell they put me in at first. I feared all the men in there and risked being put somewhere else before the faint light let them see my face yesterday morn. I ended up in the oubliette for it, but at least I was alone and untouched." Arabella felt a jolt of panic as she looked up at Lachlan. "I swear to you, no mon touched me."

Lachlan cast a quick glance at Father Gormal, who discreetly backed away. "Belle, I am glad to hear you weren't hurt. But I wouldn't turn you away. It wouldn't have been your fault."

"But I snuck out of the keep. They caught me at a tavern. They threw me in the dungeon."

"Aye. You made poor choices. But that doesn't mean you'd ever deserve a man assaulting you. It wouldn't be your fault, and I wouldn't abandon you. That would be his crime, not yours."

"But—"

Lachlan shook his head and dropped a kiss on her lips to silence Arabella. "No buts, Belle. I love you and want to marry you. Our vows will say for better, for worse, in sickness and in health. I mean it now, just like I will the day we marry and every day after that. It's not conditional. No matter what, I love you."

"Lach," Arabella croaked as tears brimmed her eyes. "How am I so lucky to have a mon with such honor love me?"

"Luck has naught to do with it. You are a kindhearted, generous, funny, caring, at times recklessly daring woman. You made a mistake, even though you usually make wiser choices. But no one is perfect. Not you, not me, not anyone. Only Christ was perfect, and there is but one of Him."

"I think you are the wise one," Arabella smiled.

Lachlan grinned and nodded. "I am because I'm

making you my wife. If your father won't agree and have the banns posted, we'll handfast. It's a family tradition."

Arabella laughed softly. "I ken. I know how Maude and Blair married their husbands, and I've heard the tales aboot your Sinclair cousins."

A single knock at the door interrupted their conversation. Father Gormal cast a glance at Lachlan and Arabella before hobbling to the door. He opened it wider once he discovered Eliza on the other side. The maid entered with fresh clothing over her arm.

"My lady," Eliza greeted Arabella. "I was so afraid. I've called for a bath, and I'll have you right as rain soon enough."

"While we wait for the hot water, assist your lady with her gown, then I will examine her," Father Gormal's soft voice belied the command in his words. "Behind the screen, Sutherland, or out you go."

Lachlan nodded but looked at Arabella before he moved. When she nodded, he walked to the screen and pulled it open. He stood behind it, wishing he could catch a peek at Arabella. He realized it wasn't lust that drove him. He was anxious about her being out of his sight, lest someone steal her away. And he feared that her injuries might be worse than she admitted. He heard the rustling of clothes and whispers, but he couldn't make out what the monk or the maid said. Lachlan wished he had room to pace. The minutes felt like hours, even though it hadn't been that long since he stepped behind the partition.

"The lass is well. You can come back." Father Gormal called out. Lachlan stepped around the screen as the priest handed Arabella a flask. "This should get you warm."

Lachlan was aghast as he watched Arabella snatch the whisky from the monk's hand and tip it to her mouth. She guzzled the contents rather than taking a sip. Even as he stomped to her side, she continued to drink. When the small jug was empty, she wiped the back of her hand over her mouth. But she didn't look the least affected by the strong alcohol. In fact, it looked as though the whisky had done little to Arabella.

"How do you drink that without it making your eyes water or making you splutter?" Lachlan demanded. He watched Arabella shrink back against the cover. Her shoulders rounded as she tried to make herself smaller, and her head turned while pulling back as though she prepared for him to strike her.

"Belle, I'm still angry with you, and I'm still scared. But I will never raise my hand to you," Lachlan softened his tone as he took a seat beside her on the mattress. When she still looked doubtful, he slid his hand beneath hers and brought it to his mouth. He kissed each knuckle before turning it over and kissing the pad of each finger. Moving slowly, so as not to scare her, he reached out his other hand and cupped her jaw. His thumb brushed over her lips before sweeping back and forth across her cheek.

"I will leave this salve and be on my way," Father Gormal muttered, but neither Lachlan nor Arabella paid attention until Eliza opened the door for the monk. Lachlan called out his thanks but didn't take his eyes off Arabella. It wasn't long after that when servants arrived with a tub and buckets of steaming water. Once the tub was full and the servants left, Lachlan helped Arabella to stand. She and Eliza looked at him expectantly. Arabella blinked rapidly when Lachlan shook his head and ordered Eliza to leave, swearing the maid to secrecy on pain of death.

"Lachlan?" Arabella stood shocked as her maid slipped out of the chamber.

"Belle, just as I promised you in the alcove, you

will leave here still a maiden, but let me take care of you." Lachlan said as he approached, then stepped around to face her back.

With some reluctance, Arabella agreed. As Lachlan helped her out of her chemise, her dress having been taken off before her examination, Arabella released a breathy chuckle. "Will you still be my lady's maid once we're married?"

"I shall be your only maid," Lachlan whispered beside her ear. His warm breath made her shiver. "I shall tend to you morning, noon, and night. Though I shall prefer undressing you in the eve to dressing you in the morn."

Arabella shivered again as her chemise slid down her body to pool at her feet. Lachlan's hands traced the path the garment had taken until they rested on her hips. He stepped closer, so his body pressed against hers, and he planted kisses on her neck.

"And will a maid scrub your back?" Arabella asked breathily.

"No one has bathed me since I was a wean. But I shall gladly accept your assistance if you're offering."

Arabella drew in a fortifying breath before she turned around. Lachlan sucked in his own breath as heat surged through his body as his first sight of Arabella's bare body.

"If I thought I could withstand the temptation, we'd share our first bath right now," Lachlan admitted. He raised his hand to touch her breast but hesitated. He was unsure of what to do. He wanted to touch her everywhere, but dared not touch her anywhere. "Belle, you are a beautiful woman, and I'm undeniably physically attracted to you. But I want you to know that I want to make love to you not because of your appearance, but because my heart demands I show you how much I love you. I know I don't have the words."

"I think those words were perfect. Lach, I've never admitted how handsome I think you are. It was never appropriate, but I need you to ken that you are the brawest, most desirable mon I have ever seen. But I love you for far more than your good looks. My eyes, and the rest of my body, are keenly aware of how attractive you are. But my mind and my heart ken what a good mon you are. And that's why I love you."

They came together in a passionate kiss, neither knowing who initiated it, but both knowing they didn't want it to end. Arabella's arms wrapped around Lachlan's waist as one of his encased her waist while the other encircled her shoulders. She tilted her head and opened her mouth wider, inviting him in. As they kissed, Arabella's frustration grew that Lachlan's leine kept her from touching his skin as he did hers. She pulled away.

"Can you take your leine off? I want to feel your skin against mine."

The words had barely left Arabella's mouth before Lachlan was unfastening the brooch that held the extra length of his plaid over his shoulder. He dropped the pin into his sporran, wrapped the swath of wool around his waist, and ripped his leine over his head. Arabella veritably purred as her hands ran over the ridges of muscles that made up Lachlan's chest and abdomen. She'd never paid attention to any of the men she saw training without shirts on. But now her eyes gorged on the sight of Lachlan's bronzed skin under her touch. He stood without moving as she explored his shoulders and arms before reaching around him to caress his back.

When Arabella's eyes drifted shut and she sighed while her hands continued to roam, Lachlan pulled her closer as his own hands became reacquainted with the soft flesh of her backside. He kneaded the globes as Arabella melted against him. The urge to lift her and guide her legs around his waist before laying her back on the bed became so strong that Lachlan stepped away. At the confusion in Arabella's eyes, he smiled sheepishly and guided her hand to his rod. She could feel the steely length through the wool.

"If you don't get in that tub soon, I may break my word. And as much as I want to make love to you, I want to honor you more," Lachlan confessed.

"I love your honor, but I don't love that you remembered it," Arabella grumbled as she moved toward the tub. Lachlan held her hand as she stepped into the linen lined wooden bath. She slid down so that the water covered her shoulders. When she could only hear Lachlan's labored breathing, she cracked open one eye and found him watching her.

"Soak and enjoy your bath. I won't rush you," Lachlan explained.

"I'm sure you won't. If you did, it would only mean I'd get dressed sooner," Arabella teased.

Lachlan pulled the stool that a servant left closer to the side and sank onto it. He trailed the back of his fingers over her collarbone before inching his hand under the water to cup her breast. His thumb brushed over her nipple until it hardened. He turned his attention to her other breast as he kissed behind her ear.

"I would keep you naked and beside me in our bed every day for the rest of our lives. I would worship every inch of you," Lachlan whispered.

"Our?" Arabella asked. Lachlan pulled back and looked at her. He realized her parents must have had separate chambers.

"Aye, ours. Belle, the couples in my family do not sleep apart. We marry for love, and we want to be beside our partners both when we're awake and when we're asleep. Unless you wish otherwise, we will share a chamber."

"I never thought aboot it before because I never let myself imagine that we might one day marry." Arabella's cheeks flamed red, and Lachlan tried to hide his amusement at her embarrassment. "I mean, I confess I've imagined us—well—you know—together. But I never thought aboot what it would be like after. When we're done and just a married couple. Or on nights when you didn't want to couple with me. I suppose I figured you'd go to your own chamber or wherever."

"Or wherever?" Lachlan let go of Arabella and sat up straight. "Belle, there will never be a wherever. If I'm not sleeping alongside you, it's because I'm either on patrol or forced to be away from the keep. The only woman I will ever touch a bed with is you."

Arabella nodded but lowered her head. She couldn't look at Lachlan; the conversation was suddenly too intense and personal. Too many insecurities and worries about disappointing him were rising to the surface, and she had no way to escape. Not with Lachlan sitting beside her, and not without something to drink.

"Couples don't always use beds," Arabella whispered.

"Do ye think I'm going to be tupping maids against a wall or in the stables?" Lachlan asked, not noticing his burr. He tried to keep the hurt and frustration from his voice. "That may be what some men do, but I never will. I will never betray ye or the vows we share. Ma word is ma honor. If it means naught, then I have none. That is nae the mon I want to be, that's nae the husband I want to be, and it's nae the laird ma clan deserves one day. And if nae by ma own choice, I'll be faithful because ma father will skelp me, and ma mother would run me through."

Lachlan tried to sound lighthearted at the end, even though he hadn't exaggerated.

"You fear your mother?" Arabella asked. "She always sounds like such a kindly woman."

"She is, but she's nae one to cross. How do ye think Maude and Blair came to be so fierce? They get it from Mama." Lachlan lowered his voice conspiratorially. "Never tell ma da, but I'm far more scared of ma mama than I am him. Always have been. He's a bit of a softy once ye get past the burly, bearded appearance."

Arabella's peel of laughter filled the chamber, and they both seemed to relax. Arabella closed her eyes as Lachlan's hand drifted over her breasts and down her belly. Her knees fell open as his fingers ran through the thatch of curls.

"Belle?"

"Aye. I'll expire if you don't."

It was the permission Lachlan sought, and it spurred him on. He dipped his middle finger into her sheath, feeling wetness he knew didn't come from the bath. Arabella's head fell back against the edge of the tub as her hips rose to meet his questing finger. When she shifted restlessly, Lachlan whispered against her neck.

"What do ye want, Belle? Tell me, and I will give it to ye. Aught you want," Lachlan offered. When her eyes flew open and looked at where his cockstand tented his plaid, he chuckled. "Nearly aught."

Arabella playfully huffed before shutting her eyes again. "Just more."

Lachlan pressed a second finger into her, marveling at how tight her channel was and how it expanded to accommodate him. When her knees bumped the sides of the tub as she tried to open them wider, Lachlan pressed deeper, but was mindful of her maidenhead. He watched as a flush crept up

Arabella's neck and flooded her cheeks. Her mouth opened slightly as she panted. He felt her straining as her hips undulated beneath the water's surface. He drew the leg closer to him out of the water and hooked it over the side. When her hands gripped the rim, her knuckles turned white, and her moans of pleasure hinted at frustration, Lachlan dared to dip a third finger into her as his thumb worked her nub. As her breaths grew shallow and faster, she grasped his wrist and tried to press him into her further. She moaned with frustration, her inexperienced body clamoring for what she wanted but unknowing of how to find it. She pressed his fourth finger into her, but Lachlan tried to pull back.

"Belle, I'll hurt ye," Lachlan worried. "Ye're too tight, too narrow."

Arabella shook her head, one hand still pressing his wrist while the other reached for his shoulder. With no leine to grab to pull him closer, she clawed at his shoulder. She pulled both feet back into the water; her legs trapping Lachlan's hand between her thighs as she pressed her feet against the bottom to raise her hips.

"Either this," Arabella jerked her chin toward where Lachlan's submerged hand continued to ply her body before looking at his cock, "Or that. But you won't hurt me. Not unless you believe you won't fit because I've stroked you, Lach, and it's much bigger than what you have in me now."

"Are ye saying that to flatter me? To tempt me?" Lachlan growled.

Arabella drew her head back and furrowed her brow. "I don't understand."

"Ye never learned that complimenting a mon on his size is a way to seduce him?"

"I—I suppose I have. But I wasn't thinking aboot what I've heard anyone say. All I was thinking aboot is how frustrated I am that I can't find that release you gave me before. How I desperately crave learning what you feel like inside me. And that having touched you before lets me know that there isn't a comparison between your fingers and your—. Well, your fingers are quite big, but your—."

Arabella squeezed her eyes shut, completely embarrassed, her arousal waning as she felt foolish. Rather than pulling Lachlan's hand to her sheath, she pushed it away. She turned her head from Lachlan's piercing stare. She whimpered when Lachlan lifted his hand, regretting pushing him away. She was unprepared for him to lift her to her feet. He looked at her and shook his head. He snatched the bar of soap from beside the stool and quickly ran it over her entire body. A wet linen followed as it washed away the soap. Her hair was still dry.

Lachlan snatched a towel from the stack beside the tub and flung it around Arabella's shoulders before grabbing another that he flung over his shoulder. He lifted her from the tub and once her feet touched the floor, he backed her toward the bed. When her thighs hit the mattress, he pressed her onto it. He used the towel he'd placed over his shoulder to dry her breasts and belly before kneeling between her thighs. He dried her left leg before hooking it over his shoulder, then repeated the process with her right. His hands grasped her hips and pulled her to the edge. He pressed his nose to her seam and flicked his tongue into her entrance. Arabella jumped, unprepared for the sensation.

"Ye shall have that release, Belle. Ma fingers and tongue will do what I willna allow ma cock to. Yet." Lachlan flicked his tongue along her entrance. "And I suggest ye find some word ye can say, or how will I ken when ye want it?"

"When I want it?" Arabella lifted onto her elbows. "I mean, I think I'll always want it any time you wish to couple. But why would I say something like that?"

Lachlan reminded himself that Arabella wasn't one of the experienced women he'd bedded in the past. Even when he imagined those women were her, they were still women who had bedded plenty of men. Her innocence was pure, and he regretted his snap judgment that she intended her words to seduce. She didn't understand the power of them.

"Ye arenae a broodmare or a bitch in heat that I'll rut whenever I want. Ye can always say nay, just as ye can always tell me when ye wish to couple." Lachlan kissed the inside of her thigh. "And ye can always tell me what ye want me to do, what ye want us to do. Never be embarrassed or ashamed that ye wish for us to join. There is no shame in it, and I confess, I long to hear ye tell me that ye want me."

"But a lady—maybe the ones you—I'm not suppose—" Arabella flopped back onto the bed, her humiliation complete. She didn't want to see Lachlan kneeling between her legs. She felt vulnerable and out of her depths. The bed dipped, then she felt Lachlan's hand brush the hair back from her temple before he kissed it.

"Aye," Lachlan whispered. "I ken what I'm doing. But I will never be with anyone else. The past is the past, Belle. I willna look back."

Arabella looked into the whisky brown eyes she was so familiar with, and she felt the air returning to her lungs as she relaxed. "I trust you, Lachlan. I'm not worried aboot that. If not because you've said so, but because I believe you're afraid of your mother—and father." Arabella grinned as she stroked her fingers along his unshaven cheek, liking the feel of the bristles. "I don't want you to think I'm the whore that my father and Beathan said."

"They are both lucky they are still breathing after that. Belle, I dinna think ye telling me what ye want or what ye enjoy makes ye a whore. It makes ye ma partner."

"Your partner?"

"Aye." Lachlan sat up and looked around. He spotted his leine and went to fetch it. He helped Arabella to sit up, and he eased it over her head. This wasn't what he thought they would be doing five minutes ago, but he realized there was much they needed to discuss before they married. He pulled his boots off and gestured for Arabella to move up to the head of the bed. He climbed on beside her and looked at her pale legs sticking out from beneath his leine. When she moved to pull them up and under the shirt, he stayed her with his hand on her thigh. "If ye're cold, then I will get ye a plaid. But dinna hide from me. Please."

Arabella nodded. "What did you mean by partner?"

Lachlan lifted her hand into his and covered it with his other. He ran his thumb over the back of it, the sensation soothing to them both.

"One day, God willing nae anytime soon, I will be laird and ye will be the lady of our clan. The Sutherlands havenae become the powerful clan we are just because of our size. Ma father was never meant to be laird. He was a third son. But his father and brothers died in battle, and the lairdship fell to him. His mother died when he was a young child, and his father was a tyrant. When he was suddenly thrust into being laird, he panicked. He rode out as soon as he knew the keep was secure and went to Dunbeath where my Aunt Kyla was. He arrived on her wedding day of all things. She was set to marry ma Uncle Liam. The day after the wedding, Uncle Liam and Aunt Kyla rode back to Dunrobin with Da to help him get the keep settled and for Uncle Liam to teach him all that his own father taught him. During the moon they were there, Da watched Uncle Liam and Aunt Kyla as they worked together to sort out everything her father left in shambles."

Lachlan lifted Arabella's hand to his lips as he remembered his aunt before she passed away. She and his mother were much alike, and had become instant friends from the tales he heard. He remembered how happy his Uncle Liam was before she died. He'd become a serious and reserved man, dedicated to his children before all else, but always a fair and powerful laird. Since becoming a grandfather, Lachlan noticed much of Liam's former joy and merriment had returned.

"Lach?" Arabella's voice broke into his thoughts.

"Sorry. I was just thinking aboot how Uncle Liam and Aunt Kyla were before she died."

"I'm sorry," Arabella whispered.

Lachlan nodded. "Da asked Uncle Liam how he and ma aunt had learned to work so well together when they'd only married the day he arrived. Uncle Liam reminded him that Aunt Kyla had been at Dunbeath for nearly a moon before they wed, and he and ma aunt paid close attention to Uncle Liam's parents. They'd been a love match, and Uncle Liam and Aunt Kyla emulated them from the beginning. In turn, Da emulated his sister and brother-by-marriage when he married Mama."

Arabella sighed as Lachlan continued to brush his thumb over her hand. The steady pace calmed her, and had she not been so interested in Lachlan's story, she would have fallen asleep.

"Ye probably dinna ken, but the Sutherlands and Rosses were in a violent feud for years because of Da's father. It wasnae long after he became laird that the old king summoned him to court. It was while he was here that he met Mama. He didna ken she was the Earl of Ross's daughter, and she didna ken he was the Earl of Sutherland. But her father kenned exactly who Da was, and they ended up in a fight. An actual brawl. Long story short, Da and Mama refused to consider aught but marrying one another. They handfasted to force ma grandfather's hand. Come to think of it, I nearly forgot that Uncle Liam and Aunt Kyla handfasted after Uncle Liam's cousin tried to hurt Aunt Kyla. Both couples didna wait to go to the kirk because they were committed to one another, and they wouldnae let anyone come between them."

"Gory, but romantic, from the sounds of it," Arabella mused.

"We're Highlanders," Lachlan stated, as though that explained everything. And Arabella supposed it did. "Maude nearly handfasted with Kieran and may as well have. And Blair handfasted with Hardi. All ma cousins did the same. Mairghread and Tristan did so after his half-brother tried to steal Mairghread away when their betrothal fell through. Callum and Siùsan did, even though they were betrothed. Beathan's bluidy uncle kidnapped her and attempted to— well, he tried to mistreat her. They didna wait until their kirking to pledge their commitment. Alex and Brighde did the same when her father and betrothed tried to claim her after trying to kill her. Magnus and Deirdre fell in love as children and pledged themselves just as they became adults. Even though her parents kept them apart, both refused to consider their handfast over, and both kept their vows. Tavish and Ceit handfasted after they both nearly died at her uncle's hand. He was the most confirmed bachelor I ken, but once he fell in love with Ceit, Heaven help anyone trying to stand in his way. He was determined to marry Ceit because they loved one another, nae because there was a betrothal arranged. The Clans Sinclair and Sutherland are like-minded in that."

"It sounds like your family has a tradition of marrying without a priest. Not a patient lot, yet you all have such discipline."

"We're nae particularly patient—or forgiving—when it comes to being kept apart from the person we love most. And that's the point of this story. Ma family has marriages made from love, and so husband and wife are partners. Ye will be ma partner in all things, Belle. From deciding how to run our clan to what we do in our bedchamber. Naught is ma decision alone. If ye wish to make love, then I will honor that. If ye dinna wish to, I will never force ye."

Arabella twisted to cup Lachlan's jaw with her free hand. She kissed him; the motions languid as she swept her tongue across the seam of his lips. He opened to her as their tongues thrust and parried. Lachlan's hand trailed along the outside of Arabella's thigh, hiking up his leine until he cupped her backside. Arabella rolled back but paused.

"I don't think you realize it, but you've sounded like a Highlander almost the entire time we've been in here. I like it much better."

"I'll show ye what a Highlander I am." Lachlan rolled toward her, bracing himself above her, his chest hovering over hers. His hand slid around to dip between her thighs. Still slick with her earlier arousal, Lachlan's fingers slipped within her. As her legs fell open, he gave into her earlier demands, all his fingers pressed into her as his thumb worked the bundle of eager nerves. It was only a matter of moments before Arabella's fingers bit into Lachlan's shoulder while the other hand clenched the pillow beneath her head. She pressed her lips together to stifle her moan.

The wave of pleasure was still lapping at her when she pushed at Lachlan's shoulder, nudging him onto his back. She followed him until she hovered above him. His hands cupped her backside once more as her hand slipped under his plaid. She wasn't brave enough to flip it back and catch sight of his cock in full light, but she wrapped her hand around it and stroked. She felt his rod swell in her hand, gaining both length and girth. Her eyes darted to his, and Lachlan's expression lacked remorse. Instead, Arabella was certain it was smug pride. She squeezed until Lachlan groaned, and his hips bucked. She continued to work his length until he pulled her in for a savage kiss and spilled his seed over her hand. Just as he had in the alcove, he hurried to wipe her hand with his plaid, fearful that his release would horrify her.

"You don't have to do that," Arabella murmured. "I mean, you don't have to be in such a rush to clean my hand. I'm not bothered by it. It's rather a sense of accomplishment."

"Sense of accomplishment? I shall show ye an accomplishment," Lachlan teased as he crawled down the bed to lie on his belly between her legs. He lowered his head and was about to lick Arabella when banging sounded on his door. "Bluidy hell. Havenae enough people come to ma door today?"

Arabella's frightened eyes made Lachlan regret his grumbling. He slipped from the bed and gathered her soiled and fresh clothes before pointing beneath the bed. He gave her a rueful expression, but they both suspected it was her father at the door. He pushed the wad of clothing underneath as Arabella scouted herself under the frame. The knocking continued as Lachlan pulled his belt loose and let it drop to the floor. It reminded him that he would need to collect his weapons from his men. He was certain they retrieved them after he stormed out of the Privy Council chamber with Arabella in his arms. He let his plaid drop; the pleats falling out as he dunked his head in the now tepid bath water. He shook it out before moving toward the door while wrapping his loose plaid around his waist.

Arabella could see Lachlan's calves as he walked toward the tub. When she watched his plaid slip toward the ground, she angled herself to look up from under the bed. She briefly glimpsed the taut backside she'd enjoyed fondling in the alcove. She regretted not having done that while they were still alone. He momentarily confused her when he dunked his head, but she soon realized he had to look like the one who had bathed to explain why the tub was there. She glanced around, ensuring she had all her belongings. Her eyes widened as her hand whipped forward to pull her boots under the bed. She watched Lachlan's bare feet pad to the door, then heard her father's voice when he opened the door.

"Where the bluidy hell is my useless daughter?"

EIGHTEEN

Lachlan stepped out of the way before Mitcholm barreled into the chamber, but he blocked the doorway when Beathan tried to enter. If Mitcholm discovered Arabella under the bed, he wouldn't let Beathan spy her in only his leine. The thought that it would incriminate them enough that they would have to marry crossed his mind, but that wasn't how he wanted to begin the partnership he swore to Arabella they would have—with her disgraced and forced. When he swore never to force her, he'd meant more than just into his bed.

"I asked you a question," Mitcholm demanded.

"Do you see her here?" Lachlan answered with a sweeping gesture around the room, his courtly accent back in place. He would do his best not to tell any overt lies, but he would if backed into a corner.

"She's not in her chamber, and we all witnessed you carrying her away," Beathan said from the passageway while Lachlan continued to keep him outside the bedchamber. Lachlan didn't spare him a glance as he watched Mitcholm stalk around the chamber.

"I suppose she's run off to find her whisky," Mitcholm grumbled. "Which mon is giving it to her?

For what it's worth, I don't think it's you. After all, if it was you, she wouldn't have been out that night."

"Thank you." Lachlan infused all the sarcasm he could muster into his tone. He hoped that keeping Mitcholm talking would distract him from his search. He slipped into his brogue on purpose to draw the man's attention to him. "Ye can see the lass isnae here. Dinna ye have better places to look? Mayhap she ran to Beathan's chamber to plead forgiveness."

Arabella nearly bit through her tongue as she fought not to make a sound. She barely breathed for fear that a floorboard would squeak, or that her breath would rattle from her lungs. She could only see three sets of feet having shrunk as far back into the shadows as she could while Lachlan answered the door. Her feet touched the wall beneath the headboard.

"I wouldn't have her," Beathan sneered, his court accent more pronounced against Lachlan's burr. Lachlan knew at least one man bought his diversion. He would keep talking with his brogue if it made Beathan focus more on speaking without his.

"Dinna fash. She's sure to turn up somewhere. And I made sure the guards ken the dungeon had better nae be where."

"The dungeon! Christ on the cross, I didn't even realize that's who you were talking aboot. When she appeared, I wasn't thinking aboot what you'd said. I just noticed how appalling she was," Mitcholm declared.

"Where did ye think she'd been looking as bedraggled as she did? She looked like she'd been dragged through a bush backwards. That's why I was so concerned. I cared enough to make sure she was hale."

"I care aboot my daughter, and I don't appreciate

you insinuating otherwise." Mitcholm came to stand before Lachlan.

"Och aye, that's why ye go a year at a time without seeing her. That's why ye'd marry her off to this dung heap, even though ye ken his reputation. That's a mile of tripe," Lachlan kept the sarcasm and added disgust to his tone.

"Sutherland," Mitcholm warned.

"Aye?" Lachlan patronized. "Ye dinna have to stay if ye dinna care for ma company. *Laird.*" He added the title as an afterthought, his tone mocking.

"Ye bastard," Beathan grumbled, letting his natural accent flavor his words.

"I'm nae the one in question," Lachlan taunted. Beathan looked nothing like his older brother or sister. There were rumors that his mother, the former laird's second wife, came to the marriage already pregnant, since she got with child suspiciously quickly after the wedding. Beathan raised his hand, but Lachlan stepped away, leaving the angry Highlander to land his blow on the irate Lowlander. "None of that. Out ye both trot."

Lachlan shoved the stunned Laird Johnstone out of his chamber and swung the door shut. Locking and barring it behind them. One of the two pounded on the door, and both called his name. He turned his back to the door and went to the side of the bed. He stuck his hand out to a dazed Arabella, who shoved her clothes at him before scooting forward and out from under the frame.

"Are ye hale?" Lachlan didn't bother to try to return to his phony accent. He was too concerned about Arabella to try.

"I'm well," she reassured him, but fell into his arms when he opened them to her. "I was so frightened he would look under the bed." Arabella whispered against his chest, terrified her voice would carry. She appreciated that Lachlan had done the same.

"We'll wait awhile until there's been silence in the passageway before I take ye back to yer chamber. Ye should dress, though. As much as I dislike suggesting that." He offered her a rakish grin. "Do ye need help with the laces? I did promise to be yer lady's maid."

"I do. Eliza chose a gown she assumed she'd help me with." Arabella blushed as she looked at the clothes Lachlan tossed onto the bed before embracing her. He'd already seen her undressed, but she suddenly felt embarrassed that she would have to strip naked to switch from his leine to her chemise. Sensing her discomfort, Lachlan turned his back and gave her space. She whispered, "Thank you."

Arabella hurried to don her chemise and stockings, then tapped Lachlan's shoulder as she pulled her skirts down over her hips. It was her turn to face away. Lachlan took advantage of the bare skin still revealed at her shoulders and upper back. He kissed one spot after another. Arabella tilted her head to the side and leaned back, appreciating his solid physique. She sighed as the kisses moved up her neck to her chin. She turned her head and canted her body so their mouths could come together. It was only the space of a heartbeat before Arabella turned to face him and pressed the length of her body against his.

Lachlan's hands found his now-favorite part of her, besides her lips and sheath. He laughed to himself as he admitted there wasn't a single part of Arabella's body that wasn't his favorite. He lifted her off her feet, and she wrapped her legs around his waist. Even though they stood beside the bed, he walked them to the far wall. His excuse, if she questioned him, would be fear that the bed would creak.

Their kisses enthralled Arabella too much to care where Lachlan carried her. When her back grazed the wall, she finally opened her eyes. She'd tunneled her hands into his hair as her ankles locked around his waist. She squeezed her thighs, encouraging him to continue kissing.

"I told ye I would take nay other woman to bed, a wall, or the stables. But I will take ye any place I can, *mo chridhe*." It was the second time he'd used the endearment, but the first when Arabella was awake.

"I don't speak Gaelic. Yet," Arabella admitted sheepishly.

Lachlan's smile was so filled with tenderness that her heart surely melted. "Why would ma Lowland lass ken? Yet." He winked at her, proud that she intended to learn the language of her future clan. "It means my heart."

Arabella swallowed several times, trying to dislodge the lump in her throat so she could speak. Her voice came out a hoarse whisper. "How do you say 'my love'?"

"*Mo ghaol. Mo leannan* is my sweetheart. My darling is *mo ghràidh*."

"And I can say that to a mon? I mean, those are terms that wouldn't be too feminine for you." She rushed to clarify. Lachlan beamed at her again, having understood what she meant from the start.

"Your first phrase can be *an duine bòidheach agam*."

"Pardon? I'll never be able to say that. It's a tongue twister. I don't even ken what it means." Arabella felt defeated before she'd started. Gaelic was more guttural than Scots, and sounds were swallowed.

"Aye, ye will with practice." Lachlan pinched her bottom. "And it means my handsome husband."

"An dun bwahay am," Arabella tried, but she knew she sounded nothing like Lachlan. But once more the expression of pride encompassed his visage. It filled his eyes and his smile.

"Nearly," he said ruefully.

"Nae even close, lad," Arabella tried to imitate his burr, which made Lachlan chuckle loud enough for them to both look at the door.

"Mayhap we start with those shorter phrases for now," Lachlan suggested before kissing the tip of her nose. "Belle, I dinna want to put ye down, but I ken I should before ye tempt me into sin." Lachlan's rakish grin returned.

"I tempt you? The devil comes in a handsome form."

"That may be." Lachlan pressed a quick kiss to her lips and pinched her backside again. "But I havenae heard aught coming from outside for some time. I need to get ye either to yer chamber or to the queen."

"My chamber," Arabella blurted. "I can't face the queen or the others. Surely, everyone in the castle kens of my fall from grace by now."

"We dinna ken that. Yer father and Beathan willna want to share that to save face. The king and his guards certainly willna. The guard in the dungeon willna speak aught again. Dinna ye trust yer maid? And she doesnae ken where ye were, just that ye needed clothes."

"You have more faith than I if you believe that. The walls have eyes and ears. People will ken, Lach."

"Then ye stay by ma side, and we make the scandal aboot us and nae where ye've been."

"I can't flaunt that before my father and Beathan!"

"Do ye wish to marry him now?" Lachlan asked pointedly.

"You ken I don't," Arabella shook her head.

"Then the talk must be aboot us carrying on together. Belle, I will take ye home to Sutherland tomorrow if I must. I hate saying this, but nay matter where ye are, yer father willna forgive ye for this for a long time. Beathan willna take a wife with a tainted reputation. He's too busy trying to prove himself as a powerful laird. He willna risk anyone mocking him. This is the only way yer father willna try to force Beathan. And it's the only way to keep Beathan from telling everyone hither and thither what really happened."

"This isn't how I wanted our courtship to go," Arabella said miserably.

"This is but a moment in time, Belle. I've been courting ye for five years. Mayhap it's time I shake a leg and make ma intentions clear. Clear enough nay one can doubt what I want."

Arabella nodded her head. She closed her eyes as another wave of exhaustion and withdrawal washed over her.

I still wish I could have a dram or ten. It would make all of this so much easier. I can ease myself off of it if I can just have one or two more drinks.

Arabella tried to convince herself that her idea was reasonable, but she knew even as she thought it, one or two sips would never be enough. She opened her eyes and looked at Lachlan. She held his gaze for a moment before it became too hard, and she feared he would suspect something. She lowered her legs, and when her feet touched the floor, she stepped around him. Once more she presented her back to him, and he quickly hurried to lace her gown. He felt her tense posture and suspected what put her at unease.

"I travel often with ma sisters, and they havenae always been together. Who do ye think they come to?" Lachlan explained. He watched her shoulders lower as she exhaled her breath. He kissed her cheek as he tapped her waist when he finished. "I love ye."

"I love you too, *mo ghaol*," she laughed at her attempt, but it earned her a smacking kiss. As they walked to the door, Arabella released a silent sigh. While Lachlan had been fastening her gown, she'd resolved to find Edwin and plead with him to go out for her whisky again. She wouldn't admit to what she was doing, and she prayed no one asked, because she realized she would lie if she had to. And that made her feel more wretched than the hours spent in the oubliette.

NINETEEN

As Arabella and Lachlan left his chamber, the bells for the noon meal rang. It was later in the day than either realized. Arabella begged to have a tray in her chamber, citing exhaustion. She wanted nothing more than to eat and sleep before she had to prepare for the evening meal. Lachlan agreed without hesitation, concerned about the deep shadows forming beneath her eyes. He hadn't asked for any specifics about her time in the dungeon, but he knew she was bone weary. There would be time later to learn what happened during the raid and her imprisonment.

Lachlan knocked on Arabella's door several hours later, looking around as he waited for the door to open. If anyone spotted him outside her door, the scandal would begin sooner than they planned. They'd agreed that Lachlan would escort Arabella to the Great Hall, and she would sit with him and his men rather than with the other ladies, her father, or Beathan. There was little chance people would overlook them sharing a meal at the same table. Beathan and Mitcholm wouldn't want to create a public scene, and the silent declaration would ensure Beathan refused to move forward with the betrothal.

The man was too prideful to accept a bride who made it clear she wanted someone else.

Rebekah's maid opened the door, her mouth hanging open as she blinked rapidly. Arabella tapped the woman on the shoulder and waited for her to move aside. Arabella stepped through the doorway, Rebekah on her heels. Lachlan bowed to the other lady-in-waiting before taking Arabella's arm and wrapping it around his. Rebekah served as an unexpected chaperone while they traversed the ladies'-in-waiting passageway, chamber doors opening as women filed out.

Arabella and Lachlan reached the Great Hall, but before stepping inside, Lachlan pulled Arabella toward the wall, and whispered, "No matter what happens, I will be by your side as long as you want me there."

"Always," Arabella blurted. Lachlan smiled down at her before chucking her chin.

"We'll get through this together, Belle."

"Thank you." Arabella breathed easier, some of her confidence returning with Lachlan's presence bolstering her courage. They entered the Great Hall, but they had barely taken a step before Arabella noticed the whispers and tittering. Some even went so far as to point at her. She kept her eyes straight ahead, but her fingers bit into Lachlan's arm. She'd guessed correctly. People were already gossiping about her. Lachlan navigated them to where his guards sat. He pulled back the bench, and Arabella eased onto it before Lachlan climbed over it. Lachlan had told his men to pick a table where they could be seen without being in the center.

Arabella placed her hands on the bench beside her, gripping the edges. The stares were making her grow anxious, and she felt her heart racing, as though it were a stallion trying to break free. Sweat formed on her brow, and she found it difficult to breathe. Nervous energy made her feel jumpy. It was only when Lachlan's hand covered hers that she felt her heartbeat slow, and the fingers of the hand he covered relaxed. But her other hand still clenched the bench. She felt a bead of sweat trickle down her temple, but she didn't dare wipe it away. She didn't want to move lest she draw more attention. She wanted to take a sip of the wine before her, but she feared it would make people talk even more. She realized she feared everything. She feared eating. She feared drinking. She feared talking. She feared moving. She feared breathing. The weight of her anxiety as she looked at the judgmental faces made her feel as though the walls were closing in on her.

"I'm here, *mo chridhe*. I'm not going anywhere. You look particularly fetching. You are the envy of every woman, and I am the envy of every mon. That's all."

"Neither you nor I believe that," Arabella muttered. "They all ken."

"Even if they do, no one will say aught."

"How can you be sure of that? They're saying plenty already," Arabella's temper fired. "I knew I shouldn't have come down. I never should have listened to you."

"Mayhap, but we're here now," Lachlan replied. He sounded unruffled, but Arabella knew her words stung him. She wanted to apologize, but she lost the ability to speak as she watched her father approach. She whimpered, and Lachlan wrapped his arm low around her hips.

"Wheest, *mo ghaol*. Partners. Remember?"

Arabella gave a jerky nod, but she feared whatever her father would have to say. She drew in a deep breath and held it as Mitcholm came to stand across the table from them.

"You little whore," he hissed, pointing his finger at Arabella. "You have ruined everything. You were seen leaving Sutherland's chamber. Everyone is talking aboot it. You had your chance to seduce him and bed him, but you waited until the mon you're supposed to marry arrives to play the harlot. It won't work, Bella. I'll send you to a convent before you marry him." Mitcholm thrust his chin at Lachlan.

Lachlan waited for Arabella to reply, but when he knew she wouldn't, he spoke up. "Call her by aught but her name, and I will cut your tongue out. Disappointed or not, Lady Arabella is still just that, a lady. And she's your daughter. You shame yourself as much as you do her. What honorable mon will respect you when you spew such filth at a woman? Where is your composure as a laird?"

Mitcholm straightened to his full height. He carried several extra stones on his frame, and being only of medium height, he was portly with middle age. Arabella nearly giggled as she imagined her father trying to put up a fight against Lachlan. She knew Lachlan wouldn't hurt her father for her sake, but she didn't doubt he would defend her. The giggle she stifled bubbled into a hysteria she struggled to control. She sucked in another breath, not noticing when she released the last one, as her father swung his livid face back to her.

"God wasted everything on you. God wasted your beauty on you. I gave you the best clothing, the most expensive jewels, music lessons, a fine horse. All for what? You're aboot as perfect as a sow in muck," Mitcholm seethed.

"Enough," Lachlan growled. "No one is perfect. Your expectation that Lady Arabella be so is your flaw, not hers. If you must pin your clan's hopes on one lass's shoulders, then you are hardly the laird you present yourself as. If you intend to wash your hands of Lady Arabella, then do so now. But you will not speak to her, or any woman, like that. The only disgrace I see is you."

As Lachlan defended her, Arabella realized he hadn't exaggerated when he said he would stand beside her no matter what. His protectiveness gave her courage to speak up for herself. She wanted to prove to him that she wasn't meek. She needed him to know she could stand on her own two feet, as she would have to as his wife. She lifted her chin and set back her shoulders.

"Father, I didn't set out to embarrass you or disappoint you. That was an accident. One I wish I could undo, but I can't. I'm sorry for what I've done, and I hope you can forgive me. But I'm not the only one to err. You are too stubborn. You've heard Lachlan say he wishes to marry me. You could have a daughter who is one day the Countess of Sutherland, but because you don't want to relent, you'd marry me to a murderer and rapist. However, you seem to have forgotten or mayhap overlooked that no priest in Scotland will marry an unwilling woman. Put me before a kirk with any mon but Lachlan, and I will refuse to say my vows."

"Very well," Mitcholm sounded as though he conceded. Arabella thought she'd made progress, but he ripped her false sense of security away with his next words. "You can say your vows in a convent. I control your dowry, and you will go where it goes. You shall become a nun."

"Father!" Arabella gasped.

"Keep her dowry. My clan and I have no need of it," Lachlan interjected.

"Sutherland, I swear to you. Keep out of it or I will make you rue the day you met my daughter."

"Never," Lachlan growled. "This conversation is over."

"It is not," Mitcholm argued. "I will take this up with the king."

"Do as you please," Lachlan sniffed. He rose and held out his hand to Arabella, praying she would take it. "Shall we go?"

Arabella didn't hesitate, nor did she spare her father a glance. She laid her hand in his and stepped over the bench. Once more, she kept her eyes ahead of her, but as they approached the table where her guards and the other Johnstones sat, she locked eyes with her guard Edwin. She knew he understood her beseeching look when it was met with surprise and a brief shake of his head. Her brow furrowed as she felt desperation tugging at her once more. Edwin must have seen it because he nodded once. Arabella exhaled slowly. She only had to wait till morning. Then she would have her whisky, and even if things continued to fall apart, at least she could manage it with calmer nerves.

———

"Are you all right?" Lachlan whispered as they entered the passageway. Arabella had gone pale as her father ranted at her, but she had bright spots of color slashed across her cheeks after standing up to him. He felt her tremble as they sat together on the bench, and the tension radiated from her as they left the Great Hall. He'd seen one of her guards' expressions, but he hadn't been able to read Arabella's. He'd noticed the nod the man offered, and it made Lachlan uneasy. He disliked feeling like he couldn't trust Arabella. It was odd and troubling, but she'd broken his trust with her recent choices. He struggled to reconcile the woman he knew her to be and loved unconditionally with the woman she'd been since he returned to court. He knew that much like his anger stemmed from fear, so did his mistrust. He was frightened of what she might do next.

"Belle?"

"Hmm? Och, aye. I'm well. Just a wee unsettled, I suppose." Arabella tried to downplay just how upset she was. She didn't want to worry Lachlan, and she didn't want to talk. She wanted to escape to her chamber and wait for Edwin to arrive with her whisky. She glanced up at Lachlan and found him staring down at her. She felt exposed and scrutinized as his piercing brown eyes bored into hers. He was far too perceptive by half, and she feared he would deduce what she was up to.

"Your guard gave you a funny look as we left," Lachlan mentioned as casually as he could.

"Oh?"

"Aye. I couldn't see the look you must have given him first, but what was he nodding his head to?" Lachlan pressed.

"Edwin and I are distant cousins, and we have known each other since we were weans. But he's a friend of one of my brothers and spent a great deal of time with my father before becoming my guard. I was hoping he might settle my father's ruffled feathers. I don't think he wants to try, but he will." Arabella didn't dare smile, fearing Lachlan would see through her imitated cheer to the brazen falsehood she told.

It's not quite a lie. I mean, I have kenned Edwin since we were weans, and he is my brother's friend. But he won't dare speak to Father. He won't get in his way, and he won't want to answer any questions.

"It seems our attempt at causing a scandal aboot our relationship worked. From what your father said, his concern was the talk aboot you leaving my chamber. He said naught aboot the gaol."

"Thank heavens. I'm not ashamed of people

talking aboot me being with you. I much prefer that. I'm proud of that." *Unlike everything else aboot my life right now.*

"Do you think your father will send you to a convent?" Lachlan asked slowly. Arabella drew her lips into a thin line before nodding.

"I do," she confessed.

"Belle, what do you want to do? You ken I'll marry you as soon as I can. We can see if we can change your father's mind aboot the convent and our marrying. We can wait, or we can handfast."

"I—I want to—. Lach, I don't know what I should do," Arabella admitted. "I know what I want. But I don't know if I dare defy my father. What trouble will it bring you and your clan?"

"None," Lachlan replied resolutely.

"You are not that naïve. Don't shield me from this, please."

"Belle, your father will return to the West Marches and will soon have a daughter who is married to the Earl of Sutherland's son, nephew to the Earl of Ross, nephew-by-marriage to the Earl of Sinclair. He will crow aboot it to anyone who will listen. He's angry now because he doesn't have the control over you he assumed he'd have. He's embarrassed and angry. But Belle, how much do you really care aboot his opinion after what he's said and how he's treated you in the past?"

"He's still my father, Lach. We aren't all as blessed as you and your sisters to come from a perfect family."

"We are hardly all perfect," Lachlan mumbled. Arabella regretted her comment. Despite the years and Maude now being happily married with three children, Lachlan carried immense guilt over causing Maude's eating disorder and self-esteem troubles when she was younger. Even though Maude reassured him that he wasn't the reason and that he'd actually saved her life, Arabella knew he was determined to be the best brother and the best man he could to make up for it.

"I'm sorry I said that. I don't want to go back to bickering and sniping. I want to marry you. Today. But I'm scared of the fallout. Can we at least wait until Beathan leaves? I don't want to pour salt in that wound for either Beathan or my father. I'd rather just stay out of sight. I ken that makes me a coward."

"No, it doesn't. It's probably the wisest thing to do. But what if your father tries to take you to a convent?"

"He won't right away. He must find one that will accept me, and he must arrange for my dowry to be delivered. Mayhap the king will even step in before then. I don't know, but I think we have a couple of days before aught else will happen."

"And in the meantime? You can't ignore your duties to the queen," Lachlan pointed out.

"I ken. We made our point this eve. I can manage gossip aboot us. I will return to my duties tomorrow, and the rumors will feed themselves. At least Bonnie Bella's fall from grace lands her beside the brawest mon she's ever met," Arabella grinned. Lachlan pulled her into his arms, uncaring of who might see them.

"Beside me, beneath me, above me. I'll have you next to me anyway I can," Lachlan murmured before their mouths sought each other. The kiss overflowed with the passion from earlier that day. Lachlan groaned as his desire to thrust inside her, claim her so that no one could separate them, roared to life. Arabella pulled away too soon for his liking.

"What if my father can't separate us?" Arabella asked. "I mean, if there's a chance I might carry the future heir to Clan Sutherland, there isn't any choice but to allow us to marry."

Lachlan stood in stunned silence. While he'd just thought about how much he wanted to do just what Arabella suggested, it shocked him to hear her say it aloud. His honor screamed that he couldn't do it even while his body encouraged him. He wrestled with what he knew was right and what he wanted above all else. He cupped Arabella's cheek as she gazed earnestly into his eyes.

"It's one thing for people to gossip aboot us because someone claimed to see us together. Everyone kens most rumors here are fabricated. There's as much room to believe it's untrue as there is to argue that it is. But that—that would destroy your reputation, and it would never be forgotten. I don't want you to live with a blemished reputation, with people looking down on you and talking aboot you behind your back for the rest of time."

"And if I want it to be true?" Arabella whispered.

"One day, when the Lord blesses us, it will be. And once we marry, I will endeavor to make that day sooner rather than later." Lachlan waggled his brows, eliciting a tinkle of laughter from Arabella. "But I won't destroy your name in the process. I will come out unscathed, while you will bear the stigma forever. And I absolutely will not have anyone speculate the only reason I married you is because we got caught. I will let no one say that I was forced into marrying you. I want it clear to any and every one that I love you, and that's why I married you."

"I trust you," Arabella murmured. Lachlan saw the apprehension in Arabella's eyes and knew she feared that he couldn't say the same.

"You broke my trust in some ways, but not entirely. It can be rebuilt, *mo chridhe*."

"I want to," Arabella blurted. "More than

aught." But in the back of her mind, she knew continuing to drink could destroy what was left of his faith in her. But the craving for whisky, the memory of how it made life easier, was even more powerful than what the alcohol did when she drank it.

"I ken, Belle." Lachlan and Arabella arrived at her door, but neither hurried to open it. He pressed a feather-soft kiss to her lips, not trusting himself to take it any deeper lest their conversation be for naught when they landed on the bed together. The shadows beneath her eyes had deepened since their encounter with her father. He knew she was exhausted. "Go to sleep, *mo ghaol*. You need more rest."

"I do. Now that I'm so close to my bed, I suddenly feel like I can barely keep my eyes open."

"Then sleep well, and I shall find you in the morn. I love you."

"I love you, *mo chridhe*." Arabella smiled shyly, uncertain whether she sounded foolish using one of the three Gaelic phrases she knew. When Lachlan's proud smile returned, she fell against his chest. His solid heartbeat and warm body beneath her cheek steadied her. His arms came around her, and he kissed the top of her head.

"Partners. Remember that. In everything. We shall get through this together," Lachlan promised, his voice muffled by her hair as he kissed her crown again. Arabella nodded, then stepped back. Lachlan watched her slip into her chamber before he turned toward his own.

TWENTY

Arabella pretended to sleep as she listened to Rebekah and her maid tiptoe around the chamber. She'd cracked an eye open and told her roommate that she needed more sleep. She would skip Mass and the morning meal, then join Queen Elizabeth and her ladies for the queen's morning walk through the gardens. She deepened her breathing, hoping the soft sighs would convince the two women that she still slumbered. As soon as Rebekah and her maid left, Arabella scrambled out of her bed and donned a gown in a muted color, then combed her hair. She'd told Eliza the night before that she intended to sleep late, so her maid had fetched a fresh ewer of water before they retired.

Arabella hurried to ready herself before slipping into the passageway on slippered feet. Much like she did any time she met Edwin, she moved through passageways usually frequented by servants, risking her safety for secrecy. On more than one occasion, she'd had to duck into the shadows to avoid being discovered alone by male servants. Her status as a lady wouldn't matter if a randy man forced himself upon her. The man would count on her keeping her indiscretion a secret rather than accusing him of a crime.

"

She eased a door open that led to the undercroft and rushed to the storeroom where she and Edwin always met. It was where the castle stored grain distributed to the villagers just beyond the town walls. Men only entered it once a week to gather wagon loads, so Arabella knew she was safe from discovery. She breathed easier when she spotted Edwin as sunlight filtered in around her.

"My lady, this must be the last time. Your father will kill me, and I do not exaggerate. He's already threatened us," Edwin declared.

"I ken, Edwin. I cannot thank you enough for what you've risked for me," Arabella replied.

"Why didn't you come to me the other night?"

"I didn't want to admit that I needed more so soon. I thought I could sneak into town and buy some on my own. The first night, Lachlan and his men caught me. By the second night, I was too desperate and too embarrassed to seek you out."

Edwin nodded but said nothing. Instead, he handed Arabella a sack that he held at the top and the bottom to keep the jugs from rattling. She took it from him before handing him a heavy pouch of coins. She'd planned to pay him extra for his troubles, but from the weight of the sack, she knew he'd brought her more than the usual three jugs.

"Six," Edwin confirmed.

"Thank you," Arabella sighed. This would last her at least until her father and Beathan left. If there was any remaining by the time she and Lachlan departed, she would give it to her guards. There was nothing more to say, so Arabella eased the storeroom door open, checking to make sure no one was in sight before she exited the room. She rushed back to her chamber.

A little nip before I join the ladies and the queen will set me to rights, Arabella reasoned with herself. She locked her chamber door, then moved to the far side of her bed where she sat on the floor. She pulled the jugs from the bag and immediately realized she had a problem. Only three jugs fit in her secret hiding place, and there were still three empty containers in there that she forgot to take with her to trade Edwin for the new ones.

With nine bottles to hide, Arabella panicked. She couldn't hide them in her chest because her maid went into it every day to pull out fresh underclothes. A servant swept under the bed on various days and would surely find them there. Arabella looked around her chamber, but she couldn't think of anywhere else to put them. She wondered if she could dig another hole in the wall or make the current one deeper or wider. She pushed against the solid wood bedframe, but it didn't budge. It made her wonder how the person who dug the hole did it. There was just enough room for her to slide under the bed to reach the loose stones. She realized her bed sat much lower than the one in Lachlan's chamber.

There's naught for it. I'll hide them in my chest at the bottom. Each night I'll pull out what I need for the next day and tell Eliza that I did it to save time in the morning so I can sleep later. But that'll only work once before she does it herself. I need to find somewhere to at least leave the empty flasks.

Arabella racked her mind as she pulled the stopper from a jug and brought it to her lips. It was the first sip she'd had in days, and the fiery burn that slid over her tongue, down her throat, and settled in her belly was a welcome and familiar feeling. It was as though she returned to a favorite spot that she hadn't visited in ages and was relieved to see. She continued to think about what she could do with the empty containers. She didn't dare ask more of Edwin, and she didn't want to ask her other guards to get involved. She wondered if she could ask Lachlan to dispose of them since he already knew about her habit. But she didn't want to do anything that might make him question whether she'd gotten more. As she worked through her dilemma, she didn't notice how many sips she'd taken until her cheeks tingled and her nose felt numb.

Och, bluidy hell! I've had more than I meant to. I'm on my way to being soused. It's all right, Belle. If you remain quiet and pretend as though you don't want to talk because you're embarrassed from the rumors, and if you pay really close attention while you're walking, no one will ken. Just keep quiet and walk properly.

Arabella toppled sideways more than leaned, but she rolled onto her belly and fished out the three empty jugs and replaced them with three full ones. Once the loose stones were back in place, she struggled to pull herself to her feet as she suddenly felt incredibly sleepy. Climbing into bed and sleeping the day away appealed to her even more as she stood upright, and her eyes drifted shut and her head bobbed forward. When she bent forward to pick up the bottles, she feared she would fall flat on her face. She reached back for the bed and eased herself onto the mattress. When the room didn't feel off-kilter, she used one hand to cling to the bedding while the other picked up the first empty jug.

She went to her chest and lifted the lid. She assessed the clothing she found and knew the containers would make the stacks of clothes uneven, but she couldn't think of any other resolution. She lifted out her stack of chemises and stockings, laying them on the bed. She laid the empty flask on its side. She slid her feet along the floor as she walked back to the other containers. Having learned her lesson the last time, she squatted to pick up the other two empty ones. She placed those in the chest and spread the stacks of clothes over them. Even to her bleary eyes, it didn't look right. She prayed her father departed soon, or that Eliza was more loyal to her than to her laird. She returned to the other three jugs that still remained on the floor. She lifted the one she'd been drinking from and realized it was already half empty.

That explains the state I'm in. How did I not notice? Because you're a drunkard, Belle. You've grown so used to it that now not only don't you notice the taste, you need more. This has to stop.

Arabella's self-recrimination gave her a moment of sobriety, so she hurried to gather the other two jugs. She looked at the wardrobe where she kept her gowns. She knew her satchels were in the bottom. If she could fit the jugs into her satchels and pushed them all the way to the back where they were less likely to rattle, she might succeed in hiding them. She tested the stoppers before kneeling down and placing them in the bags. She pushed her gowns apart and set the satchels all the way against the back. She fluffed out her gowns until they hid her contraband.

There. That does it. Arabella turned away but stopped. *Mayhap just one more sip. I feel much better than I did before. Another dram won't make a difference.*

Arabella kneeled down again and drew out the bottle she'd already started. She took two quick swigs before putting it back. She went to the table that held the pitcher and ewer. Beside them were several sprigs of mint. She broke off two and chewed them quickly. She cupped her hand in front of her mouth and breathed on it. She could only smell the slightest hint of alcohol. She grabbed another sprig to chew as she made her way to join the ladies as they were leaving the keep for the queen's morning constitutional. She felt like she'd lived an entire day already. She fell into place between Laurel and Caitlyn but kept quiet. As the bright sunlight dazzled her eyes, she regretted the extra drink she'd thought wouldn't make a difference.

She felt unsteady on her feet as she squinted to shut out the blinding light. A pounding head replaced the nice tingle in her cheeks. Despite the physical discomfort, she finally felt calm after days of anxiety.

It was worth it. I can do this now. Even if I see my father or Beathan, I can make it through. And for now, keep quiet and speak only when spoken to. Mayhap no one will say aught to me, anyway.

The thought had barely crossed her mind when Laurel linked her arm through Arabella's and leaned over conspiratorially. "You made quite the announcement last night by entering the Great Hall with Lachlan and walking right past your father and Laird Gunn. I thought for sure either or both of them would have an apoplexy when they saw you. It made me wonder if the rumors were true. Are you and Lachlan—?" Laurel gave her a pointed look.

Arabella feigned a look of innocence she'd perfected as a child. She would never tell anyone about what she and Lachlan shared in his chamber. She shook her head, but regretted it when it felt like a bell tower with her brain as the clapper rattling back and forth. "We did naught that left me any different from before my father arrived."

"Does that mean you two have been—well—since before then?" Laurel whispered.

Arabella appreciated that Laurel kept her voice down, but despite that, they were drawing attention. Arabella shot Laurel a warning glance, but her friend appeared too eager to recognize it. Arabella grew suspicious, wondering if Laurel was the one feeding the rumors. They'd only become friends within the past two years; before that, Arabella had avoided Laurel. They weren't close enough for Arabella to share her deepest secrets. They based their friendship more on length of acquaintance than being likeminded.

"I am still a maiden if that's what you wish to ken. I haven't done aught with anyone to be ashamed of, nor am I guilty of aught with any mon," Arabella assured Laurel. She was growing warm, and she knew it wasn't from the outside temperature. The whisky swished in her empty belly with each step. Her heart was beating harder, but the walk was no more arduous than normal along the flat path.

"Then why would anyone see you leaving his chamber?" Laurel pressed.

"Who said that they did?" Arabella countered.

"Mary Elizabeth," Laurel answered. She'd named a lady-in-waiting who'd been at court for less than a year, but who had become the self-appointed leader. She had the same nasty and spiteful demeanor that Madeline MacLeod had possessed, and much like Mary Kerr, Madeline's predecessor as the ringleader of the most vindictive of the ladies. Laurel had once been part of that circle, and Arabella feared she'd returned to her old ways. "Bella, if I don't know at least some truth, I might say the wrong thing. I don't want Mary Elizabeth to keep spreading these rumors. I'll deny them if I can, but I don't want to accidentally give something away. If I know what I'm hiding, then I know what not to say."

Arabella considered what Laurel said. It was reasonable considering they had grown closer, but she still didn't trust the other woman enough to share anything private with her. She tried to come up with something to say, but her mind felt like it was suddenly drowning in a bog. Clear thoughts wouldn't come to her, and her blinks grew longer as she wished she could catch a moment of sleep with each one.

"Bella? You don't look well. Your face has grown red, and you look like you're overheated," Laurel whispered. Even in a low tone, Arabella's head rang. She didn't dare shake it.

"I feel a wee off today. That's why I slept later than usual," Arabella explained.

"You don't sound right either," Laurel pointed out. "Do you need the healer?"

"Nay, but I think I should return to my chamber. If I have the ague, I wouldn't want to pass it to anyone." Arabella was grateful to have an excuse to escape. She knew she needed to sleep off her overconsumption. She knew Lachlan would finish in the lists soon, and she wanted to flee before he found her. He would know immediately that she'd imbibed again.

I want to hide from the mon I love. What have I—don't, Belle. Don't ask yourself that yet again when you already know the answer. You are the wretched failure Father said. You are a disappointment to Lachlan, just like you are to Father. He's just being kind to you because he feels sorry for you. He must feel stuck. He doesn't want to marry me, but he thinks he has to protect me. He doesn't really want me. I'm useless to him, to Father, and to my clan. They'd be better off if I drank myself into oblivion and floated away on the River Forth.

"Do you want me to walk with you?" The concern in Laurel's voice drew Arabella back to their conversation. She saw the worry in the other woman's eyes and knew she'd failed in her goal to remain unnoticed. Not only had she drawn attention to herself, she'd done it in a way that would make others ask about her later.

"Nay, I'm fine," Arabella slurred. She gave her head a little shake and pulled away from Laurel. "Please let the others ken I'm not feeling well."

Arabella didn't wait for Laurel to answer. She turned away, picking her skirts up and hurrying back to the castle. She made her way inside, and once she was alone, she leaned against a wall to catch her breath. Everything spun around her, and she wanted to retch. Keeping one hand on the wall to steady her and using the other to hold up her skirts, she made her way to her chamber. She darted to the chamber pot and barely made it before her stomach emptied of all the whisky that had swirled around inside her. She kicked off her slippers and barely made it onto her bed before her eyes closed.

TWENTY-ONE

Lachlan left the lists feeling better than he had in days. He'd had a good training session, and despite his worries, neither Beathan nor Mitcholm showed up to spar. He'd released the pent-up frustration from the situation with Arabella and felt relaxed after days of worry about the woman he longed to see. He noticed the ladies-in-waiting lingering at the entrance to the garden while Queen Elizabeth stood speaking to some of her matronly attendants. She rubbed her swollen belly, and Lachlan wondered how long it would be until she gave birth. There'd been talk about both his father and his uncle serving as godfathers and his mother becoming the bairn's godmother, but they had settled nothing. He turned away from the women but turned back when he heard his name.

"Lachlan," Laurel called once. She glanced around before making her way to Lachlan. While she glided gracefully toward him, her pace unhurried, Lachlan could see the strain on her face even from a distance. He didn't need Laurel to tell him it involved Arabella.

What now? Lachlan tensed. *Lach! That's horrible. Ye love her, and she's in trouble. Be more gracious. But she's been naught but trouble since I arrived. Can I really bring such a woman home as ma wife? How can ye doubt what ye've kenned for years? Because she's nae the woman ye thought ye kenned for years. All the more reason to help her.*

Lachlan's mind swirled with doubt and guilt as Laurel came to stand before her. He took a deep breath, preparing himself for whatever the woman had to say. He already knew he wouldn't like it.

"Something isn't right aboot Arabella. I don't ken if she's coming down with a sickness, but she wasn't at all herself. She's distracted, and she didn't come to Mass or the morning meal today. When she joined us for the walk, her eyes were glassy, and she broke out in a sweat from a walk we take every day. And when she spoke, her voice wasn't normal. It was as if each word came out slower and slower, like she really had to think aboot them. She wouldn't let me summon the healer."

Lachlan knew she wasn't ailing from some sickness, unless drinking too much could be considered one. Laurel might not realize she'd just describe an intoxicated person, but Lachlan did.

"Where is she now?"

"She went to her chamber to rest," Laurel explained.

"Thank you for telling me. I'm certain she will be right as rain soon enough," Lachlan reassured. But he felt his temper boiling within. He nodded to Laurel and turned toward the keep. His bath and fresh clothing would have to wait. He had a wayward sweetheart to find. He prayed she made it to her chamber before someone found her. He wound his way through the labyrinth of passageways until he came to Arabella's door. He didn't bother to knock, pushing the door open, and stopping short when he found Arabella sprawled across her bed. He sniffed the air in the chamber and recognized the scent of strong whisky. He knew without tasting it that it was an inferior quality with a high-alcohol content.

"Belle," Lachlan whispered as he shook her shoulder. When she didn't make a sound, he stared at her chest. When he saw it rise and fall, he released the breath he hadn't realized he was holding. He shook her shoulder more firmly, but she still didn't move, not even a twitch. He spoke louder the next time. "Arabella."

He infused command into his tone and deepened it. She attempted to roll away from him, but his hand on her shoulder pinned her in place. He said her name again, shaking her shoulder roughly. He feared for a moment that he would hurt her, but his anger and worry soon made him forget his guilt.

"Arabella," Lachlan's tone was demanding as he tapped her cheeks. He was careful not to be rough. He didn't want to leave marks, and he drew a line at slapping any woman. "Belle."

Arabella's eyes fluttered open, and he read the confusion in her expression. She blinked several times as her brow furrowed. She swept her eyes around the chamber but closed them with a wince. She waited a moment before she pried them open once more.

"Lach?" Arabella's voice was hoarse.

"Aye. How much did you have to drink, Belle?"

"Too much," she moaned. But she tried to jerk upright when she realized what she confessed. She moaned again, and Lachlan watched as her face went ghostly pale. He rushed to the chamber pot, finding it filled with the contents from Arabella's earlier episode. He had no choice and held it under her mouth just in time. She gripped it, her hands covering his as she cast up her accounts.

When they both were convinced there was nothing left to come up, Lachlan set it aside and brought a wet linen square and a sprig of mint to Arabella. She wiped her mouth before folding the cloth over and wiping her face and neck. Lachlan took the cloth back as he traded it for the mint. He soaked the cloth once more, ringing it out and folding so he could place it at the base of her neck. She laid back and shut her eyes.

"Go away."

"No," Lachlan's voice was resolute.

"Leave me, Lach. Go back to Dunrobin," Arabella hissed.

"No."

"Yes."

Lachlan realized he wouldn't leave Arabella for anything in the world. He wasn't prepared to give up and seeing her in her current condition only made him more resolved to stay. His earlier doubts fled as his heart ached for her. He'd never seen her in such a state, and it wasn't just the aftereffects of the alcohol. She'd given up.

"You can do better than a drunkard. You deserve better. Leave and find someone who deserves you," Arabella muttered.

"And if I refuse?" Lachlan countered.

"Stop, Lach. I don't want to fight you aboot this. Just go home. Go wherever. Just leave me alone."

Lachlan sat beside Arabella on the bed and slid his arm beneath her. When he rolled her toward him, she didn't resist. He moved the still-cool cloth to her forehead and held it there. He didn't know what to say, and he didn't want to argue either. Instead, he offered her the strength that he had and that she needed. They sat like that as Arabella dozed. Lachlan kissed the crown of her head periodically as he stroked her hair, finding it calmed her. Eventually, she wrapped her arm around his middle. He knew she didn't realize what she was doing, but she sought the comfort he offered.

Arabella came awake feeling more like herself and knew she'd slept off the effects of the alcohol. Her chamber was dim, and she realized it was late afternoon. She'd been sleeping for hours. Something solid but comfortable sat propped beside her, her arm slung over it. She didn't need to look up to know it was Lachlan. He continued to stroke her hair, and she closed her eyes again, reveling in the tenderness. She knew he'd noticed she was awake when he slid down so that they lay eye-to-eye.

Arabella's eyes filled with tears as she looked at Lachlan. His expression was so filled with worry that guilt swept through her. She tried to draw in a breath, but it felt as though her lungs had quit. Lachlan pressed a soft but lingering kiss to her forehead, and her sobs began. She cried for all the years she'd done her best to please everyone, for the rebelliousness that led her to turn to alcohol, the shame of now needing it, and the fear that Lachlan would leave just as she told him to.

"I'm nae going anywhere, *mo chridhe*," Lachlan promised as though he'd read her mind. She fisted his leine as she clung to him, his burr somehow the most comforting sound she'd ever heard.

"Lach, I have a problem," Arabella confessed.

"I ken, little one. I ken," Lachlan whispered.

"I don't want to be like this, but I don't know how to stop. Even now, I feel so miserable, and all I want is a drink to make me feel better, which only makes me feel worse. Does that make me hopeless?"

"Nay. Ye need help, and I amnae going anywhere. I promise ye. I will do whatever I can, but I think the first step was ye asking. But I need to ken, do ye mean it? Or do ye fear that I will go, and ye're saying it so I will stay?"

"Both," Arabella sobbed once more. "I want to stop, but I don't know if I can do it without you. And I feel even worse that I want your help. I don't want to trap you, Lach. Never have I wanted that."

"I'm nae trapped if I'm where I want to be," Lachlan reasoned.

"How can you still want me? How can you stay when I'm such a disappointment?" Arabella asked.

"Because yer choices and yer actions can disappoint me without the whole of ye being a disappointment. I've kenned ye a long time, Belle. Never have ye been like this before. I'm scared and I'm angry too. I confess that I had a moment of doubt, but I kenned as soon as I walked in here that I canna and willna leave ye."

"My father has washed his hands of me. I wouldn't blame you if you did the same," Arabella whispered.

"I wish yer father didna keep hurting ye as he does. But, Belle, even in the best of situations, if ye marry a Highlander, it would be rare for ye to see yer clan once ye move north. He wouldnae be part of yer life anymore, anyway. We can go as soon as ye wish, his blessing or nae. Ye dinna have to face him again if ye dinna wish."

"I don't want to slink away as though I ran away in disgrace," Arabella countered as she shook her head. It no longer felt like a hammer striking an anvil.

"We will do what ye want, Belle. But ye willna be well as yer body purges itself of the need for whisky. Ye canna be here to do it. That's too big a secret to hope to keep. Ye will look like ye are vera ill, so someone is bound to summon the healer. I trust Father Gormal to keep yer secret, but people will doubt his healing skills if he comes and ye dinna get better."

"I don't want to jeopardize his reputation, or the faith people have in him. I can't hide in my chamber without the queen growing angry or without everyone talking."

"Aye. We have to leave, even if ye dinna want to go to Dunrobin."

"I want to go to Dunrobin," Arabella blurted, then slowed down. "But I don't want your parents to meet me like this, or when I'm looking like I'm on death's doorstep."

"Will ye let me speak to the king and queen? I will ask for King Robert to dissolve the agreement between yer father and Beathan, and I will ask Queen Elizabeth to let ye go from her service. But I need to tell them why."

"Yes, but I want to go too. Lachlan, this is my responsibility. You may be the rock I'm leaning on, but I won't hide behind you."

"Vera well. But it needs to be sooner rather than later," Lachlan warned.

"Do you think we could gain an audience with them again?" Arabella asked.

"We can try the antechamber once more. We'd be pushing our luck, but it's the most likely way to find them together and alone." Lachlan glanced at the window embrasure and the shadows cast on the floor. "We will need to go soon."

Arabella bit her bottom lip, and Lachlan felt all the blood rush to his cock. He pulled her lip free, and heat filled the look they exchanged. Their mouths neared one another's, but they both paused. "I love you," they said as one, both smiling before they kissed. Hunger flared within them both, and Arabella clung to Lachlan as his hand grabbed her backside none too gently. He pulled her against him. With a grumble, he pushed his sporran out of the way. Arabella's instincts told her to hook her leg over Lachlan's hip, bringing them closer. She felt the length of his rod brushing against her mound.

Arabella paused and drew back from their kiss. "Am I the whore my father said for wanting you so much? I'm a maiden. I shouldn't ken such desire, but it's burning a hole into me."

"Do nae *ever* use that word to describe yerself again, Belle. I dinna want to hear it. Ye are nae one. Ye are a woman, one who I pray loves me as much as I love her. There is naught wrong with desiring the mon ye love, the mon who wishes more than aught to make ye his wife."

"But women aren't supposed to be this way," Arabella argued. Her face crumpled when he chuckled.

"Och, Belle. I'm nae laughing at ye, but at what ye said. Maude has three bairns, and she's been married barely four years. Blair has a bairn on the way and only married a couple of months ago. Ma parents had three children and would have had more had Mama's pregnancy with Blair nae been so trying. It terrified Da into swearing to be more careful, but that hasnae slowed them down. Embarrasses Maude, Blair, and me nearly daily. Uncle Liam and Aunt Kyla had five children. Mairghread has four, Callum has three as does Alex. Magnus and Tavish each have one with another on the way. Ma family isnae so big because the women turn their husbands away. Wait until ye meet ma cousins. Ye will see within a moment of meeting them that their wives are vera demanding." Lachlan grinned and waggled his eyebrows. "I hope ma bonnie bride is just as demanding."

Lachlan froze when he realized Arabella might

not appreciate the phrase bonnie bride if it reminded her too much of being called Bonnie Bella. She smoothed back the hair from his temple and kissed Lachlan's cheek.

"I much prefer being called your bonnie bride than Bonnie Bella. 'Bonnie bride' is a title I can be proud of," Arabella assured him. "And if a demanding wife is what you wish, then I aim to please. Kiss me again, Lach. Please." She added the courtesy at the last minute before Lachlan's mouth descended on hers. Lachlan gripped her thigh, keeping it wrapped around his hip as he rolled Arabella onto her back.

"One day soon, I shall show ye the real passion that lies between us, Belle." Lachlan thrust his length against her mons, imitating what he wanted to do without their clothes in the way. Arabella moaned as she ran her hands over his back until she reached his buttocks. She gripped the hardened muscles, feeling them flex under her fingers. She pressed Lachlan against her as she rocked her hips beneath him. She could feel the friction pushing her toward the same sensations she'd felt when he brought her to release.

"Don't stop," Belle panted.

"Do ye feel it too?" Lachlan asked as he felt his climax tightening his bollocks.

"Aye." Arabella barely breathed the word before her head tilted back, the chords in her neck straining as pleasure drew her core into a tight knot before it radiated throughout her. Lachlan groaned as he rocked his hips faster, his release surging through him until he spilled within his plaid.

"The next time, I will burry maself inside ye because ye will be ma wife."

"Aye. I want that too." Arabella cupped his cheeks and kissed him with all the love she could pour into the exchange. She felt Lachlan receive it and reciprocate. He held her in his arms as they both drifted back down to earth. Reluctantly, Arabella tapped Lachlan's back. "If we are to attempt an audience with the king and queen before the evening meal, we must go. And I still have to change into an appropriate gown."

Arabella bit her bottom lip again but released it with a grin when Lachlan growled a warning. He rolled off her and stood, offering her his hand. She went to her wardrobe and selected a gown, then turned back to Lachlan.

"I need help, please," Arabella confessed.

"Lord, ye do test me," Lachlan muttered. "I'll unlace and lace ye, but ye had better go behind the screen to dress. I can only withstand so much temptation, lass."

Arabella raked her eyes over Lachlan, making it clear that he was not the only one struggling with restraint. Lachlan made quick work of undoing her laces, and Arabella disappeared behind the screen. They were ready to leave in less than five minutes. Arabella peered into the passageway and noticed no one nearby. She led Lachlan through the servants' passageway, the same way she'd gone to meet Edwin. He raised an eyebrow, but said nothing. When they came to the royal antechamber, they squeezed one another's hand before Lachlan pulled the door open.

TWENTY-TWO

"You are making a rather nasty habit of entering where you are not welcome, Lachlan. I'm certain your mother taught you better than that," King Robert snapped. Lachlan and Arabella stood before him and Queen Elizabeth. Lachlan and Arabella had interrupted the royals' conversation but hadn't intruded upon another private moment.

"I ken, and I apologize, Your Majesty." Lachlan bowed. "May we have a word with Uncle Robert and Aunt Elizabeth?" Lachlan signaled that he wished to talk to them as members of his extended family rather than as their sovereigns.

"Nay," King Robert snapped. "You and your sisters are making this an all-too-frequent habit."

Lachlan stiffened to his full height and raised his chin. "I am nearing six-and-twenty. In all my life, I have asked for three audiences as your godson. My sister Maude could have begged for you to make the other women cease their harassment, but she never did. She dealt with it herself. Maude only wished to marry the mon she loved. Blair only wanted the same and to help the mon she loved when his clan threatened to destroy him. You said yourself my family has a habit of marrying for love. That's why I'm here."

"My dear," Queen Elizabeth laid her hand on King Robert's forearm and leaned to whisper something in his ear while Lachlan and Arabella waited. King Robert's lips turned down, but he nodded.

"Your godmother pointed out that not only do you speak the truth, but if I'm not prepared to be your godfather from time to time, I never should have accepted the privilege and the duty. What is it that you seek?"

"Your Majesty," Arabella spoke up. She swallowed. "It's not Lachlan who seeks something. I mean, not him alone. I need to confess something to the queen before we can move forward."

Arabella glanced at Lachlan before stepping away. She moved toward the queen but stopped a respectful distance from her. She kneeled before Queen Elizabeth and bowed her head. She swallowed again, forcing herself to find the strength to confess what she'd only told Lachlan.

"Some time again, I developed a fondness for the drink, whisky in particular. It started out as a wee dram once in a while to calm my nerves before the evening meal. I didn't notice the stares and whispers as much. When I realized the evenings I had a tipple were easier to manage than those when I didn't, I started having a dram or two before the nightly meal. When I drank, the attention from men and the snide questions from women no longer made me self-conscious. Then my father informed me by missive that he was looking for a betrothal." Arabella looked back at Lachlan. "I didn't—I don't—want to marry anyone but Lachlan. I became anxious that my father would marry me off before I could see Lachlan again. Then each time he came to court, neither of us dared confess how we felt for fear of hurting

Maude and Blair. I started needing more than just a dram each evening to feel the same ease."

Arabella stopped speaking for a moment as she sniffled, trying to keep her composure despite her humiliation.

"The more my father pressured me to find a mon, then threatened to find one for me, the more anxious I became. He expected me to be perfect. Everyone did because of how I look. I became scared of choosing the wrong gown, doing my hair in a way that wasn't flattering, of saying something idiotic. I wasn't perfect, but everyone kept saying I was, kept expecting that of me."

Arabella paused again to catch her breath. She felt the tears pricking at her eyelids, but she didn't dare cry before the royal couple. She was already making a fool of herself by having to confess her sins. She wouldn't add to it to by being a watering pot.

"I've gotten to where I need at least one stiff drink to get through the day. I was in the gaol because I went to the Merry Widow to buy more whisky. I was too ashamed to ask the person who usually bought it for me because it was too soon. I thought I could slip out and return with no one knowing. Obviously, that was a grave error on my part. But even after two nights and a day in prison, I still crave it." Arabella looked up at the queen and blinked several times. "Your Grace, I missed Mass and the morning meal today because I went to collect more whisky. I left our walk early because I was too drunk to walk through the gardens. I've been absent all afternoon because I was sleeping off the drink."

Lachlan stepped forward and gripped Arabella's elbow as he helped her to her feet. He pulled her against him and turned her face into his chest. He shot the king and queen a warning glare, but he saw the shock and sorrow in both of their faces.

"I am not pretending when I say I want to marry Arabella. I have since I met her, but we made the scene last eve to distract from anyone learning aboot her time in the dungeon. I learned of Arabella's problem when I arrived here with Blair and Hardi. I didn't realize how serious it was until the sheriff arrested Arabella. Uncle Robert, you heard how Mitcholm and Beathan spoke to Arabella, but you didn't hear what Mitcholm said to Belle last night. It was horrible. It made me want to drink. If that's what Belle has heard even once, I don't blame her for the pressure she feels to be perfect."

"Lady Arabella," Queen Elizabeth reached out her hands as Arabella turned to look at her. Arabella stepped away from Lachlan and accepted the queen's gesture. "It's no secret how I came to be married to the king. My father and King Edward pinned their hopes on me remaining loyal to them, to me sharing the king's secrets. We know what became of me for choosing my husband over my father and the English king."

Queen Elizabeth grimaced as she recalled her eight years under house arrest. She, King Robert's daughter and sisters, and Isabella MacDuff had all been part of the failed escape. King Robert lost two brothers for their attempt to aid the women. King Robert lowered his eyes as he too recalled one of the darkest moments in his life.

"I tell you this because I understand what it is to have your family's hopes and plans pinned onto your shoulders. It's a significant burden to bear, especially for someone so young. I turned to prayer because it was all I had. But I confess I can easily see how you turned to the drink. I likely would have too, had it been available. Solace and oblivion is what we both sought. I wish I had known sooner. I have failed to look after the women who attend me, and that is my failing as your queen." Queen Elizabeth looked at Lachlan, pulling one hand free to offer it to him. "It was a tremendous honor when your parents and your aunt and uncle asked us to be godparents to you, your sisters, and your cousins. It hasn't been easy to balance our relationships when we're at court, but I should have done more for you and Maude and Blair. I regret that. I offer you my humble apologies."

Lachlan squeezed the older woman's hand and leaned forward to kiss her cheek, just as he had as a child. He stepped back and wrapped his arm around Arabella's waist as Queen Elizabeth released her hand. "Thank you, Aunt," Lachlan whispered.

"I disagreed with Beathan Gunn as your father's choice, Lady Arabella. But it is a tenuous line that I must tread with allowing lairds to choose their alliances. Unifying Scotland has always been my goal. When a Lowland laird wishes to marry his daughter to a Highland laird, it strengthens that unification. The individual isn't what I must consider as king. But as a father and a godfather, I ken that what I want and what is good for Scotland are often at odds. When you and Lachlan came to us before, I felt it was too late to jeopardize severing the alliance your marriage to the Gunn would form. Your father still is not wholly trustworthy. I don't fear him allying with the English, but he seeks power in the Marches. Granting the marriage and holding that over him reels him in," King Robert explained.

He looked at Lachlan and shook his head. Lachlan noticed for the first time just how much the king had aged since seven-year-old Lachlan once tailed after the king, his father, and his uncle to go hunting. He hadn't been able to sit for a week. Duty, war, and great family loss had worn away the once youthful warrior and left a wisened but aged monarch.

"Mitcholm and Beathan's behavior in the Privy Council chamber worried me before you showed up, Lachlan. Once Lady Arabella joined us, I was deeply perturbed. And while I didn't hear what Mitcholm said last night, I've heard of it." King Robert cast a long, hard look at the couple before nodding. "Lachlan, you spoke the truth. Your family nearly never asks for aught from us. When you have, it has always been with a just reason. Lady Arabella, your story troubles me. I know the lure of whisky and how it eases pain no one can see. You are a brave young woman to confess so much, especially when you do so before your king and queen. Your humility convinces me that you will be an excellent Countess of Sutherland when the time comes."

Lachlan's mouth fell open before he wrapped his arms around the king. His tight embrace squeezed the wind from King Robert's chest. But the monarch returned the embrace, remembering what it had felt like when Lachlan was a child and clamored on his lap, begging for more war stories, the gruesomer the better.

"Thank you, Uncle Robert," Lachlan whispered as he eased his hold on the older man.

"You remind me so much of your father when he fought alongside me all those years ago. While I pray that my auld friend remains with us for a long time, I ken you will make a powerful Earl of Sutherland in your day." King Robert clapped Lachlan on the back, the sound echoing through the quiet chamber. "There is still much to resolve with the Johnstone and the Gunn, but you have our blessing to marry."

"Thank you, Your Majesty, Your Grace," Arabella whispered as she curtsied.

"Lady Arabella," Queen Elizabeth smiled softly.

"Once you marry Lachlan, you will be my god-daughter-by-marriage of sorts. While we don't make it north as often as we would like, I would very much appreciate it if you address me as Aunt Elizabeth when we visit Dunrobin and Dunbeath."

Arabella nodded, stunned at the gesture. She didn't intend to address the queen by anything but her royal title, but the offer left her speechless. Lachlan grinned at Arabella and drew her back into his embrace, knowing she was feeling overwhelmed by everything that transpired.

"Do you wish to marry here or at Dunrobin?" King Robert asked.

"Dunrobin," Arabella answered without thought. Lachlan turned to look at her, and she nodded. Her hopeful smile lit up her face, and in that moment, there was nothing Lachlan would have denied her.

"I will send a messenger ahead of you to have the banns posted. I will speak with Mitcholm and Beathan after the evening meal." King Robert announced. "Now, we shall adjourn. Lach, you ken how I dislike missing my evening meal. I did that more than enough times over the years."

"Aye, Uncle Robert. Thank you to you both." Lachlan paused as he looked at the man and woman that he'd known since birth. He hadn't understood the significance of their position or the honor of their familial connection when he was a child. But he knew he'd cared about them both for as long as he could remember. "I love you both."

"As we do you, Lach," King Robert clapped his hand on Lachlan's shoulder again before he and Queen Elizabeth led the way to the Great Hall.

TWENTY-THREE

Arabella's heart felt lighter than it had in months. She lay in bed knowing that the next few weeks would be among the most challenging of her life as she left her self-destructive habit behind. But she felt optimistic knowing that not only had the king granted permission for Lachlan and her to marry, Lachlan hadn't abandoned her in her darkest hour.

The evening meal had been trying as her father and Beathan glared at them. Arriving at the Great Hall on the king and queen's coattails had caused a stir, but it was sitting with Lachlan for a second night in a row that had everyone's chin wagging. She stuck with watered ale all night, and she found that the slightly fuzzy-headed feeling was enough to replace the normal carefree feeling whisky provided. Lachlan whispered that he understood that while they were still at court, she would do better to have a little alcohol each day than to cease drinking abruptly. It would begin weaning her without throwing her into the depths of withdrawal with an entire royal entourage watching.

Arabella recalled dancing once more with Lachlan. They kept their conversation light, but they enjoyed one another's company. They moved together with such ease that the music seemed to carry them on magical winged notes. She'd danced with a few other men and been polite, but she'd hurried to Lachlan's side when she noticed Beathan approaching. Lachlan had dropped his hands from his partner's with barely a polite apology and pulled Arabella into his. They moved around the other dancers and slipped out of the Great Hall.

Arabella closed her eyes, the memory of their goodnight kiss lingering. Lachlan had taken all the whisky jugs, full and empty, when he left. Arabella's conscience felt clear for the first time since she began drinking. She still yearned for a taste, but she didn't feel the compulsion to drink that she had for so long. While the evening hadn't been perfect, it had been better than any she could remember since the last time Lachlan visited. Despite the long nap that afternoon, the evening exhausted her. Her eyes drifted closed as she pictured Lachlan lying beside her as he had earlier that day. Except they both lay there without a stitch on.

"Wake up, you ungrateful wretch," a deep voice barked in the dark. Arabella opened her eyes and found a shadowy figure standing beside her bed. "Move yourself, lass."

Arabella recognized her father's voice, but she didn't understand why he was in her chamber. She looked up at him in time for the gown he flung at her to land on her head. She ripped it away and glanced at Rebekah. She knew immediately that her roommate was awake but didn't dare to make a sound.

Arabella knew it was Rebekah who'd alerted Lachlan, and she was confident the younger lady would do so again. She just didn't know how soon Rebekah would get to him.

"Get dressed," Mitcholm hissed. Arabella rose from the bed and pulled on the gown. It was one with laces in the back, so there was no way she could fasten the entire length on her own, but she did what she could to tighten them. She was grateful that she slept in a chemise, so the fabric would cover her back despite the gown not being on properly. A thunk beside her feet told her that her father had dropped her boots nearby.

"I need stockings," Arabella whispered.

"Hurry."

Arabella slipped to her chest and opened the lid. She pretended to rummage around, but she bought herself time to find one of her dirks. She owned two *sgian dubhs* along with the longer blade she'd carried the nights she went to the Merry Widow. The gown her father chose in the dark wouldn't allow her to hide the larger knife, but she tucked one *sgian dubh* into a hidden pocket before pulling out the stockings. She went to the bed and sat near her pillow. She turned away from her father as though she sought privacy while putting her stockings on. She'd pulled on a thigh bracer Maude and Blair gave her just after Lachlan taught her how to use a knife. She reached under her pillow for the other *sgian dubh* and slipped it into the holster. Sleeping with a knife under her pillow was another precaution Maude and Blair taught her, despite having lived at court for a few years before the sisters arrived.

She stood again, and despite the dark, caught her cloak when her father tossed it at her. She looked over at Rebekah as her father opened the door. Light from the passageway illuminated her roommate's bed just long enough for Arabella to see Rebekah nod. Once in the passageway, Arabella blinked several times as torch light shone before her. She found her three guards waiting for her, along with two of the men who'd arrived with Mitcholm. None of the men would meet her eye, and Arabella's trepidation mounted. She knew in that moment that wherever they were going, it wasn't to her home at Lochwood Tower.

Arabella didn't dare speak as the men surrounded her, and her father led the way. The men were all warriors and moved without making a sound. With their silent tread, they heard every noise coming from the closed chamber doors, but Arabella had heard a door open behind them. She prayed it was Rebekah watching them. But she also prayed the lady-in-waiting had enough sense not to follow them. When they arrived in the bailey, Arabella found her father's other men waiting with their horses saddled. She turned toward her mount, but Edwin blocked her way.

"I'm sorry, Lady Arabella," Edwin whispered. "But the laird ordered you to ride with me."

"Then why is my horse with us?" Arabella murmured.

"Too valuable to leave behind," Edwin explained.

"Where are we—"

"Enough!" Mitcholm bellowed loudly enough that everyone shifted uncomfortably. "You will ken when you get there."

Edwin helped Arabella into the saddle. She moved as far back as she could, allowing Edwin to mount in front of her. She didn't feel right riding with Edwin's arms wrapped around her. Despite the ominous situation, it didn't feel appropriate after what she'd shared with Lachlan and now that the king gave his blessing for them to marry. She would ride pillion instead. They walked their horses out of the bailey onto the road leading away from the castle. Once clear of the gates, the party spurred their horses to a gallop.

"I honestly don't know," Edwin said as he strained to his voice low. "But I suspect a convent like your father has been threatening."

Arabella sat in stunned silence. She assumed King Robert had spoken to her father and informed him that he supported Lachlan marrying her. Her father was acting in defiance of the king. As they left the city limits, they turned west, and Arabella feared she knew where they headed. A rock settled in her stomach that bounced with each step the horse took. Fear tried to take hold, but she made herself think of Maude and Bair, asking herself what they would do. If she was to become a Sutherland, she needed to think like one.

———

Lachlan's eyes opened in the dark, and he reached for his sword. The sound of his chamber door opening woke him. A tiny figure slipped into his chamber but didn't advance. He waited to see if the shadow of a weapon would appear, but the person didn't move.

"Who's there?" he demanded.

"Och, thank the blessed Christ. You're awake," Rebekah sighed.

"I am now. What're you doing here, lass? You need to leave before someone sees you."

"Laird Johnstone just came and forced Arabella

to dress. He made her go with him. I saw her, her father, and five men in the passageway. She had her cloak and boots on. The men looked prepared to ride. I waited until they wouldn't be able to see or hear me, then I followed them, assuming they were going to the bailey. They just rode out."

Lachlan reached for his leine, which he'd fortunately left at the end of his bed. He pulled it on as Rebekah spoke. He rose from the bed, and she spun around. He didn't bother to reassure her, focusing on pleating his plaid and getting it wrapped around him. He pushed his sword into its scabbard and slung it onto his back. He tugged on his boots before going to the small locked chest he'd brought with him. It carried the coin he had with him. He shoved it into his satchel before throwing in the rest of his clothes. He suspected he wouldn't be returning to court again. He would find Arabella and ride for Dunrobin.

"Return to your chamber as though naught has happened, but be at the kirk when the queen arrives for morning Mass. Tell her what's happened. Tell her my men and I have gone after Lady Arabella. Her father threatened to take her to a convent, and I believe he's making good on that. Let Queen Elizabeth know that I'm riding to Inchcailleoch Priory then Dunrobin."

Rebekah gasped, recognizing the convent often called "the island of old women." It was renowned for its severity, the sisters swearing vows of silence. Their vow of poverty was extreme, and the nuns were known to wear hair shirts and practice self-flagellation. Rebekah nodded in the dark and spun on her heels. She slipped through the door before Lachlan crossed the chamber. He stepped into the passageway and watched Rebekah run toward the wing where the ladies-in-waiting slept.

He rushed to the barracks and roused his men.

Much like the last time he'd had to wake them, they all scrambled to ready themselves without question. Lachlan tapped his satchel, and the men dumped their belongings into their own. As his four guards finished preparing to leave, Lachlan went to the stables and found the stable boys preparing to return to their beds.

"Do you ken where the Johnstones headed?" Lachlan asked as he offered the youngest lad a coin. The boy's face lit up as he nodded.

"The island of auld women."

An older boy boxed his ear. "You don't tell people's business," the older boy admonished.

"She didn't look like she wanted to go," complained the younger stable hand. "She kept looking at the castle like she hoped someone was coming."

"She was hoping it was me," Lachlan stated. "You did right to tell me, lad. She didn't leave by choice."

Lachlan said no more as his men arrived and they led their horses from the stables. The men mounted and charged out of the bailey. Lachlan pointed west as soon as the road widened, and his men followed. He briefly explained what he knew and to where they rode. None spoke at they raced to catch up to Arabella and her clansmen. Lachlan knew her father wouldn't dally, but he prayed they weren't moving as fast as he and his men. He was banking on Mitcholm Johnstone believing no one would follow him, at least not that soon after they left.

As the minutes turned into hours, Lachlan doubted whether he was going in the right direction. He wondered if the Johnstones had paid the stable boy to tip them off. They picked up the trail soon after leaving Stirling, but within an hour, there were too many prints on the road to determine which belonged to the horses Arabella and the Johnstone men rode. He pushed the Sutherland warriors and their horses as they charged over hill and dale. The priory was a day's ride from Stirling Castle, but Lachlan didn't want to be apart from Arabella that long. He had no way to know what condition she was in or how her father was treating her. Neither Rebekah nor the stable hand mentioned Beathan, but Lachlan knew the man could have been waiting to meet them somewhere outside the city gates. Lachlan didn't know how many men he might face to win Arabella's freedom.

"Lach," Wallace, the most experienced tracker, pointed to the road before him. "The ground evens out just ahead. I may find their tracks again."

The five men reined in and Wallace jumped down from his horse. He knelt down, his hand hovering over the ground as though he might feel something rising from the earth that would tell them what they needed to know.

"It's them. I recognize the hoofprints from several of the horses. But I can't tell how long ago they made them. If they're riding like we are, stopping only long enough for the horses to have a drink, then they will remain ahead of us. From how deep the prints are and the kickback of dirt, I'd say they are riding hard, too."

Lachlan nodded and looked into the distance. The moment Wallace mounted, they spurred their horses again. They continued riding west, stopping every few hours to rest the horses. It was sundown as they approached Inchcailleoch Priory, and they still hadn't caught sight of Arabella or the other Johnstones. Lachlan wouldn't question Wallace because he didn't doubt his friend. But his frustration grew when they failed to catch up. The men were weary and dirty as they rode into the priory's center court.

As he walked his horse into the stable, he noticed several horses that were too fine to belong to the nuns. They weren't workhorses. They were warhorses. Lachlan had found the Johnstones' mounts; now he needed to find the Johnstones.

TWENTY-FOUR

Arabella stood in the refectory, looking around and unsure of what to do. The prioress had pointed her in the dining hall's direction before leading her father to the outer parlour, the room set aside for her to meet with outsiders. Arabella didn't dare move since no meal was being served, and she was alone.

"Bella?" A soft voice made Arabella turn around. She looked at a face she recognized but never thought to see again. It was familiar, yet very different to what she recalled.

"Madeline?" Arabella walked toward Madeline MacLeod, stunned to find the woman dressed as a novice. She knew Maude's husband and Madeline's brother, Laird Kieran MacLeod, brought Madeline to the priory, but she hadn't thought she might see her again. The woman possessed the same moss green eyes Arabella remembered, but a wimple covered her raven hair. A simple habit replaced the once lavish court gowns she wore. Madeline had worn a perpetual sneer when she wasn't in the queen's presence, and even when she'd smiled, there'd been smugness about it. The woman who walked toward Arabella appeared serene.

"Aye, it's me. I ken I don't look the same, do I?" Madeline's smile held genuine warmth, and Arabella didn't know what to make of it. "This is my home now, and I've found peace in my work."

"You like it here?" Arabella blurted, then covered her mouth with her hand. She glanced around but relaxed when Madeline's smile didn't falter. It put her more at ease.

"I didn't at first. I was resentful. The nuns terrified me just from the stories I'd heard. It didn't take long for me to realize that if I was respectful and did my share of the work, the rumors were exaggerated. I've accepted that Kieran was wise to bring me here. This is a far better place for me than court." Madeline embraced Arabella, and it was a moment before Arabella responded. It shocked her to find comfort in Madeline's arms, but she supposed it was the sense of familiarity after the hair-raising ride from the castle.

"Are you now a nun?" Arabella tried to remember what she knew of monastic life and becoming a nun.

"Not yet, but soon. I was a postulant for two years, and I've been a novice for two. I shall take my final vows in a few months. Then I will be a nun," Madeline explained.

"Are you still called Madeline?" Arabella wondered since she knew some nuns changed their names.

"Aye. Though I haven't decided whether I will renounce it for something else when I take my vows. But Bella, what are you doing here? Are you in need of respite for the night?"

Arabella looked around, unsure of who might hear them. She wanted to trust Madeline since she seemed so different, but it scared her to. She hadn't seen the woman in years, and they hadn't been friends when Madeline left Stirling. Arabella looked back at Madeline and continued to debate what she should tell her.

"Come with me," Madeline suggested. "We can talk in my cell. No one will listen."

"Cell?" Arabella balked. After her experience in the castle's dungeon, she didn't want to go near any place called a cell.

"It's what we call our chambers in the dormitory," Madeline replied.

"I don't know if I dare. The prioress sent me here while she speaks to my father," Arabella said as she shook her head. She felt her uneasiness growing as she continued to look around her. Her father's anger hadn't abated despite a day's ride. He'd barked at her to remain silent as they rode into the priory's courtyard. She didn't know if Lachlan was aware of where they headed, and she didn't know if he followed. She wanted to believe he did, but a niggling part of her feared it would relieve him to be done with her. As her fear edged into terror, the need to drink made her edgy and jumpy.

"We can step into the gardens. We'll see if the Mother Abbess comes toward the refectory." Madeline leaned closer to Arabella and whispered. "Whatever it is has you terrified, and you don't need anyone listening in." Madeline steered a reluctant Arabella outside into the twilight. Madeline led them to a garden just outside the building that held the refectory and was next door to the outer parlour. "What's happened?"

Arabella weighed what to tell Madeline and opted for the most basic parts of her story. "You may recall that Lachlan Sutherland and I formed a friendship when his sisters arrived at court." Even in the dim evening light, Arabella saw how Madeline's face went up in flames. There was no way the woman pretended the amount of remorse that filled her eyes. Madeline nodded, and Arabella watched her fight back tears.

"I've never been able to apologize," Madeline's whisper was hoarse. "Please go on."

"Over the years, it became something more than friendship, but we never thought to do aught aboot it. Neither of us wanted to spoil our relationships with Maude and Blair. My father arranged a betrothal to Laird Beathan Gunn. When it became obvious that time was running out, Lachlan and I finally were honest with one another aboot how we feel. My father is irate that I've made things difficult for him to complete the betrothal with Laird Gunn. And King Robert spoke to my father last night and told him that the betrothal can no longer go forward. King Robert has given his blessing that Lachlan and I marry, and my father is angrier than I've ever seen him. He took me from Stirling Castle in the middle of the night and brought me here."

"So, you were brought here as punishment too. You and I aren't the only ones, Bella. You're in good company," Madeline said as she offered a soft smile. "Do you think Lachlan will figure out where you are?"

Arabella nodded. "I do."

"Do you think he'll come for you?"

"I believe so, aye." Arabella wanted to believe the words she spoke, but her self-doubt made her wonder if Lachlan would forsake her.

"I ken Beathan Gunn, and he's not a mon I would suggest any woman marry. He's far better than his aulder brother or uncles were, and better than his father. He could be a good laird if that's now his position, but he'll never be a good husband. He's like his brother Arlan. He uses women and hurts them because it makes him feel more powerful. I wouldn't wish a lifetime with him on any woman. If Lachlan comes for you, and you wish to be with him, I will help you."

"Madeline, I can't ask that of you. You'll get in trouble. You'll have to wear a hair shirt and beat yourself with a cat-o'-nine-tails," Arabella said aghast.

"Nay. Those are auld tales from long before I arrived here. Mother Abbess is a kind soul. If she learns of who your father wishes you to marry and learns of the mon he is, she will accept you here to protect you. If I help you leave with Lachlan, she'll understand. We may be in the Lowlands, but the Sutherland name carries significant weight everywhere. No one questions their honor. It runs too deeply in their veins for there ever to be any doubt. If Lachlan wishes to marry you, then Mother Abbess will ken you're a fine woman."

Arabella was about to thank Madeline when a party of riders passed through the gate. Arabella recognized Lachlan immediately. She moved to run and catch up to him, but Madeline caught her arm. From the other direction, the prioress and Mitcholm approached the refectory. The two women slipped back into the building, even though Arabella kept looking back over her shoulder.

"Do not say you saw Lachlan. Do not go to him yet," Madeline warned. "Wait until your father is nowhere around."

"But if he starts yelling, Lachlan will hear him and come looking for me."

"Your father would yell in a convent?" Madeline's eyebrows shot straight up.

"I wouldn't put aught past him these days," Arabella sighed.

"Mother Abbess won't allow it. Stay beside me

and don't look toward the door. Does your father speak Gaelic?"

"No. No one in my family does. Why?"

"I'm still a Hebridean, Bella. And the Mother Abbess is a Highlander." Madeline didn't have the chance to say more as the prioress and Mitcholm entered the dining hall. Mitcholm narrowed his eyes at Arabella, suspicious of why she spoke to a woman who looked like a nun.

When the older man and woman came to stand before the two ladies, Madeline bowed to the prioress. Arabella curtsied and turned to her father. Keeping her voice low, she explained, "Father, this is Madeline MacLeod. She was a lady-in-waiting with me some years ago."

Madeline dipped a bow to Mitcholm, then turned her attention to the prioress. She hurried to speak in just more than a whisper. "*Màthair Abbess, chan eil fhios agam dè a chuala thu, ach tha an t-uachdaran an dùil a pòsadh ri fear as aithne dhomh a 'toirt ionnsaigh air boireannaich agus a mharbh co-dhiù aon. Tha mi air a bhith eòlach air bho bha mi nam nighean òg.*" Madeline told the nun, "Mother Abbess, I dinna ken what ye've heard, but the laird intends to marry her to a mon I ken assaults women and has killed at least one. I've known him since I was a young girl."

"*Tha fios agam, leanabh. Dh 'aithnich mi an t-ainm nuair a dh' innis e dhomh. Ma tha an duine càil coltach ri a chàirdean, tha e ri sheachnadh. Bhiodh i na h-uan don mharbhadh.*" Continuing their conversation in Gaeilic the prioress replied quickly, "I ken, child. I recognized the name when he told me. If the mon is aught like his relatives, he's to be avoided. She'd be a lamb to the slaughter."

Madeline rushed to tell the prioress, "The brother of the woman ma brother married is who she wishes to marry. He just arrived. He will be looking for ye soon. He's a good mon." *"Is e bràthair a 'bhoireannaich a phòs mo bhràthair a tha i airson pòsadh. Ràinig e dìreach. Bidh e a 'coimhead air do shon a dh' aithghearr. Tha e na dhuine math."*

The only sign that the prioress registered the potential trouble was a slight flaring of her nostrils. She nodded her head. She opened her mouth to speak, but Mitcholm interrupted.

"What gibberish are you going on aboot?"

"Sister Madeline and I were making arrangements for Lady Arabella to share her cell. She will take your daughter there now, and I will show you to the guest house." The prioress turned away from the doors they used earlier and led the group toward the back of the refectory. Arabella prayed that whoever greeted Lachlan sent him somewhere other than the guest house, or there would be an almighty scene that even God couldn't stop.

Lachlan looked around the chamber he was shown to in the outer parlour. He was impatient to speak to the prioress, since he knew the Johnstones were there. He struggled not to storm out of the building and tear apart the convent as he searched for Arabella. When the door opened, he whirled around. Before him stood a woman in her middle years with a kind face and knowing eyes. When she stood before him, Lachlan reached out his hand, palm up. She placed hers over his, and he bowed to kiss her ring. The Mother Abbess noted the difference in how the young man greeted her to the laird who'd demanded an audience.

"Tha i an seo ach tha a h-athair. Tha Madeline MacLeòid air do bhean a thoirt gu seòmar Madeline. Tha i sàbhailte an sin gus an urrainn dhut falbh còmhla." The

prioress revealed "she's here, but so is her father. Madeline MacLeod has taken yer lady to Madeline's chamber. She's safe there until you can leave together."

Lachlan nodded, surprised to hear a Gaelic-speaking nun in the Lowlands, along with what he learned. The woman smiled softly before switching back to Scots.

"I was a Gunn many years ago. I'm the sister Elizabeth, Tomas, James, and Farlane forgot. I committed an indiscretion in my younger days, and my penance was life here. Little did my family know, I much prefer it here. But I ken what the men are like in my family. I won't sentence any woman to that. I will help you," the prioress explained.

"Thank you, Mother Abbess. Lady Arabella is all I seek. I don't want to cause any trouble for you or the sisters," Lachlan replied.

"I ken, lad. I kenned your aunt and uncle well. The Gunns and Sinclairs didn't get along even back then, but it was to them I fled when Tomas threatened me. Laird Sinclair ensured my safe escort here. I owe my life to your family. I'm certain I wouldn't have survived if I'd remained at Clyth Castle. I pray Beathan is a better leader than the men before him, but I doubt he is a better mon."

Lachlan witnessed the sadness in the older woman's eyes and could tell she was lost in her memories for a moment. While he wanted to hurry her, so he could reach Arabella sooner, he didn't dare end her wistfulness before she was ready. She looked up at Lachlan and nodded.

"Laird Johnstone and his men have gone to the guesthouse. I will take you and your men to the cellarium. You can wait in the undercroft until I can fetch Lady Arabella. Compline will begin soon, so you and your men must be out of sight. I will come to you before I go to your lady. When I do, send your men to ready the horses while I go into the dormitory. You must ride as soon as Lady Arabella joins you. It'll be a few hours before Matins. Rest while you can," Mother Abbess instructed.

"What will you do when Laird Johnstone discovers Arabella gone?" Lachlan asked.

"I have many hours to solve that. The Lord will provide me with the right answer," the prioress reassured. "Come now."

Lachlan followed the woman in the swishing robes as she walked with her hands steepled together. It surprised him how quiet her tread was. If she'd been a man, she would have made a fine warrior. Once they entered the courtyard, he signaled to his men to leave the shadows and follow them. The hours spent in the cellarium were tedious, and he couldn't lower his guard enough to sleep despite his exhaustion. He waited on edge until he saw two feminine forms coming toward him. One was dressed as a nun and the other wasn't. He scrambled to his feet, but shock made him take a step back. It was the Mother Abbess and Madeline MacLeod.

TWENTY-FIVE

Arabella gazed down at the habit she wore. She'd traded her clothes for Madeline's, and she found she preferred the simplicity. She wasn't interested in becoming a nun, but it reminded her of the gowns she'd worn as a girl growing up along the border. It was a time long before her parents sent her to court with extravagant gowns and lavish jewels. She reached up to touch the wimple that now covered her auburn tresses. That was the item she was most grateful for from the entire ensemble. It would give her the anonymity that Madeline and Mother Abbess offered. She'd understood Madeline's meaning as soon as the former lady-in-waiting suggested they trade outfits.

Arabella wanted to pace, but there was little room to do that in the cell. Two cots occupied most of the room, and she was relieved to see one was a spare that Madeline said she could rest on. She'd caught a couple hours of sleep before she woke to the sound of the cell door opening and Mother Abbess entering. Now she waited for the Mother Abbess to return for her. They'd agreed it was best if people witnessed Lachlan depart with a raven-haired woman rather than with a redhead. She would slip through the gardens and leave through a small hatch in the wall. It would put her near the woods where Lachlan and Madeline would meet her. She and Madeline would exchange clothes, and Madeline would return to her cell. Madeline wouldn't appear until the morning meal, leaving plenty of time for rumors to spread that she left with Lachlan. There was little that could be done once Laird Johnstone learned that Arabella had disappeared, but the confusion should buy them some time.

Arabella turned toward the door when it eased open, and she found the prioress waving to her to follow. The nun pressed a finger to her lips, warning Arabella to be quiet. They hurried out of the dormitory, through the cloister, out to the end of the garden. Arabella kept her chin tucked, but her eyes scanned her surroundings. There was no one in sight, but that didn't mean no one saw them. She tried to walk with the grace that Mother Abbess exhibited, but she wanted nothing more than to sprint to the wall.

"Go with God, my child," the prioress blessed her with the sign of the cross.

"Thank you," Arabella mouthed before passing through the wooden door in the wall. She looked around before running into the trees. It was only moments later that Lachlan's arms snared her, and he lifted her off her feet, his mouth demanding she return his kiss.

"You haven't time for that," Madeline's voice interrupted. Arabella looked at the woman she'd once loathed, and she couldn't help but feel gratitude for what Madeline risked. Arabella feared how her father would react when he learned of her escape and if he learned of Madeline's involvement. As though reading her mind, Madeline reassured, "Don't worry. Kieran is still my brother, and that carries weight even to a Lowlander. He is Laird MacLeod of Lewis, and one of the Lord of the Isles's most favored lairds. That carries sway, even with a border laird. I am safe."

Arabella embraced Madeline, surprised at the warmth she felt for a woman she'd imagined she would always detest. But time at Inchcailleoch Priory had wholly changed Madeline. There was little left of the woman who'd once been a lady-in-waiting. Arabella regretted there wasn't time to get to know the newer version of Madeline. She suspected they might have become friends. When Arabella released Madeline, she reached to pull off the wimple, but Madeline's hand caught her forearm as she shook her head.

"Your hair is too noticeable. If your hood blows back from your head, anyone would see your mane of auburn hair," Madeline grinned before growing serious once more. "Travel as a nun for as long as you can. The disguise will protect you as much as Lachlan will. I have another habit in here. Help me undo the laces, then put the gown in the satchel. It holds some food."

Madeline pulled out a habit, then handed Arabella the bag. They ducked behind the trees as Arabella helped Madeline strip out of the gown. Arabella hastily folded it and shoved it into the leather carryall while Madeline dressed once more as a nun. They exchanged another brief embrace before Lachlan helped her mount and swung into the saddle behind her. Arabella glanced back as they rode away, but Madeline had already disappeared within the priory.

The party didn't speak, except for when Lachlan arranged their ferry ride off the island. The ferry operator looked sideways at Arabella and squinted. Lachlan explained the woman who appeared as a nun was his cousin and was leaving the priory to attend her father's funeral. The old sun-weathered man nodded and said nothing. Once they were on the mainland, Arabella distributed the bannocks and dried beef she discovered in the satchel. She offered the men apples and pears, but they declined, saying they would save them for later. Arabella hadn't argued and made do with her own bannock and chewy strip of meat.

They had nearly a fortnight's ride ahead of them, and Arabella dreaded being in the saddle for so long. The longest stretch she'd ever ridden was the five days it took to reach Stirling from her home at Lochwood Tower. It relieved her to see that Lachlan freed her mare from the stables and brought the horse with them. She'd feared riding double would slow them, even with Lachlan's powerful steed beneath them. Once she mounted her horse and watched the smaller animal fighting to keep up with the larger destriers, she worried her horse would never last the arduous journey that would take them through the Cairngorm Mountains. Her horse was used to the flatter terrain of the Lowlands. The mare also wasn't accustomed to charging alongside stallions. Arabella wondered if there was a way to circumvent the mountainous region, but as she pictured the map of Scotland she'd once seen, she realized it would add days to their journey.

When they stopped the first time to rest the horses, Arabella was certain it was for her and her horse's sake. The men and their mounts barely looked winded. Lachlan helped Arabella down, his hands lingering at her waist as they gazed at one another. Lachlan moved them to stand among the horses as they drank. It was the only privacy they had. He pulled her against him, but it was Arabella who initiated their kiss. It was hungry with a need to reassure one another that they were both hale and that nothing had changed between them.

"I love you, Belle," Lachlan swore as they broke apart.

"But it's not possible that you can love me more than I love you," Arabella replied before she pressed the fingers in his hair against his head, nudging him for another kiss. "It was only a day, but how I missed you."

Arabella tucked her head and rested her forehead against Lachlan's broad chest, catching her breath from their passionate exchange. He ran his hands over her back and arms, but it wasn't a lover's caress. She knew he was checking to see if her father or his men had injured her. She went onto her toes to kiss his neck, then whispered in his ear. "The only thing that ails me is the ache I have for your special attention. Only your ministrations will heal me."

Lachlan's fingers bit into her backside as he groaned. "*Mo chridhe*, you're torturing me."

"Aye," Arabella grinned. "Misery loves company." But she soon sobered as she cast her eyes around them to see if anyone could hear them. Her cheeks flushed a deep red as she dropped her hands.

"Shh, little one. There's naught wrong with what you said, and no one but me heard. What your father said isn't true. You're not one. I pray you will never be afraid to tell me what you want."

"But doesn't that make me wanton?" Arabella asked.

"If you were to offer yourself to every mon, it might. I ken you've never said such things to anyone else. I want you with a ferocity that makes me fear being too rough with you. But it pleases me to no end to ken you desire me, too."

"It is a good feeling to be wanted," Arabella admitted. Lachlan nodded, but she knew the moment he intended to change the subject, and she could guess what he wanted to discuss. She was certain he didn't want to ask, but she also understood he was justly worried about her. "My father didn't beat me. He came into my chamber and insisted that I get dressed. After that, he barely spared me a word. I rode pillion with Edwin because he didn't trust me on Firelight." She felt compelled to tell Lachlan that she hadn't ridden in Edwin's arms, so his response surprised her.

"Don't ride pillion again, Belle. It's too easy for you to be thrown. If you share a horse, always ride where the mon can brace you."

"You want me to ride in another mon's arms?" She asked, surprised by his declaration, but Lachlan grimaced at her question.

"I'd prefer you not. No mon could ride with your backside rubbing against him and not have his body react. But I'd rather that than you break your neck."

"If that's the case, I don't want you riding with any woman but me in your lap," Arabella huffed. Lachlan grinned as he tickled her waist.

"Jealous?"

"Yes," Arabella snapped. She refused to feel remorseful.

"Belle, aught rubbing a mon's cock will make it stiffen. And you're a beautiful woman, we ken that. Put those together, and while a mon may not wish for that reaction, I would say it's rather inevitable."

"But doesn't that mean he wants to couple?" Arabella whispered.

"I think most men would give their sword arm for a chance to do that," Lachlan grinned.

"Just because I'm pretty," Arabella whispered. The conversation hadn't gone in the direction she expected, and she felt worthless knowing that men only found her appearance attractive. "So that would happen if you rode with a woman before you?"

"I've ridden with my sisters plenty of times, and no, that doesn't happen. A mon must find the woman appealing."

"This is entirely confusing. You ken a mon would become aroused if I ride in front of him, and that doesn't bother you because a mon can't help being attracted to me because I'm bonnie. But I'm supposed to believe you wouldn't react the same if a beautiful woman rode with you? And you wonder why I'm jealous." Despite her conflicted feelings, she recognized that Lachlan trusted her. And her jealousy stemmed more from thinking another woman would be fortunate enough to ride with him than any mistrust she might feel.

"Belle, the only point I meant was aye, a mon might become aroused, but I'd rather that than you fly off the back of the horse and die."

"And that's what you would say when you ride with another woman."

"When? Unless it's my mother or my sisters, there won't be any other women riding with me besides you." Lachlan appeared truly mystified.

"Then why do you assume I'd ride with another mon? I don't intend to do that."

Lachlan fought to keep from sighing. He understood Arabella's naivety, but he knew they needed to get back on the road. He hadn't started the conversation intending to steer it in this direction, but he had. "*Mo chridhe*, there may be times when you must ride with a guard. You must understand this to some level because you said you rode pillion with Edwin."

Arabella nodded. "That is why I rode pillion. It

just didn't seem right to be wrapped in another mon's arms. It didn't feel appropriate, and I suppose I knew why, even if I didn't actually think it."

Lachlan kissed her forehead, then the tip of her nose. "Don't think that just because I want you safe doesn't mean I wouldn't be jealous. But your well-being will always come first, Belle. It's what matters most to me; that and your happiness."

"Bluidy hell, Lachlan. I love you," Arabella swore before fisting his leine and going on her toes to press a quick, hard kiss.

"And I love you. Now we must be away," Lachlan said as he tapped her backside. They mounted and cantered away from the stream. Once they were on the open stretch of road, they pushed their horses to run faster.

TWENTY-SIX

rabella opened one eye as she came awake during the middle of their second night traveling northeast. She lay still beside Lachlan, whose heavy arm kept her pinned against his chest. She'd shivered so badly the night before that Lachlan woke her to make sure she wasn't ailing. After that, he cast propriety to the wind and insisted that she sleep tucked beneath his plaid and against him.

She was certain she heard movement, but she lay still and heard nothing more. The longer she lay with one eye open, the more she couldn't ignore the need to relieve herself. She tried to ease out from under Lachlan's arm by rolling on her belly and scooting out from under the plaid, but his fingers tightened around her waist.

"Where're you going?" His voice was rough and groggy.

"Just to the bush on the other side of the fire. I'll only be a moment," Arabella whispered her reply. She jumped when she looked back and saw both of Lachlan's eyes were open wide, and he didn't appear to have just been sleeping. "You're awake?"

"The moment you woke," Lachlan explained.

"How?" Arabella's brow furrowed, but then she shook her head. Her sense of urgency only increased by the moment. "Never mind."

"I'll come with you," Lachlan offered.

"That's not necessary. Give me just a moment. You won't have a chance to miss me."

"Of course I will." Lachlan's smile was exceedingly rakish when combined with his deep and rasping voice. Arabella tutted quietly and slipped from beneath the plaid. She looked back when she sensed Lachlan's movement. He'd sat up and was leaning to see around the fire. Arabella skirted around the slumbering men, but she wondered if they too woke from her movement. She suspected they were awake, since they were trained warriors like Lachlan. She was both embarrassed and remorseful to wake them while she crept to the bush.

As Arabella lowered the skirt of the habit she still wore, she was certain she heard something that sounded more like a man's tread than a ground animal. She froze for a heartbeat, trying to determine from which direction it came. She lifted her foot to take her first step back to the camp when a hand came over her mouth and nose. She tried to scream, but the sound was too muffled to travel. She was certain the man had ham hocks for forearms as his hand slipped down to cover only her mouth as the fingers from his other hand pinched her nose. She struggled against him, but as her vision blurred, she settled. She fought off the haze as she tried to conserve what air she still had trapped in her lungs. She knew it was less than a couple minutes before her eyes slid shut. She'd gone to a bush just past where she knew Lachlan could see because she'd been too modest. Now she would pay for that.

Her unidentified assailant carried her to a waiting horse and flung her belly down. The impact was enough to knock the remaining air from her and bring her eyes open. She attempted to wiggle free and drop from the horse's back. As she tried to free herself, she noticed a pair of bare calves walking toward her. She couldn't see the man's face, but she registered the uncovered legs were beneath the hem of a plaid. Unable to see the pattern she could only guess who was abducting her. Beathan Gunn's fist slammed into the back of her head, and everything went black.

Lachlan was on edge the moment Arabella disappeared from his sight. The longer she was away, the more anxious he became. Even if she needed more time than she suggested, Lachlan reasoned she should have returned by now. He rose and drew a log from the fire, singeing his knuckles, but he had a torch. He moved in the direction Arabella went, but paused when all four of his men sat up.

"Aye, she's been gone too long," Wallace grunted.

Lachlan looked at his friend and most experienced warrior among the group. He nodded before glancing at the others. Without a word, the men began folding their bedrolls and pulled logs from the fire before kicking dirt into it. Lachlan's heart thudded because he knew he wouldn't find Arabella. He carried the torch into the bushes, holding it toward the ground in front of him. He spotted her footprints and found the bush she'd used. He also discovered the disturbed brush and leaves where Arabella must have struggled. He squatted and pushed aside the loose foliage to find the footprints beneath. Someone had covered them. He noticed a man's size boot print along with Arabella's smaller one. They were smeared as if there was a scuffle. He turned away from the camp and searched for the direction the prints went. He found it, but there was only one set. Lachlan whistled softly, and his men appeared like wraiths. The fire was out, and he knew there would be no sign of their stay. The Sutherlands followed the footprints a short distance until they ended and hoofprints began.

"There's only one set," George noted. He was close in age to Lachlan, but he was a mountain of a man. The warrior often reminded Lachlan of his cousin Magnus. Both men had tree trunks for legs and shoulders board enough to carry Atlas's rock. "Whoever it was must be meeting his men further away. Didna want to risk us hearing too many of them."

"Aye. And that someone is Beathan Gunn. I would bet ma last groat," Lachlan replied. He never bothered hiding his burr when he was among his men. His father had never lost his and didn't even attempt to hide it. Lachlan found he could concentrate better on trying to reason where Beathan headed when his speech wasn't his focus. He looked back and found Tarran and Lellan, the other two guards with him, had the horses. Each man carried a torch, more concerned with finding Arabella than remaining invisible. None wanted to miss any sign, or worse, her body, by stumbling through the dark. They followed the hoofprints until they found the cluster of several more. The men looked around, but the trail seemed to disappear.

"They're sweeping away their tracks," Wallace noted as he once again kneeled and hovered his hand over the ground. He shone his torch in every direction before facing west. He inched along until he placed his palm on the ground. "Here. I can feel the imprint even if they smoothed over the top. It's deep, so it must be the horse carrying Lady Arabella and whoever has her."

The men walked in the direction Wallace pointed, even though they couldn't see any prints. The tracker periodically touched the ground again. Lachlan was growing restless, wanting to mount his horse and charge after Arabella. But he knew he needed to be strategic, or he was likely to ride off in the wrong direction. Lachlan understood Beathan chose a western path thinking to throw the Sutherlands off his trail, but inevitably, he had to turn east before long. Riding in that direction didn't guarantee they would find Arabella and the Gunns. They needed a more exact route to follow.

Lachlan's patience was rewarded five minutes later when hoofprints became visible with no attempt made to hide them. They pointed east toward Loch Tay. It would be three quarters of a day's ride to reach the waterway, but Beathan didn't have that great a head start. The men swung into their saddles and kneed their steeds into a gallop.

TWENTY-SEVEN

rabella's ears rang as her head pounded. It was worse than any headache from overconsumption. Her chest flopped against the horse's shoulder with each stride, and her stomach churned as she watched the ground pass beneath the charging horse. Before she could stop herself, the rabbit and bannocks she'd had before going to sleep spewed forth, splattering the horse's legs. The odd sensation made the animal rear and whinny. A hand grabbed hold of the back of her clothes as she felt herself sliding. Another wave of nausea crashed over her, and her stomach emptied.

"Ye stupid bitch," a gravelly voice came from above her. The sun had risen several hours earlier, and Arabella recognized Beathan. He no longer sounded like the man at court. His burr didn't have the soothing effect Lachlan's did. She squinted as she watched, fearful she would lose hours again if she slipped back into unconsciousness. She felt one of Beathan's hands still grasping her clothes while the other tugged on the reins as he brought his horse back under control. He pulled the horse to a stop and swung down, pulling Arabella with him. He tossed a waterskin at her, and she put it to her lips, grateful for a drink. She spluttered as whisky flowed into her mouth instead of water. Unprepared for the alcohol, it surprised her, but only a moment later her craving overtook her sense. She took long drags from the flask, both thirsty and wishing to escape the nightmare she found herself in. After several long swigs, her sense came back to her.

What're you doing? You were just praying not to pass out again, and now you're drinking yourself to where you'll black out. How will you defend yourself from these men if you're soused? How will you escape if you're too drunk to put one foot in front of the other? How will you get back to Lachlan if you can't pay attention to where you are?

"Uh-uh, lass. Drink up." Beathan ripped the wimple from her hair and fisted her locks. He forced the flask back to her mouth despite her attempts to push against him and to turn her head away. He yanked her head back and pushed the opening of the waterskin into her mouth. She feared she was about to drown as the liquid scorched a path down her throat, bypassing her tongue. She gagged until Beathan gave her a moment's reprieve. "Dinna think I forgot aboot why ye ended up in the gaol, ma little wayward bride."

Arabella turned wide eyes toward him and tried to shake her head. She stopped swallowing, the liquid pooling in her mouth. When there was enough to dribble from her lips, she spat it in Beathan's looming face. He dropped the flask and swung his hand until his palm connected with her cheek.

"Ye'll think twice before ye do that again, lass. Wed ye and bed ye is all I need to collect yer dowry. I forced yer father to lower the bride price, but I'll still collect yer entire dowry. Yer father needs the wee bit of coin and wants ye off his hands even more. Ye're mine now." Beathan made a lewd gesture as his hand slid beneath his sporran and he thrust his hips forward.

Arabella felt the effects of the alcohol washing over her, but she was still aware enough to be terrified that Beathan would follow through on his threat. If she was too drunk to argue, she might find herself before a priest willing to marry her to the odious man. Then she would find herself beneath him as he slavered over her and claimed his husbandly rights. She didn't doubt that if Beathan gained proof that he consummated a marriage between them, her father would be bound to hand over her dowry. Once that happened, she would be no use to him. She was likely to be dead before they could arrive at Clyth Castle.

"I can see yer wee mind whirling away as ye work it all out. I'd wager ye ken I dinna need ye once yer dowry is on the way. But I will swive ye a few times just for the pleasure of having Lachlan Sutherland's woman. Tell me, has he broken ye in yet? Or will I be the one to rip through yer maidenhead? I like it when they scream," Beathan sneered before licking her neck.

Without thinking, Arabella's foot landed against his shin and then her knee aimed for his bollocks. Beathan laughed as his palm connected with her cheek once more. He held out his hand and gestured for one of his men to come closer. He pointed to the waterskin, never taking his eyes off Arabella. He shoved it back into her mouth, releasing her hair in favor of plugging her nose. It forced her to swallow even when she tried not to. It wasn't long before she'd drunk the entire container. Her eyes shut as her head wobbled on her neck. She tried to open her eyes, but what she could see was blurry. She closed them once more, hearing sounds and sensing movement around her, but she only remained on her feet because Beathan held her up.

Arabella jerked out of her semi-asleep state when Beathan nudged her forward. One of his men supported her as he climbed into the saddle. He pulled her in front of him, and deciding he couldn't afford another chance of her vomit spooking his horse, he kept her upright. Arabella registered the hint of a thought. Something Lachlan told her. She struggled to work through it until she recalled him saying it was safer for her to ride in front of a man. She blinked several times as the horse lurched forward. She was in disagreement with Lachlan's argument. At that moment, she would have much preferred the horse throw her. She'd take her chances breaking her neck if it meant Beathan Gunn no longer held her captive.

Lachlan scanned the horizon, but there was nothing to see but open landscape. They'd been following the trail for most of the day and still hadn't caught up to Beathan, Arabella, and the Gunn escort. They'd determined there were six men riding with Beathan, which made it seven Gunns to five Sutherlands. The Sutherlands were confident in their odds, having fought and bested the Gunns on more than one occasion. As the sun passed over the zenith and moved to shine at their backs, they approached the village of Killin at the foot of Loch Tay. Lachlan and his men had already discussed their best course of action was to either catch Beathan or overtake him. They rode to the shore and searched for birlinns they could hire. Lachlan wanted to groan when he discovered the only boats along the docks were fishing boats. They wouldn't be able to take their horses. Without the steeds, there would be little they could do to intercept Beathan even if they got ahead of the Gunns.

"Have a nun and a mon, along with his escort, boarded any boats today?" Lachlan asked. Several men shook their heads. "Have they passed by this way?"

"Aye," an old man with gnarled fingers and a toothless smile nodded. "An hour or so past. They stopped to water their horses."

Lachlan looked at his men and raised his eyebrows. "If there arenae any boats, then we must ride. I dinna think we can catch them while it's still light, but we may find their camp if we ride through the night. We take her from Laird Gunn just as he took her from me." Lachlan was cautious not to use Arabella's name, but he had no qualms about having people discuss Beathan kidnapping a woman.

"Ye're Sutherlands, arenae ye?" Another man asked as he came to stand beside the ancient fisherman. Lachlan nodded slowly. There was little way to hide the fact since he and his men wore their plaids, but Lachlan was suspicious. "The woman wore a nun's robes but had bright red hair. She looked worse for wear. She had a bright bruise across her cheek."

Lachlan fisted his hands as he ground his teeth. Any chance that Beathan would survive their inevitable fight ended with that news. He would kill him and not lose a wink of sleep. He waited for the man to say more, but when nothing was forthcoming, Lachlan thanked him and prepared to return to his horse.

"She didna look like any nun I've seen," the old man said.

"She's nae. She's ma betrothed," Lachlan replied.

"Runaway from the convent, has she? Caught by the wrong mon?" The younger fisherman asked.

"Nay. She dressed as a nun to protect her from

the vera mon who stole her," Lachlan answered. He walked to his horse and put his foot in the stirrup. He grasped his saddle and was prepared to pull himself up when one fisherman called out to him.

"There are birlinns a wee distance up the shore. Ye can sail them north. Tell them Samuel sent ye," the older man stated. Lachlan once again thanked him, and the Sutherlands rode away from the village. They kept close to the banks and easily found the larger crafts. The fishermen were apt to haggle until Lachlan mentioned Samuel's name. They nodded and said there was no fee. They would ferry Lachlan and his men for nothing. It made Lachlan wonder what position Samuel held that gave his name such influence.

Accustomed to boats, the Sutherland horses boarded without trouble. It was minutes later that they raised the sails and were under way. Lachlan scanned the terrain they passed, straining for any sign of Arabella. If they reached Comrie Castle after sailing to the far end of Loch Tay and up the River Tay without spotting the Gunns, Lachlan would enlist the Menzies help. A clan that normally remained neutral in clan issues that surrounded them, Lachlan knew they would lend their help to the Sutherlands. It was a debt owed and never repaid from generations ago. Proud Highlanders, Lachlan knew it was manipulative, but their honor would demand they ride alongside him.

As the sun dipped beneath the horizon, and the first stars twinkled, he was certain they'd overtaken the riders despite seeing no signs of them. He wondered if Beathan spotted the boats and knew they were aboard, or if he'd ignored them. There was the possibility that the Gunn hadn't seen them at all. While the horseback riders would have to make camp, Lachlan and the other men continued to sail throughout the night. It was another three-quarters of a day's ride to traverse the length of Loch Tay on horseback, but only a few hours by water. Beathan's party could have only ridden a couple hours past the village before having to stop. Sailing through the night meant Lachlan would arrive with time to spare, or rather time to recruit the Menzies.

TWENTY-EIGHT

"That's it. Down the hatch," Beathan chuckled as he tilted Arabella's head back and pinched her nose, much like he had earlier that day. The whisky flowed down her throat as she struggled to swallow fast enough. He'd plied her with alcohol off and on the entire day, keeping her in a continued state of semi-consciousness. He'd tried to let his hand roam over her breasts, but she'd dug the nails of one hand into his forearm and pinched the back of his hand with the other. She'd drawn blood from his arm and left a bruise on his hand. Arabella was certain riding at a fast canter kept Beathan from lashing out at her.

He'd tried a second time, but she grabbed handfuls of the horse's mane and yanked. She felt guilty abusing the innocent animal, but the horse shimmied sideways and shook his massive head. Beathan tried to spur him on, but the horse shook his head again. With several oaths, Beathan abandoned his attempt to fondle her. It was wasting time he didn't have to spare. Instead, he kept her drunk and compliant. She prayed a litany of thanksgiving that the man's sporran kept her from feeling anything that might have shown riding with her and touching her aroused him. Though it was foggy, she recalled what Lachlan told her. The sporran rubbed against her backside and made it sore, but she appreciated the barrier knowing now what she did. She supposed the conversation came in handy after all.

As she fought to keep from feeling like she would drown, her body felt like it weighed too much to support. She was pleased to see the other men making camp. She was sore from the long hours of riding and too intoxicated to remember any landmarks they passed. Even when she'd been able to pay attention, what she saw was of little use to her. The landscape all looked the same, and she wasn't familiar with the Highlands. She knew they rode alongside a loch she'd heard called the Tay. They'd seen boats sailing near the shore, but they'd been too far away for her to see any faces. Her constant blurry vision didn't help. There'd been a moment when she'd spotted movement on the ship's deck, and Beathan snarled something in Gaelic. But the road took them away from the loch, and the water became a distant shimmer.

Now she sat tied to a tree while Beathan and his men moved around the camp. She wondered if they would feed her anything. She doubted it when one man took the rabbits on the spit off of the fire and divided them among the men. Arabella knew Beathan intended to keep her hungry, so she wouldn't grow sober. He'd only feed her whisky to keep her going. As her eyes grew heavy, she welcomed the oblivion she used to seek. It was her only friend at the moment.

Arabella drifted in and out of sleep throughout the night. She heard Beathan's voice as he spoke with the man who seemed to be his most trusted warrior. She couldn't understand what they said because they used Gaelic the entire time except for when they gave her orders or doled out insults. During the middle of the night, she had a nightmare that Lachlan was on one of the boats she'd seen. She'd run toward him, but she was too unsteady on her feet to move fast enough, swerving and weaving as she tried to make it to the shore. Beathan caught her and held her up so Lachlan could see as he ran a blade across her throat. Lachlan hadn't been able to get to her in time, and she hadn't been able to escape. Even in her dream, she knew they'd been close to happiness, but her drinking tore them apart.

She'd woken with a start and mumbled in her drowsy state. Beathan crossed the camp and once more plied her with whisky until her eyes rolled back. She remained in a semi-state of wakefulness, aware of what happened around her for the rest of the night, but still asleep. When the sun peaked through the foliage above her, Arabella moaned and thrashed her head. She tried to block out the light by having her hair tumble in front of her face, but the liquid swilling in her stomach threatened to make a return. The ropes around her body, her wrists, and her ankles fell away as one guard cut her free. He reached out his hand as if he would cup her breast, but Arabella snarled and snapped her teeth at him like a feral animal. She felt like one: filthy, untrusting, and angry.

"Cease, or ye will feel ma hand across the other cheek. And I dinna mean the one on yer face," Beathan barked.

"Then make your hound heel," Arabella spat. She rubbed the rope burns around her wrist as she glared at Beathan. "You've filled me so full of liquid, I'm likely to float away. Unless you'd like to smell pish all day, I need a moment of privacy."

"Nae bluidy likely. I stole ye while ye had yer moment of privacy. I'm nae aboot to lose ye like that fool Sutherland did. Hold it, or I come with," Beathan offered.

Arabella needed relief too badly to care what Beathan did. She jerked her head up and down, then turned away from the camp. She found a bush close to where they'd tied her. She made sure she angled herself to have the most privacy she could and did what was necessary. Her balance was still off, and she nearly tumbled forward as she tried to stand. Beathan's none-too-gentle grip on her arm righted her. Manners drilled into her for years made her say "thank you," but she spat on the ground beside his feet afterward. She'd spat twice in the past two days, which was more than she'd ever done in her life. But she would have gladly done it over and over to make her loathing clear to Beathan. He led her back to the horses and lifted her into the saddle. They were back on the road, and Arabella's head was back to feeling like it was swimming. But the alcohol kept her from being terrified. It kept her from being furious. It kept her from being much more than numb, and that kept her going.

"Menzies," Lachlan gripped forearms with Laird Cathal Menzies as the man greeted Lachlan warmly. It didn't fool Lachlan into thinking it was a genuine welcome. He'd known Cathal since he was a young boy, and the laird was shrewd. It was how he kept his clan prosperous and out of feuds. "It's been a long time."

"It has, Lachlan. What brings ye to Comrie?" Cathal inquired.

"Beathan Gunn."

Lachlan watched as Cathal struggled not to allow his disgust to show. He'd been at the last Highland

Gathering that the Grants hosted, and he'd witnessed the standoff between Farlane and his son Arlan against the twins Ewan and Eoin Gordon. He'd learned what Arlan Gunn did to Cairstine Grant years earlier. Cathal had been one of the men to support Eoin's demand for single combat when Arlan threatened Cairstine once again. The Menzies were among the clans that ensured the Gunns left without further trouble after the Gordon twins slayed their laird and heir.

"Apple doesnae fall far from that tree, does it?" Cathal asked.

"Nay, it doesnae. Beathan is proving to be more judicious in clan affairs than his father or uncles, but he is the same when it comes to how he treats women," Lachlan explained.

"So this is aboot a woman?" Cathal studied Lachlan. "Yer woman."

"Aye. He's abducted Lady Arabella Johnstone. Her father was in the midst of arranging a betrothal, but King Robert favored ma suit over Beathan's. He didna take defeat graciously."

Cathal laughed. "Nay Gunn ever has. They have a propensity for kidnapping women. It's nae as though nay other Highlander has ever committed bride stealing, but that clan doesnae think aboot who they go up against. Twice they've tried to take women from yer cousins and now yer own lady. Nay sense at all."

Cathal passed an assessing gaze over Lachlan, and he knew the older laird wouldn't make any serious offers until Lachlan stated what he wanted. But he was just as patient as Cathal was shrewd. He stood looking at the man. As the seconds ticked by, Lachlan cocked an eyebrow and glanced at the keep before returning his gaze to Cathal's. They stood before one another, silent and contemplative.

"It's only the wee hours of the morn, but I suppose ye're looking for a place to catch some shuteye. Yer men can bed down in the barracks, and I'll have Enid arrange a chamber for ye," Cathal said as he made to turn away.

"Ye ken that isnae why I came. Why would I sleep now when ye ken I was on a boat all night with little to do but sleep?" Lachlan countered. "I have four men with me, and Beathan has six. The odds favor me, but where Arabella is concerned, I willna take any chances. Ye ken I've come to ask for help, and I ken ye willna turn me down."

"Ye ken that, do ye? Upstart," Cathal grumbled. He looked at Lachlan's expectant face, and both men knew Lachlan didn't need to mention the outstanding debt for Cathal to agree. "How many do ye want?"

"Half a score," Lachlan responded without hesitation. "They'll still be riding along the loch until at least midday. We should be able to meet them at the sharp bend in the river near Taymouth. I think that's the best place to make our stand."

"Aye, I can see that. But mayhap there be another way." A speculative gleam entered Cathal's eyes, and Lachlan prayed he and his men would survive whatever Cathal plotted. "I'm guessing ye saw signs of ma patrols along the river. What if I send one out that happens to find Beathan and yer lass? It'll be nearly sundown by the time they ride within spitting distance of here. Ma patrol extends our Highland hospitality to Beathan, and kenning him as I did his uncles, he willna turn down a bed and a meal paid for by another mon's coin. Once he's here —" Cathal shrugged "—ye have the entire Menzies army to back ye."

Lachlan considered what Cathal suggested, and it made far more sense than trying to launch a surprise attack along a river that had little high ground. He loathed allowing Arabella to remain within Beathan's reach the extra hours they would have to wait, but he knew it was the soundest approach. It was also the safest one for Arabella. He nodded his head.

"Fine choice, Lachlan. Come inside and have something to eat. Ye must be half-starved. The size of ye and only wee rabbits to fill ye. The woods between here and Stirling must be empty by now." Cathal led the way into the keep, and Lachlan didn't bother to mention the detour to Inchcailleoch Priory. The fewer questions asked, the better.

The morning passed into the early afternoon, and Lachlan paced along Comrie Castle's battlements. He'd gone into the lists that morning at Cathal's invitation. Swinging his sword helped ease his nervous energy and pass the time, but his mind was never far from thinking about Arabella. With every swing, thrust, and parry, he imagined running Beathan through. With every lift of his targe, he pictured shielding Arabella. The hours of the afternoon didn't pass nearly as quickly as those of the morning.

It was Lachlan who spotted the approaching riders before the Menzies guards. Arabella's hair shone like a radiant beacon as they approached. He rushed down the stairs before any of the Gunns or Arabella could recognize him. Cathal had already instructed his men not to mention the Sutherlands' presence. Lady Enid Menzies knew her part. She was to fuss over Arabella like a mother hen until she could separate her from Beathan. She would take her to a chamber where Lachlan waited. If Beathan insisted on accompanying Arabella, then so would some of Cathal's guards. They would detain him once Arabella was safely with Lachlan.

Once Arabella was abovestairs with Lachlan, assuming Beathan didn't follow her, Enid would inform

Beathan that she arranged a bath and food for Arabella but that the poor lass had fallen asleep before taking advantage of either. In the meantime, Cathal's daughter Millicent would sneak them through the keep and out through the postern gate where his men and the half a score of riders Cathal promised would be waiting. The Menzies warriors would accompany the Sutherlands and Arabella until they were safely into the mountains. All the while, Cathal would ply Beathan with whisky until he was deep in his cups.

TWENTY-NINE

Lachlan took the stairs by twos and threes as he hurried to reach the chamber Enid told him to wait in. He kept the door open a crack since the chamber offered a view of the Great Hall, and voices wafted up to him. He didn't have long to wait before a commotion tempted him to leave the chamber. He strained to see and gasped when he spotted Arabella barely standing on her own two feet. Her head flopped from side to side, and she stumbled with each step. Lachlan knew whatever excuse Beathan gave, Arabella was dangerously intoxicated. He suspected Beathan had plied her with whisky to make her obedient.

"Been sick as a bluidy dog the entire ride. I didna ken ma bride canna sit a horse," Beathan's voice boomed. "The trouble with marrying yerself to a Lowlander. Weak they are."

Lachlan heard laughter, but he suspected it only came from Beathan's men. Lady Menzies was a former Armstrong and still held strong ties to her clan of origin. The Menzies knew better than to laugh at jests made at Lowlanders' expense. Lachlan laid on the floor and pulled himself across the passageway on his belly. There was no light in the corridor, so he didn't fear it giving him away.

"The lass looks nearly dead on her feet," Enid fussed. "I'll have her put to rights with a bath and some food." The older woman reached out for Arabella, but Beathan pulled her away.

"A right bampot. Her father didna tell me the lass is barmy. She mutters nonsense and can be a right she-cat. Stuck with her, I am," Beathan said woefully. "Best she stays close to me. She's calm with me."

Lady Enid Menzies looked over Beathan from the top of his head to the tip of his toes and back up again. She stepped before the man who towered over her and put her hands on her hips. "That's the greatest pile of pig shite I've ever heard. The lass is drunk as a skunk. I can smell it. I don't know how she came to be that way, but she is."

Enid grasped Arabella's arm and gave it a little shake. Arabella's head lolled back as her eyebrows rose over closed eyes. Arabella had heard everything going around her, but her head had weighed too much and she was too sleepy to say anything. She forced her eyes open a crack and took in the resolute woman's expression. She tried to nod but moaned instead.

"That's it. I don't like liars, Laird Gunn. Hand the lass over to me, or I'll have her taken from you." Enid turned her attention back to Arabella and softened her voice. "Do you want to come with me? I'll be sure you get food and a bath."

Arabella tried to follow what the lady said, but only parts of it made sense to her. She tried nodding again, but she lost her balance. She tilted toward Beathan, making it look like she preferred him. Beathan cast a smug smile at Lady Enid.

"*Tu es un morceau de bouse. Je prie pour que vous*

mouriez bientôt d'une terrible maladie qui pourrit vos intestins et vous fait chier," Enid spat. Arabella pushed back her hair and stared at Enid, her eyes wide. It was the most sober she'd felt in days as she listened to the genteel looking woman spew, "You are a piece of dung. I pray you die soon of a terrible illness that rots away your bowels and makes you shit yourself."

Arabella coughed as she attempted to swallow the hysterical laughter that threatened to bubble forth. She pushed against Beathan's side and took a step away from him. His arm around her waist kept her close, but she put some space between them. *"Vous avez raison. Je souhaite la même chose au salaud."* Arabella told Lady Enid, "You are correct. I wish the same for the bastard.

"Votre homme vous attend dans une chambre. Il est là pour vous éloigner de ce porc. Vous devez venir avec moi." Lady Enid hurried to explain to Arabella that "your man is waiting for you in a chamber. He's here to take you away from this swine. You must come with me."

Arabella blinked several times, trying to wrap her mind around Lachlan being so close but not coming for her. Her glassy eyes darted around the Great Hall and toward the stairs. She struggled to focus, but she was certain she saw the shape of a head on the floor of the landing. Even without seeing clearly, she was certain it was Lachlan.

"I don't feel right. I think I shall be sick," Arabella whispered. She looked at Enid, who gave a nearly imperceptible nod, which looked more like she turned her head to look more squarely at Arabella. She flexed the muscles in her stomach and throat until she gagged twice, then vomited on cue. Beathan pushed Arabella away as filthy Gaelic curses spewed from his mouth as though it was his turn to vomit, only it was words that came forth.

"Ye willna speak like that in ma home," Cathal bellowed. "Ye change yer tone or ye will be out on yer arse. The lass stays with us."

"Ye canna take a mon's bride from him," Beathan argued.

"Canna I?" Cathal's gimlet stare made Beathan pause. Suspicion crept into Beathan's gaze as it shifted to look around the Great Hall. But Cathal's next words settled him. "Lady Menzies was set to marry another, and as ye can see, she is ma wife. I amnae opposed to bride stealing. Are ye?"

"Ye already have a bride, auld mon," Beathan spat.

"There ye go again. Oaths and insults in another mon's home. Ye test the bounds of Highland hospitality, lad." Cathal crossed his brawny arms. Middle aged, but still fit enough to pose a threat to Beathan, he leaned forward. "I have a son yet to wed."

As Cathal and Beathan argued, Enid eased Arabella away from Beathan. She wrapped her arm around Arabella's shoulders and steered her toward the stairs. They were halfway across the Great Hall before Beathan called out for them to stop. Arabella stumbled as Enid pushed her forward, reassuring her that Beathan couldn't get to her before the Menzies stopped him. As a guest, Beathan had left his sword and at least some of his dirks with a guard at the gatehouse. Beathan took a menacing step forward before he remembered he was virtually unarmed, while the laird's personal guard waited nearby with hands ready to draw their swords.

"Vera well. She's disgusting anyway. Take her and make her presentable," Beathan ordered. When it was Cathal who took a menacing step forward, Beathan turned his attention away from Enid and Arabella.

"Ye're mother did a lousy job of teaching ye yer p's and q's. Try again, lad."

Beathan cast him a scathing look as he muttered, "Please."

Enid called back over her shoulder, "I'm doing it for the lass. I hope you choke on your own tongue."

THIRTY

L achlan scrambled to crawl back into the chamber and shut the door without a sound. He stood behind the door with a dirk drawn in case a threat crossed the threshold rather than Enid and Arabella. Now shut in the chamber, he couldn't be sure whose hand moved the handle. The air whooshed from his lungs as Arabella stepped into the chamber, but she froze.

"Lachlan?" She whispered with desperation. "Lach? You said…" Arabella sobbed and fell to her knees before Lachlan could catch her. He stepped around Enid and helped Arabella to her feet. She fell against him as tears streamed down her face. She clung to him; his scent recognizable even as she cried inconsolably. Lachlan lifted her into his arms and carried her to a chair before the fire.

"The bath will be here shortly along with food," Enid whispered before slipping from the chamber. As the door closed behind the woman, Lachlan brushed the hair back from Arabella's face.

"Shh, little one. I'm here, and I'm going nay where," Lachlan soothed.

"You promised that before," Arabella stammered.

"Aye. And so I came after ye. But ye arenae leaving ma side again, Belle. Nae to sleep in another chamber, nae to ride another horse, nae aught." Lachlan kissed her forehead then each cheek, before lifting her chin to kiss her mouth. Arabella tried to pull away.

"I'm filthy, Lach. You don't want to do that," Arabella mumbled. But Lachlan disregarded her warning and pressed a soft kiss to her lips.

"We shall have ye right as rain soon enough. Then ye will climb into that big bed and sleep the rest of the day away." Lachlan didn't wish to make such a promise. He wanted to get Arabella away from Comrie Castle and Beathan as soon as he could, but she was in no condition to travel anywhere until she ate and rested. A knock on the door made them both look toward the portal, and Arabella felt herself grow more sober by the minute as she struggled to appear less intoxicated than she was. Lachlan set Arabella on her feet, taking her hand. He led them to the door and pressed himself against the wall beside it before nodding his head.

Arabella opened the door and allowed a wave of servants into the chamber. She stood beside the open door, blocking Lachlan from sight and keeping anyone from trying to close it. Men carried a tub into the chamber with women following with several buckets of hot water and one with tepid water. A tray of food also arrived and was set on the bed. No one spoke as the servants worked, but Arabella thanked them as they left.

Once the door was shut, Lachlan wrapped his arms around Arabella's waist, and she leaned her back against his chest. Her head fell back against his shoulder as her hands covered his. The solace she found after her ordeal was immeasurable. She found she had hope again simply by being in Lachlan's arms. She grumbled when he pulled one hand away, but he moved her hair aside and kissed her neck. Her head fell to the side as Lachlan brushed his lips along the column of her neck. Her hands fell away and gripped his plaid. Lachlan's hand settled on her breast, kneading the firm mound. Arabella moaned softly as she pressed her bottom against Lachlan's sporran. She fumbled behind her to move it aside before pressing the cleft of her backside against the ridge beneath his plaid.

"I told ye the last time we did this that we would be married the next time. And I promised to bury myself in ye," Lachlan whispered against her skin, his warm breath tickling her.

"I remember," Arabella breathed. Lachlan turned her in his arms and pulled her into his embrace. It wasn't a passionate hold, but rather tender and loving. Arabella sighed as she wrapped her arms around his waist and rested her head on his chest. "I love you, Lachlan. All I could think aboot, when I could think at all, was how to get back to you. That I wasn't aboot to give up our future together."

"We were of a like mind. I love ye, and there isnae aught I willna do to be with ye, Belle. I would have ye as ma wife before the moon rises. Tell me true, Arabella, do ye wish to marry?" Lachlan held his breath as Arabella leaned back.

"I have never wanted aught more than to marry you, Lachlan. I've dreamed of it, wished for it, prayed for it for years. We don't have a priest though, and I'm afraid to leave this chamber, Lach."

"We dinna have to have a priest to marry, Belle. Mayhap ye dinna do it this way in the Lowlands, but we have two choices. We can handfast, but would have to marry in a kirk within a year. Or we can have an irregular wedding and marry by declaration. That is binding, just like at a kirk."

"Then by declaration. I won't choose aught that could let someone take me from you ever again. If declaring it is all that needs to happen, aren't we married already? We've said we wish to marry more than once," Arabella reasoned.

Lachlan grinned and shook his head. "Were that it was so easy. We must have two witnesses to bear testimony that we married, and that the bride did so willingly."

"Lady Menzies," Arabella suggested.

"Aye, and either Cathal or their daughter Millicent," Lachlan added.

"Is that really all that it will take?" Arabella asked skeptically.

"In the eyes of the law, aye. In the Highlands, there's nae always a priest available because of distance or weather, so we've come up with solutions over the generations. But I would like to say our own vows before God." Arabella could hear the hope in Lachlan's hushed tones. She nodded her head enthusiastically and threw her arms around his, squeezing so hard that she pinned them to his side. "For a wee lass, ye are stronger than ye look. Stronger than anyone could imagine."

Lachlan tucked hair behind her ear, but wrapped the lock around his finger, mesmerized by the different hues of red, orange, and gold that shone in the light coming from the window embrasure and the fire. He considered all that Arabella endured from her father's abusive words, to life at court, her addiction to alcohol, and her time with Beathan. He pressed her chin up and looked into her emerald eyes.

"Nay one can ever deny ye are beautiful beyond compare, but that is such a small part of who ye are,

Belle. Ye can be reckless and daring, but ye are also brave and resilient. I am proud to ken I'll be yer husband. There is nay mon luckier than me. Ye have a kindness and strength our people will need."

"Our people?" Arabella whispered. "You think of me as a Sutherland already?"

"I think a part of me has since the day I met ye. It's grown with each visit, each time we've talked, each time we've danced, every minute of missing ye when we were apart. I pray I willna become laird until I have gray hair, but one day I will. Ye are who I need and want at ma side."

"I wish I could wipe away all that I've put you through in the past moon. I don't ken if my conscience will ever let go of all my guilt, but I want naught more than to marry you. I will stand behind you no matter what, Lachlan."

"Never behind. Always at my side," Lachlan corrected. "It's as partners that we will get through this."

Arabella nodded and tried to swallow the lump in her throat. "Then it's as partners that we enter this marriage."

Even with their mouths sealed, love and passion filled the kiss they exchanged. Lachlan plucked at the habit's ties at Arabella's neck, loosening it until the robe nearly slipped from her shoulders. He gathered the material in his hands and drew it up her body and over her head. He'd ignored the bruise on her cheek, not wanting to draw attention to it or grow any angrier than he'd been when he first spotted it. But as he took in the magnificence of her body, he looked for any sign that Beathan had manhandled her. There were a few light bruises, but nothing spoke to abuse.

"He did naught to me," Arabella whispered. "No mon has."

Lachlan took her hand and as they walked to the

tub, he told her, "That is far from important to me. Ye are with me, and ye are safe. That is all that matters. There is naught that would ever turn me away from ye. Whatever state ye came to me in, as long as ye came, I would've welcomed ye with the fullness of ma heart."

Arabella cupped his cheek as she looked into the chocolate-colored eyes she loved gazing into. "You are a good mon, Lachlan. I am blessed we found one another. It's your eyes I hope to look into every night as I fall asleep, and it's your eyes that I hope to see when I open mine each morn."

Lachlan helped Arabella into the tub, and she slid beneath the surface of the water. The water was still hot, and she wondered if it would have scalded her had she gotten in sooner. She'd feared it would be cold, but it was just right as it eased her aches. She pushed her head to the surface and leaned back, recalling the last time Lachlan helped her bathe. He kneeled beside the tub with a bar of soap in one hand and a lathered linen square in the other. He began at her neck, drawing the cloth over her as his hands rubbed away the tension from her shoulders. He lifted her left arm and wiped the soapy material over it. Then he repeated the process with her left leg, her right arm, and finally her right leg. With the soap in his hand, he washed her chest, moving unhurriedly over her breasts, his free hand trailing the one with the soap. He massaged the small globes, his tongue peeking out between his lips. His hands ran down her ribs and over her belly. He placed the soap in the dish beside him before he used the cloth to wash between her legs.

Arabella watched as the linen floated to the surface just before his fingers slipped inside her. His movement surprised her even though she anticipated it. A moan slipped from her as she flexed her hips, inviting him to give her more. His thumb swirled around her nub, as three fingers worked her sheath. He cupped her breast, massaging it as Arabella arched her back. Her nipples puckered in the chamber's cool air. Free from the water covering them, Lachlan lowered his head and suckled. His tongue rasped over the sensitive bud before his teeth grazed it and bit down with just enough pressure to make Arabella's hand press his head closer. He opened his mouth wider, appearing to consume her entire breast. His groan was purely masculine, and Arabella purred as he continued to work her body.

"Come for me, Belle," Lachlan whispered.

"Come?"

"Find yer release, *mo chridhe*," Lachlan clarified.

Arabella's eyes drifted closed, even though she was more sober than she had been in days. She realized she'd barely felt the effects of the whisky once she reunited with Lachlan. Her hips undulated in the water as she struggled to leash the sensations within her core, so she could climax as Lachlan asked. She knew seeing her pleasured aroused him as much as it did her. She reached over the side of the tub and fumbled with the buckle to Lachlan's belt. He didn't stop her, so she twisted to use both hands. When it fell free, she tugged at his plaid. It took more than one yank to release the yards of wool. But when Lachlan kneeled naked beside the tub, her breath caught. The muscles in his arms, chest, and abdomen flexed and strained as he continued his ministrations. Arabella's hand run over his biceps to his shoulder before trailing down his chest. His abdomen twitched as her fingernails grazed the taut skin. She wrapped her hand around his length, stroking him as he'd shown her all that time ago in the alcove.

Arabella couldn't help staring. She reveled in the glorious sight of his naked body. He brought to mind drawings she'd seen of Romans and Greeks in bathhouses in a book she'd been forced to read to the queen. The images had seemed so scandalous at the time. Now she had her very own god whose body she had free roam of. Lachlan's hips rocked as her hand moved over his shaft.

"Belle, I canna last much longer. I've craved yer touch too much, too often. I want ye to fin—" Lachlan groaned, unable to finish as jets of his seed splashed against the side of the tub. Watching his cock pulse then trailing her eyes over his straining body up to the ecstasy on his face, Belle's body exploded as her core spasmed, and her body went rigid. Lachlan fell forward, resting his body on the edge of the tub. He ran a soothing hand over her body and thighs before once more massaging her breast. He'd once thought he preferred her backside the most of her attributes, but he couldn't get enough of her front side.

Feeling boneless and suddenly sleepy once more, Arabella leaned forward with Lachlan's guidance as he scrubbed her back and then washed her hair. When she was clean, Lachlan helped her from the tub and wrapped her in drying cloths and handed her three sprigs of mint. He chewed one too. He'd brought the satchel Madeline packed with him, so he withdrew a clean chemise, and slipped it over Arabella's head. She struggled not to yawn as she sat before the fire and Lachlan combed her tangled hair. Every so often, her hands reached behind her, enjoying the feel of his still-naked body. When her hair was mostly dry, Lachlan carried her to the bed. He tucked her in before retrieving a clean leine from his own satchel. He climbed onto the bed, laying on top of the covers. Arabella snuggled closer, even though she'd already fallen asleep. Even in her sleep, she sought him. He wrapped her in his arms, kissing her forehead over and over as he shut his eyes but didn't dare fall asleep. It would be a long time before he let his guard down and risked losing her again.

THIRTY-ONE

The weak late summer light cast thin beams through the window embrasure as Arabella continued to sleep. She'd had a few restless moments, but Lachlan's soothing voice and gentle touch soon calmed her. She'd mutter "I love you" in her sleep before her breathing deepened again. Lachlan rested with his eyes closed, but his ears strained for any sounds that would warn him of someone entering the chamber or lurking in the passageway. Once Arabella had fallen asleep, he'd peeled his arm out from beneath her and retrieved two dirks that now laid beside him.

When a light tap came at the door, he grasped the hilt of one. He was positioned on the side of the bed closer to the door to protect Arabella, but he once again had to slide himself away from her, so no part of his back was to the door. It opened a crack, but Enid's smiling face quickly peered around it. She crept into the chamber with her daughter Millicent behind her.

Enid nodded at the blade in Lachlan's hand. "Didn't want that coming whizzing at my head but didn't want to intrude either. How's the lass?"

"She's well," Arabella rasped as she sat up and

wiped the sleep from her eyes. She blinked several times at Enid, as if she tried to recall where she knew the woman from. As her memory from the morning fell into place, she blurted, "You speak French."

"Aye, Lady Arabella. My mother insisted upon it before I went to court as a lady-in-waiting many moons ago," Enid explained.

"You told me Lachlan was here," Arabella said it as if to clear her memory rather than make a statement. "I remember wanting to run to find him, but my body barely felt like my own."

"It wasnae. The bastard must have nearly killed ye with whisky. Ye're a slight thing, but ye swayed like a drunken sailor," Millicent grinned. At Arabella's surprise, then scowl, Millicent laughed. "I didna mean offense, ma lady. Ye just appeared a wee off-kilter. I dinna think ye saw me, but I was by the doors to the kitchens. Saw all of it. I'm glad ye're away from him."

"Millie, *tais-toi*," Enid snapped as she told her daughter to be quiet.

"*C'est bon.*" Arabella reassured that it was all right.

"*Mieux vaut trouver l'humour que la tristesse*," Lachlan said philosophically as he told them, "it's better to find humor than sadness."

"*C'est vrai.* That's true," Enid nodded. She walked to the foot of the bed and looked at the tray that remained untouched. She raised a scolding eyebrow at Lachlan, but Arabella waved her hand.

"It's not his fault. After I bathed, I was too tired to do aught but sleep. But I'm famished and could eat a leg of mutton, then the rest of it." Arabella looked at the tray for the first time, and her eyes widened as she noticed the array of food. There was enough that it should have fed them both, but she suspected she could eat all of it herself. But before she made a move toward it, she recalled what she and Lachlan discussed before her bath. She looked at him expectantly and nodded when he returned her expression.

"Lady Enid, we would like to marry this eve," Lachlan said cautiously.

"Aye. That would be for the best. You ken we're in the Highlands. You only need two of us," Enid replied.

"You knew we'd want to marry by—" Arabella looked at Lachlan. "What did you call it? Declaration? You knew we'd want to marry by declaration?"

"If neither of you mentioned it, we would have," Millicent interjected.

Lachlan slipped from the bed and went to one of the satchels. He pulled Arabella's gown out. It was hopelessly wrinkled, but still serviceable. Arabella slid off the bed and took the kirtle Lachlan held out.

"I would have married you in my chemise, but I admit I would prefer looking a bit more presentable," Arabella smiled.

"We'll help you while your mon dresses. I don't think he wishes to marry in his leine either," Enid chuckled. She, Millicent, and Arabella ducked behind the screen while Lachlan hurried to pleat his plaid. A thought occurred to him when the women reappeared.

"We havenae seen hide nor hair of Beathan. I'm surprised he hasnae come storming in yet," Lachlan mused.

"Cathal has him spinning tales as he drinks our buttery dry. The bluidy mon has hollow legs, but he's been in his cups for a few hours. Told Cathal his entire life story and just aboot every secret his clan has. Lucky for the toad, Cathal has him in his solar rather than blaring his business like a town crier," Enid explained.

"But his voice carries," Millicent added. "Mama and I could hear him from outside Father's door. I learned words today that I didna ken existed."

"And I'll wash your mouth out with soap if you repeat them. You may be four-and-ten, but your father will still take a switch to your rump," Enid warned.

With an unrepentant grin, Millicent bobbed a curtsy and said, "Aye, Mama."

"Right," Enid's tone turned serious. "Let's get you wed, fed, and bedded."

Arabella's cheeks turned scarlet, and Lachlan shifted from one foot to another. They'd been alone all afternoon in a bedchamber, so it would have been reasonable for anyone to question what they'd done to pass the time. But Enid's frank comment embarrassed them both.

"You're a healthy mon, and you're aboot to be a wife. Don't pretend as though my words are shocking," Enid looked down her nose at them down despite Lachlan being more than a foot taller than her. "Shall we be on with it?"

Lachlan turned to Arabella, and she offered him her hands. Her fingertips feathered his palms before they turned their hands and entwined their fingers. They gazed into one another's eyes, savoring the moment before either spoke. Lachlan's thumbs ran over Arabella's.

"Arabella Johnstone, do ye wish to wed with me?" Lachlan asked, his deep voice soaking into Arabella as though it might wrap its warmth around her.

"Aye, Lachlan Sutherland. I wish to wed with you," Arabella responded. They were the words he'd waited five years to hear, and none had ever sounded better.

"We will bear witness to your marriage," Enid said as she shooed Millicent toward the door. Once her daughter was in the passageway, Enid turned back to them. "I will be back before morn to see the sheet."

She didn't wait for either of them to respond, nor did she make any more mention of a bedding. Lachlan and Arabella knew what she suspected, and that Enid wasn't interested in how blood got on the sheet as long as there was something that they could use to prove consummation.

Arabella glanced at the bed and wondered if Lachlan would suggest they couple immediately. She'd enjoyed every touch and every intimacy they'd shared, but she had a moment of trepidation as she thought about his sword fitting in her sheath. She was curious and eager, but she was also nervous.

"Belle, this isnae how either of us imagined we would marry. If ye arenae ready, then we can wait," Lachlan offered.

"Nay!" Arabella's eyes widened. "I mean, we can if you prefer that. But not on my account." Her cheeks once more grew rosy as she looked away from the bed, but couldn't bring her eyes to meet his.

"Ye havenae eaten in I dinna ken how long. Let's have our repast and see where things go," Lachlan suggested. He didn't understand why Arabella suddenly grew agitated and looked on the verge of tears. He wrapped his arm around her and murmured, "What's wrong?"

"I thought you'd want to—" Arabella turned her head toward the bed. Even before he spoke, Lachlan's wolfish grin made her realize she'd just conjured a fear out of nowhere. Lachlan lifted his plaid and took one of her hands. Her fingertips brushed against his hardened cock before wrapping them around it. Lachlan's sigh sounded like pure bliss. He cast her a knowing glance before closing his eyes.

"Christ on the cross, Arabella," Lachlan panted

as she stroked him. A few minutes later, he caught her wrist and pried her hand loose despite her resistance and humph. "I just meant for ye to ken I want ye. I didna mean for ye to make me spill the second ye touched me."

Lachlan cupped her skull as he kissed her. His tongue flicked her slightly parted lips, and she opened to him. As his tongue inched into her mouth, she lured him in with her own. Once she could, she sucked softly on it. Lachlan growled as he tore at the laces to her kirtle. She fumbled for the second time that day as she unfastened his belt. As his plaid dropped to the ground, Lachlan pushed her gown down her arms and over her hips. She reached up and pulled the ribbons of her chemise loose. It followed her kirtle to the ground. Lachlan yanked his leine off before returning his mouth to Arabella's. Their naked bodies pressed together as Lachlan slid his thigh between Arabella's. She rocked her hips as she straddled the muscular limb. Lachlan pulled her higher until her thatch of curls brushed against his. Her nails bit into his shoulders as her need made her restless.

"*Sard*," Lachlan muttered once they'd inched their way to the bed. He released Arabella and swept the tray of food off the bed. He looked around before settling with placing it on the chair where Arabella had sat while her hair dried. Arabella watched as he walked toward her, his cock swaying with each step. As his arm came around her waist, she encircled his length with her hand. Lachlan dipped his fingers between her thighs, pleased to find her as aroused as he was. Moisture coated the tops of the inside of her thighs, and her nether lips were dripping with arousal.

"Lachlan," Arabella said his name softly. When he nodded, she glanced down between them. "I liked earlier. But do we—um—have to do that much be-fore we can?" She turned her face toward the bed.

Lachlan wrapped his forearm underneath her bottom while bringing her breast to his mouth. He lifted her off her feet and walked to the side of the bed. He laid her gently on the mattress, but Arabella scrambled to move into the center. Her bent legs dropped open as she reached for him.

"Nay, we dinna have to do that much," Lachlan said as his hand guided his cock to her entrance. As the tip brushed her folds, he forced himself to slow. He lowered himself onto his forearms as he pressed the head of his cock into her. He waited for her to shy away or show she was in any pain. She looked at him in confusion. "I'll go slowly, Belle. I dinna want to hurt ye any more than is unavoidable."

Arabella shook her head. "It hurts now." She squeezed his upper arms as he tried to pull away, horror written across his face. "That's not what I meant. I ache for you, Lach. So much that it hurts. My body keeps saying open to you, take you into me even though my mind says I don't know what I'm do-ing. I ken it'll hurt differently soon enough, but right now, it's agony."

Lachlan brushed the hair from her throat and kissed her neck where it met her shoulder as he pressed forward. Arabella wrapped her calves over his and tried to tilt and lift her hips to him. "Lach," she cried in desperation. He shushed her before molding his mouth to hers and thrusting into her. Her body arched off the bed as her fingers released his arms and splayed wide in the air.

"I'm sorry," Lachlan gasped. Shame washed over him as guilt snapped at his conscience. He knew it would hurt, but he never imagined it would be so bad that her body would react as it did. "It's done. I'll stop."

"Done? Stop?" Tears dribbled from her eyes as she squeezed them shut. Her voice croaked as she spoke. "Don't I feel right?"

"St Columba's bones. Belle, naught has ever felt more right. I just canna stomach kenning that I'm hurting ye."

"I may hurt you," Arabella snapped as she shifted restlessly. "It was shocking, and it was painful, and it's over. But I don't want this to be over." Arabella waved her hand up and down between them. Lachlan slowly pressed his hips forward, testing to be sure Arabella showed no signs of discomfort. Instead, the look of a siren entered her eyes as she tested moving beneath him. When he drew back then thrust into her, her moan was purely carnal. As he grew braver, he surged into her with more confidence and more eagerness. Arabella pulled him down, so they lay chest to chest. Their kiss reflected the passion their bodies enjoyed. Lachlan's hand grasped her hip as he moved faster. Her quiet, breathy sounds encouraged him until she asked for more.

"I love you," Lachlan whispered before burying his face in her neck as he fought not to climax. He wanted to draw out their experience, and he refused to finish before Arabella had her first taste of pleasure from making love.

"I love you doesn't feel like enough," Arabella whispered. "It's starting. Lach, oh." Arabella closed her eyes and focused as her body moved in tandem with Lachlan's. He watched her furrowed brow and lips compressed into a line. She'd never looked more beautiful to him. As her core tightened around his shaft, and he drove himself into her with abandon, her emerald eyes snapped open. She strained, and her forehead came up to rest against his shoulder. With one more thrust and a tilt of her hips, they came apart in one another's arms.

Lachlan couldn't look away. Arabella's eyes had gone a deep moss green, like Highland grass after a summer storm. Her cheeks were flushed, and color suffused her chest and neck. Tiny beads of sweat slipped along her temple. As she wrapped her arms around him, he eased his weight onto her, mindful not to crush her. They sighed on the same breath as they laid, still joined, basking in the peaceful calm after their explosive joining.

"Is it always—" Arabella wasn't naive. She knew there'd been women before her, even during their acquaintance. He'd admitted as much. Even though she never wanted any specifics, she couldn't help her curiosity. Only one of them had something to compare.

"Never." Lachlan didn't hesitate to answer. "I didna ken it could ever be so—so intense. Ma chest felt like ma heart would break through. Every time I looked at ye, I wanted to be closer to ye. It was unlike aught else. It certainly wasna just lust. I ken it can only be love."

"You say the most wonderful things," Arabella smiled. The softness in her eyes made Lachlan want to run away with her and hide her from anything that would make it fade. Her hand cupped his cheek. "I've never wanted to love someone else as much as I do you. I would do aught to make you happy. I mean to make your life as good as it can be."

"Belle, it already is. I'm yer husband now. I finally understand the feeling or sense I have when I see Mama and Da together or Maude and Blair with their husbands. It always seemed like happiness, but with something more. Now I ken."

"Lach, I saw it with Blair and Hardi, and Maude and Kieran. But I thought we'd never be together. I assumed it was an opportunity that passed me by. I was a little jealous, but I was mostly sad because I believed I would never have that. I longed to tell you that I love you, to tell you how much I want to be with you. But I didn't dare. The one thing I've ever really wished for, been willing to beg and barter with God for, has finally come true. I love you so much."

"There is naught finer than being yer husband, and with God's grace, one day being the father of yer bairns."

"Our bairns," Arabella corrected.

"Our bairns." Lachlan paused, cautious about his next question. "Ye liked this enough to want to do it again?"

"Can we?" The excitement in Arabella's eyes made him chuckle. His cock twitched within her, and he felt himself hardening.

"I didna think so soon, but, aye. Keep tightening around me, and I'll finish before we start." Lachlan nipped at her neck. But a quiet but insistent knock interrupted them.

"Lachlan, Lady Arabella," Enid's muffled voice floated beneath the door. Several more knocks followed. Lachlan sprang from the bed, grabbing his leine from the floor as he passed it. He glanced back at Arabella and found her beneath the bedding and pulling the covers up to her chin. He opened the door, and Enid rushed in. She took one glance at Lachlan, then rushed to the bed. "You must hurry and dress. You must leave. Now. Beathan is demanding to see you, Lady Arabella. He's getting ornery and loud. Cathal still has him occupied, but you need to make haste while it's still dark."

Enid tossed Arabella her chemise before laying the gown across the bed. She looked around and found the tattered habit that lay near the forgotten tub. She scooped it from the floor as she hurried to the fireplace. She tossed an extra block of peat into the fire and brought it to a crackling roar. She flung the garment into the flames, poking the logs as though encouraging them to devour the fabric. She dashed back to Arabella's side and helped pull the laces tight as Lachlan donned his plaid and gathered their meager belongings. Arabella helped him pull back the covers, revealing the stained bedsheet. They stripped it off the bed together, Enid nodding as they worked together. Lachlan shoved it into a saddlebag.

"It's not much, but enough to wrap around your hair and shoulders," Enid said as she handed Arabella a swath of Menzies plaid. Covering her hair would always be the most crucial part of hiding her identity. If she could pass as a Menzies, even with Lachlan wearing his Sutherland plaid, they might draw fewer questions.

"Thank you," Arabella whispered as they hurried to the door. Enid opened it, and they heard Beathan bellowing from the Great Hall.

"Hurry," Enid pointed. "Millicent is in the shadows. She'll take you to the postern gate where your men should already be waiting. Go and don't look back."

"Thank you, Lady Menzies," Lachlan said in a hushed tone. Arabella pressed a quick kiss to the older woman's cheek. They knew how much the Menzies risked helping them. While the Gunns lived far to the north, there was no doubt Beathan would cause trouble once he knew Arabella was gone. Lachlan took her hand as they ran toward the dark end of the passageway.

"Follow me," Millicent's soft voice said as she materialized from the shadows. No one spoke again until they reached the postern gate. A Menzies guard opened it for the couple. "Good luck."

Arabella turned back to say thank you, but the portal was already closed. The Sutherlands and Menzies were mounted and waiting for them.

Lachlan tossed Arabella into the saddle on Firelight, and they set off before Lachlan settled in his. The men surrounded Arabella, and it relieved her that Firelight could follow the horse in front of her since Arabella could barely see anything. A cloud cover kept the light from the moon and the stars from illuminating the land ahead of them.

While it aided their cover, it made it difficult to navigate. Arabella had no way to gauge distance or time, so it surprised her when they began their ascent into the foothills. She hadn't expected to reach the beginning of the Cairngorms so soon. She wondered what awaited them once they were in the mountains, since she'd never traveled through any. As the first rays of sunlight spread around the peaks, she discovered what lay ahead of them. It was the making of her newest nightmare.

THIRTY-TWO

Lachlan nearly went flying over his horse's withers as it stumbled to a halt, a line of warriors standing before them where the path widened. With their swords drawn and Gunn plaids flapping in the morning air, they were a menacing sight. Lachlan scanned the two-man deep row of them and counted nearly a score. That didn't mean there weren't more that remained unseen. When Arabella gasped, it tempted him to take his eyes off the men to check on her.

"That's Graham," Arabella whispered. "He traveled with us. I saw Beathan talking to him several times, but I couldn't understand any of it. They've been planning this."

Lachlan eased a dirk from his boot. Reaching for his sword would only antagonize his opponents, but the dirk made the Gunns aware he would fight and defend Arabella.

"Ye seem lost, Sutherland," The man named Graham called. "But I see ye found ma laird's bride. Troublesome bitch."

Lachlan didn't flinch. He wouldn't show any sign that the man's insult enraged him, nor would he give away that Arabella was now his wife. He sat and waited for Graham to continue talking. His silence unsettled Graham, who shifted nervously in his saddle.

"Ye're outnumbered four to one," Graham called.

"He can count," Lachlan muttered, and his men laughed, understanding his strategy.

"What's that?" Graham called. Lachlan merely blinked as he sat like a statue. Graham turned his attention to Arabella, but she followed Lachlan's lead. Her eyes met Graham's, silently challenging him to look away first. She felt a deep sense of satisfaction when the Gunn warrior shifted his attention back to Lachlan. "Surrender now, and yer death willna be so painful."

"Canna say the same for yers," Lachlan said, a little louder this time, so Graham heard his voice rather than saw his mouth move. But Lachlan's adversary still couldn't hear him. The Sutherlands laughed again.

"Nae brave enough to share yer jests, Sutherland?" Graham taunted.

"The only jest today is ye, Graham," Lachlan called. He caught the surprise on the man's face when Lachlan addressed him by name.

"Been having a chat with the lass, have ye? Passing the whisky back and forth, I'd say. She drinks like an auld tart."

Lachlan was immensely proud of Arabella as she sat on her horse, not moving a muscle. She remained calm, and her horse remained settled, unlike the steed beneath Graham. The animal danced from side to side, bumping into the horses on each side. Lachlan continued to watch Graham, but his mind whirled as he tried to think of a way to get Arabella to safety rather than have her drawn into the center of a battle on a mountain path. He wished the Menzies men that joined them as they left the keep were still with them, but they'd turned back less than an hour ago. Lachlan suspected the Gunns knew that and had waited until their numbers dwindled.

His peripheral vision caught Lellan lurch forward as an arrow protruded from his back. Graham's laughter carried to him as Lachlan looked back to find Beathan and the men who'd accompanied him into Comrie Castle racing toward them. The Gunns sandwiched the Sutherlands between their two groups.

"Lele?" Lachlan asked.

"I'll survive, but the bastard who shot me willna," the Sutherland warrior groaned.

Lachlan didn't wait another moment before he plucked Arabella from her saddle and pulled her in front of him. "Lie low over his neck," Lachlan commanded as he drew his sword. He spun his horse around, using his knees to command the animal, his men following suite. His best chance was to ride toward Beathan and the smaller group, making his way downhill with greater speed than Beathan could ascend. The Sutherlands maneuvered in silent understanding as Lachlan's horse shifted positions within the group, moving Arabella away from Beathan's path.

Arabella wanted to look back to see what was becoming of Firelight, but she didn't dare. She clung to the stallion's mane and gripped the beastly sized horse's flanks with her knees. Lachlan prepared to swing his sword if a Gunn warrior got too close. Wallace and Tarran cut a path ahead of them, while George and the injured Lellan remained close to Lachlan's sides, defending Arabella as the Gunns launched their defense. Beathan and his six men charged uphill, but their horses were no match for the Sutherlands barreling downhill. Wallace injured three while Tarran unseated two. That left Beathan and one other man. Lachlan continued to steer his horse away from Beathan, as his men closed ranks. The four men created a wall as Lachlan guided his horse off the path and onto uneven ground.

As an arrow whizzed past his shoulder, he leaned over Arabella, protecting her back and making himself a smaller target. He glanced beneath each arm, looking back at Beathan, who now lay on the ground, and the larger group that was advancing on his men. He whistled sharply and heard the hoofbeats following him. He and his men traversed this mountain path frequently since he made regular trips to court to visit his sisters. They knew the lay of the land, and Lachlan was confident his men's knowledge exceeded the Gunns'.

As the five horses raced across the rocks and shale, Lachlan whistled once more. Arabella spied the Sutherland men fanning out, their horses kicking up rocks with every step. She watched as the steeds strained to climb the mountainside without a path to follow. She feared once more what became of Firelight. Her mare wasn't built with the endurance these Highland warhorses possessed. As more arrows impaled the surrounding ground, Arabella squeezed her eyes shut and clung to the horse, grateful Lachlan's enormous frame kept her pinned to the animal.

"*La petite fille!*" Lachlan called out. Arabella didn't understand why he yelled "the little girl." But she opened her eyes and spied George and Tarran nodding. She couldn't see Lellan or Wallace. She prayed Lellan was still with them. Lachlan brought his mouth close to Arabella's ear. "Sutherland warriors ken all the Gaelic names of these mountains in French for this vera reason. The Gunns dinna speak French, but ye ken they speak Gaelic. If I use the mountain's real name, *A' Bhuidheanach Bheag*, they'll ken where we're going. Just hold on, *mo ghaol.*"

"I trust you, *mo ghràidh*," Arabella said against the wind in her face. It was the Gaelic phrase for "my darling."

"Ye'll be a fine Highland lass soon enough." Arabella heard the pride and merriment in Lachlan's voice. The tone sent conflicting emotions through her. She was pleased that he appreciated her attempt, but the good humor terrified her as their daring escape continued. She saw no jocularity in their situation. "Dinna fash. I'm just trying to make ye feel better."

Lachlan's comment came just as her unease grew. She nodded and closed her eyes again. She placed her faith in Lachlan without hesitation. She would believe in him and his battle-hewn skills to keep them alive. An arrow landed too close to the horse's hoof for its comfort, making the steed whinny as it skirted away only to have another land between its front and hind quarters. It reared from fear, and it was only Lachlan's weight on top of Arabella that kept her from slipping.

"Come on, *Spiorad*. Now isnae the time to act scared. Ye'll embarrass yerself in front of yer lady. Let's go, lad. Ye've done this before," Lachlan coaxed his horse, whose name meant "Spirit" in Gaelic. His voice was authoritative yet soothing. Arabella didn't know how it could be both, but even she felt calmer as she listened. The stallion nodded its head and continued its headlong charge. As they climbed, the cloud cover grew denser and surrounded them, giving them a cloak of near-invisibility. Lachlan raised his torso enough to see their surroundings. When no more arrows soared toward him, he looked around.

The other Sutherlands had disappeared, but the

echo of their horses' hoofbeats carried to him. They were in front of him, which made sense to him since their horses only carried a single rider. Lachlan strained to hear anything from behind. With the low visibility, Lachlan knew everyone was moving slower, but he had no desire for his enemy to catch up to him.

"Stay quiet, Belle," Lachlan whispered beside her ear before he dismounted. He grasped his horse's bridle and led it along the rocky ground. He was certain he heard Spiorad breathe a sigh of relief to have only one rider. Lachlan looked back at Arabella, who still laid over the horse's withers but watched Lachlan with wide eyes. They continued their ascent in silence, and soon Lachlan couldn't hear anything around him. That worried him more than if he heard Gunn's army chasing them.

***

The cloud cover opened, and Arabella had a breathtaking view across the Cairngorm Mountain range. While they weren't the tallest mountains she'd heard of, they were still spectacular. As Lachlan's steed lumbered beneath her, she was reminded of the tale she'd read about the North African invader, Hannibal, who marched into Rome with elephants he'd brought through the Alps. She patted Spiorad's neck and said a prayer of thanksgiving that she was on horseback and not elephant back.

They continued in silence for another quarter hour before Lachlan stopped beneath an outcropping of rocks and helped Arabella down from the saddle. They wrapped one another in their arms and embraced, both relieved that their death-defying mountain climb was over. Arabella rested her head against his chest and listened to Lachlan's heartbeat.

The strong, steady, and slow rhythm calmed her own racing heart. Her nerves were still fraught with anxiety, and she longed for a drink despite nearly drowning in a barrel's worth of whisky for two days. A tremble began in her hands as she thought about the taste and the warmth it would provide her against the blustery wind that whipped around the mountaintop.

"Belle?" Lachlan looked down at Arabella. "You're shaking."

"Just chilled," Arabella answered. Lachlan tightened his hold, and it wasn't long before Arabella felt like she was sweltering.

"I ken ye're nae still cold, Belle. What's wrong?" Lachlan pressed. Arabella shook her head and tried to look away, too ashamed of her weakness. "Are ye wishing for a drink?"

Arabella gasped, her embarrassment morphing into humiliation. She tried to step away from Lachlan, but he kept her at his side.

"Belle, I dinna want anyone to see ye. We're protected here, but if ye step out, ye will be a target if anyone is nearby," Lachlan warned. He cupped her face and pressed a kiss to her lips. "Dinna hide from me, *mo ghaol*. I will always find ye. If ye need some space, say so, and I will give it to ye as best I can. But if ye're hiding because ye fear what I will say or do, I dinna want that to come between us."

"It's both," Arabella confessed. "I'm restless and jumpy from the attack, and it's only made worse by how badly I need a drink." She looked away from him. "I hate telling you that, and I despise myself for being so weak. I want to push you away and pull you closer. I don't know what I want."

Lachlan released her but took one hand in his. He brought it to his lips before letting go. He didn't move away, and neither did she, but he wouldn't crowd her. Arabella turned tearful eyes to him, and the look would haunt him for years. She looked nearly as distraught as she had the morning he'd found her sprawled across her bed. "Dinna give up, lass. I never will. Arabella, I need ye too much to lose ye."

Arabella heard the emotion in Lachlan's voice, and the hurt and fear she saw in his eyes confounded her. She never imagined seeing such vulnerability in the man she believed could move mountains if he tried. It wrenched at her heart to know she caused it, but it proved a depth of feeling that his words simply couldn't.

"For you, I won't," Arabella promised.

"It canna just be for me. It has to be for ye too. It has to be what ye want."

"Don't you think I want to be sober? Don't you think I hate myself for who I am?" Arabella hissed. Her temper sparked, and she wanted to lash out at someone, something. The venom in her voice didn't make Lachlan flinch. Her emotions found it patronizing, even while her mind reasoned that he was being the support she needed. Instead of answering her, Lachlan pointed past her.

"Do ye see that mountain? It's *Meall a' Chaorruinn*, or the Hill of the Rowan Tree, and it's a wee more than a mile from here. Badenoch isnae far past it. Just a ways to the northwest. There's a cave in *Meall a' Chaorruinn* that ye will only find if ye ken where to look. We need to pass over the summit of *A' Bhuidheanach Bheag*, and we should find Wallace and the others. If we do, then we'll make for the cave. I'll send the men out to hunt, then down to the village of Dalwhinnie. I dinna think Beathan will think to look there, as the village is easy to miss. George has distant cousins there, and we sometimes stop for the night." Lachlan took Arabella's hands again. "Once we have food in the cave, ye and I will stay while the men are in Dal-whinnie."

"Why?" Arabella's emerald eyes were wide with confusion and apprehension.

"Because ye are going to be vera ill for the next few days as yer body purges its cravings. I dinna want anyone to see ye like that. I would spare ye the em-barrassment. But ye willna be able to travel much longer before ye start feeling poorly. The cave is the safest place within a few days' ride where nay one will notice us. There's a stream near it with fresh wa-ter, and the cave is deep enough that I can build a fire without smoking us out or signaling the Gunns, if they're still in the area."

"What will it be like?" Arabella whispered.

"I dinna ken for sure. I've only heard what hap-pens, and it's different for different people. But ye may feel like ye have a fever, likely throw up, have a headache. Ye will sweat and shiver. Ye willna want to eat for a couple of days. Ye may become vera angry and jumpy. Some people see things that arenae really there," Lachlan explained.

"For how long?" Arabella was terrified to hear the answer.

"The worst may last aboot two or three days. Ye should be on the mend after five or six days, a sen-night at most, I think."

"You think?" Arabella snapped. She covered her mouth and shook her head. "I'm sorry. You already told me you've never witnessed it. I shouldn't treat you like this. Leave me with enough water when we get to the cave, then go with your men."

"Ye're bluidy out of yer heid if ye think I'm going anywhere without ye. And I most certainly amnae bluidy well leaving ye alone. Ye can do us both a favor and put that notion right out of yer bonnie little heid." Lachlan didn't intend to growl at Arabella, but he was growing frustrated.

The past month with Arabella had been little more than one disaster after another. Lachlan was tired. He wanted to be done with the fear for Arabella's wellbeing, the fear of someone taking her from him, the fear of her doing something thoughtless. He wanted nothing more than to have the woman he knew still lurked within Arabella to re-emerge, and he wanted to go home.

"I don't want you to see me like that," Arabella confessed. "I'm scared you'll reach the point where you've had enough, and you can't keep forgiving me."

Lachlan stifled the sigh he nearly released, realizing it would only make Arabella more agitated if she heard him. He knew this was a situation of her own making—to an extent. She was as much a victim as she was to blame. And laying either of those at her feet would get them nowhere.

"What kind of husband would I be if I walked away at the first sign of trouble? Life willna always be easy. I could lose an arm or a leg in battle and be a cripple for the rest of ma life. Ye might have to take care of me like a wee bairn. Will ye leave me if that happens?"

"You know I wouldn't," Arabella shook her head as she spoke.

"Then none of this foolishness. This isnae easy, and this isnae how I hoped our life together would begin, but this is where we find ourselves," Lachlan's gaze bore into hers, daring her to refute what he said.

"When we come out of this on the other side, there will be naught we can't face together," Arabella said.

"Ye have the right of that, lass."

Arabella stilled as she looked up at Lachlan. She

took in the face she knew so well, the physique she was learning, and the steadfastness he always showed. "Thank you."

They were two of the simplest words, but they conveyed so much of how she felt in that moment. Lachlan nodded, then his face eased into one of his boyish smiles that she saw so rarely. She was used to his rakish grins, his brotherly smiles, and his deep rumble of laughter. But the smile she saw now was unlike any of the others. She'd only glimpsed it a few times, and it felt like a secret only she knew. She ran the pad of her thumb over his lips before rising onto her toes. Their foreheads rested together before they exchanged a quick peck. Their lingering look expressed how they both wished for more, but they had a mountain to finish climbing.

THIRTY-THREE

Lachlan held Arabella's hand while the other held his horse's reins. As they crested the summit, they had another expansive view of the land surrounding them. On three sides were more mountain peaks, while to the west the rolling hills of the Highlands stretched before them. Lachlan whistled a bird call, and it was only a moment later that they heard a response. Wallace and his horse seemed to appear from nowhere as Arabella twisted and turned to see where he might have been hiding. The other men appeared too, and a frisky mare nickered and tried to pull away from George.

"Firelight!" Arabella exclaimed. The horse stomped its hoof, nearly landing on George's foot. He released the reins, and Firelight appeared to prance toward Arabella. She wrapped her arms around her horse's neck as she rubbed the long bridge of her horse's nose. Lachlan watched her fondly as she chattered quietly to her horse, promising the animal all the carrots, apples, and sugar she could eat. He motioned his men to come closer, but they knew to stand where all five of them could see Arabella.

"Any sign of the Gunns?" Lachlan asked.

"Nay," George shook his head. "Last we saw, Beathan was bleeding from where I stabbed him. The men with him fell, and he was gushing blood like a bubbling spring."

"We havenae seen hide nor hair of them," Lellan said. Lachlan noticed only a small portion of the arrow protruded from his back. Someone had snapped the shaft. He cradled his left arm across his chest, but he looked as if the wound barely fazed him. He assured Lachlan, "It'll come right. Wallace'll take it out once we are somewhere he can clean and seal it. Aches, but it's nae too deep."

"Do you think Graham and the other men stayed at the base with Beathan?" Lachlan asked.

"Likely," Wallace said. "They dinna ken these hills like we do. I havenae seen any sign of them, so I imagine they're regrouping and planning what to do next."

"I'm taking Lady Arabella to cave in *Meall a' Chaorruinn*. I need ye to hunt enough to last us a sennight. I can take her to the brook, but I dinna want to be away from her as long as it would take to hunt."

Four faces turned toward Arabella. As though she sensed their gazes, she turned around. Four sets of eyes studiously avoided hers. She glanced at Lachlan, but his smile assured her that all was well. She suspected they were discussing her, but Lachlan had to tell his men the truth. They deserved to know the plans that involved them all. She turned back to Firelight.

"Before aught else, ye need to ken Lady Arabella and I are wed. Lady Menzies and Lady Millicent stood as our witnesses. We married by declaration." Lachlan lowered his voice for his next comment. "I have the proof. So nay one can claim she is meant to marry another mon. She is ma legal wife."

While the men kept their voices low, they congratulated Lachlan with warrior handshakes and claps on the back. When Arabella looked back at them again, she had a grin that matched Lachlan's. She continued to talk to Firelight as she walked around her horse, checking the mare's legs and flanks. Lachlan continued explaining to his men what would happen next.

"Ye ken Beathan kept her drunk the entire time he had her, and ye ken she had problems with the drink before that. We're going to *Meall a' Chaorruinn*, so she can recover from her need for whisky. I want her safe and with privacy. Ye will go to Dalwhinnie and wait for us there."

"Lachlan," Wallace shook his head.

"I willna be gainsaid on this, Wall," Lachlan warned.

Wallace stepped closer, and all five men leaned in. "Ye need us closer than that. If Beathan finds ye while she's ill, ye willna be able to move her. Ye canna defend her alone. If she's as ill as ma uncle was when he got off the drink, then ye may need more than one set of hands."

Lachlan knew his friend and guard made sound points, but he didn't want the men in the same space as where he hoped Arabella could fight past her demons. He nodded slowly. "Go to *A' Bhuidheanach*. It's less than a mile from *Meall a' Chaorruinn*, and it's taller than this mountain or *Meall*. Ye'll have a better view of anyone coming or going."

"We can make do there. We'll take shifts, two with ye and two on *A' Bhuidheanach*," Tarran spoke. The quietest of the men, he observed much and spoke little. "If ye dinna want her to ken, she'll have nay idea we're there."

Lachlan shook his head. He wouldn't keep secrets from Arabella. He called out to her, and she gave

Firelight one last stroke between her wide-set eyes. She smiled at the men as she took her place beside Lachlan. He explained the change in plans, and she nodded, softly agreeing that it was wiser for them to stay close together. They were prepared to start walking when Arabella coughed out a nervous laugh.

"If *A' Bhuidheanach Bheag*," Arabella struggled to say. "Means the little girl, does *A' Bhuidheanach* mean the girl or the little?" Arabella asked timidly.

"The girl, ma lady. Ye did vera well with that. They arenae easy names for someone who doesnae speak Gaelic," Wallace offered. Then he grinned. "Yet."

"Aye, yet. I told Lachlan some time back that I would like to learn," Arabella admitted. She looked questioningly when Lachlan snapped at the men in Gaelic, and they laughed riotously. "What?"

"Lachlan told us we canna be the ones to teach ye," Lellan guffawed. "He doesnae trust us nae to teach ye the foulest words first."

"Would you?" Arabella sounded a little too eager, and Lachlan cast her a stunned look. It only made the men laugh harder.

"We shall see, ma lady," Lellan chortled.

George held the reins to Firelight and his own horse while Tarran took Spiorad's reins along with his horse's. Lachlan helped Arabella scramble over the rocks, since she needed at least one hand to lift her skirts out of the way.

"I envy ye yer plaids," Arabella grumbled as she clutched bunches of fabric in her hands before leaping from one boulder to another. The men chuckled while Lachlan explained some benefits of the *breacan feile* that she hadn't realized. He described how he could pull the great plaid's extra length of wool over his head and shoulders if the weather was foul. He explained how getting the wool damp before it rained or snowed helped to keep him dryer. Arabella had never understood why the great plaid, or *breacan feile*, was so long. It made sense to her now as she considered how much of Lachlan's life must have been spent outdoors. He'd spent the better part of the past two months on horseback.

"Dinna fash, *mo chridhe*," Lachlan smiled. "Mama will teach ye to wear an arisaid, and then ye'll have yer own plaid."

Arabella nodded but turned her head to whisper, "Can it be one of your plaids?"

Lachlan looked into her earnest face and realized that having one of his plaids, rather than just any Sutherland, meant a great deal to her. "Ye may have aught ye want. But ye could make two arisaids from one of ma plaids. We need to get some more meat on yer bones, lass."

"I shall ask ye soon enough whether ye think there's enough meat on these bones," Arabella playfully huffed as she mimicked his burr. She sucked her lips in and ducked her head when she realized the others heard what she said and were trying not to laugh. Try as she might, she couldn't contain her own laughter. When she couldn't smother it, the men felt less guilty about joining in. They were a much lighter-hearted group when they reached the cave.

THIRTY-FOUR

Once Lachlan and Arabella were settled into the cave with waterskins filled from the nearby stream and several rabbits and squirrels for their coming meals, the Sutherland warriors left the couple alone. Arabella didn't know who stood watch or when they changed, but it reassured her to know that there were others nearby and not all the responsibility fell on Lachlan's shoulders. She'd remained quiet during the rest of their walk to the cave because a pounding headache had begun behind her eyes. She hoped that water and dim light would help, but she recognized the pain for what it was. The beginning of her withdrawal. Throughout the first night, Arabella alternated sweating and shivering. Lachlan soothed her as best he could, but he was mainly a quiet figure who tended to her as best he could.

As the first night moved into the second day, Arabella ran to the mouth of the cave several times, heaving over and over, but there was little to purge. Her belly cramps and the need to vomit only made her headache worse. She felt herself growing short-tempered, and she longed to have a drink. Her body craved it as much as her mind. She wanted to slip away from the misery she and Lachlan endured. When she wasn't standing at the cave's entrance, she huddled near the fire. Lachlan moved around on silent feet or sat near her. When she needed his comfort, he moved closer. When she grew restless and fidgety, he gave her space. Throughout their ordeal, Arabella fought against the tears that threatened. She refused to indulge in self-pity, since she reasoned she had no one but herself to blame for her condition.

It was their third night in the cave, and Arabella woke to find herself sweating profusely. She was certain she smelled whisky. She sniffed, and her mind urged her to investigate. She sat up, finding Lachlan still sleeping next to her. Or at least, pretending to sleep. He'd been gracious about giving her privacy when she needed to relieve herself, as long as she remained where he could see at least the top of her head. He wouldn't embarrass her by making it known that he was aware she moved around.

She stood and continued to sniff, but no matter where she went, she smelled whisky but found none. She knew that Lachlan had none with him because she'd pulled all the contents from their bags during one of her angry outbursts. As she moved around the cave, she pulled off the extra plaid Lachlan gave her for when she had the chills. With the men out of sight, at least to her, she'd given up and stripped down to her chemise. She tugged at the neckline, feeling as though the light garment was strangling her.

When she'd swept through the entire crave, her frustration grew until she wanted to throw or break something. She tucked her chin and inhaled, trying to calm herself. As she did, she caught the strongest scent of whisky yet. She turned her head from side-to-side as she inhaled. She realized she was what smelled like whisky. She didn't know if she imagined it or if she was sweating out whatever lingered in her system. She turned back toward the fire, prepared to give up and settle back against Lachlan's broad frame. She stopped short and released a short, high pitched scream. Lachlan was on his feet and running to her before she stopped. She waved her hands at him as it to tell him to stop.

"Lach, no! They'll bite you!" Arabella screamed. Lachlan continued to run toward her as she trembled.

"What will?" Lachlan asked as he wrapped his arms around her. Her entire body shook like an autumn leaf waiting to break away from its branch.

"Those." Arabella pointed to the ground, but there was nothing there but stone and dirt. "The adders. Don't you see them? You ran through them. How did none bite you?"

Lachlan looked at the ground, then back to Arabella. He knew she was hallucinating. When she tried to pull away and back toward the cave's mouth, Lachlan walked with her.

"Don't you see them?" Arabella demanded. But before Lachlan could respond, she writhed and swept her hands over her arms as though she were scraping something off them. "Spiders!"

Arabella pushed at Lachlan's chest, and he released her. She twisted and twitched like an entranced pagan priestess as she tried to knock the invisible bugs from her arms. She ran her fingers into her hair and shook it as though the infestation would fall from her locks.

"Ants, spiders," Arabella gasped. "Get them off me. Get them off!"

Lachlan's attention was on Arabella until he caught a movement from the corner of his eye. George and Lellan stood at the entrance to the cave. Lachlan shook his head and shooed them away. They disappeared just as quickly as they had appeared. Lachlan lifted Arabella into his arms, and despite her flailing, carried her to the stream. He assumed his men were a discreet distance from them and not watching, but he didn't take the time to investigate. He stripped Arabella's chemise off her and yanked off her boots. She hadn't bothered to wear stockings in days. He lifted her again and waded into the brook, boots and plaid still on.

"Shh, Belle," Lachlan crooned. "We'll wash them away."

He eased her into the water until her shoulders were nearly submerged while he held her in a seated position. She splashed water over herself, but she continued to scratch and whimper.

"Lach!" George called from behind him. Lachlan turned his head to see his guard and scowled. George held out his hand. "Take the soap. Let her think ye are washing them away."

George tossed a bar of soap to Lachlan, and he nodded his thanks. George scrambled out of the water and faded back into the boulders. Lachlan ran the soap over Arabella's arms and shoulders, watching as she calmed. In the few minutes that had passed since her visions began, she'd scratched deep lines into her arms and neck. He would dress her in a spare leine to keep her from inflicting more harm if the hallucinations continued.

"Tip yer head back, *mo ghaol*. I'll wash yer hair," Lachlan offered. Arabella unexpectedly shoved at Lachlan's chest so hard that she toppled from his arms with a splash.

"No! Don't touch me. Don't ever touch me. Your fingers. They're worms. You're trying to hurt me. Get away, Lach," Arabella ranted. Lachlan curled his hands into fists, hiding his fingers, and raised them in surrender.

"I'll stay here, just to be certain you dinna float away," Lachlan offered. Arabella jerked her head in agreement before dipping below the surface. She came up spluttering and looking around wildly. She stood up unthinkingly, not remembering that Lachlan's men must be nearby. She glanced around wildly before meeting Lachlan's eyes.

"Lach? They're all gone," she stammered as she stumbled toward him. Lachlan didn't move. He was prepared to catch her if she tripped, but he didn't reach for her. She took in his raised fists and shuddered. "They were never really there, were they?"

"Nay, little one. There was naught here or in the cave to hurt ye," Lachlan whispered.

"I—I thought your—your fingers—I told you to —to go a—away," Arabella stuttered between sobs. "I p—p—pushed you." The tears she'd repressed for days became wrenching sobs, but still Lachlan didn't move. He was uncertain what to do. He wanted nothing more than to hold her, but he feared making her trauma worse. She made the decision for him, when she lurched forward, his chest catching her as she pulled his arms down and around her.

"What's wrong with me?" She sobbed.

"Naught but drying out from the whisky. I feared ye might start seeing things, but I amnae surprised. I only feared it for how it would upset ye," Lachlan explained.

"But the things I keep saying. It's as though my mouth starts moving before my mind knows what it's going to do. I'm so sorry," Arabella's voice trailed off to a whisper.

"I ken, Belle. I ken this isnae easy for ye, and ye are brave to be doing it. This is why I kenned we needed to leave court and why we needed the cave."

"How did you know?" Arabella leaned back to look at Lachlan. He sighed but smiled gently.

"I'll tell ye everything, but ye shall grow cold out here. Do ye wish to wash yer hair? Finish bathing if ye wish, then let's go back to the fire," Lachlan suggested. Arabella nodded and squatted in the water. She was quick, scrubbing the soap into her hair, then dipping back under the water to wash it out. When she finished her toilette, Lachlan stripped his leine off. When she was done, Lachlan lifted her onto the bank, and she donned his shirt. He used the extra length of plaid to wrap around her as he carried her back to the cave. She held her boots in one hand as the other played with the hair at his nape. Arabella gasped when she noticed George inside their temporary shelter. He stood, stoking the fire.

"Wanted to be sure it was warm enough for ye, ma lady," George said as he tossed the stick into the fire. He wiped his hands against each other and made to walk to the entrance.

"Thank you," Arabella stated. She asked Lachlan to put her down before she walked toward George. "Thank you for tending the fire, and thank you for the soap. It didn't register with me at first, but I ken you brought it and gave it to Lachlan for me. Thank you and my thanks to the others. You are sacrificing a lot for me, and I've hardly made it easy. Please know that I appreciate each of you." Arabella stuck out her hands, and George gently clasped them but shot a glance at Lachlan, who nodded. Arabella squeezed his hands before letting them drop.

"I'll tell the others, ma lady," George bowed before hurrying out of the cave.

"Did I make him uncomfortable?" Arabella asked. She wasn't certain what to make of his responding smile.

"Aye, but ye made him feel good too. George likes the ladies as long as the ladies dinna like to talk aboot feelings. Lellan is a charmer and doesnae listen to aught but nods, so women think he's sweet on them. Tarran is rather brooding and quieten, but from what I've heard, women——-" Lachlan put his hands up in front of him as if he didn't know what to say, but his grin said everything. "Wallace married a woman he's loved since he was a lad. Took him years to convince her to marry him, but now she'd flay anyone alive who said aught against him."

Arabella nodded as she walked to the fire. She patted the spot beside her, and Lachlan sat down. She lifted his heavy arm and draped it around her as she burrowed closer. Lachlan kissed her forehead, then her lips. Arabella's arms wrapped around his waist and neck as she welcomed his affection and passion. When they pulled apart, Arabella rested her head against Lachlan's chest. The rumble when he began speaking soothed her.

"Ye asked how I ken. There is much Da has taught me over the years kenning one day I will be laird. He's told me a great deal aboot people's different natures. He's told me signs to look for, both the ones I can see and the ones I canna. He told me aboot how his older brothers and father used to drink too much. Da explained some of the reasons why people turn to whisky, and he told me what his brothers and father were like when they were drunk. They werenae always violent toward Aunt Kyla, but they were cruel with the things they said. According to Da, half the time they couldnae remember what they said, and the other half they pretended to be repentant. We've had people from time to time in the clan who drink too much. Mostly men. And they mostly pick fights with other men. A few have made the error of turning their fists on women. Da doesnae tolerate any of that. He saw what his father did to Aunt Kyla, and he has never stopped blaming himself for nae intervening. Now, he intervenes on behalf of any woman in our clan who is mistreated or receives threats of mistreatment. Few men make that mistake, and those who do, only do it once."

Arabella nodded as she listened. She'd met Hamish Sutherland several times over the years, and as she became better friends with Lachlan's sisters and fell more in love with him, she often envied the two sisters and brother the relationship they had with Hamish. She wished he were her father. What she knew of their mother Amelia made her want to become part of their family, if for no other reason than to have two loving and kind parents. Her own mother wasn't as sharp-tongued and belligerent as her father; instead, she was indifferent. As Arabella grew older, her mother only took an interest in dressing her up and parading her around like a doll. She could still hear her mother's words in her head. *Well-brought up young ladies have poise and grace. Only the uncouth act like peasants, or worse, Highlanders.* Arabella shifted her attention back to Lachlan after he paused to kiss her forehead again.

"Wallace told us aboot how his uncle handled coming off the drink. He's explained more to me while ye've been sleeping. He warned me that ye might see things, even hear things. He warned me nae to believe things ye say in anger because ye arenae yerself. The need for whisky takes over yer mind and yer body, makes ye do things ye never would. It messes with yer heid," Lachlan explained, tapping his temple.

"Did Wallace's uncle survive? Did he stop drinking?" Arabella wondered.

"Aye. Apparently, this happened when we were lads, but Wallace says he remembers it vividly. His uncle stayed with them while Wallace's mother tended to him because she's his sister. Wallace said his father nearly murdered him after his uncle swung at Wallace's mother while seeing visions. It was only his mother's threat to leave him that made Wallace's father back down." Lachlan shook his head as he wiped the silent tears from Arabella's cheeks. He knew she was riddled with guilt and remorse. "I ken Wallace's uncle as the mon who taught me how to care for ma horse. He's the stable master and has a way with animals I've never seen the like of."

"Lach, even if you kenned what to expect, I still feel horrible for the things I've said. I'm sorry I'm putting you through this. I never imagined when I started sneaking a sip here and there that it would ever get so bad."

"This wouldnae have been pleasant regardless, but Beathan's mistreating ye made this far worse. We're lucky he didna poison ye with all that alcohol."

"Thank you for still loving me," Arabella gazed into the brown eyes that she adored. "Do you ken, your eyes are the same color as aged whisky? I think I will be very happy to look into your eyes any time I think of it. I prefer you to it, anyway."

Lachlan's gentle touch trailed along her temple and past her ear until his fingers slipped around her nape. Their kiss was languid as they indulged in their first chance for intimacy since they left Comrie Castle. Arabella had been too unwell for either of them to think about making love.

"You said I can tell you anytime I wish for us to join," Arabella murmured, and Lachlan nodded. "I would very much like to do that right now. Can we?"

Lachlan's soft chuckle blew his warm breath against her ear, making her shiver. "Ye dinna have to ask, *mo ghaol*. Ye should tell me. Do ye remember I said I expect a demanding wife?"

Arabella laid back until her back and head were on the ground. As she reclined, she curled her finger in a beckoning motion. He followed her down, pushing his leine high up her thigh as Arabella lifted his plaid. Lachlan's hand glided over the satiny skin of her outer thigh as she bent her leg.

"I want to see you. All of you," Arabella said with command, but her smile made it difficult to take her seriously. Lachlan pulled back onto his knees and unbuckled his belt. He teased her as he slowly unraveled his plaid. She stuck her tongue out at him when she grew impatient and stripped off his leine. A glimpse of her naked body made Lachlan forget about taunting her. His plaid landed beside them.

Arabella stared up at him once she laid back again. She'd never imagined a man's body could be as magnificent as Lachlan's. She'd always assumed that they would be hairy and coarse all over, feeling more like the bristles from a man's beard. Lachlan's body was smooth, each muscle showing as he kneeled above her and raked his eyes over her. When he moved, the muscles bunched and rippled, showing his strength and belying the gentleness he used. Arabella knew his greater size and strength could crush her, and yet he handled her as though she were more precious than gold. His gaze now was reverent as his fingers trailed between her breasts until his palm swept over her belly. It slid back up her ribs until he cupped her breast. He lowered himself to take her nipple into his mouth. He squeezed gently as he opened his mouth wider, once more devouring her. She'd always been secretly envious of Maude's ample endowments. She relied on Eliza cinching her kirtle especially tight over her shoulder blades to hold her breasts higher and to make them look fuller. But as Lachlan's eyes drifted close, and Arabella could see the pleasure he took in lavishing his attention on one then the other, she no longer feared they were too small.

Arabella slipped her hand between them, cupping his bollocks and rolling them in her hand. It was the first time she'd explored the sack she'd seen hanging between his legs. When he groaned and pressed his hips upward, she knew he enjoyed her touch. She eased her other hand between them and wrapped it around his rod. With both hands, she worked him until his hips seemed to move of their own accord. With a suddenness she didn't expect, Lachlan rolled them over so that she straddled him.

"Like this, ye control how we make love. Ye can set the pace and what ye want," Lachlan explained as his hands lifted her. She reached down and guided his sword to her sheath. She looked questioningly at Lachlan, and he nodded. His hands rested on her thighs as she eased her body down as her core consumed his length. She didn't move as she adjusted to the new feeling of fullness. It differed from the first time they made love, but she was just as uncertain. She lifted and lowered herself on his length before testing out rocking her hips like she had when he was on top. She found she could manage a combination of the two, and her body began to hum.

"Lach, this feel so—different—so good but different," Arabella said.

"I ken," Lachlan grunted.

"Ye feel even bigger," Arabella said with awe. "Or mayhap it's just deeper. But I can't imagine how since I thought you would rend me in two the last time, and I was certain you could reach all the way to my heart."

Lachlan groaned, her words both exciting him and making him melt. Her tone was a mixture of surprise and wistfulness. As she leaned forward to kiss him, he wrapped his arms around her, his hands able to touch his opposite shoulder since her figure was so slight compared to his hulking upper body.

"I like it when you hold me like this," Arabella

whispered. "You make me feel tiny and protected." She reached behind her and pulled one of his arms down until she could find his hand. She guided it to her bottom and pressed it until he squeezed. She pushed her hips back, her sheath swallowing him whole. He ground his hips into her pubic bone, and she felt the beginnings of the twinge she knew led to release.

"And you make me feel desired, but not just with lust. With love too," Arabella murmured.

"Because ye are. I love ye nay matter what. When ye're strong and when ye're vulnerable. When ye look yer bonniest and when—ye dinna," Lachlan grinned. Arabella caught his chin between her thumb and fingers and pressed a relentless kiss to his mouth. Their movement become more frenzied as the time for sharing their feelings and teasing was over. Arabella felt the early twinges of her release and moaned. Lachlan held her and let her guide them at her pace. Her inner muscle tightened around him as she moaned her climax.

"Roll over," she panted. "Want to see your shoulders."

Lachlan looked confused, but he did as she wanted. He watched as her eyes lit up as her hands ran over his shoulders. He could feel his muscles flexing with each surge of his cock into her, and he realized that seeing him move above her aroused her even more. The gleam in her eyes was pure feminine hunger.

"More," Arabella demanded.

"Nay. Ye're still new to this. I dinna want to hurt ye, little one," Lachlan worried.

Arabella shook her head. "Please. I want—" Arabella struggled to find the words she needed. She wanted him to lose control, to show how much he desired her with an abandonment that edged on rough. After what they'd been through, she needed to feel he still wanted her as fiercely as she wanted him. She didn't doubt his words for a moment, but as her mind needed the words, her body need the motion.

"Ye want to feel just how much I need ye," Lachlan supplied. Arabella nodded. "Then promise me to tell me if it's too much."

Arabella nodded again, but her eyes slid shut as her heart thundered beneath her breastbone. Lachlan's movements were without finesse, just pure unadulterated, nearly savage, instinct. Arabella's body met every thrust and every surge, their motions melding together as though they'd been making love for a lifetime already.

"Lach!" Arabella cried out as pleasure overtook her. The waves of release washed over her, leaving her boneless and out of breath as Lachlan thrust thrice more before bellowing her name.

"Belle!" Lachlan rolled them over with a speed that made Arabella squeak, but he knew he couldn't support his weight much longer. He didn't want to crush her, but neither did he want to pull away. They lay together, panting and their bodies glistening with sweat. Lachlan caressed a lazy hand over her back as Arabella nuzzled his neck. They both laid with their eyes closed as they fought to catch their breath. Lachlan felt around for his plaid and draped it over them before they both fell asleep.

THIRTY-FIVE

Arabella blinked as she came awake. She couldn't understand how she was shivering while sweat poured from her hairline. She looked around and couldn't decide if she wanted to throw off the plaid that covered her or add more layers. She opted for both, or at least trading the woolen plaid for Lachlan's linen leine. She pulled the shirt toward her but froze as a frog hopped out from beneath it. She snatched the leine from the ground, shaking it out and watching one frog after another fall from it until there were at least a dozen beady-eyed toads staring at her. She reached over to Lachlan and shook him, never taking her eyes off the animals. She kept shaking Lachlan, but he didn't budge. Struggling to her feet, she pulled the leine on but then shuddered as she thought about the amphibians using it as their nest. She shook from fear and revulsion as she backed away.

"Arabella! Belle!" Lachlan yelled as he lunged to wrap his arm around Arabella's thighs, lifting her off the ground and rolling away from the fire. She'd nearly walked backwards into the flames.

Lachlan watched as she stared toward the back of the cave with sightless eyes. He realized that she was in the throes of a nightmare or hallucinating once again, possibly both. He shook her shoulder, but her attention never turned toward him. She sat quietly for a moment, and Lachlan relaxed. Suddenly, she grasped a handful of dirt and threw it toward the back of the cavern. Next came a handful of pebbles that sprayed across the width of the cave, the sound of them hitting the walls creating an echo.

"Belle? What do ye see?" Lachlan asked calmly, even though his heart hammered.

"Toads. So many toads," Arabella whispered.

"Shh. Come lie next to me. Did ye ken they go away if ye dinna move?" Lachlan soothed as he tried to guide her to lie next to him. He felt trapped, not knowing if he should keep her away from the side where she believed the frogs sat or away from the nearby fire.

"No. They'll hop all over us. They'll give us warts! And they're so slimy. We have to go. We have to go," Arabella sobbed. It was the middle of the night, and Lachlan wasn't about to take Arabella into the mountains in her semi-lucid state.

"Look at me, Belle," Lachlan crooned. He waited to see if she could see him yet. When she turned her head, her eyes were vacant like they had been a moment ago. He suspected she'd been dreaming at first, but the false visions continued even now that she was awake. "Look at me, *mo chridhe*."

He ran his hand over her leg and backside as she laid on her side. His hand slipped under the leine until he could slide his hand up her back. She released a shuddering breath as he continued to sooth her. His hand alternated between gentle circles and long sweeps from her shoulders to her backside. When his hand slowed, then cupped her backside, she wriggled closer to him. Lachlan was torn. He knew how he could distract her, but he feared she'd see it as him taking advantage of her when she finally came round. He slid his hand to the top of her thigh, letting his fingers drift between her legs. When she moaned, he eased his fingers along her seam.

"Belle, they aren't there anymore," Lachlan promised. "We're safe. I promise."

Arabella tried to prop herself up on an elbow and look over Lachlan's shoulders, but she dropped back down and huddled against him. "They are still there. They're watching us."

"No, little one. I won't let them come near you. Shh. Think about where my hands are, how I'm touching you. Don't think aboot them." Lachlan rolled Arabella onto her back and drew his hand up and down her leg. As his fingers drew higher, he could see her arousal glistening in the firelight. He closed his eyes and steeled himself against temptation as his cock throbbed. He pressed the flat of his hand over her mound, his fingers traveling over her nether lips but not dipping within. His palm and the heel of his hand trailed over her nub, and she shifted restlessly

"Did they go away," Arabella asked.

"Aye, ma sweet lass. They're gone," Lachlan assured her.

"Are you certain? Let me see." Arabella tried to sit up, but Lachlan used it to press a kiss to her lips as he blocked her view. As he gazed into her eyes, he noticed her pupils were back to their normal size, and she didn't seem disoriented anymore.

"Belle, what do you feel?" Lachlan asked softly as they pulled apart.

"You. You kissed me."

"Aught else?" Lachlan pressed. He watched Arabella's brow furrow. He added pressure to his hand as he continued to rub her mons. She looked down at his hand, confusion clear on her face.

"Lach? What're you doing?" Arabella whispered as her legs moved apart, a silent offering.

"Distracting you," Lachlan answered.

"From what?" Arabella's eyes flew open, and she sat up so abruptly that she narrowly missed crashing her head into Lachlan's. "I remember. I thought there were frogs everywhere."

Lachlan didn't move. He waited for her to continue, but she turned a questioning expression to him, as though she didn't trust her recollection. "Ye did. But I swear there werenae any."

"Like earlier with the adders and bugs," Arabella said morosely.

"Aye. I think ye were having a nightmare, and ye only woke up part of the way. Ye were still seeing things when ye stood up. Ye almost walked into the fire," Lachlan explained slowly, gauging her response to each of his words.

"And now?" She waved her hand toward his where it rested on her thatch of curls.

"I rubbed yer back, and now I'm touching yer thighs and yer cunny," Lachlan spoke the truth. "Aught to distract ye and bring ye back to me."

"Would you have coupled with me while I didn't know what's happening?" Arabella demanded. She wasn't sure how she felt about what she discovered.

"Nay. I will never take advantage of ye, and I willna ever force ye. But I will do whatever I can think of to make ye feel better, to keep ye with me and nae lost to the recesses of yer mind." Lachlan's voice held an edge he didn't mean to have. "I didna do more than what ye can feel now. It brought ye round, and ye arenae terrified of toads attacking us. If ye were still hallucinating, I wouldnae have gone further. I would have dumped ye in the stream before raping ye, Arabella."

Arabella's eyes widened as she really gave

thought for the first time to how this experience was affecting Lachlan. She nodded her head and swallowed. She stroked his arm as she gazed into his eyes, really seeing the depth of his pain for the first time. She slid her hand up to cup his cheek as she pressed a soft kiss to his mouth before resting her forehead against his. She felt the shuddering breath he took.

"Lach, I know you ken I don't want to be like this, that I regret what I've done. I think you ken how grateful I am." Arabella dropped her hand and moved to sit crossed legged. She needed to keep her concentration on what she said, and touching Lachlan made that impossible. "I know this isn't what you ever imagined, and I feel guilty aboot that. It's why I've told you to leave more than once. But each of those times, it was really more aboot how I felt. I realize that now. I know you love me enough that you won't go anywhere. But I need you to know that I'm realizing how much this must hurt you. I never, *ever* imagined I could put you through something like this. I would never have touched a drop of whisky if I could have foreseen how you would suffer, too."

Arabella shifted, realizing that she didn't think as well as she assumed when she wasn't touching Lachlan. She unfurled her legs, inching her way to sit between his before draping hers over his thighs. She took his hands and wove their fingers together.

"Everything you've done since you returned to court, everything you've ever done where I'm concerned, has been for my good. I just questioned your honor, and I shouldn't have. Not if I say I trust you. I have to mean those words. I know the mon you are, Lach. I know you have limits, lines you would never cross. But I know you'll do anything and everything to help me. I can't promise I'll never question you again, but I can promise I'll never question my faith in you or your integrity."

"I willna lie," Lachlan sighed. "This isnae easy. It pains me to see ye suffering and nae being able to do aught to end it. I'm frustrated and I feel helpless. I confess, I am still a wee angry at ye for some of yer choices, even if I understand why ye made them. But that anger still comes from fear. Since returning to court, I have lived in constant fear of losing ye. Losing ye to whisky, losing ye to a bluidy prison, losing ye to a convent, losing ye to Beathan. I'm worn thin, Arabella. But there will always be just enough of me that I willna break. I will always be at yer side."

"I don't ken how you can be so strong. I ken it's not just because you're a mon. There are far lesser men than you. Mayhap it's because you're a Sutherland. Or mayhap it's just because you are you. But I ken our gracious and merciful God blessed me when He sent you into my life. I never want to take that for granted again."

"We'll get through this together, Belle. If it hasnae broken us yet, then naught will," Lachlan swore.

"Isnae that endearing?" Beathan Gunn sneered as he stood at the mouth of the cave. Behind him stood men trying to wrangle and restrain the four Sutherland guards. "Thought we'd give up? Nae bluidy likely. Ye might have lost us for a day or two, but ye canna disappear. Now the lass is mine, and ye will die."

Arabella and Lachlan scrambled off the ground. Arabella instinctively moved behind Lachlan, who reached for the sword propped against a rock nearby. Arabella looked around, but it was hard to see in the dim light behind Lachlan. She had two thoughts: get dressed and get into the back of the cave. She felt around in the dark until she found the satchel that held her filthy and tattered but still serviceable gown. When she'd donned the gown at Cromie Castle, it had relieved her to discover her knife was still in the hidden pocket. Lachlan had encouraged her to continue wearing the thigh strap that carried her other knife. While she hadn't been wearing it since they arrived at the cave, she intended to not take it off again until they reached Dunrobin. She fished it out of the satchel. As Lachlan and Beathan exchanged words, taunting and insulting one another. Belle slipped into the back of the cave. She fumbled in the dark, but she soon had the dirk strapped to her leg and her gown on, even if the laces weren't tied.

"Enough!" Beathan snapped. "Grab the lass and bring the bastard with us."

Arabella remained tucked in the shadows, but she crouched and found a rock for each hand. She watched in horror, as two men swung their swords at Lachlan. He blocked them with ease, but while the first two engaged Lachlan, two more slipped around him and came for her. When she could make out the silhouette of the first man's head, she launched the rock in her right hand. It hit him squarely in the face.

"Fucking whore broke ma bluidy nose," the man yelled. "That's it. I dinna care whether ye live or die."

"I do, ye eejit," Beathan called. "A dead daughter doesnae get us a dowry. Keep her alive until her dowry arrives. Then I dinna care what happens to her."

The man whose nose she broke stomped toward her. She gathered another rock before she backed away further. When her back hit a wall, she knew there was nowhere left for her to go. When he reached out to grab her arm, she smashed one of the rocks into the side of his head. She launched the other at the man who followed him. She evaded the stunned men, running toward Lachlan as she reached into her pocket. She kept her hand wrapped around the hilt but didn't draw it. She wouldn't let any of the Gunns see she was armed unless she had to use the knife. Arabella hadn't seen three more men advance on Lachlan. A wall protected his back, but he now fought off five men. Arabella knew it was only a matter of time before two or more well-timed swings would cut him down.

"Stop! I'll go. Leave Lachlan alive, and I will go. Beathan, if you kill him, the Sutherlands, Sinclairs, and Mackays will massacre your people. You know I'm not exaggerating. If they don't kill every last one of them, they will run them off the land like the Campbells did the MacGreggors or harry you like the Bruce did the Comyns. You will not survive this, Beathan. Leave him, and I'll leave with you."

Arabella pulled away from the men who tried to restrain her, walking toward Beathan on her own. As she passed, Lachlan, she kept her voice low and said in French, "I know you will come for me. Just don't get yourself killed in the meantime. He won't kill me until he knows he'll get my dowry. He can't know that until he tells my father he has me. He's been in these hills too. He couldn't have told him, and no messenger will have reached my father yet."

Lachlan responded, "*Je vais chercher mon père. Nous allons chercher nos cousins. Son donjon est plus au nord que le nôtre. Les autres viendront.*" He told her, "I'm going for my father. We'll fetch our cousins. His keep is further north than either of ours. The others will come."

Arabella understood "the others" were the Mackays. Beathan Gunn had just unleashed a clan war that he couldn't hope to survive. Through marriage, the Sinclairs were tied to the Mackenzies, and the Sutherlands were connected to the MacLeods and

Camerons. Most of the northern Highlands would soon descend upon the Gunns' doorstep. There was no chance to say more before a man shoved Arabella toward Beathan. He wrapped his arm around the back of her neck and tipped her backwards, so he could kiss her. Arabella jabbed her fingers into his eyes and stumbled backwards as he released her.

"Ye will rue the day ye did that," Beathan barked.

"No more than I rue the day my father heard your name," Arabella spat back. Beathan snagged a fistful of her hair and pushed her toward the mouth of the cave. She fought against his hold and managed to look back at Lachlan. She nodded as best she could, and he returned it. Arabella feared the Sutherlands might run their horses into the ground, but they would travel faster than the Gunns. She just had to keep herself alive long enough for Lachlan to rescue her. Again.

THIRTY-SIX

Lachlan had never ridden so hard as he had for the past four days. For the first two days, he and his men rode parallel to the Gunns, taking turns riding ahead to scout their nemesis' progress. But they were forced to pull ahead, so he could reach Dunrobin with time to ready his clan. It should have taken the Sutherlands six days to travel from the mountains to their home, but they rode through the nights and only stopped when they feared they would kill their horses if they didn't. When they reached Dornoch Firth, Tarran and Wallace broke off and rode to Castle Varrich to seek the Mackays' help. It was nearly an eight days' ride from the Cairngorms to the northern coast, but Lachlan knew his men would continue to push themselves and their horses, just like he, Lellan, and George did. It would be another three days from Varrich to Clyth. It was likely that any battle between the Gunns and the Sutherlands would be over, but Lachlan couldn't be certain. He knew his cousin Mairghread would geld her husband Tristan if the laird didn't ride out, and he knew Tristan would be on horseback the moment he saw Sutherlands approaching.

It was a day's ride north from Dunrobin to reach the Sinclairs at Dunbeath, and just a little more than half a day's ride further north to Clyth. He prayed his father and their army could make it to the Sinclairs in time to stop and ask for their help before the Gunns traveled past. In Lachlan's mind, the most ideal scenario would be to catch the Gunns as they passed close to Dunbeath, but he would track Beathan to Clyth, if he had to.

Lachlan had never been so happy to see his home as he was when he crested the last hill. He and his two guards clattered into the bailey as his parents stepped out of the keep. The bells ringing alerted his clan to his return. He leaped from Spiorad's back before the horse came to a stop. He sprinted to his parents and didn't bother with a greeting.

"We need to talk," Lachlan said as soon as his parents could hear him without yelling. "Beathan has Arabella."

Without a word, Hamish and Amelia turned to lead the way to Hamish's solar. Once they were behind the closed door, Lachlan explained. As he watched his parents' faces, he realized it didn't surprise them to learn that he loved Arabella. He saw a flash of hurt in his mother's eyes as he told his parents about his impromptu wedding. While he spoke rapidly and without unnecessary detail, he recounted everything that led to Beathan kidnapping Arabella a second time. Guilt nipped at the back of his mind for telling Arabella's secret without asking her first, but he had to be honest with his parents. If he would risk the lives of the clan's warriors, his parents had to know what they faced.

"I'll have food packed and fresh clothes in yer saddlebags," Amelia said as she rose. She leaned forward and kissed Lachlan's cheek. "I'm glad to see ye son, and ye ken I worry for ye, but I have faith in ye."

Amelia squeezed his shoulder as she rushed out of the solar. Lachlan turned to look at his father, who had risen too. He watched the man he most admired and trusted above all others pull open a drawer to his desk. Hamish lifted out a box and flipped the lid open. Inside lay two matching dirks. They had been a gift from Robert the Bruce for Hamish's service to him during the Wars of Independence.

In recent years, the Sutherlands hadn't seen too many conflicts. When warriors rode out, as Hamish's tánaiste, Lachlan usually led the way while Hamish remained at the keep. But when they rode to the Camerons a couple months earlier, Hamish gave Lachlan one of the dirks. There was a silent and sacred bond between father and son as they carried the matching set of weapons. As they prepared to ride into battle, Hamish held out Lachlan's dirk. Both men sheathed their dirks into their belts. Without a word, the men embraced, both praying that they returned together just as they left together.

Arabella gritted her teeth as Beathan attempted to push the waterskin into her mouth that she knew he'd filled with whisky. She hadn't suffered for days only to have her progress undone by even the slightest drop of alcohol. As Beathan's fist swung toward her, she feared he would win if he knocked out all of her teeth. She dodged away from him, his fist swinging through air where her head had been a moment ago. He grabbed her hair and pulled until her back bent like a bow. He plowed his fist into her belly, making her mouth open as she gasped. He was quick and poured whisky into her mouth, but he didn't anticipate Arabella spitting it back at him. He released her as his hands went to his face, trying to wipe away the alcohol that burned his eyes.

"Yer days are limited, bitch," Beathan grunted.

"Do you like being laird?" Arabella asked with sickly sweetness. Her question caught Beathan off guard. He narrowed his watering eyes at her. "If you do, then you'll need to stay alive. Hurt me, and there is no way you will live. If it isn't Lachlan who kills you, it will Laird Sutherland or one of his men. Mayhap it'll be Laird Sinclair, or Callum, or Tavish, or Alex, or Magnus. Don't forget Laird Mackay is likely to show up. So may Laird Cameron and Laird MacLeod. If they miss the fight, I'm certain their pish will water the flowers on your grave."

Beathan seethed as he leaned closer to her face, thinking his size would intimidate her. Arabella was sober and refused to cower before him. She'd welcomed the chance to hide from reality when he plied her with whisky the last time. But now she refused to cower or run away, even if it was only in her mind.

"Think what the king will have to say when he learns you've stolen me not once, but twice, from the man he granted permission for me to marry. Do you think what you want supersedes the king's wishes? That is what he will think you believe when he hears of this. And how will the queen react in her fragile condition when she learns of what has befallen one of her longest serving and most loyal attendants? I can only imagine what she will say to the king. Imagine how he will feel with a pregnant and irate wife. I doubt he will forgive you for that alone."

Arabella grinned as she continued to provoke Beathan. She knew it wasn't the wisest course of action, but as long as she was talking, it meant he wasn't pouring whisky into her.

"Have you told your clan where you wish to be buried? Do you have a spot already picked out? Or is there a family tomb? Och, we're in the Highlands. Mayhap a family cairn? If you haven't thought aboot that yet, this would be a good time. You don't have much longer to decide."

"Shut yer gob, wench," Beathan snapped.

Gladly since a mouth shut is a mouth without whisky.

Arabella cast him a speculative glance, as though she was thinking about what to say next. Beathan grunted and stomped away. She swept her eyes around the camp they'd made less than an hour earlier. They'd been traveling for five days, and she suspected they had to be drawing near Dunrobin from what she remembered Lachlan telling her. She assumed Beathan wouldn't expect Lachlan to arrive at his home before the Gunns passed it. She also assumed they would give Dunrobin a wide berth. She wondered if Lachlan had been successful in reaching his home yet.

Of course, he has. He and his father will have ridden out already. They must be close to the Sinclairs by now. They will be ready. I ken it.

As Arabella continued to look around, her hand rested on the outside of her pocket where she could feel the outline of her knife. As she shifted her weight, she rubbed her thighs together, and the dirk strapped to her leg gave her a sense of reassurance. She thanked God over and over that no man had searched her, and since she remained unmolested, none had discovered the weapon beneath her skirts. Plenty of the Gunn men ogled her, but none dared make any advances, knowing Beathan claimed her.

She'd reminded him more than once that not only had she and Lachlan married, but there was already the chance that she carried his heir. He'd threatened to murder Lachlan, then marry her. She'd tapped her chin and asked, "will you mind if it's Lachlan's son who becomes your clan's next laird? I mean, if you bed me now, you'll never ken if the lad is yours or Lachlan's. Can you imagine if it is Lachlan's? Then he would be laird to both the Sutherlands and the Gunns. Can your clan get used to being called Sutherland?"

Beathan had spewed curses in Gaelic that she didn't understand, but from his men's reaction, she knew they had to be vile. She'd sat atop her horse and grinned. She'd pretended to be mostly cooperative, so they hadn't restrained her. When the Gunns captured the Sutherland guards, they'd taken Firelight from them, so Arabella had her own mount. She would continue to go along to get along, only making enough trouble to remind Beathan that he hadn't won yet.

"Ye think ye can outwit him," Graham sneered as he stepped from behind her. She cast him a haughty look before turning her head away in disinterest. "Be a bitch. I dinna care. He will kill ye eventually. That ye can be sure of, but nae before he lets me have a rut or two on ye. Ye've clearly heard the stories aboot him and how he likes to take his women. Who do ye think introduced him to how to control a whore? Yer sweet little arse will be raw by the time I finish with ye."

Arabella sniffed, pretending to curl her lip in disgust. She wouldn't allow Graham to know how his words terrified her. She risked her life with her next words, but she prayed it was enough to make him walk away. "I thought it was only men who like to bugger lads who do it that way. I don't see any lads here, so is that why you want it that way with me? I am as small as an aulder lad. Mayhap you'll close your eyes and can think I'm one."

"Stupid whore," Graham growled. His hand whipped out to strike her, but Beathan called out.

"Nae until after I'm done with her. Then she's

yers. Until then, only I get to play with her." Beathan flicked his tongue in a vulgar gesture that Arabella sensed she understood. She thought about what she and Lachlan had done together, and she grew certain she understood. Arabella remained quiet the rest of the night, and no one approached her. They were back in the saddle before sunrise. She survived the next two days on horseback, but as they cantered down a hill into a meadow, glimmering metal in the distance made her wonder if any of the surrounding men would survive to see the next.

THIRTY-SEVEN

As Lachlan sat atop Spiorad at the crest of the hill, he had an unobstructed view across the valley. Arabella's red tresses was the beacon calling him home. He could see she was riding Firelight, her horse's chestnut coat shone nearly as brightly as Arabella's hair. Sinclair scouts informed them an hour ago that the Gunns approached and that Arabella rode her own mount. They reassured Lachlan that no one had bound or restrained her, and that despite the situation, she looked well. Lachlan knew the report came from spying her from a distance, but it was enough to breathe easier.

He looked to his left, where his father sat on his giant stallion beside him. The beast made Spiorad look like a colt. Hamish's horse sired Spiorad, who was only six. Lachlan was confident his horse still had a couple years left to grow. Beyond Hamish were the Sutherland warriors who rode out with them. Two score men in Sutherland plaid with their swords resting upon their laps awaited his order.

Lachlan looked to his right, where his Uncle Liam's horse nickered beside his. Liam Sinclair was a legend in his own right, both for the great love he shared and continued to carry for his deceased wife and for his prowess on the battlefield. As a child, Lachlan had revered his father, been in awe of King Robert, but idolized his uncle. Liam looked sideways at him and cast him a knowing smile. Lachlan couldn't help but grin.

"What's so funny?" Callum demanded.

"Dinna be mardy," Liam warned his oldest son. Lachlan chuckled, knowing Callum disliked the word "mardy" as much as Lachlan did. Deep rumbling laughter came from Alex, Tavish, and Magnus. The four brothers waited side by side, descending in age the further they were from their father. The four brothers had their own reputations, mostly from before they each married. But as a united force, there were few who were foolish enough to take on the Sinclair brothers. More than one man had stopped fighting on a battlefield to watch the Sinclairs tear through their opponents.

"He canna help it, Da," Tristan Mackay called from the end of the line. "He misses Siùsan too much. He doesnae ken his heid from his arse without her to tell him."

Every man within earshot guffawed. Callum leaned forward to shoot a murderous glare at his brother-by-marriage. "And just what do ye think ma wee baby sister will think when ma wife is consoling me for the horrid things ye say?"

It was Callum's turn to hoot with laughter as Tristan swore. His horse danced about, sensing its owner's displeasure. Lachlan leaned back and looked over his shoulder at the Sinclair and Mackay warriors assembled. Tarran and Wallace had met the Mackays as Mairghread and her husband traveled to visit the Sinclairs. There were newborn bairns at Dunbeath, and Mairghread and Tristan came to see their nieces and nephews. Tavish and Magnus hadn't hesitated to ride out, but Lachlan kenned they worried about their wives who had given birth only days apart. Lachlan had sworn they would finish their business with the Gunns and be home in time for the evening meal. Five female voices had floated into Dunbeath's Great Hall from the second floor, announcing they would hold him to that pledge.

While it was taking every ounce of restraint not to spur his horse and gallop toward Arabella, he was proud of his family and their bonds. No one, not a member of his family or their clans, had hesitated to take up his cause when he arrived at Dunrobin and Dunbeath asking for help. He knew he'd been blessed to be born into such an unusual family. His hand slipped into his sporran, and his fingers ran over the carving he always carried with him any time he left his home, even if only to ride out to a nearby village. The eve before his first battle, Hamish had presented him, Amelia, Maude, and Blair with identical carvings that depicted their family. The five of them stood arm in arm. It was each family member's most prized possession. He'd carried the treasured item for more than a decade, some parts smooth from his fingers rubbing over them. He looked at Hamish when his father placed his hand on Lachlan's knee.

"I am proud of the mon ye are, Lach. I couldnae ask for a better son. I dinna care what Uncle Liam says. There is nay finer warrior than ye. He can keep his lads, and I will keep mine." Hamish squeezed his knee before drawing his hand away.

"Thank ye, Da. I just strive to be like ye. If I am even a little, then I can respect maself," Lachlan whispered. He turned his eyes toward the meadow. He knew the moment Arabella spotted him. The men surrounding her continued to canter forward as they passed her. Firelight was slowing to a trot, allowing the Gunns to move ahead of her.

Lachlan raised his sword arm over his head. When he saw Beathan's attention turn to Arabella, looking to see where she'd gone, Lachlan dropped his arm. He spurred Spiorad and calling out, "*sans peur*," the Sutherlands' battle cry of "fearless." He heard it echoed to his left while the Mackays let loose their battle cry, "*Bratach Bhan Chlann Aoidh*" unifying their men under the call for "the white flag of Mackay." Not to be outdone, the Sinclairs called out "*Girnigoe! Girnigoe!*" Their war cry harkened back to their Norse ancestors.

Warriors from the three clans charged down the hillside as the Gunns entered the center of the meadow. Lachlan released an ear-piercing whistle, the signal for the warriors to fan out and wrap around the Gunn party. In a matter of only minutes, the Gunns were surrounded. Beathan looked around wildly until he spotted Arabella. He nudged his horse to move closer to hers as the Sutherlands, Sinclairs, and Mackays fought the few Gunns who put up a fight. Arabella was prepared. She'd pulled her *sgian dubhs* from her pocket and her thigh holster. When Beathan neared her, she took a deep breath.

"Ye're coming with me, lass," Beathan hissed. Holding the reins in one hand, he reached out the other to wrap around Arabella's waist. She drew her left hand up then plunged her knife into his forearm.

"I'm going nowhere with you. You bampot. You may have returned me to Lachlan," Arabella crowed. "But you are going to die."

As Beathan stared at the knife quivering in his arm, he was slow to react to Arabella's words. With her hand wrapped around the hilt of her second *sgian dubh*, she turned her palm up and thrust the short but fatally sharp blade into his neck. Blood sprayed forth, covering her face, chest, and hand. It splattered across her gown. The scent so close to Firelight's nose made the already agitated horse frantic. Untrained for battle, the tiny mare bolted. Arabella barely had time to grasp the reins before they slipped beyond her reach. She let Firelight run until she broke through the circle of warriors who came to rescue her. She reined in her terrified horse, cooing at her and patting her neck.

When Firelight settled, Arabella looked back at the nonexistent battle. More than a hundred sets of eyes looked at her, but she only saw Lachlan. He spurred Spiorad forward, going through the break in the line of men that Firelight created with her headlong flight away from the blood and noise. Arabella swung down from her horse as Lachlan brought Spiorad to a stop. He leaped from his horse as his steed nodded his head and pawed the ground as if he agreed with Lachlan and Arabella's reunion.

Arabella flung herself into Lachlan's arms as he lifted her off the ground. They clung to one another, neither saying anything, just rejoicing in the feeling of holding one another. Arabella leaned back until they looked at one another. They said more with the expressions in their eyes than they could with words. She cupped his jaw, and their mouths fused together. Their kiss seemed to last forever. Arabella's head swam with much the same feeling as when she drank too much. But this time she was drunk from Lachlan's kisses. Neither cared about what went on around them, they had eyes only for one another. When they were both breathless, Lachlan lowered Arabella to the ground, but neither let go.

Lachlan brushed the hair back from Arabella's face before clasping the cuff of his sleeve in his hand and used it to wipe away some of the splattered blood. Arabella looked at the red on his shirt as he drew his arm away.

"I can't believe I did that," she murmured with disbelief.

"Neither can I," Lachlan chortled. "When he reached for ye, I feared I wouldnae get to ye in time. Then ye stabbed his ruddy arm. I thought he would snap ye in half for that, but then out of nowhere came yer other dirk. I shall give Firelight every apple from the Sinclairs' orchard that I can find. I dinna think ye heard Beathan's bellowing because Firelight was determined to escape. Beathan stood in his stirrups, raised the arm with yer knife in it, started yelling, then toppled dead from his horse."

"He's dead?" Arabella asked, glancing around Lachlan's shoulder but unable to see past the rumps of so many horses.

"Dead and on his way to hell," Lachlan replied. "Once he fell, his men surrendered. Only Graham and a few others didna make a sound choice. They shall be food for the crows, just like Beathan. The rest will come back to Dunbeath and take up residence in Uncle Liam's dungeon until we decide what to do with them."

"I saw you on the hill. I don't know how I knew which one you were, but I did. I tried to fall back, to stay out of your way when the fighting started, but Beathan noticed. He threatened me, which raised my hackles. I'd had enough. I acted without really thinking. All I knew was that I wanted to be away from him and get to you."

"Ye did just that, little one," Lachlan grinned. "Took at least a dozen years off ma life, but ye bested him."

"Don't fear. I have no intention of doing aught like that again. I was just so angry. Angrier than I ever imagined I could be. He tried to make me drink like last time, but I wouldn't. I did everything I could to keep from swallowing any whisky." Arabella bit her bottom lip as she looked down between them. "I didn't trust myself. I was scared that if I had a little, I would want a lot. I was scared that I would give up like I did before, and I didn't want that. I wanted to be aware. And I wasn't going to throw away everything we went through to get me past needing it."

"I'm so vera proud of ye, Belle," Lachlan whispered as his face neared hers. Their lips touched over and over in tiny kisses until they melted into one another again, their mouths becoming one.

"Do ye think ye can let the lass breathe long enough to get her home?" Tavish crossed his arms over his pummel and leaned forward.

"Nay, I dinna," Lachlan snapped before returning to kissing Arabella. He drew one arm away from Arabella's waist and made an obscene gesture behind his back. The men roared with laughter, making Arabella pull away. She looked at seven men who muttered to one another in Gaelic. A man of middle age smiled kindly at her. She assumed he was Laird Liam Sinclair because the four younger men around him bore a striking resemblance to him, and those men were nearly identical to one another. A fifth dark-haired man was beside Tavish. He didn't look enough like the five Sinclair men to be one of them, but he blended in. Arabella realized she was looking at Laird Tristan Mackay, who offered her a warm grin as he called out something in Gaelic that made the younger men laugh and Lachlan blush.

"What did he say?" Arabella asked softly. Lachlan look mortified as he shook his head.

"He said welcome to the family, lass," Laird Hamish Sutherland said as he walked up to the couple. Arabella shot Lachlan a look that told him she wouldn't forget to ask again later. She sank into

Hamish's embrace; it was the most fatherly affection she'd ever experienced. She didn't want to let go.

"Ye can have a hug anytime ye wish, *nighean*."

"*Nighean*?" Arabella tried to repeat the word the way it sounded coming from Hamish.

"It means 'daughter,'" Lachlan explained as he opened his arms to his wife and father. "Thank ye, Da."

"Yer mama and I are happy to have a third. The keep is so lonely now that yer sisters are gone," Hamish chuckled.

"Da!" Lachlan admonished. He playfully pouted. "I'm still there."

Hamish tutted with a smile before looking back at Arabella. "I welcome ye to Clan Sutherland, Lady Arabella." Hamish formally bowed, and Arabella dropped into a curtsy befitting a royal. She supposed Lachlan and his family practically were royalty, since they were so close to King Robert and Queen Elizabeth. "Lachlan, yer mama will be at Dunbeath by now. We should return."

"Mama? But she stayed home." Lachlan looked at his father in confusion.

"Ye have much to learn, lad. Would yer sisters have stayed home?" Hamish asked.

"Nay. They dinna listen," Lachlan mused.

"And who do ye think they get it from? Certainly nae me. I'm the model of obedience. I do just as yer mama says," Hamish grinned. Arabella listened to the banter between father and son, and the love in Hamish's voice as he spoke about his wife. While they weren't on Sutherland land yet, she knew she'd come home.

THIRTY-EIGHT

Arabella spotted six women of varying heights, builds, and hair color standing on the top step of the keep. The oldest woman was nearly a mirror image of Maude, so she recognized Amelia immediately. She'd met Lady Sutherland several times over the years, but she hadn't let herself believe that Amelia would one day be her mother-by-marriage. She noticed Ceit and Deidre both held tiny swaddled bundles in their arms. A toddler clung to each of them, and Arabella realized that the women's older and younger children must have been nearly exactly the same age.

As though reading her mind, Lachlan whispered, "Aye. Tavish and Magnus have always been competitive. Magnus's older child is two months older than Tavish's, but the bairns are just days apart."

Arabella nodded as her eyes landed on a woman with nearly white-blond hair with three children standing around her. The woman was breathtaking, and her hair was the perfect contrast to the strawberry blonde who stood beside her, their arms around one another's waists.

"The redhead is Siùsan, Callum's wife. The blonde is Brighde, Alex's wife. Their bairns are quite close in age too. The tyke over there running down the steps is Wee Liam. As ye can see, the lad isnae so vera wee, but we call him that so he isnae confused with his grandda. He's Mairghread and Tristan's oldest, and the first of the next generation."

Arabella nodded as she watched the family gathered around waiting for their warrior husbands and fathers to return. She slipped her hand over her belly, realizing that her children with Lachlan would be part of what he called the next generation. The idea warmed her from the inside out. But recalling that the reunions taking place as the Sinclairs ran to their wives and Tristan enveloped Mairghread in his brawny arms were because they'd rode out to save her, she wanted to retreat.

"Dinna fash, *mo chridhe*. There isnae a woman on those steps who hasnae had a rough start to her marriage, and none of them are timid. More than one has defended herself like ye did today. Nay mon underestimates them anymore. Ye'll be trading war stories before ye make it to the dais. They will welcome ye just as Da did."

"They won't be angry that I put their husbands' lives at risk?" Arabella asked with disbelief.

"Ye married a warrior, just like they did. They understand there's always risk, but they value family above all else, just like their husbands do. Ye are family." Lachlan kissed her temple before climbing down from his horse. He helped Arabella to the ground and tucked her under his arm. She watched as the men greeted their wives with passionate kisses that would have shocked even the most scandalous members of court. Arabella even watched Hamish lift Amelia off her feet. He turned his back to the crowd, but Arabella could tell where the older man's hands went.

"Told ye they embarrass me and ma sisters daily," Lachlan chortled. Arabella nodded, but Liam caught her eye. He was the only man in the family who didn't have a wife to greet him. He smiled indulgently at his children and their spouses as the grandchildren flocked to him. Arabella heart felt like it would burst as she watched the man she'd just seen charging toward the Gunns with his sword raised, looking fiercer than most, toss his grandchildren in the air and tickle them as they clamored all over him. Her mouth dropped open when he scooped up six of them and carried them up the steps toward the keep's door. He did it with ease, and Arabella supposed he did so often. She'd never seen a man so engaged with children before. She looked up at Lachlan.

"One day, *mo ghaol*," Lachlan promised. Arabella concentrated really hard as she formed the words she wanted to say in her head. She recalled the quiet pledges Lachlan had made while she struggled through her recovery in the cave. She rehearsed the words so many times that she nearly missed her chance. Lachlan moved to step toward his family, but she put her hand on his chest to stop him.

"*Tha gaol agam ort nas motha na rud sam bith*," Arabella said, carefully forming each word to sound like Lachlan had as she said, "I love you more than aught."

Lachlan stopped short and looked down at the petite redhead he'd loved for years. He swept her into his arms and kissed her as he moved toward the keep's steps. He ignored his cousins' teasing or his parents calling out to him. When he reached the top of the steps, he turned to his family.

"We'll see ye in the morn." Lachlan didn't wait for a response, and Arabella buried her face in his shoulder, mortified.

"Newlyweds in this family are all the same," Arabella heard Liam say with resignation. When she heard a woman's voice call out, she lifted her head to watch as the Sinclairs, Sutherlands, and Mackays entered behind them.

"I bet ye that there will be a bairn born in nine moons in the middle of the month," Mairghread said as she held up a dagger.

"Nae this time, sister," Tavish grinned. "I say eight and a half." Tavish nodded then jumped when his wife swatted his arm none-too-gently. She tugged at him until he leaned over and she whispered something to him. Arabella couldn't help her amusement as Ceit waved toward them as she scolded Tavish about something. When the barrel-chested warrior stood upright, his cheeks were ruddy. "I meant ten and a half moons."

Mairghread veritably cackled. "Too late!" She gloated. "Ye made yer bid. What say the rest of ye? I've had the dirk the longest again. Any of ye think ye can best me?" Arabella couldn't hear Callum, Alex, or Magnus answer, but she could tell they were negotiating.

"They've had that dirk since they were children. They place bets, and the dirk is the prize. Mairghread has the gift of second sight, or so her brothers claim, because she's had it most often and for the longest. Maude says it's because Mairghread is more observant than her brothers and reasons through things better. Blair just flat out says Mair is smarter than her brothers. I'm inclined to agree with both of ma sisters."

"Because they're smarter than you," Arabella giggled as she kissed Lachlan's cheek.

"That they are," Lachlan merrily conceded. "But I'm going to show ye what I've observed and reasoned through aboot ye while I make love to ye for the rest of the night. Mama and Da can go back to

Dunrobin in the morn. But Uncle Liam shall have to host us for at least a sennight because we're nae leaving our chamber before then!" Lachlan declared as he bounded up the stairs and hurried down the passageway to the chamber he'd used whenever he visited since he was a child. He kicked the door shut behind them, lowering Arabella to the ground before locking and barring the door.

Arabella pulled her lips in as she struggled to contain her laughter as she watched her husband double check that the door was secure. She pulled her gown down over her shoulders and let it fall to the floor. She was about to strip off her chemise when several pounding knocks came from the other side of the door. The rhythm told her several people were there. Five female voices demanded, "Lachlan, open up."

Mairghread's voice drowned out the others. "Lachlan, open this door and let us in with the tub and soap, or ye will learn how I used to get into this chamber and put lizards and fish in yer bed."

"Lizards and fish?" Arabella mouthed.

"Aye. Maude and Blair only had one brother to keep up with. And they had each other. Mairghread had four and nay sisters. She's braver than anyone else I ken. A daredevil too. Dinna go along with any of her suggestions. They're likely to wind ye up in trouble. Uncle Liam couldnae bear to punish her because she reminds him too much of Aunt Kyla. She didna take advantage of him, mind ye, but she got away with far more than her brothers. Or me." Lachlan added for good measure.

He unbarred the door and unlocked it. He barely moved aside in time as the door swung open. Mairghread, Siùsan, Brighde, Deirdre, and Ceit hustled inside followed by a team of servants who brought in the largest tub Arabella had ever seen along with buckets of steaming water. Mairghread walked over to Arabella and smiled. She dropped a soft kiss on Arabella's cheek.

"Welcome to our family, Arabella," her voice kind as she offered a sisterly embrace. When she straightened, a mocking smile shone on her face. She looked at Lachlan and tipped her head toward the tub. "Ye can thank me later. A ride on Spiorad should do."

"Nae on yer life. Ma wee beasty willna survive the way ye ride," Lachlan teased. "Besides isnae it a family tradition for the newlyweds to tuck themselves away for a sennight?"

"I can wait." Mairghread's tinkle of laughter followed her as she left the chamber, the other wives and servants disappearing as quickly as they appeared. Arabella looked at the tub and couldn't believe what she found. The servants had filled the enormous wooden barrel more than halfway, and there were rose petals floating in it. The scents of lemongrass and lavender wafted to her. A stack of washing cloths and drying lines sat beside the tub, and a shiny bar of soap lay in a dish on a table she hadn't seen being brought in. She noticed someone had turned down the bed too. She marveled at how so much was accomplished without her observing and in such little time.

"Will you fit?" Arabella asked seductively.

"Havenae I shown ye I do already?" Lachlan replied as he toed his boots off and dropped his clothes to the floor. When they stood before one another naked, Lachlan trailed the back of his fingers over her collarbones to her shoulders then down her arms before returning to run them over her chest. She wrapped her arms around his waist, unable to wait another moment before they had full skin-to-skin contact. Lachlan lifted her, and she wrapped her legs around his waist. His cock found what it sought and slid into her. Lachlan walked them to the tub before climbing in. He settled them, helping Arabella find a comfortable position. As the water lapped around them, Arabella leaned against Lachlan's chest. They were both content with the moment of solitude. But it was the calm before the storm. Arabella shifted at the same time Lachlan did, and it ignited a maelstrom of need and passion.

Lachlan grasped Arabella's backside, his fingers biting into her flesh as she rocked her hips, riding his cock as their desire spiraled beyond control. Arabella's moans filled the chamber. The more she made the more she noticed Lachlan's excitement. He whispered, "ma Belle" over and over, worshipping her body and her soul. When their release engulfed them, it was cataclysmic in strength.

They soaked in the tub until the water turned cool. Forced to hurry, they scrubbed one another with the lavender and lemongrass soap. As they helped dry each other, what they'd assumed was a satiated hunger flared back to life. Their hands roamed everywhere as they stumbled to the bed. Lachlan playfully tossed Arabella onto the bed before prowling toward her. He settled with his shoulders between her legs, and the wolfish grin that made her core ache reappeared.

"I am famished, and there is only one thing I wish to feast upon," Lachlan purred. "Do ye ken what that is?"

Arabella shook her head as she watched him lower his face to her mound. His tongue flicked out, laving her from stem to stern. Her body twitched, unprepared for the sensation. She rested on her elbows as she watched Lachlan.

"It's yer honey." Lachlan winked before

launching his attack. But he was unprepared for Arabella's response.

"Does that mean I can feast on yer sausage and taters afterward?" She asked as she infused a burr into her accent. Lachlan's stunned expression at his wife's randy comment made Arabella giggle, but she was soon gasping when Lachlan growled and launched his attack on her senses. His tongue flicked her bud over and over before laving her once more. He rubbed the bristles from his unshaven face over her sensitive nerve endings, making her hips buck off of the bed. His teeth grazed the nub before he sucked it into his mouth as he pressed three fingers into her passage. Arabella's hips rose and fell as she struggled to get closer to Lachlan. Her fingers fisted in his hair as she pressed his face to her mound. When his tongue pressed into her along with his fingers, she was certain she would expire. When he bit her nub with just pressure and no pain, her tether snapped, and her body gave in as pleasure coursed through her.

Arabella gasped as she tried to catch her breath, astonished by what had just happened.

She watched as Lachlan inched up the bed and settled beside her. His eyes were on her the entire time, a note of worry in his expression as he listened to her labored breathing. He was wholly unprepared when she launched herself at him. Her tongue flicked his lips, demanding entry. She tasted herself on his tongue, and while she wasn't sure what to make of it, her desire brought her attention back to Lachlan's body. She slid her hand down his belly until she wrapped her hand around his rod. She stroked him as his fingers danced over her backside. She watched as his eyes drifted close, the chords in his neck straining even though his face appeared relaxed.

Lachlan made a strangled sound when he felt her tongue swirl around the head of his cock before flicking the opening at its tip. She licked him from the root back up to the bulbous head. He watched her, his head lifted off the pillow but the rest of his body frozen, his entire concentration on what she was doing. Arabella licked her lips and studied Lachlan's cock before sinking her mouth onto it. She closed her eyes and recalled how his mouth on her had felt. She tried to think how she could mimic the things he'd done that she liked the best. Drawing a blank, her mouth mimicked what her hand had done. Lachlan's groans were a blend of agony and pleasure.

I think he's enjoying it. He hasn't told me to stop, so I must be at least fair to middlin' at this. He looks like he's in pain one moment then in heaven the next. Is that how it's supposed to be? Maybe I'm not doing this right after all.

Arabella began to pull away, but Lachlan's strangled plea made her pause. "Please, Belle. Dinna stop. Christ on the cross, this is the most glorious torture known to mon." Lachlan panted as he watched Arabella slide her mouth down his length until he felt it brush the back of her throat. She stroked him as her mouth and hand worked in tandem. "I canna last much longer, but I want to be inside ye, Belle. I want us to be together."

Lachlan lifted Arabella and positioned her to straddle him, but she shook her head. "You on top."

Lachlan rolled them over, grasping one of Arabella's legs and hooking it over his shoulder. He plunged into her as she clawed the sheets. Another new position, another new feeling. Arabella was overwhelmed by the intensity, her eyes squeezing shut.

"Belle?" Lachlan slowed his pace, and her eyes flew open. "Am I hurting ye? I'll slow down, stop if ye need me to."

"Nay. It's just different. I'm still learning," Arabella smiled timidly. "But I like it."

"Only what ye like, Belle. If aught doesnae feel good, tell me, and we'll try something else. Dinna do aught just because ye think it's what I want. Promise?" Lachlan's earnest expression made Arabella's heart flip-flop. She knew in that moment, that no matter what, Lachlan would always put her ahead of himself. She opened her arms to him, and without question, he lowered himself into her embrace.

"I love you so very much, Lach. I just want to hold you. Is that all right?"

"Aught for you, Belle. And I like this too. Being this close, yer skin against mine. There is naught better than being this close to ma bonnie bride," Lachlan confessed.

"*An duine agam*," Arabella attempted. My husband. Lachlan turned his head, and a swirl of emotions filled their kiss. Their bodies moved together in synchronicity until they were both too spent to move. They drew the covers over themselves and drifted off to sleep in one another's arms.

THIRTY-NINE

As midmorning light shone into their chamber, Lachlan gazed at his slumbering wife. His thumbnail trailed along her back between her shoulder blades. It was the first time he'd really looked at Arabella's body since their whirlwind romance began. The times he'd seen her as bare as she was now were always precursors to intimacy. His bride attracted him in every way, and he'd lusted for her for years. But as he lay beside her, he swept an assessing eye over her. He noticed how sallow her skin had grown since they left Stirling. He brushed his hand over her ribs and realized that she'd lost significant weight in the past few weeks, her bones showing beneath the taut skin. While her hair was still a fiery red, some of its luster had faded. Deep shadows cast smudges beneath her eyes. He turned his attention to her legs, noticing how bruises mottled them. He knew they came from her captivity and when she thrashed about in her delirium. He spied the rope burns around her ankles from where Beathan had restrained her. It made him take a peek at her wrists only to find the same marks were healing on the fragile, paper-thin skin.

They'd operated in a state of panic for days, and

while their reunion the day before seemed to breathe new life into Arabella, Lachlan wasn't fooled into thinking they were free of her demons. Her recovery would take longer than just the intense days of withdrawal. He feared she might still grow ill from the strain she'd endured, not only since leaving Stirling, but all that came before it. There was still the matter of her father to resolve, and Lachlan feared how the stress of informing her father of their marriage and the inevitable fallout would affect her. He knew Arabella wasn't close to her family, but she still felt loyal and compelled to please them. Even from a distance, Lachlan understood they held control over her.

Arabella rolled over in her sleep, nestling her backside against Lachlan's groin. He stifled the groan that threatened to slip from his throat as his cock sprang to life. They'd woken throughout the night, sharing tender and passionate touches, making love thrice. But Lachlan would do nothing now to disturb Arabella's slumber. As much as he desired her, taking stock of her physical changes made him determined to focus on encouraging her to eat and sleep as much as she could.

"Lach," Arabella's groggy voice mumbled. Lachlan raised up on his elbow to look over her shoulder. Her eyes were still closed, and her breathing even. He draped his arm over her waist, and she sighed with contentment. Lachlan found he was just as content to hold her while she slept, but as the hours crept on and she barely moved except to change position sometimes, he grew concerned. He was torn between letting her sleep for as long as her body needed and waking her to ensure she ate.

As afternoon slipped into evening, and the couple remained in bed, Lachlan realized he'd napped several times throughout the day. He conceded to himself that the past month's unexpected adventure had exhausted him. As he reflected on the summer that was nearly over, he realized it was more like a season of adventures rather than just a singular month. He'd arrived at court toward the beginning of summer to pay his clan's taxes. He'd been excited to see Blair and spend time with his sister, but it had been all too brief. Just as he prepared to return to Sutherland, Hardi arrived. They hadn't seen much of one another since Hardi returned to his clan after his years training with the Sutherlands. It hadn't come as a surprise to learn Blair and Hardi fell in love. Most of the Sutherlands had seen it blossoming when they were youths, but Blair's younger age prevented the couple from becoming more serious before Hardi returned home.

But then Blair had disappeared for a month, or at least her family feared that. Intercepted missives and nefarious plots left Blair's parents and siblings in the dark about her whereabouts and safety. The fear that something had happened to Blair was the beginning of Lachlan's nerve-wracking summer. He, his parents, Maude and Kieran, and their clans' warriors had ridden to Tor Castle unknowing whether they would find Blair. The relief of seeing his little sister had been incalculable. Never had he been so happy to see her mischievous grin and be on the receiving side of her sharp tongue.

He'd returned to Dunrobin for a brief time before riding back to Tor Castle to accompany Blair and Hardi to Stirling. It was from there that everything fell apart. He figured out that he'd operated with a sense of impending danger for months. As he worked through these thoughts, it no longer came as a surprise that he was tired. He'd ignored the emotional turmoil and physical strain of traveling and fighting because he'd been singularly focused, first on Blair, and then on Arabella.

"Lach?" Arabella once again said his name, her voice raspy from sleep. She'd been sleeping on her stomach, facing away from him. She turned her head and offered him a weary smile.

"Aye, little one," Lachlan stroked her back.

"I'm starving," Arabella confessed, but her smile was still weak.

"I'm nae surprised. It's been ages since ye've had a proper meal. And I'd wager they barely fed ye the last couple of days."

"That's true. He only offered me whisky. When I refused, he refused to give me aught else." Arabella never wanted to say Beathan's name again.

"I'll request the kitchens send a tray up," Lachlan suggested. Arabella struggled to sit up, and Lachlan propped pillows behind her.

"I feel like we should go down to the Great Hall since we've been hidden away in here all day. My introduction to your family was not exactly gracious or polite."

"Is that what ye want to do?" Lachlan asked, surprised at her suggestion.

"Not really, but it feels like the right thing to do. They'll expect us."

"The only thing ma family will expect is for ye to rest and be well."

"But I'm a guest in their home. I owe them more courtesy than that."

"Nay, ye dinna. Brighde showed up at their gates in the middle of a storm. Alex carried her to his chamber where she slept for days. When she woke, she refused to tell him who she was because she feared her father finding her. She ran away from here because she was terrified she'd bring trouble to ma family's door." Lachlan slid his arm beneath her shoulders, and she inched closer to him. "If they didna fault her for running away from the people who'd fed and tended to her injuries, then they willna fault ye for needing yer sleep."

"But—" Arabella started, but Lachlan shook his head.

"That isnae how ma family works. And ye're part of it now. They will only want what's best for ye. They willna expect aught from ye."

"Everyone expects something of people," Arabella argued.

"Mayhap later," Lachlan shrugged. "But for now, their only wish will be for ye to get better."

The notion that no one would hold her to a standard of perfect behavior and perfect appearance was new and disconcerting. She nodded as she tried to accept Lachlan's reasoning, but it felt too foreign. She still thought she owed his family at least a brief appearance to express her gratitude. When someone knocked, she feared whoever stood on the other side was there to demand their presence. She shot a pointed look at Lachlan, but he smiled and shook his head. He wrapped his plaid around his waist, and Arabella couldn't help but be distracted by how enticing it was to see the woolen garment sitting low on his hips.

"Mama," Lachlan greeted Amelia as he held the door open for his mother. Arabella gawked before scrambling to pull the covers up over her shoulders. She looked around wildly, wondering where her clothes were, embarrassed that Lachlan's mother found her obviously naked and still in bed.

"Och, lass! I thought ye would still be sleeping. I feared waking ye, but I kenned ye'd both be hungry sooner or later. I brought only cold plates, thinking it would be awhile before ye would be ready to eat."

"Thank you," Arabella said, her cheeks feeling like they emitted flames. "I'm sorry for the trouble. We were just aboot to come belowstairs."

Amelia cast a disapproving glare at Lachlan, and her son held up his hands in surrender. "What did ye say to yer wife that makes her think she needs to be moving aboot so soon?"

"Naught, Mama. I swear." Arabella thought Lachlan sounded like a little boy terrified of being punished for a crime he didn't commit. She remembered that he'd admitted that he feared his petite mother far more than his bear of a father. She recalled how gentle Hamish's hug had been the day before, and she realized Lachlan's parents were as kind and loving as he'd described.

"It wasn't his idea, Lady Sutherland. I feel I should make more of an effort to be polite."

"More effort to be polite?" Amelia turned a stunned visage toward Arabella. "I feared I was the one being rude if I woke ye. And it's Amelia."

"You are very thoughtful to bring up the tray, Lady Amelia," Arabella compromised on Amelia's title. "But you shouldn't be bringing trays up to us."

Amelia shoved the tray at Lachlan, who barely grasped it in time. She approached the bed with such a motherly smile that Arabella feared she would burst into tears and sob against Amelia's shoulder. That's exactly what she did when her mother-by-marriage sat on the edge of the mattress and held out her arms. Arabella wept until her throat was raw, but Amelia said nothing. She cooed and stroked Arabella's hair, but she let her release years of hurt and all the fear she'd faced recently. She cried harder than she had when Lachlan found her drunk in her chamber.

When Arabella's tears were spent, Amelia continued to stroke her hair, rocking them as she kissed Arabella's head. They sat together, Arabella's labored breathing the only sound in the chamber. Lachlan stood back, watching the woman he loved more than anything receive solace in the arms of the woman he'd depended upon most for his entire life. As he watched them, he realized his father hadn't exaggerated the day before when he called Arabella "daughter." His parents welcomed his bride as though she'd always been a part of their family.

Arabella leaned back and looked over Amelia's shoulder. Lachlan's expression was a mixture of emotions, but the clearest was his worry for her. "I feel much better now, *mo chridhe*."

The smile filled with pride once again beamed from Lachlan's face, and she believed he'd never looked finer. She knew her small efforts meant more to him than the actual words. She wanted him to know that she didn't take him for granted, and that she wanted to be part of his life in the Highlands. She held her hand out to him, and he walked around the bed to take it.

"That's vera good," Amelia commented. "Has Lachlan been teaching ye?"

"A few things here and there," Arabella nodded.

"We'll have ye sounding like a proper Highlander in nay time," Amelia grinned as she patted Arabella's hand. Lachlan embraced his mother when she rose, finding the same comfort in her arms that he had as a child. It always amazed him how Amelia knew exactly how long he needed the affection, and she never pulled away before he was ready, even now that he was an adult. She kissed his cheek before leaning over to kiss Arabella's forehead. "Eat and sleep as much as ye need, Arabella. We figure it'll be at least a sennight before ye're in fine fettle, so dinna feel ye need to go anywhere unless that's what ye wish. If ye tire of his nib's company, the others are happy to visit. But nay one will intrude. If ye wish for a change of scenery, ye may enjoy the gardens. Siùsan does a fine job tending them. They're as lovely as when Kyla was still with us. And it's still Amelia."

Amelia turned, but Arabella caught her hand. When the older woman looked back at Arabella, the younger lady squeezed it. "It's Belle."

Lachlan watched as something passed between them, and he couldn't remember the last time his heart had felt so light.

FORTY

Arabella tilted her head back and enjoyed the feel of the sun on her face. The clanking of steel-on-steel filled the background while the sound of children's voices surrounded her. She opened her eyes and glanced toward the lists. She didn't expect to see Lachlan while he trained, so it pleasantly surprised her when her muscular and agile husband shifted into her view. His lithe movement and the power she could see even from a distance fascinated her.

"Never grows old, does it?" Ceit mused as she watched Tavish sparring with Lachlan.

"I don't think it will," Arabella agreed, but the children's antics around her drew her attention back to them.

She and Lachlan had been at Dunbeath for a fortnight, giving her time to recuperate. Much to Lachlan's distress, she'd suffered another bout of fever and delirium four days after they arrived. It lasted nearly a full week, but Amelia assured him that Arabella would pull through. She explained that the stress of Arabella's second abduction interrupted what would have likely happened, anyway. Amelia had helped Lachlan throughout the ordeal, bathing

Arabella, feeding her, telling her stories about Lachlan as a child. She encouraged Lachlan to get fresh air and spend time with his cousins, but he steadfastly refused to leave Arabella. The fear that had abated when he believed they'd survived the worst of it returned. It frightened him that if he left, something would happen, and he wouldn't be there to help. A fear that she might die while he stepped out lurked in the back of his mind.

It was only the during the last three days that she'd been well enough to leave their chamber and return to the land of the living. She felt stronger than she had in months. It wasn't just her body that had time to rest and heal. Her mind had too. It surprised her how open and welcoming the Sinclairs were to her. Just as Hamish and Amelia made her feel as though she'd always been their daughter, Lachlan's cousins and their families acted as though she'd always been part of their kin. It was a wholly different experience than what she'd had at Lochwood Tower. Her distant mother, demanding father, arrogant brothers, and competitive sisters made Arabella feel like she was under constant scrutiny. She hadn't dared jest or tease like she'd started to do with the Sutherlands and Sinclairs. Even Tristan, with his dark and brooding appearance, had teased her about finally bringing Lachlan up to snuff.

She jumped when Lachlan dropped a kiss on her cheek. She hadn't heard him approach, his silent warrior tread still surprising her. He tousled Wee Liam's hair as he spoke to Mairghread, bragging about the young boy's ability with a wooden sword. Arabella knew Mairghread was more than aware of her son's burgeoning skills, but as a doting mother, she beamed and oohed and awed for Wee Liam's sake. Arabella wondered if she and Lachlan would have children. She thought about it a great deal during her lucid moments and over the past few days. Her cycle had been erratic since she started drinking. They hadn't come at the times when she'd expected them, and they were far lighter than she was accustomed to. She feared she might have damaged her womb from all the whisky she consumed. The Sinclairs' healer had visited her more than once during her illness when her fever made even Amelia nervous. She asked the old woman about her fears, but the healer assured her with time, her body would return to normal. Arabella wanted to believe her, but guilt gnawed at her.

"Walk with me?" Lachlan whispered. Arabella nodded. They crossed the bailey and left the keep through the postern gate. They walked in companionable silence, holding hands until they reached the cliffs overlooking the North Sea. Lachlan turned to face Arabella as she gazed up at him, thankful that his towering height blocked the sun that would have otherwise blinded her. Lachlan reached into his sporran and withdrew a green ribbon that was nearly the same shade as her eyes. He held it up for her to see, rubbing his thumb over a spot. He stared at it for a long moment before handing it to her. "I know I've said it before, but I dinna think I'll ever stop saying it. I'm so proud of ye, Belle. Ye've fought to cease yer drinking, and there are many lesser men who never try and never succeed. Ye didna give up, even when ye were tested over and over. I ken it hasnae been easy, but ye have the determination of a warrior. Ye've fought yer battles and found victory."

Lachlan tucked hair behind Arabella's ear, but the breeze defied him, making the hair whip around Arabella's face once more. They shared an amused smile before Lachlan continued.

"I thought for sure ye would beg and plead for even just a wee drop to help ye through, but ye havenae asked for aught. Nae ma time, nae ma patience, nae ma love. But ye ken I give all of those willingly, and I ken ye appreciate it."

"I do. More that I ken how to say," Arabella responded. "I never want to take you for granted, but I want to prove to you, Lach, that I'm strong enough to be your wife."

"I never doubted that," Lachlan insisted.

"Then prove I'm worthy enough."

"Ye went through a rough spell, but I never thought ye were weak or unworthy. Ye made a mistake. I told ye once before that I can be disappointed in yer choice without being disappointed in ye as a person. I am proud of ye, and I dinna want ye to feel like ye must prove aught to me."

Arabella nodded, uncertain what to say. She believed Lachlan and that he believed what he said. But she still didn't have that much confidence in herself. She was still riddled with self-doubt and anxious about making a good impression with those around her. However, she still feared her imperfections would keep that from happening. But unlike before, her doubts didn't consume her; they didn't make her want to run and hide. She felt strong enough to face them, live with them, without the crutch that whisky had become. She knew she owed a part of that to Lachlan for the things he'd done like rescuing her from Stirling Castle's gaol, taking her away from Inchcailleoch Priory, freeing her from Beathan, and staying with her in the cave and in their chamber throughout her battle with withdrawal. But more than anything, she felt she owed him for his unwavering faith in her and for being at her side through it all.

"Belle," Lachlan drew her away from her thoughts as he gave the ribbon she held a brief tug. "It's been a fortnight since the last time ye had a drink. Ye havenae asked for any, and I ken ye havenae tried to sneak any."

"Because I've been too poorly to do much more than lay abed," Arabella mumbled.

"Be that as it may, ye still reached a fortnight without a drink. I want ye to have this ribbon as a reminder of yer accomplishment, of how far ye've come," Lachlan explained as Arabella looked down at the emerald ribbon in her hand. The ends fluttered in the wind coming from the sea. "I thought mayhap every month I could give ye a ribbon to remind ye of yer success. If ye'd like." Lachlan grew uncertain when Arabella didn't react. She stared at the ribbon for a long time before looking up at him.

"And if I fail?" She whispered. "If I can't go without it after all? If I'm weak?"

"I pray that doesnae happen, but I understand it can. I hope that if ye feel tempted ye will seek me out, or Mama or Da. If ye slip, we will stand around ye and catch ye." Lachlan shrugged as he lifted the end of the ribbon. "Then we start counting over and use a different color ribbon."

Arabella bit her tongue to keep from responding that she'd have a rainbow of ribbons if that was the case. She wanted to believe that she would never drink again, but she was also afraid to think that. But in the meantime, she drew strength from Lachlan's certainty.

"Thank you, *mo ghràidh*." She'd been practicing more each day, the other women helping her. Brighde was a Lowlander by birth, so she shared some tricks she'd used to help her learn Gaelic. Arabella held out her wrist. "Would you tie it for me? I would keep it with me as a reminder, just as you do your carving." Lachlan had shown her the carving one evening while they'd rested in bed between her sweats and shivers. Lachlan nodded and wrapped the length of ribbon around her slender wrist. They kissed on the top of the cliffs, the sea crashing beneath them, seals calling to one another, but the world around them slipped away until it was just the two of them.

Arabella caught sight of Lachlan's smile as she walked toward him, the Sutherlands parting as she made her way to the kirk. They'd been back at Dunrobin for a fortnight, and now they were celebrating their wedding before the kirk and their clan. It had surprised Arabella how easily she'd started thinking of the Sutherlands as her clan. They'd welcomed her much like Lachlan's extended family had. The clan shared in the newlyweds' excitement, and they anticipated the feast that would celebrate Lachlan and Arabella's official church wedding. As she neared the steps, she noticed Amelia and Hamish stood with Blair and Hardi to her left. Across from them, holding her infant daughter, Maude stood with Kieran, who held up their twins, so the toddlers could see. She'd passed the Sinclairs who stood on both sides of the path.

But once she stood before Lachlan, her focus was solely on him. As they took each other's hands, the priest wrapped an emerald ribbon around their wrists, binding them. It was the ribbon Lachlan presented her that morning to commemorate her first full month without drinking. Her original green ribbon encircled her neck, a bow tied at the side.

In just a fortnight, she'd discovered she had more confidence than she imagined she could possess. They'd arrived at Dunrobin to find two missives waiting for them. King Robert sent a missive wishing them well, but demanding an explanation about why yet another Gunn died at the hands of the Sutherlands and Sinclairs. The second missive was from Mitcholm. It also wished them well, alluding to his pleasure that Arabella would one day be a countess. But it hinted at a warning that he'd washed his hands of her and that she shouldn't return if her marriage failed. Lachlan sent a return missive saying that the Johnstones were to keep Arabella's dowry or they could donate it to the priory, but since Arabella was now a Sutherland, they were in no need of anything from the Johnstones. She'd worried that Amelia and Hamish would be angry at Lachlan's response and they would expect payment for taking her into their family. They quickly disabused her of that idea once they got past the horror that she feared their rejection. The remaining time had been a whirlwind of meeting various clan members, riding out to villages so Lachlan could introduce people to their future Lady Sutherland, and preparing for the wedding.

As Lachlan and Arabella stood together reciting their vows, Arabella was overcome with a sense of lightness. It was as though someone lifted a heavy weight from her shoulders that had been crushing her. As she looked into Lachlan's eyes, she saw nothing but a future with him. Her past faded away as though it were only made up of dull memories from long ago. When the priest pronounced them married, they filled the kiss they shared with hope and tenderness. It was the most perfect moment of Arabella's life.

Arabella handed Lachlan the mug of whisky as she listened to him complaining about the Gunns demand for recompense. It had been nearly a year and a half since she slayed Beathan, but the Gunns still clamored for vindication. Hamish had offered to meet them again on the battlefield to settle their differences, but as expected, they shied away from the challenge. They wanted to reinstate their Viking forefathers' *weregild*, insisting the Sutherland and the Sinclairs pay blood money. As Arabella took a seat beside Lachlan in Hamish's solar, Lachlan explained that the Gunns argued the Sutherlands and Sinclairs had unjustly murdered Tomas, James, and Beathan over the past several years. He shared that he and Hamish had shared a raucous laugh before Hamish tossed the missive into the fire.

"They are out of their heids if they think we'll pay a penny. They're lucky we havenae overrun them and taken everything from them after what they've put our family through," Arabella mused. She no longer noticed when Highlander phrases slipped into her speech. She rubbed her swollen belly as Lachlan continued to tell her about his meeting with Hamish as he sipped his whisky. The drink's scent had once filled her with anticipation, but now it did nothing but occasionally make her feel queasy. It had taken months before Arabella could convince Lachlan that it didn't bother her if he drank in front of her. She smiled to herself as she recalled that he'd finally relented days before she learned she was expecting. She'd teased that it was a good thing he'd given in because he needed to calm his jittery nerves about becoming a father.

"Their feathers will settle soon enough, and they'll turn to the Oliphants to cause trouble with. Ye would think they wouldnae be so daft as to keep antagonizing us when the Sinclairs, the Mackays, and the Sutherlands surround them. Where do they have to go but into the sea?" Lachlan shook his head as he reached out his hand to rub Arabella's belly. "How are ye and our wee lass today?"

"I don't ken how you can be so certain it's a girl. What if you have a son?" Arabella asked over dramatically.

"As long as they look like ye, I dinna mind if the bairn is a lad or a lass," Lachlan repeated for the hundredth time.

"And if I want a bairn who looks like you?" Arabella countered as she did each time. Lachlan plucked her out of her seat, just as he had often done before she'd grown round. He settled her on his lap, his hand on her belly. She covered his and leaned her head against his shoulder. They sat in silence as they enjoyed feeling their child's kicks. While the half-filled mug that sat on the table beside Arabella no longer tempted her, she'd come close to succumbing to temptation more than once during the early days at Dunrobin.

She'd been devoted to Lachlan for what felt like forever, but the moment the midwife confirmed she was with child, the thought of drinking again never came back. As the midwife finished her examination, she'd realized as she lay on the bed she shared with Lachlan each night that she had a new purpose. Discovering she would be a mother made her see in an instant that her life was no longer just about her. Even as close as she was to Lachlan, she wasn't bound to him as she was a child. With sudden clarity, she knew every choice she made needed to be one that would protect and nurture her children. That would never be possible if she returned to drinking.

Instead, she had a collection of nineteen ribbons of varying shades of green to celebrate her first fortnight and every month since. She wore at least one each day to remind her of what she'd overcome and to remind her of what she had to look forward to.

Lachlan and Arabella sat together, musing about their unborn bairn and sharing news from different members of their clan. To others, it might have appeared mundane or ordinary, but to Lachlan and Arabella, it was perfection.

Celeste Barclay, a nom de plume, lives near the Southern California coast with her husband and sons. Growing up in the Midwest, Celeste enjoyed spending as much time in and on the water as she could. Now she lives near the beach. She's an avid swimmer, a hopeful future surfer, and a former rower. When she's not writing, she's working or being a mom.

Visit Celeste's website, www.celestebarclay.com, for regular updates on works in progress, new releases, and her blog where she features posts about her experiences as an author and recommendations of her favorite reads.

Are you an author who would like to guest blog or be featured in her recommendations? Visit her website for an opportunity to share your insights and experiences.

Have you read *Their Highland Beginning, The Clan*

Sinclair Prequel? Learn how the saga begins! This FREE novella is available to all new subscribers to Celeste's monthly newsletter. Subscribe on her website.

www.celestebarclay.com

Join the fun and get exclusive insider giveaways, sneak peeks, and new release announcements in

Celeste Barclay's Facebook Ladies of Yore Group

A Spinster at the Highland Court
BOOK 1 SNEAK PEEK

Elizabeth Fraser looked around the royal chapel within Stirling Castle. The ornate candlestick holders on the altar glistened and reflected the light from the ones in the wall sconces as the priest intoned the holy prayers of the Advent season. Elizabeth kept her head bowed as though in prayer, but her green eyes swept the congregation. She watched the other ladies-in-waiting, many of whom were doing the same thing. She caught the eye of Allyson Elliott. Elizabeth raised one eyebrow as Allyson's lips twitched. Both women had been there enough times to accept they'd be kneeling for at least the next hour as the Latin service carried on. Elizabeth understood the Mass thanks to her cousin Deirdre Fraser, or rather now Deirdre Sinclair. Elizabeth's mind flashed to the recent struggle her cousin faced as she reunited with her husband Magnus after a seven-year separation. Her aunt and uncle's choice to keep Deirdre hidden from her husband simply because they didn't think the Sinclairs were an advantageous enough match, and the resulting scandal, still humiliated the other Fraser clan members at court. She admired Deirdre's husband Magnus's pledge to remain faithful despite not knowing if he'd ever see Deirdre again.

Elizabeth suddenly snapped her attention; while everyone else intoned the twelfth—or was it thirteenth—amen of the Mass, the hairs on the back of her neck stood up. She had the strongest feeling that someone was watching her. Her eyes scanned to her right, where her parents sat further down the pew. Her mother and father had their heads bowed and eyes closed. While she was convinced her mother was in devout prayer, she wondered if her father had fallen asleep during the Mass. Again. With nothing seeming out of the ordinary and no one visibly paying attention to her, her eyes swung to the left. She took in the king and queen as they kneeled together at their prie-dieu. The queen's lips moved as she recited the liturgy in silence. The king was as still as a statue. Years of leading warriors showed, both in his stature and his ability to control his body into absolute stillness. Elizabeth peered past the royal couple and found herself looking into the astute hazel eyes of Edward Bruce, Lord of Badenoch and Lochaber. His gaze gave her the sense that he peered into her thoughts, as though he were assessing her. She tried to keep her face neutral as heat surged up her neck. She prayed her face didn't redden as much as her neck must have, but at a twenty-one, she still hadn't mastered how to control her blushing. Her nape burned like it was on fire. She canted her head slightly before looking up at the crucifix hanging over the altar. She closed her eyes and tried to invoke the image of the Lord that usually centered her when her mind wandered during Mass.

Elizabeth sensed Edward's gaze remained on her. She didn't understand how she was so sure that he was looking at her. She didn't have any special gifts of perception or sight, but her intuition screamed that he was still looking.

A Spy at the Highland Court **BOOK 2**

A Wallflower at the Highland Court **BOOK 3**

A Rogue at the Highland Court **BOOK 4**

A Rake at the Highland Court **BOOK 5**

An Enemy at the Highland Court **BOOK 6**

A Saint at the Highland Court **BOOK 7**

A Beauty at the Highland Court **BOOK 8**

A Sinner at the Highland Court **BOOK 9**

A Hellion at the Highland Court **BOOK 10**

An Angel at the Highland Court **BOOK 11**

A Harlot at the Highland Court **BOOK 12**

THE CLAN SINCLAIR

His Highland Lass **BOOK 1 SNEAK PEEK**

She entered the great hall like a strong spring storm in the
northern most Highlands. Tristan Mackay felt like he had
been blown hither and yon. As the storm settled, she left
him with the sweet scents of heather and lavender wafting
towards him as she approached. She was not a classic
beauty, tall and willowy like the women at court. Her face
and form were not what legends were made of. But she
held a unique appeal unlike any he had seen before. He
could not take his eyes off of her long chestnut hair that
had strands of fire and burnt copper running through
them. Unlike the waves or curls he was used to, her hair
was unusually straight and fine. It looked like a waterfall
cascading down her back. While she was not tall, neither
was she short. She had a figure that was meant for a man
to grasp and hold onto, whether from the front or from
behind. She had an aura of confidence and charm, but
not arrogance or conceit like many good looking women
he had met. She did not seem to know her own appeal. He
could tell that she was many things, but one thing she was
not was his.

His Bonnie Highland Temptation **BOOK 2**

His Highland Prize **BOOK 3**

His Highland Pledge **BOOK 4**

His Highland Surprise **BOOK 5**

Their Highland Beginning **BOOK 6**

The Blond Devil of the Sea **BOOK 1 SNEAK PEEK**

Caragh lifted her torch into the air as she made her way down the precarious Cornish cliffside. She made out the hulking shape of a ship, but the dead of night made it impossible to see who was there. She and the fishermen of Bedruthan Steps weren't expecting any shipments that night. But her younger brother Eddie, who stood watch at the entrance to their hiding place, had spotted the ship and signaled up to the village watchman, who alerted Caragh.

As her boot slid along the dirt and sand, she cursed having to carry the torch and wished she could have sunlight to guide her. She knew these cliffs well, and it was for that reason it was better that she moved slowly than stop moving once and for all. Caragh feared the light from her torch would carry out to the boat. Despite her efforts to keep the flame small, the solitary light would be a beacon.

When Caragh came to the final twist in the path before the sand, she snuffed out her torch and started to run to the cave where the main source of the village's income lay in hiding. She heard movement along the trail above her head and knew the local fishermen would soon join her on the beach. These men, both young and old, were strong from days spent pulling in the full trawling nets and hoisting the larger catches onto their boats. However, these men weren't well-trained swordsmen, and the fear of pirate raids was ever-present. Caragh feared that was who the villagers would face that night.

The Dark Heart of the Sea **BOOK 2**

The Red Drifter of the Sea **BOOK3**

The Scarlet Blade of the Sea **BOOK 4**

Leif **BOOK 1 SNEAK PEEK**

Leif looked around his chambers within his father's longhouse and breathed a sigh of relief. He noticed the large fur rugs spread throughout the chamber. His two favorites placed strategically before the fire and the bedside he preferred. He looked at his shield that hung on the wall near the door in a symbolic position but waiting at the ready. The chests that held his clothes and some of his finer acquisitions from voyages near and far sat beside his bed and along the far wall. And in the center was his most favorite possession. His oversized bed was one of the few that could accommodate his long and broad frame. He shook his head at his longing to climb under the pile of furs and on the stuffed mattress that beckoned him. He took in the chair placed before the fire where he longed to sit now with a cup of warm mead. It had been two months since he slept in his own bed, and he looked forward to nothing more than pulling the furs over his head and sleeping until he could no longer ignore his hunger. Alas, he would not be crawling into his bed again for several more hours. A feast awaited him to celebrate his and his crew's return from their latest expedition to explore the isle of Britannia. He bathed and wore fresh clothes, so he had no excuse for lingering other than a bone weariness that set in during the last storm at sea. He was eager to spend time at home no matter how much he loved sailing. Their last expedition had been profitable with several raids of monasteries that yielded jewels and both silver and gold, but he was ready for respite.

Leif left his chambers and knocked on the door next to his. He heard movement on the other side, but it was only moments before his sister, Freya, opened her door. She, too, looked tired but clean. A few pieces of jewelry she confiscated from the holy houses that allegedly swore to a life of poverty and deprivation adorned her trim frame.

"That armband suits you well. It compliments your muscles," Leif smirked and dodged a strike from one of those muscular arms.

Only a year younger than he, his sister was a well-known and feared shield maiden. Her lithe form was strong and agile making her a ferocious and competent opponent to any man. Freya's beauty was stunning, but Leif had taken every opportunity since they were children to tease her about her unusual strength even among the female warriors.

"At least one of us inherited our father's prowess. Such a shame it wasn't you."

Freya **BOOK 2**

Tyra & Bjorn **BOOK 3**

Strian **VIKING GLORY BOOK 4**

Lena & Ivar **VIKING GLORY BOOK 5**